Faceless

A Novel of Love and Identity
in a Changing America

B. J. QUANDER

ISBN: 979-8-88653-426-9

Published by Satin Romance
An Imprint of Melange Books, LLC
White Bear Lake, MN 55110
www.satinromance.com

Cover Design by Caroline Andrus

I dedicate this story to everyone who has taken the time to read this book.

Nota Bene

Hello Reader, I appreciate your reading a tale that I had long considered but wondered if I had the skill to apply to page.

Here I present a two-fold story.

Half of it is a tale of romance passing through, that comes upon many of us when we least expect it, while also delving into the philosophies of life. This section of the book spans from over the course of the summers from 2022 to 2024.

The other half of the story follows the hero, Briseis in the winter of 2024, after the USA Presidential 2024 Election.

Although the first half has no political affiliations or social connections with the second, the lessons the hero learns from both aspects of her life will propel her forward in her identity and dreams.

To give respect, the tour bus that Briseis rides around the city is inspired by an actual tour bus. In this tale, the bus 'Kite & Key' is inspired by the Phlash Bus. So, if you ever rode on that bus, when in Philadelphia, it is the inspiration behind the bus in this story.

As such, I hope, as you turn the page, you can find yourself within the story. As well as let us not find ourselves alone.

I dedicate this book to my wonderful parents, family, the excellent readers who chose to read this story, and all who helped me publish this book.

A special thanks to Glad, who encouraged me to write this book, and very much also to El for helping me so much with the research! I would be lost without you both.

The actual novel is approximately 320 pages.

After this book, there will be a *very* lengthy Afterword, to give future generations an explanation of what happened in American History between January 2020, to January 2025.

Very much aware that this book might not be read by anyone for many years to come, it is to give future generations a personal account of someone who lived during politically turbulent times.

If the USA has a future, I hope that the next generation might read this, so they understand us a little better.

Also, never shall I forget all the tourists who visit Philadelphia. By coming to my city, you bring new life into us, as well as bringing the world to those of us who cannot always go to it. You have saved our lives.

Lastly, I give credit to the ultimate inspiration. To the Face Changer who came to the USA, and I was able to see perform. I say this to you: wherever you are and whoever you may be, you have been the main reason that drove me to write this tale. Never will I forget you, for I owe you so much.

Now, read on, and thank you again for everything.

—B. J. Quander

The flame is not out, but it is flickering.

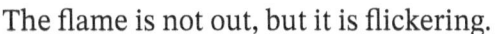

— Ken Burns

Chapter 1
The Remains of the Day

December 1, 2024

W henever you choose to go on an adventure, the first thing that comes to mind is how to plan it all, and what is the best way to undertake it.

When travelling across land and ocean, between money, luggage, identification, and all the essentials, there is so much to consider.

Some of us dive into the task, eager to go to the world, with arms wide open. Others of us want nothing to do with the foreign, either because we are quite comfortable where we are, or because we are trained not to accept anything different than what we have been raised to.

And then there is the third kind: we don't travel anywhere, because we can't. Either because we are too busy, or we lack the ability to *afford* going anywhere.

I was the third kind—and I was both...

"That's why I'm going," I said to my co-worker, Vella, as

I was rushing to get my coat on, "If I can't be a tourist somewhere else, at least I can be it in my own city."

I had just gotten done telling her about why I was riding a tour bus to the major tourist sites in downtown Philadelphia, despite that I had already been to all these places.

"Good!" Vella said, as she was finishing counting the money in the register, "I was waiting for you to give me a logical reason for what the heck you are doing. Because, until now, I was living off assumptions, and none of them made sense."

I gave a fake dramatic sigh.

"Oh, you have been worried about my sanity—while also showing that you care about what I do. How nice."

"I sell stuff at a tourist gift shop all day; I need to find my joys where I can."

"I'm interesting?" I asked, putting my hat on.

"Not really," she replied, smiling, "that just goes to show you how boring this day has been."

"Darn," I replied, "and just when I thought that I was finally beginning to have an identity."

"It's 2024; does anyone ever know what their identity is?"

I raised an eyebrow.

"Good point," I admitted, "See you soon?"

"Tomorrow?"

"You know me; I never know that I'm working until the night before."

"Check your schedule more often."

"Why would I do that? When not knowing when I am working, until the last second, is one of the last great surprises that I have left."

Nodding to her, I rushed out of the store, just as two tourists came past me.

"Excuse me," the woman said, with an accent, "are they giving away free maps in there?"

"Yes, they are," I answered, buttoning my coat up, "Just ask for one, and they will give you a gazette. Inside of it is a free map. And yes, there are bathrooms in there."

The woman smiled.

"Thank you!"

Time has taught me to always give that information without the tourist asking first. When it comes to visiting a new city, you view every place that has a public bathroom as being a port in a storm.

"Where are you from?" I asked her.

"Italy."

"Oh," I said, smiling, "Bon Giorno!"

Her face widened and she responded with the same. And I was both happy that I learned that word—and embarrassed that I hadn't learned any other Italian words. That would not be the first time that I felt like an uncultured idiot—as you will see.

"And thank you for being the inspiration that named us," I elaborated, "you do know that America is named after an Italian explorer?"

"Yes," she said, "Amerigo Vespucci. You are the feminine version of his name."

"We are," I said, speaking to her over my shoulder as I walked to the bus stop. "And that's where it all began."

"You're welcome!" she said, going into the gift shop, with the man who she was with.

That is what it means to be a tour guide:

You meet the person.

You establish a quick relationship with them.

You make them comfortable.

And then you walk out of their life forever.

The only problem is that it becomes part of who we are. We come.

We enter your life.

We give you a quick spark of something new.

But after the exotic aspect of us wears off—what are we?

Some of us know how to start a relationship and keep it going.

But for the rest of us, we are what I call drive-by novelties. We enter, we give you something fresh—and then have nothing more to give you. No more conversations, no more experiences—because the truth is, you were the conversation. *You* were the experience. Outside of that, what else are we when we stop being a reflection of yourself? That was me. That was what I was growing into. And that is what I was afraid of.

Turning the corner, I dashed down Arch Street, worried that I had missed the tour bus, and was happy to see that there were people waiting.

Inwardly, I found satisfaction from the little things, the mundane that is a marvel to those of us who did not have much to our lives.

I had not missed the bus.

That, to a woman of no importance, was a small kind of accomplishment. An achievement. How pathetic I was.

———

Reaching 239 Arch Street, I stood at the bus stop, waiting to ride to more of the same, while knowing that it was all that I had.

"Excuse me," a woman said behind me, "are you waiting for a bus?"

"Yes, I am," I replied, "Which bus are you waiting for?

The Big Bus? The Philadelphia Sightseeing one? Or the Kite & Key bus?"

"I think it's the bus that's purple and pink."

"That's the Kite & Key bus." I smiled warmly at her, "That's the one that I'm waiting for. My co-worker told me that it will get here in six minutes. We didn't miss it."

"Good."

Like the previous woman, she also had an accent.

"Where are you from?" I asked her.

"Puerto Rico."

"Ah! You're Puerto Rican American."

"Yes, I am."

"Lovely flag."

"Thank you!"

"Red, white, and blue," I said, raising up my fist, in solidarity—after all, both our flags had those colors, because we were two nations, but one family. "Brothers in arms."

"And sisters in arms."

"Very well phrased. Mind if I steal that idea?"

"Steal away."

"Puerto Rico is lovely. It's a beautiful place."

"Oh, you've been there?"

Again, from my conscious to subconscious, came the inner shame of lack of experience. Of making choices in life that did not guarantee that I would be able to encounter more nations besides my own.

But time taught me wit. Drive-by wit, to put it better. I can be a delight for a few minutes, but soon after, the jokes die, the wit dissolves, and I become the most boring individual. Fortunately, she will not know me long enough to learn that. After all, we only had six minutes. That was the longest that could be provided as a tour guide who had no tour.

"Nothing is more annoying than saying the word 'no', but it's the only answer you will get," I replied. "I did not, because that's the path of a person who lives from paycheck to paycheck—we can't visit anywhere, so we have the internet to save us from ourselves. I look at Puerto Rico online and get to see it from the computer screen. There are some parts of it that are very lovely."

"The good thing about that is that you can enjoy our nation without having to deal with the pains of meeting people."

We both laughed.

"Don't worry," I professed. "I'm an American—you guys don't have people that we have never seen before. Welcome to Philadelphia."

"Thank you. I am enjoying it."

"Thank you," I said, sighing, always happy to hear that people liked my city. "Tell us that, from time to time. We need to hear it."

The woman went back to talking with her friend—which was the perfect time for us to speak before I had no more words to give.

Leaning against the gate of the courtyard, they conversed in Spanish.

I knew only ten Spanish words—another shortcoming of mine.

As they spoke, I could not help but look upward at the building we were next to as we waited for the Kite & Key tour bus.

It was the Betsy Ross House.

Small and quaint, stood the home of the woman who was known for making the first official American Flag.

The flag that began it all—a new experiment that entered, and showed us something different on the horizon, that many nations took part in creating. All that began with a shot heard around the world.

And the world responded.

Because the world came to help us as we built ourselves.

And so, a new nation was born.

Looking up at the red and white stripes, and the blue with the thirteen stars that marked the first thirteen British colonies that became American states, for the longest time, I took our flag for granted. After all, it was only a flag.

Only time, and accepting my own foolishness, would I begin to understand what it meant. And what it symbolized.

To me, I was born at a time when the flag was already old. It had seen many years.

However, when you begin to research history, you truly see how young it was, compared to so many other flags that came before it.

And when looking up at it, sewn by a woman who made it in her bedroom, at nighttime, risking her life, since she was committing treason, time began to unwind, I saw the idea of Betsy sewing all the American flags that she continued to make throughout the war, and how young those stars were.

Sewing something where there wasn't something before.

Beginning something new from the old.

Beginnings.

Looking up at those three colors, as the flag flapped in the wind, refusing to lay limp, but show itself boldly amongst those who would see it, I remembered.

For that was where it all began, three years ago...

Chapter 2
The Beginning

April, 2022

"This is the home of Betsy Ross," I said, as I was leading a tour through Old City—which was the name of the historic areas of Philadelphia. At first, I had met the group outside of the National Constitution Center, a museum that was focused on the foundations of the United States, our Constitution, and how we had to struggle to confront the mistakes of our past. The tour group were high school kids, and so far, I was just so happy that they were nice to me, that I was able to use their energy to stay excited in my narration. So far, they were still paying attention, which was another small kind of accomplishment. When we reached the Betsy Ross House, the wind was not blowing and the flag was laying, motionless, on the pole. "According to the story passed down by her descendants, this is where three men, George Washington amongst them, asked her to make the flag."

"Sometimes," one of the students asked, "people say that she didn't actually make the first American Flag."

"They say that because there is no evidence that she did," I answered, "but there's a lot of circumstantial evidence that shows that either she made it or were among the first set of people to make the first flags. For example—"

"Excuse me," their teacher interrupted me. With an apologetic expression, she felt sorry that she cut off my explanation, but it was not to be rude. A few of the students had to use the restroom, and she was wondering if they could go into the Betsy Ross gift shop.

Not upset, I agreed, and led them into the museum while the rest of the students followed, to window shop.

Wholly aware that a tour guide will never be more interesting than all the lovely trinkets that you could buy in a quality shop, I shrunk to the background and leaned against the wall.

"Bri!"

I turned in the direction where my name was called, and saw my past employer, Shelby, wave to me. She was the supervisor who had hired me for a survey-collecting gig, in the brief four months when I needed more work.

As a temporary worker, I worried that I would be forgettable, but fortunately, Shelby had remembered me and bore no ill will when I needed to leave, due to having too many conflicts. After all, she also had her share of part-time jobs.

"Shelby!" I called, approaching her happily, "how's it going?"

"Good," she said, raising up her hand and showing a ring on her third finger. Smiling, I displayed excitement.

"Congratulations!" I said, going behind the desk and giving her a hug.

"Thank you. Any chance you want to go to the wedding?"

"Damn straight I do. And you know me. I will only need one invitation, because I have no date to speak of."

"Still giving men a wide berth?"

"Not as much as just my heart is. I'm still waiting to fall in love again. But I don't think it will happen. Don't worry, I'm not sad over it. Maybe I'm just free of it."

"Well," Shelby said, "I won't judge. Sometimes, where there is no man, there is no cry."

"That's how I look at it."

"Before you go, have you heard? The Chinese Lantern Festival is coming back this summer, and they need people to work the MC position?"

"The MC position?" I asked, with a raised eyebrow. "What's that?"

————

Filing out the Betsy Ross gift shop, the teacher was organizing the students so that we could continue the tour through Old City.

Usually, when it comes to high school groups, the students ignore us tour guides until they have no choice.

What I was unaware of was that one of the students had overheard my conversation with Shelby.

"What is the Chinese Lantern Festival?" the student asked—the same student who questioned if Betsy Ross had really been asked to sew the flag. My surprise in her asking about it did not last more than a couple seconds. Every now and again, you stumble on those who are the naturally curious sorts, and you don't fear those types. Actually, us guides prefer them.

"It's fun actually," I explained, "it's a festival that we have, in Philadelphia, every summer. It takes place in one of our parks, Franklin Square, where we have Chinese Lanterns that turn on at night, and there are shows. I can't explain it very well, because the performances change every year. There are Chinese folk dancers, acrobats, plate spinners, tea demonstrators—and sometimes, there is a Face Changer. It's a person who changes the mask on their face in literally a second. It was a big thing every year, until the pandemic hit."

"Yeah, Covid killed everything."

"It did. After the virus brought this country, and the world, to its knees, we couldn't have the festival here. But now it's coming back—if that's not a sign that 2022 is going to be better than the last two years, than I don't know what is."

"Don't the Chinese hate us?" she asked. "And we hate them."

I chuckled, shaking my head.

"Get off the internet sometime," was all that I could advise her. "Hate types faster than love. And the world hears the former more than they hear the latter."

"You don't understand my generation." She chuckled.

"Do you understand mine?" I asked, amused. "Call me old and I will say 'so what?'"

She chuckled some more.

"So what?"

She walked off. Again, I didn't hate her or despise her sort. They asked the questions that everyone was thinking.

The rest of us have learned to be too polite to ask them.

We just got older and realized that there's politics and people.

And then there's people, and politics.

You can be at odds with the second, and still like the first. She just needed to reach my age to understand that... as many younger folk are prone to suffering under.

I always felt a deep pity for her generation. Her time in history was no worse than mine, no more horrible than mine, or any other generation, for that matter. That is the side effect (and joys) of researching history. You begin to realize that times were always bad, so you try to get a few laughs in, when you could. The difference between her generation and mine was close, but also wide. We had the same problems, but with her, she could learn of every frightening thing within a matter of seconds. In our time, we could go weeks before discovering things, we didn't have such instant exposure to everything, and so, we could be removed from horrors for durations of time.

Life, daily, had more highlights than lowlights. More chances to stay a kid for longer. We knew that, when you came home with nothing bad to report, that it was a good day.

Were any of the students that I was leading around ever taught what a good day was?

They had access to all the corrupt, the unconscionable, and terrifying aspects of life at all times of the day. It reached such an extent that they became immune to it all. And maybe even welcomed it. How much of a chance were they given?

As they all filed out of the Betsy Ross Gift shop, I saw four of the boys in the group, emerging with pennies that they had pressed in the penny machine, stamping a land-mark on them.

Comparing their pennies, the boys laughed, showing which stamp they had chosen. Any technology that they had was stored in their pockets—but they were distracted from an old machine that had done something so simple.

I knew that they were happy.

I was thus given a glimmer of hope.

When arriving at the remains of the day, the good moments will reach around the grim, tipping off the bad that fills the cup and then the overflow will be something wholly unexpected.

However, I suspect that someone did not come to my tale for there to be a quick succession of busy good moments. We all want those moments in life, but we do not wish for those in people who are sharing their history.

I would have you know of all the mistakes that I have made, in life—for there were many. Most of them occurred from me biting off more than I could chew and having to swallow the disappointment that comes with approaching something that I was not right or skilled enough for. And of disappointing others—which I have done.

But the conclusion and aftermath of all those occurrences were now where I lived. And where I dwelled. How you find me is during the final result of a woman who was on the other sides of her largest mistakes.

No more would I do that again.

No more would I suffer under my own stupidity.

No more would I fail.

No more would I cause damage.

No more would I be the problem!

I was tired of being the problem. And I would not stick around to cause any collateral damage, where someone suffered from the chaos that I left in my wake.

However, what no one mentions is—or rather, what no one prepares you for is the next question: what happens next?

What happens when you overcome your worst mistakes and reached the point where you have stumbled on the wisdom that you sought so much, and you've reached the summit of completion?

You are at the top of the mountain.

The emotional and mental climb is now at its apex and have achieved the highest peak.

Therefore, there is nowhere else to go.

No one prepares you for that!

For when you discover yourself, all paths seem to end. You are locked in stasis, where there is no desire to go anywhere else.

Life gets less curious.

Life gets more mundane.

And you have no more stories.

No more roads to tread.

You've achieved serenity.

While also losing something else. And you don't know what that 'something' even is.

All you can do is sit around and be happy that nothing wrong is going to happen in your life, which could not be said of many.

But find completion somewhere—usually in your dreams, where you seek love than you cannot possess. Or where you come up with imaginary obstacles to upset your life, to stand in your way and prove to the world that you are worth more than anyone bargained for.

You ask for a crisis that you would never want in real life.

You ask for adventure that would be so upsetting if it actually happened.

You ask for a passionate love that would leave you wholly unsettled.

You now ask for the impossible.

But then you blink, you take a step on actual ground, and you come back to the present.

I began to lead my tour group to Arch Street Meeting House, to have an early lunch.

Outwardly, I was explaining how the Meeting House was one of the largest Quaker Meeting Houses on the East Coast of America and giving a history of how it was originally a burial ground, especially during the time of the Yellow Fever epidemic that swept through Philadelphia in 1793.

Yet, inwardly, I was still thinking of the summer and the lantern festival that was now coming back to our city.

When first hearing the news, my outward response was enthusiastic. Although, my internal reaction was bland, as everything else was when I first hear of it. I faked a positive interest in it, because for me, it was just another event that was occurring.

Then something unique happened.

As my group entered the Quaker Meeting House, the supervisor there gave them the rules on how to behave, I discovered that I was feeling something that I did not believe I would: expectation.

It was not a loud and boisterous one that was swelling inside of myself.

Although it was still alive.

Small, but alive.

Subdued, but alive.

Subtle, but alive.

It began and ended under the instinct that I felt like my city was beginning to settle into a state of normalcy.

After all, when the pandemic in 2019 and 2020 wreaked

so much devastation, Philadelphia and Pennsylvania were caught in its evil clutches.

But for the Lantern Festival to return, it was a sign—a symbol if you will!

And an end to any questions of who was to blame for the plague that took many lives.

With that being the reason, I was not surprised that was where my wishes lay; a happiness to return to normalcy.

Little did I know that something else would begin.

For how was I to know?

He was coming.

Chapter 3
Another Market Street Tale

December 1ˢᵗ, 2024

"Here it comes!" I said to the two Puerto Ricans that I had been waiting at the bus stop with.

Standing up by the gate that led to the Betsy Ross courtyard, their expressions brightened up, as they were saved from the monotony of waiting around.

Passed a few cars, the color purple and pink was a sight for sore eyes as the Kite & Key Bus arrived at the curb right in front of us.

I let the tourists get on first. When stepping on, I removed my public transit card from my wallet, because anyone who had a Septa transit key card in Philadelphia could travel on the Kite and Key bus for free.

After greeting the bus driver, I saw that there were copies of maps of the bus route on the window. Taking one of them, I sat down and looked at the stops that the bus took.

After the Betsy Ross House, which was Stop #16 on the

map, the bus was headed to Stop #1, which was the Independence Visitor's Center, the very middle of the tourist hub.

As we stopped at the red light on 3rd and Arch Street, I spotted two women sitting in the seats opposite me. One held the bus route schedule, and the other had a map of Old City.

After all, they had no choice but to be curious, for nothing could be more natural than for them to assume that I was a tourist, like them.

"Traveling alone?" One of them asked me, with no hint of thinking I was strange for doing it. Since I was a child, whenever anyone went anywhere alone, people wondered at it, marveling at the prospect that one could be happy in the state of me, myself, and I.

However, I, being an instinctive loner, would walk for miles at a time, alone.

I would go to restaurants to eat alone.

Go to the movies, alone, wholly not intimidated that everyone else in the theatre was with their significant other, or their family.

You learn not to be offended at the question, even when it was offensive.

But since the world has grown large enough to embrace ideas passed the status quo, their comprehension of what makes sense has widened, and they understand those who go out, by themselves. And even travel to other places, by themselves. That was their tone.

"Yes, I am," I said, "but I suppose I cannot say I'm traveling, because I already live here. I am a Philadelphian, born and raised."

"You are?" The second one asked me, placing some

strands of blonde hair behind her ear that had fallen from out of the hair tie.

"Yes," I replied, "I have always wanted to travel and see the world. But I don't have the money to do that. Yeah, I'm the 'living from paycheck to paycheck' kind of gal. So, I figured that, since I can't go to other places, at least I can visit my own city. See what's on my doorstep, as it were. Do I sound ridiculous?"

"Not really. There are parts of our city that we still have not seen. No one bothers to look at one's doorstep. But instead, we look at different horizons."

"I get it, and for those of us working in the local area, we appreciate that. Sorry! After all these years, I'm still bad at placing accents. Where are you from?"

"Stockholm," the first one responded, "It's a city in—"

"Sweden," I responded, as the bus drove passed the Arch Street Meeting House on our left, and the large bust of Benjamin Franklin on our right.

Next to that was the Fireman's Mural, as well as a fire station, where there were usually firemen in the front of it, either tending to the trucks, or sitting down casually. Often, I wished to see a dalmatian dog there, but life is not always meant to be so cliché.

"Yes," they confirmed, their eyes alight at the fact that I actually knew that. Faith, I should not have been surprised. Both women had fair skin, flaxen straight hair, and physical features, that was unique to people of Scandinavian heritage.

"Isn't Stockholm Sweden's state capital?" I asked, "and that it is spread across 14 islands."

"Yes, it is."

"That is so cool!" I responded, "and welcome back home."

The women looked between each other, slightly confused.

"Sorry," I said, as the bus turned off Arch and was riding toward Market Street, the main street in center city. "What I meant was that Philadelphia, and Pennsylvania, went through a lot of hands before we became American. First, we really are the home of the Lenni Lenape people. That's the native tribe that this land belongs to. Then the Swedes came to this territory, and we became New Sweden."

When hearing that, the women dropped their maps and were looking at me in earnest, leaning forward, lessening the gap between our seats ever so slightly.

"You all were?"

The bus driver stopped abruptly and apologized to us that he had to wait for a homeless person to cross the street in front of the cars and his bus. Happy that no mishap occurred, and no life was lost, we were all more relieved.

"Yes, we were," I elaborated, turning back to the women, "That's why the Philadelphia flag has Swedish colors. Our city has a flag, and the colors are light blue and yellow, from the Swedish flag. It's a reminder when we were a part of Sweden. That's why one of our oldest churches in the city is called 'Old Swedes'."

"How do you know all this?"

"I'm a tour guide—who decided to see her own city." I chuckled, "Have you gone to the Philadelphia Museum of Art? At the top of the steps is the American flag on the left, and the Philadelphia flag on the right."

I jerked as the bus moved forward again. That was another thing about me—I got shocked easily, when it came to the small things. But when it came to the larger things, I was solid as a rock. The irony of that tendency was not, nor ever would it be, lost on me. Then again, since we humans often encounter smaller conflicts in life, and not the enormous ones, we respond to what we are used to encountering.

"We want to go there soon, to run up the steps," the second Swedish women said.

I grinned, still amazed about how that tradition of running up the Art Museum Steps, reached all corners of the world.

"I had no idea that people in Sweden knew about that tradition," I said, "it's the one bright spot of Philadelphia that cannot be touched by anything that people make fun of us about. When you walk up the steps, don't worry about feeling like it will let you down," I assured them. "When you get to the top, turn around, and you will feel it."

"Feel what?" The first woman asked.

"*It*," was all that I could reply. That's the only answer that I could give.

———

The bus finally reached 5th and Market Street, but it stopped at the red light so it could not turn.

"This is our next stop," the women said. "We have tickets to see Independence Hall."

"I hope you like it," I said, still sitting down.

"I'm curious," the second woman said, "why did you wait till now to tour, instead of the summer?"

Scratching my chin, I suddenly felt nervous.

"I don't know," I answered, "For some reason, it just made sense to go now."

"Oh."

She was a very discerning person. Her head titled to the

side, she gave me a 'I think I know what you are avoiding telling me', kind of look.

She was right. She just knew that I didn't want to talk about it.

"I understand," was all she said simply.

Gently, but heavily, I nodded.

"Besides," I smoothed over, "even if I want to go in the summer, it would be an occupation hazard. For you guys, the summer is your vacation. With us guides, it's our work-time. We are very backwards in that way. During the day, I was guiding, and at night, I would sometimes work at the Chinese Lantern Festival."

When hearing me mention it, their eyes brightened.

"We saw the festival!"

"You did?"

"Yes. Well, I saw it two years ago, before the pandemic. So, we saw it."

"I was there," I said, my eyes downcast, "on their last day."

Shifting in their stance, they deduced that the mood had died in me, somewhat. The average person is deductive when it comes to reading another person. And then there are the rest, who are not that way, because they avoid any sort of contact with someone that they do not care enough about.

"You miss it, don't you?" she asked.

I felt the heaviness in my chest swell up, knowing what was gone, and what would never be.

"Yes," I answered. "I miss it very much."

We reached the front of the Independence Visitor Center.

We said goodbye to each other as they got off, and new tourists got on.

The life of a tour guide:
Come.
Connect.
Leave.
Don't linger.
And that's the end.
That was how my days always went.
That's our lives.

————

With a new set of people who arrived on the bus, I turned my head, directing my attention to across the street, and rested my eyes on a succession of three historic sights, or locations, that were always the most immediate attraction to our city.

Did we have stretches of stone ruins that gave hint of an old city that lay underneath the new one, like Mykonos, on the Island of Kusadasi?

Not at all.

For as a city, we were too young.

Did we have large and beautiful temples like those in Turkey, in Istanbul?

Not at all.

Being created by an amalgamation of European colonization, and invading forces that had quite eradicated any history that had been here before—we were formed under too many influences for ancient culture to cling to us.

Thus, being born on the ruins of conflict with those eager to claim the land, we must resurrect what is younger, in the eyes of history, but what is old to us.

For what is regarded of us Americans is a statement,

tried and true: to us, 100 years, is a long time. For others, 100 miles is a long distance.

Across the street is a frame structure of a spot that was the President's House. The home once boasted of being America's first White House, where our first presidents, George Washington, and John Adams, lived.

Being torn down for a series of reasons, but the largest of all was indifference: no one protested to preserve it. As such, my mind unwound, as can happen in our imagination, when I dashed over decades long past, and saw many construction workers, in the 1830s, tearing down a house that appeared to be of little value. Thus, commerce gave way, and the property was recycled for shops.

Materialization is frowned upon.

Yet materialization is human.

Eventually, after the turn of the 21st century, regret began to wind itself onto the heartstrings of the city, we repented the errors of human nature gone past, and we realized that part of our history should never have been demolished.

An important bit of our history is gone, because of indifference and money.

For that was another aspect of human nature: the past gets sacrificed for the wheel of change. The only problem is that it's the correct sort of past which gets sacrificed, and the wheel of 'forward' does not roll over the part of our history that we ought to leave behind.

One day, we will get it right.

As such, there was a frame structure that now outlines where the house was, giving the history of the place, elaborating on the good and bad that happened in those presidential halls.

I did not run from what our Founding Fathers were. For there was one thing that I never feared nor suffered under: the truth. I acknowledged the good of what they achieved and never concealed the bad that they committed. After all, what were they that they were not raised to be?

Behind the President's House, was the Liberty Bell Center, which stored the most famous bell in our history: a bell that cracked soon after it first rung. A crack that became symbolic of our democratic republic, which was that we are a nation founded on ideals, but the practices behind them are not perfect—a concept that is cracked. But it has the chance for that crack to be repaired. Becoming a symbol across the world for a uniform liberty and equality, there was always much history about social and political movements inside the building, that many people rush past to get to the bell to take their picture.

No one judges them. For why would we?

Then came the last building in the line.

Independence Hall.

Originally it was called the Pennsylvania State House, that was built to House the government of the British colony of Pennsylvania.

Then it turned around to be the building that became symbolic of America's fight for Independence from Mother England. A year after the iconic document, the Declaration of Independence, was read to the public, the British armies marched into Philadelphia, taking over the city. They turned the building into a prison and stable for their horses. When the Continental Army reclaimed the city a few months later, they came to a vandalized building, broken windows, and horse crap all over the floor.

By rights, that was the beginning of the many moments

that showed that we would lose that war, for what was a band of uncouth and undisciplined militias to do against the greatest army of the time?

That was the moment where history saw the rebels out of the corner of its eye and chose to bow down to the underdog that were the American States.

Next, the Kite & Key bus closed the doors as the other tourists got on, and waited for the streetlight to turn green, so that it could continue down Market Street.

Yes, friends! That was the first impression that tourists glimpsed when they came:

A torn down building that was subjected to shortsightedness and was resurrected by brick framework.

A cracked bell that got louder with the more silent it became.

A government building that had to be repaired after being vandalized and could either be regarded as a place of revolution and the beginning of so much, or a site of treason.

That was the foundation of the beginning of the American Experiment.

Then, to the left of all three buildings was a healthy green, a small field that left a view wide open for tourists to take a picture, for there to be concerts...and political protests.

For if there was one place for someone to speak up, preaching for equal rights, for a better tomorrow, for a free space where you could voice your principles without fear of being thrown in prison, it was the green to the left of a cracked bell, and in front of a building where independence was sought.

As such, the days fell back upon the natural course of

time, and only in the mind can you go back to your past, and see things stretched out for you to analyze.

There, on the green, I returned to three years ago, on my first day where I worked at the Lantern Festival...

Chapter 4
The Knife of Indecision

June, 2022

Walking passed the Jewish Museum, on 5th Street, I felt my nerves tightly wound under the concept of walking to a job where you didn't know what to expect.

My job title was to be the M.C., an abbreviation that meant Master of Ceremonies.

I was briefed on the fact that it was a fancy way of saying that I was an announcer.

The Chinese Lantern Festival took place at Franklin Square, on 6th and Race Street.

Like much of the city, Franklin Square had been a good idea that rose through the ashes of being a disgusting part of urban habits.

Originally, it was one of the five open-park spaces that our city's founder, William Penn, had organized and planned in 1682. Then it was overseen by his wife, Hannah Penn, who made sure the city was built, and was, to our knowledge, the only female 'governor' of the colonies in the 1600s.

But as time went by, it grew into a park where drug addicts went there to overdose, make deals, alcoholics dwelled, and was in the epicenter of criminal territory.

But, at some point, there is always one political official, who looks out of their ivory tower, and was elected because they do care about the city they control, and said the immortal word, 'enough!'

The park was cleaned up, returned to its original glory, and was turned into a park for children to enjoy a playground, a fountain, well-kept grass for people to play volleyball, a minigolf course, a fountain in the middle, and a small restaurant.

Wherever William Penn was, we gave him and his wife reason to smile at their city that still stands, and the parks that were established so that people could enjoy country life in a modern 17th century city.

Thank the stars for an Englishman who learned from the mistakes of what led to the Great Fire of London in 1666. He didn't want us to be overcrowded, easily capable of going up in flames in the same way and lacking in green scenes of nature.

When crossing Market Street, going past the Synagogue of the American Revolution, I heard declarations taking place.

There, on the green, that was next to the President's House, and in front of Independence Hall, were two Asian men, in white robes with a flag next to them with red stripes against a blue sky, white triangle, with a sun over it, and lions in the bottom middle.

What I do not know could fill a very large book, but I knew enough to know that it was the Tibetan Flag.

My guess was confirmed when, between the two men was a sign saying:

FREE TIBET!

They were the traditional Tibetans who got permission to peacefully protest against China's occupation over Tibet, in front of Independence Hall.

For a time, I, like the rest of the world, was unaware of what Tibet was going through.

All their attempts to make the world enlightened of their grievances and suffering had been suppressed and even extinguished under the great wheel of governmental power to snuff out a cry in the wilderness.

For many years the Tibetan people had been subject to oppression, torture, imprisonment against freedom of speech, and the slow extinction of their culture, religion and language. Each generation was born into the crisis to maintain their identity, and their freedoms.

While any attempts to try and reach the world about its struggles led to a significant number of Tibetans being thrown in prison, here they could not be touched, and not silenced.

"Free Tibet!" They shouted into a microphone. "Tibet Independence."

As they kept preaching, trying to make the world informed of a movement that we are not given the right to learn about, there were many passersby who moved around them, avoiding eye contact.

Why do they ignore them, you might ask?

The answer is simple, because the second you start caring for one, you must care for everything. We're all considered cowards when we don't take sides when it comes to foreign conflicts. Or indifferent. But that is not so.

No. Often it is because we are scared. Scared of caring about something and then it turns out to be the wrong thing to care about.

Also, we go the entire day happy that we came home alive, so what of other lives? What of other cares?

Standing across the street from the peaceful protests, which Tibetan protestors were known for, I stopped, turned to them and did something they were not accustomed to; I made eye contact.

The Tibetan who was speaking into the microphone, saw me looking on, and stopped his protestations.

Wholly foreign a concept it was for someone to be willing to face them—to lock gazes, and to see them, it was a shock.

Should I go across the street and speak to them?

Should I be brave and take the first step?

I was no hero, often.

And sometimes... I could be a coward. Unwilling to get further involved than mere empathy, and not action, I smiled at him and nodded my head.

What was he to think that I did not do more? That I was not eager enough to do more.

Just to acknowledge.

As two people, one with a cause, and one wholly unconnected to a situation that I could never see firsthand, what could there be, but a nod? For my part.

Although the moment, among the many other moments that have occurred on the Philadelphia Streets, would just be a passing thing, of no significance, could still render itself worth notice.

The Tibetan smiled in return and nodded as a response. He understood—that was all that I could give him.

Sighing, I felt better at him forgiving my cowardice.

He knew, deep down, he knew; on some level, under the many layers of my inaction, there was an attempt. No matter how flimsy that attempt would be.

In my eyes there was immense appreciation and elation. Especially since he did not ask anything of me, except for acknowledgment of his situation. He did not ask me to take up his cause or die for it.

Just to understand.

Connect.

Don't linger.

Then leave.

Tearing my eyes away from him, I walked down the street, turned the corner and walked away from another moment that took place on Market Street.

Chapter 5
Mystery

W alking past the National Constitution Center, I picked up my step. The eagerness in my walk had nothing to do with confidence, but nervousness.

I was walking into the unknown, however trivial the situation was. As I approached 6th and Race Street, Franklin Square came up on my left. Even if I didn't know where I was going, I would be aware that I had found the right place.

In front of the park was a sign with the name written above.

PHILADELPHIA CHINESE LANTERN FESTIVAL

There was security and staff there to check people's tickets, and even grander—there was a large dragon placed over and around the top of the park's opening. Flashes of red and gold, it radiated from the lights within it, as it bore down with its penetrating eyes.

When I arrived, it took a couple of minutes to convince the security that I worked there.

After being given admittance, I walked into a wonderland that only needed for the sun to set for it to reach its magnificence. When making a festival, you can't be subtle. You have to come in big and strong.

The first brick pathway of the park had been outlined by a long overhang of beautiful lanterns, of different vibrant colors.

They were in long rows and columns, that rendered the visitor speechless, taking out their cell phone or camera (finally, cameras were making a comeback!) and I had to move around them to keep going.

To the left of the lantern pathway was a large red dragon that was immense, three stories tall, and six stories long from its head to its tail. Behind it was the stage where the performances took place. To the right was a large clam lantern that opened and emitted bubbles, and some frog lanterns that were around some pink flowers.

All the lanterns were life-size, and some of them dwarfed the tallest person. Up ahead, was the centerfold of the park, which was the fountain.

As I walked past it, there were large lanterns of birds, frogs and aquatic plants.

Running around me were children, who were rushing toward the gate in chase of bubbles that were being ejected from a machine, which added ambiance.

So began all!

All around the park were more lanterns of animals, dragons, trees and flowers, even hanging over the minigolf course. Description and detail be damned! I could explain everything, and it would not do it justice.

At first, I walked over to the minigolf course, checked in with my supervisor, Matthew, who was to tell me what to expect.

"The M.C. works at the performances," Matthew explained. "There are three performances each night. The first performance is 7:30 p.m., the second is 9:00 p.m., and the last one is 10:15 p.m."

"How long do the performances run for?" I asked.

"About half an hour," he answered.

That meant that I was not leaving till 10:45 at night.

And I was not a person who ever used the Uber or Lyft system to call a car to take me home. In fact, I didn't even have an Uber app on my phone. So, I was going to be riding the trolley and train, at 11 in the evening.

I think I had a death wish!

———

Looking at my phone, I saw that it was now 7:20 p.m., and it was about time that I started walking to the stage, but Matthew had more instructions.

"When you get back there, you have to change the background of the stage. You go on the computer and click on what scene that you want in the background. It will change from giving the times of the show to a beige screen with a Chinese temple behind it. There is a script backstage where you announce each performance. When done, you can leave and enjoy the festival, until you have to return for the next performance."

"Will I be alone at that side of the stage?" I asked, feeling nervous as hell. I was not used to speaking in a microphone.

"No," Matthew responded, "You will have Kaori with you. She's the one who controls the microphone and music. And she speaks English, so she can always translate if the performers want to speak to you. Two of them only speak

Chinese. The other performers are Pierre and his assistant, Ally, and they speak English."

"Pierre and Ally?" I questioned, raising an eyebrow, in suspicion. "They are not Chinese, are they?"

"No," Matthew responded, giving me a 'yeah, whoops, but that's the way that it has to be' face. "Two Chinese performers are all that we could get this year."

Two of our performers were not actually Chinese? At all?

After a few seconds, I adjusted to the surprise of us not getting enough Chinese performers.

"Makes sense, the more that I think about it," I acknowledged, slinging my bag over my shoulder, as I was about to move around the fountain, to the stage. "After Covid-19, we're lucky if we get any Chinese to come and perform anymore."

"Yeah, Coronavirus killed more than you would know."

"Quite frankly," I said, "I'm amazed that we're even making a comeback. Is life always like this after a global pandemic?"

"Hello!" he blurted out, pointing to his youthful face. "Do I look like the kind of person who has been through a plague before? I'm a baby, just like you. And with the other performers, there is Tsai. She does the Peacock dance and another folk one. Oh, and then there's the Face Changer performer."

My eyes widened again. Did he say what I thought that he said?

"We've got a Face Changer to come back to the festival?"

"Oh yeah! The performers are all good, but you always gotta have a Face Changer."

I bit my lip, anxious.

I had seen the Chinese Lantern Festival and remembering loving it. The lanterns aglow at night was enough to make you feel like you had been born again, yes.

But the chief attraction was the show, where different incredible acts were presented. From plate spinning to folk dance, to acrobatics, but one act never failed to be the favorite.

The Face Changer!

"His name is Jin."

Wholly distracted that I would see a Face Changer again, I was not paying attention to what Matthew said.

"Sorry," I squinted, coming back to reality, "what did you say?"

"When in costume," Matthew continued, taking out some tools, "he looks very distinct, but out of costume don't be surprised if you don't recognize him. He looks like a teenager."

"How old is he?"

"No idea."

"And I was not paying attention before. What's his name?"

"Cheong-Jin. Cheong-Jin Chang."

———

Now my nerves were bubbling under the surface of my skin as I walked to the stage. Already, a crowd had formed, and all the benches were filled up.

When doing so, I had considered how, but a year ago, the whole world was in hysteria, Covid-19 was in full swing, people were dying, or deftly sick. And where sickness comes, so does crime.

Being a tour guide, one learns that when plagues come to devastate the human population, the best and worst of humanity walk up to your door, sit on the porch and wait to pounce on you, during an unguarded moment. History is full of that, and no one was a greater victim of that sad habit than the United States of America.

We were a nation who was shaken to no end. There was death, riots, vandalism, racism, a president who ignored the problem and spread false information, and then there was a quiet, but true contempt for the nation that the virus first came from. Some of our politicians were very blatant about it, and it led to the Chinese residents in the USA having to bear the brunt of that.

For so long, we did not see an end in sight, a visible light at the end of a dark tunnel and felt that the darkness would not be overcome.

However, as quickly as humanity is about falling into chaos, how much quicker the world can be to recover, and forget about national humiliation.

The great irony of my life was that my time during Covid was a time of neighborly peace.

No one on my street, or on many blocks around us, wanted strife.

When one of our supermarkets had been vandalized, people from the area came to help the supermarket clean up and recover.

For every crime, there was a caretaker.

For every horror, there was someone who knew to come in as the hero, to dare the world to label every event as only bad, but not virtue to be found anywhere.

However, in our neighborhood, during the plague, I encountered people smiling more, appreciating their homes as they were confined to them, forcing them to stop taking passersby for granted, for we felt our mortality dripping down the drain.

We learned not to overlook a kind person. We greeted each other as fellow passengers on the way to the grave (as Charles Dickens put it. Mind you, I am aware that he was a horrible husband). Thus, in the part of my city, we were tucked away, from many horrors, only to see that they existed on the television, far away from us, as we rested in a part of Philadelphia that still belonged to an obtainable hope.

I was kept safe from seeing the world fall apart and was able to distance myself from the realities by the barrier of a TV screen.

I lived during the time of the COVID epidemic, but I didn't experience it. Although, I did share the humiliation that comes from being associated with savagery. For a long time, during the pandemic, the USA was an embarrassment.

Dared we hope to believe that we could recover?

And now that I stood there for a few seconds, looking at the crowd in front of the stage, and more people walking up to sit on the ground to find any space, I saw it.

We were recovering.

Our political system was recovering.

We all wanted to forget.

Rather, we needed to, or we would continue to go mad. As such, we did so, and I was content to leave it all behind.

As long as we don't leave it to the dusty pages of forgetfulness, or history will repeat itself. We tour guides know *that* vicious cycle better than most.

To sojourn on, always.

But forget, never.

At last, I looked at the stage where the show would begin soon.

———

A day in early summer would guarantee that it was still light out. Thus, sun and shadow fell on the stage, and over the audience as I faced it. Anxiety and apprehension overcame me as I walked to the left of the stage, went backstage, where all the props were.

Preparing myself for an awkward meeting, to face all the performers and learn their names, I felt my spirit rise and my courage shrink.

There were tents backstage, but there was no one.

At first, I felt the emptiness of the scene to be like a haunting kind of foreshadow.

In each tent, the performers must have been in, secluded and focusing on their upcoming performance. That was only natural. But it only made me wonder if this was how I was to spend my time there this summer: they tucked away, until they came out to perform, and disappeared again.

Before coming, I had decided to make an effort to exert myself better, to meet someone of new horizons. For when you are tied to one place, the largest event was the entrance of another person.

The foreigner—was not to be feared.

In the same manner that the tourist was your trip.

But there was no one.

Just backstage, tents, and me.

Slowly, I walked the narrow pathway behind the stage, careful not to trip over the foundations that kept the platform up and chose to count my blessings. It was best that I had been met with nothing. I had escaped the awkward glances, and I might have felt like nothing short of a person that they probably did not want to know. If I had been extraordinary, then maybe that could have saved me from their cold stares, and I would have been spared from feeling like an unwanted sort of character.

Yes, this was better!

After all, what had I always been preaching of never pressing your presence on where it was not wanted?

Sometimes, we don't all practice what we preach—especially people like me. One thing that you must know about me is the sad tendency to have to be told something four times before it begins to make an impression. Many of my life's lessons came later and all that I could do was look back on my teenage years, and early twenties, and see nothing but regrets.

Too many things said, that never should have been.

And other things not said that ought to have been.

And some things done—that I will never do again.

I was interesting once, yes, but I was not in the mood to be that way now.

To be bad—well, let's just say that the media finds you to be precisely the kind of person that you want and is the true source of stories. Sadly, that leads to our national undoing. To be better is boring. As such, forgive me if I am dull. For that is the price of enlightenment.

When going to the left side of the backstage, I was met with a crude computer—since technology hates me, I call all computers crude—two plain stools, and a sound system that had been safely tucked away in a black shed. This was done to protect the equipment from whenever it rained, I assumed.

Placing my bag down, I looked at the computer screen, to figure out how to work it, and then I noticed something around me.

The bane of humanity...mosquitoes! They were everywhere. It was like the devilish little buggers had converged right in the backstage and haunted the place.

Harpies!

Where are bats, when you need them, to decrease the surplus population of those little spawns? Bats eat mosquitoes. Despite being afraid of bats, I do wish that they at least helped out, in this circumstance.

Thank goodness I had chosen to wear a long dress, and brought a shawl with me, to keep the damn things away.

Just as I reached down, to pull my shawl out of my bag, to protect my delicious arms, I was met with two legs.

I froze.

"Um, hello?" came a pleasant voice, with a Chinese accent.

Recall how I said I didn't want to begin awkwardly? Well, I believe this is what they would call an incomplete pass. Looking up, I was met by a very beautiful woman, in her early twenties. Her black hair came down to the middle of her back, and was neatly parted, framing her face.

Immediately, I felt insecure.

Standing up, with my shawl in my hand, I felt rather than knew that my cheeks had turned red.

"Oh," I began, "sorry." I waved awkwardly, but kept the smile plastered across my face, in hopes that she would be kind about it all. "Hello. My name is Briseis. Briseis Cunningham."

"I'm Kaori," she said, "It's nice to meet you."

"It's nice to meet you too." I gestured to my shawl. "I know, it's hot, but I didn't know that there would be—"

"Mosquitoes?" she said, moving around me, putting her bag down, and beginning to work the sound system.

"Yes," I replied, thinking it best to pick up the script that

I was going to use, to give the announcements. If I looked busy, like she did, it might calm my nerves.

Quickly, I wrapped the shawl over my shoulders, cursing that I had worn a halter dress. My legs were safe, but my arms and back were like a smorgasbord for the critters.

"Are they always like this?" I asked her.

"Oh yes," she said, "there are so many people in the festival, but the mosquitoes love it right here. Did you spray yourself?"

"No," I replied, embarrassed. "It's obvious how new I am, huh?"

"If it helps, I'm new at working this place too."

"Oh, you don't usually travel with the festival?"

"I'm still in college. This is a summer job. How about you?"

I chuckled. "My whole world thrives around summer jobs. That's when I get the most work. I work myself to the grave, to make up for when I don't get enough work throughout the year."

"What do you do?"

"I'm a tour guide. We get some tours in the fall and spring, but it's during the summer that we get the most work." Looking away from her, I focused on the script. "But next time, I will definitely spray every inch of me and will not let the bugs defeat me. No, I shall not!" That last sentence was spoken with a very bad British accent, with a dramatic tone. I was so desperate to break the ice wherever I could, that I might have been walking to the edge of the social cliff. "It's strange. I have not been to a Chinese Lantern Festival since before COVID. And now, here I am, backstage, seeing it from a different angle. Who would have thought, huh?"

Pause.

"I'm rambling, aren't I?" I asked. "Like really rambling. Almost to the point of being annoying?"

Kaori looked away from the sound system and faced me. Her simple, but effective beauty made me a little uneasy.

At first, I was prepared for her to give me an equally uncomfortable answer. Or she was going to say nothing at all. Time helped me get used to people not answering my questions, sometimes. I stopped letting that affect me, eventually.

Thus, I was prepared for anything and everything. Everything else but what she said.

"Are you nervous?" she asked.

I blinked, astonished.

It wasn't a question that was delivered like a conviction, or like a criticism. It was simply asked, and I quickly grew to appreciate her immediately. Of course, it was a plain question, and so it deserved no more and no less than a plain answer.

"Yes," I answered, rubbing my bottom lip. "That's probably what's happening right now. Sorry about that."

"It's okay."

"Thanks."

Looking down at the script, I knew what the next best thing was to do. "I should start going over this, first, shouldn't I?"

"That will be a good way to start," Kaori agreed.

"Yes, it would."

Raising up the script, I began to read it in my head. Growing familiar with the words is always a proper way to begin before you have to say the lines out loud.

I studied it, almost a little too hard. The more that I could focus on the script, the less that I was talking, which was a good thing.

Time and experience had helped me to never be intimidated by women who were vastly prettier than I was. Because that was always the way things were.

With my friends in middle school, they were prettier.

High school, they were prettier.

College, much prettier. I'm still amazed that I had two boyfriends during that whole four years.

And, in every job I worked, there was always women of superlative beauty. It reached a point where I never felt jealousy or insecurity. After all, one thing that I learned was that men could still focus on plainer women as much as they do on pretty ones.

But with Kaori, it was a little disarming. I felt a little wrong to be in her presence. Reading the script helped me quiet that part of myself and studied on how I could defeat those voices within me.

"Now!" Kaori said, giving the indication that the show was going to begin.

"Oh crap!" I gasped, rushing to the computer, to change the background of the stage, to make it look like a Chinese temple.

When hearing me swear, Kaori laughed quietly.

Chuckling too, I felt better.

That was another skill that we tour guides learn, which I was stupid for forgetting:

Meet

Greet

Access

Then laugh at your mess

It breaks the ice every time.

Now I knew how to be in her presence, and we could begin to get along. Once I got the background changed, I rushed back to the microphone and turned to Kaori. Gesturing to the mic, I nodded.

She nodded back, indicating that she had turned the microphone on and that I now could speak.

Turning back, I pushed away all nervousness, raised the script to my ear, and began my job as an announcer.

"Good evening. Welcome to the Philadelphia Chinese Lantern Festival here in Franklin Square!"

Immediately, my first two sentences were followed by cheering. Now, we could begin. After giving a brief explanation of how old the tradition of Lantern Festivals was, and what happened at them, now was the moment to introduce the first act.

"We begin the show with the wonderful art of Face Changing. Where performers change their masks quicker than the blink of an eye, in this 300-year tradition of the Szechuan Opera."

Once I finished speaking, Kaori began to turn on the music. Happy to be done, I lowered the script and now could focus on the performer.

From the other side of the stage were a set of steps where the performer entered. Because of the lighting, I was unable to get the best view as a man, completely covered, walked up the first step. Yet with each step, his outline became more defined. Donning a stunning Chinese costume, he was, in his own manner, hypnotic.

At first, I took in his legs, which were covered in black pants with a beautiful pattern that were along his thighs, knees, and down to his ankle. Because of the distance, I could not make the design out, but it was of little matter.

On his feet were black slippers, also equally designed and ornate. On his chest was a black tunic with vibrant colors, from gold to pink, red, blue and green flashes across.

This was added by a jacket with a cape on the back, which was a flamboyant pink, a circular design in the center, gold tassels along the edges, and red sleeves underneath, with a gold pattern running through it.

He wore a headdress, where there was a bit of a crown on the front, that flowed down in the back, with two flaps that came down the sides, and thus came another main touch: The humble and effective fan.

In my mind, his movements to climb the stage were slow, as we can so easily alter the course of action in our thoughts.

What is a matter of two seconds in reality, can turn into half a minute within the *coinage* of your brain?

His movements were swift, but I found myself arrested under his sudden arrival into my life. At the time, I could not account for why I wished to cherish every movement that he made, for what was he but a stranger to me? All that I could consider and determine was that I wanted to commit him to memory, and rushing through my first time was not good enough.

Emerging onto the stage, with his large red fan in front of his face, the Face Changer moved, gracefully and energetically, to center stage, his face hidden.

Since it had been so many years since I had seen the performance, this was as new to me as if I had never witnessed it before.

Ruffling the fan in front of his face, he was practically teasing the audience, to know what he looked like. The curiosity was building, and would continue to do so, until the very end of his dance.

At last, he lowered his fan to reveal—nothing.

On his face was no mask

No feature

No expression

Only black!

Along his face was a thin black sheer material that revealed nothing, where he saw all from underneath, and we saw nothing from the outside.

Now, I remembered.

For that was how every performer began the dance.

They began it as a mystery.

They began it faceless.

Chapter 6
From Out of the Ashes

December 1, 2024

B lack.
  That was the color of the newly paved street that I looked on as I stared out of the bus window.

As the Kite & Key bus moved along, further away from what we call Old City, we reached 7th and Market Street, and had to stop at the red light, as traffic drove past the bus, to get to Arch Street.

"I think that's it?" said a voice behind me.

Hearing their unique accent, instinctively, I turned my head to see two people, who I presumed were a husband and wife. Guessing by their appearance, they were in their fifties and bore the appearance of a couple who stopped caring about what others thought of them long ago. People who have that thought process tend to have a natural confidence in their nature, are comfortable with some definite weight on their bones, and dress simply.

The woman had red hair, and the husband's hair had

turned gray. The woman had tourist brochures on her hand, trying to analyze what they were looking at.

Without thinking, I spoke up before they even looked at me.

"You mean the Declaration House?" I asked.

"Yes," the woman said, "that's it, isn't it?"

"You're right. That's the house that Thomas Jefferson, our Third President, stayed at, in 1776, when he wrote the Declaration of Independence."

The couple looked out of the window, raised their camera and eagerly began to take pictures.

"The house where the man wrote your declaration," the husband said, "and it's right across the street from a Dunkin Donuts."

"Yes," I said, chuckling. "It's just a touch anachronistic, I know."

And it was! On 7th and Market, was the home of where Jefferson wrote the iconic document that changed the course of our history. It was a thin, beautiful brick building that looked as if it never left the 18th century...and right across the street was A Dunkin Donuts, where people went to get coffee, donuts and breakfast food.

Right in the middle *of modern times*, was an old building that had stood the test *of time*.

"While Thomas Jefferson definitely wrote most of the Declaration of Independence," I added, "there were actually five men on the committee who also contributed to it. Him, Benjamin Franklin, President John Adams, Robert Livingston, and Robert Sherman. And even after that, Jefferson had to watch the rest of Congress edit the document right in front of him."

"He must have hated that!" the woman said.

"Oh, yeah, Jefferson totally did."

The light turned green, and the bus got moving.

"And who wouldn't be?" I continued, looking back at the couple. When I realized that I butted in on their discussion, I thought it was best to explain. "Sorry! I'm a tour guide."

Their looks changed from curiosity to comprehension. At first, they wondered why I knew such an obscure fact, but they understood now that it made sense.

"Ah, well that explains everything," the man said.

"Yes, that explains me," I responded. "Didn't want to leave you all wondering what the heck I am."

They chuckled.

"Where are you from, by the way?"

That question is the question of the tour guide. We ask it at least forty times a day.

"We are from Australia."

When hearing it, my eyes lit up.

"Australia!" I smiled. "Well, as Britain's one-time penal colony, to another of Britain's fellow penal colony, hello and again!"

We all laughed loudly, which drew the attention of the other people on the bus.

Quick to explain our outburst, my reason was briefly put.

"When Britain was colonizing the U.S.A and Australia, they sent their prisoners to both places, and we were penal colonies."

"Yeah," the woman said, "that's us for you."

"And now look at us," I added, sharing the camaraderie. "We both began as penal colonies, and then we made something of ourselves."

"We did. In fact, one of my ancestors on my father's

side, was one of those convicts that were shipped over. Most of them were not even very bad characters."

"Same with us. And my story is not that different than yours," I added. "On my father's side, my ancestors were also brought to the American colonies. They weren't prisoners, but it was in a different way."

"Ah," they both said, understanding what I meant, without saying it. "Yeah, I get it."

"Neither of our ancestors deserved the hell that they got, but since we are where we are now, it worked out for the best, for us."

"True. I like being an Australian."

"And I like being American. Well, I used to like being one."

They nodded to me, understanding why I said that.

"When it came to Thomas Jefferson," the woman said, "he wrote about equality, but didn't he own slaves?"

"Yes, he did. In 1776, though, it was complicated. He was from Virginia, where the slaves' laws were really strict, and it made liberating them impossible. At first, Jefferson really did hate the idea of enslavement, and his original Declaration even brought up the evils of slavery. But the other delegates forced him to remove those passages."

"They did?"

"Yes. They said, unless he removed those passages, they would not sign the declaration. And if they did not sign, we would not be united. And if we did not unite, then there would be no war."

At this point, they both were looking at me, enthralled. I was not giving them a dream or a nightmare. I was just telling them 'this is simply the way it was', with no judgment attached to it.

"So, that's how the war continued?" the man asked me.

"Yes. Our war of Independence waged on, because certain passages speaking for freedom, and against slavery, were removed. That's life for you: irony."

"Oh..." the man stuttered, "I mean—well..."

I looked at him, with a raised eyebrow. Truly, I had a feeling that I knew what he was considering saying but was afraid to say it.

"What?" I asked. "Penny for your thoughts?"

"Well, it's just...how does that make you feel? Knowing that's how it really happened."

This should have been a hard question to answer, but it was not. With it being easy, it was not because of wisdom on my part, but experience. I had been asked that question so many times that I learned how to give an answer.

"I know I should be angry, but I let go of anger a while back. While I wish that things had been different, and I do, I know that history can never be. There are too many humans involved, for it to be anything else. I'm just hoping that they don't try to erase our history now. Also, back then, they were not given certain principles and morals. So many people were never even given a chance to be better than what they were pressured to be. Then there's the other thing."

"What other thing?" she asked.

"If I hated us for being that way, then I have to hate every nation that created us, in *its* image. That's too many people to be angry with. Too many nations that resulted in making us. Quite frankly, I don't have the energy to do that."

"Do you have any more reasons?" the husband asked, intrigued.

"Yes. All historical figures, I have learned, who are what we consider good, at some point, were an asshole."

Rubbing my cheek, I knew that I was still giving only the half-truth. So, here came the rest of it.

"And the truth is, I used to tell myself that if I had lived back then, I would have been better than all of them. I would have understood what was right, and what was wrong. I would not have been like them. But then I realized..."

"What?"

"Maybe I would have been brainwashed, like them. And just assumed that life was like that, so it must be correct. Maybe I would have been *just* like them."

———

This was the moment.

This is always the moment. Where you wonder what will happen? How will they react? And how they will now see you as a disappointment. How you ruined the image in their brains. I awaited what they were going to say, and I was prepared to be damned. They had no choice but to despise me. They leaned back into their bus seats, looking at me. At last, the man opened his mouth to speak.

"Sorry," he said.

"You're sorry?" I asked, my eyes wide in wonder. "Why?"

"Because we made you confess that. Sorry about that."

I sighed, and though I did not smile, my tone was calm and sincere. "It's okay. Sorry, if I put you in a weird place."

"We began it. *We* began it."

"Well, I won't make it hard on you," I said. "Where are you headed to next?"

"Oh, we are going out to eat, and we were told to go to a market."

"Reading Terminal Market?"

"That's the one. Of course, it's your job to know that place, huh?"

"I'm a Pennsylvanian; it's all of our jobs to know it."

Just as we reached 10th and Market, I stood up from my seat. "I just have to show you something," I said pointing out of the window, toward 10th and Arch Street, which was right after the street we were on. "Right there! Look."

The Australians, and a few others, followed my gesture and they rested their eyes up ahead.

"That's the China Gate," I said, as they glimpsed a far-off view of the Chinese Archway that was the entrance to an old neighborhood in our city, "that's the entrance to Chinatown."

Everyone on the bus squinted, trying to see the beautiful archway that could not be described, no matter how best I tried. For when describing true art, even a thousand words could never do it justice.

The Archway was almost 42 feet high, and 34 feet wide.

It was adorned with dragon motifs, small animal sculptures, floral patterns, and ornamental roof tiles.

"It was designed by Sabrina Soong, and was built in 1984," I narrated, "it was dedicated as a commemoration of the friendship between Philadelphia and Tianjin, our sister city. The tiles came from Tianjin, and a team of Chinese engineers and artisans built the pieces of the arch."

"Tianjin?" another tourist asked.

"It's one of the nine central cities, located in Northern China," I said, "Philadelphia is her American sister city. Our Chinatown is not as large as New York's is but is around the size of Boston's. But it's still very old."

"How old?" the Australian woman asked.

"It began around the 1870s. The USA wasn't even 100

years old yet, when Chinatown was born here. If you get the chance, eat at one of the restaurants there, before you go back home."

"Do you have any recommendations on where to eat?"

"I don't have to," I replied, pleasantly, "they all can cook. Just go into whatever business where the hostess smiles at you first. At this point in time, go to whatever business that wants you."

Eventually, we reached Reading Terminal Market. The driver announced it, and I pointed out where the couple should walk into, they waved to me, stepped off and the bus doors closed behind them.

The door closed.

I would never see either of them again.

No awkwardness ensued.

Briseis, that was well done!

As I sat down, I looked at Reading Terminal Market, while the bus driver waited for the light to turn green.

To the untrained observer, you would have walked right passed it. All you see is just a street with a lot of windows to a building with a sign over it, bearing the place's name. Then you went inside, and it was like walking into a whole new world of hustle, bustle, and rushed beauty.

Opening in 1893, it was a large set of floors that had 800 spaces for merchants to sell their food and goods. From there, it became one of the vital organs that made up our city. During The Great Depression, when our country had fallen into hell, Reading Terminal Market still prospered. When food was harder to come by, farmers brought their produce to sell at the market, keeping the city from mass starvation.

It was the same thing during World War II as well.

Eating there was the *only* good thing about when I was

called in to do jury duty, a few years back. Literally, when summoned to report to serve on a jury, the municipal building was right across the street from Reading Terminal Market. When you were paid your eight or ten dollars to report for service, you always ended up going to the Market to eat lunch there. It was the bright aspect of spending hours sitting around strangers who don't want to be in the same room as you, only to be told that you weren't needed the entire time. Thank God for that slice of pizza that you had to eat while walking back to jury selection. Oh, heaven preserve us!

"How do you know so much about Chinatown?"

The question penetrated my thoughts, and I fell out of my walking down memory lane.

Turning to who asked me, I saw a man who was wearing a business suit and was holding a suitcase.

Telling the difference between a local and a tourist is obvious. This man, like me, was local, and was clearly riding the Kite & Key Bus because it took him close to somewhere that he needed to go next.

"Sorry," I said, "I was daydreaming in such a hardcore way. What did you say?"

"I asked how you knew so much about Chinatown?"

"Nostalgia," I said, and I meant it. This was one of those times where research had nothing to do with. "When growing up, I used to go to Chinatown with my family."

"Yeah, my mom would bring me down here too."

"No matter what you do," I said, "you can't escape the whirlpool that is *nostalgia*. It's the one thing that the bad parts of the world can never touch."

"By the way, I heard that the city is considering building a stadium for the Basketball team, on 10th and Market Street. Right where Chinatown is."

When hearing that, I was prepared for a potential argument coming my way. Too often, I have found that people bring up issues for two reasons.

First, they need to get something off their chest, while also acknowledging that they do care about what goes on in the world. Sometimes, those of us who shut ourselves off, are not cowards. Usually, it all has to do with self-preservation; if you don't show the world everything that you care about, then the world will not roll over you, in its' constant course. The only side effect is thus…the world also passes you by.

And second, they bring up such issues because they seek either compliance or conflict. They are secretly hoping that you do agree with them, to support their voice and their views. For no one ever wants to be alone, and what are prophets without their disciples?

But then, for others, they want conflict. They want someone to argue with them, for through disagreement, they can rise to distinction.

They do not like you, because, in their eyes 'they are enlightened, while your eyes are shut'. That philosophy only works if they are *actually* enlightened. That's not always the case.

If it is the first set, then I can understand, because those sorts usually come in peace.

If it were the second set, I would have to be on my guard.

I didn't want to have a fight on the bus.

"Yes," I said, "but the city still has to get full permission to do that."

"What do you feel?" he asked me, "About the stadium being put there?"

Now came the moment of decision. He put the discussion out there, without showing what he was for, or against. He had put me in the position of deciding what direction that we were going to. Did I agree with whatever viewpoint that he was for, or was I against him? Now I had to choose my words carefully.

"You wonder if I do or do not like the idea of a basketball stadium being placed literally right next to, and almost on top of, a neighborhood that has been here for over 120 years?" My answer was in the question.

"I understand," was all that he said. In his eyes, was a slice of coldness toward me. It was of a man who was about to disagree with me, while also informing me. "But you might be wrong—"

"I respect your views," I said simply, "and I always will. But please, respect mine."

He didn't respond to that either, for a few seconds. He was forming a counterattack, even though I had already given him a safe way out. Now, I was wondering if he ever wanted one.

"Please," I urged, "I'm not in the mood to debate with you. I just disagree. I do not believe it is right to put a stadium so close to this neighborhood."

"But I thought that your type would have wanted it. After all, opening that stadium would bring work and more money to that area, especially for you all."

Why did it all have to be about that! Money is not everything.

"I'm a tour guide. I've researched what it means to be a displaced people," I said, "Many cultures suffered that. I don't believe in doing it to someone else. I'm not about to think it's right to infringe that on a neighborhood, just to put up a stadium when our sports team already have one."

The man continued to look at me, so I figured that I would rattle on until my point was done.

"And those who are like me," I uttered, "but think the opposite, need to open a history book. Being displaced happened to many people. Including mine. How did we forget that it's not just *our* pain that matters?"

The man shifted in his seat, discomforted.

He didn't expect that answer, I could tell.

"Also, many of us have ideas," I stressed, "other ways on how that space can be used to gain more popularity, more revenue for the city, and make it into a tourist attraction, if only the city councils will listen to us." Looking at him, I knew that nothing I said would persuade him. Some people don't want to be moved. "I could still understand if you believe differently. I don't have to be your enemy."

"You don't think that I know that!" he asked, needing to be angry at me for pointing out the obvious.

"I didn't say that either," I replied, keeping my voice even. I was dealing with a spooked animal, and quickly I changed the scene where we were not humans, but it was like a fox facing a rabbit in the corner. But the rabbit still was skittish and was looking for a means to come out of the situation, alive and victorious.

However, I had no intention of pouncing or devouring anyone. Unfortunately, it did not matter. He had the image placed in front of us, and there was no removing it.

"Well," the man continued, "I suppose that you were there, marching with them on the protest they had a couple a weeks ago."

I looked down at the bus floor, immediately perturbed. I did not show it though; I didn't want to give him the satisfaction.

On September 7th, there was a protest. Hundreds of

people, both Chinatown residents and other Philadelphians, did a peaceful march and rally, to save their neighborhood from it being marred by a newly erected stadium.

Why was I distraught? Because it was not a satisfying answer, from my part.

"No," I responded, "I was working that day, and well... I also didn't know it was going on."

"How didn't you know? It was advertised a lot. The march was on the news."

"I know...but that's the side effect to tour guiding; when you are done performing, you shut yourself off, push the rest away, don't pay attention to the news around you sometimes, so that you can recover and keep going the next day."

It was the truth. It was not a satisfying answer, but so it was. When being a guide, you push all your energy into being social. Except your attempts are extreme.

As such, when you are done, often you have nothing left to give, and you leave the world behind so that you can remove yourself from all the anxieties that plague and pester you. But who is there to always understand? Is anybody there? Can anybody see? Or understand?

Some do.

And some don't.

Guess where he fell?

"Well," the man said, "how convenient for you, huh? For all your views and beliefs, when a moment of action comes, you somehow have no idea what is going on. So, you couldn't do it? I wonder if you are telling me the truth, and that you actually did know about the protest, and you just didn't have the courage to join it?"

Reaction is very rarely pinned down to one standard response. But that is not so and cannot be attributed to myself.

One reaction is red, and hot. You are fuming, and you want to respond, to retaliate, and seek retribution for being so wholly offended.

The second reaction is blue and cold. It's to freeze and refuse to be moved or affected.

Your emotions go to that realm to die, and your heart is not worn on your sleeve, as is the case with the red. You don't want to give your opponent the satisfaction.

The third reaction is that of the yellow. Yellow is often viewed as the color of a coward. I don't know where that concept came from. And maybe you are correct. But yellow can always mean another thing for me: it is to do both. To retaliate, but also to give nothing away.

Yellow can sometimes mean that you are mixed.

Red.

Blue.

Yellow.

What was it to be?

Turning away from him, I looked out of the window.

I chose blue.

Eventually, the man got off the bus, much to my happiness.

I saw into his mind; he felt that he had won.

No matter what I did, no matter what course of action that I took, it didn't matter.

With people like that, they always feel like they win.

The bus rode on, reaching 8th and Market Street, where I knew, just a couple of blocks down, was Chinatown, with its unforgettable archway.

As I recalled, very vividly, the many colors on the ornaments and decorations, I blinked, as I thought back on the flashes of red and gold on the Face Changer's arms, as his dance began...

Chapter 7
The Man in the Material Mask

June, 2022

Faceless!
   With his fan moving seamlessly through the air, the Face Changer struck up a familiar chord that lay dormant within me, but was ever present, and ever existing. The performer moved along the stage with elegance, passion and precision.

Every action could be rendered by the term of staccato: direct, sharp, and striking.

A Face Changer cannot live on subtlety, or you shall sink below the waves of the music and spectacle that surrounds them. They must come forward and make strong their stance, emerging through the mundane and declaring themselves to be magnificent. Confidence and control *must* be their subject, and they *must* rule it.

The best Face Changer cannot merely stand there and change their masks. The best can be dancers and have some technique in martial arts. They must have dominance over every aspect of their body, be limber, fluid and move through the air as if there is nothing to deter them.

What about this Face Changer?

What of Jin Chang?

Raising his fan in front of his face, and removing it, the black cover on his face gave way to a red mask with lines on it to add features and I saw his eyes.

The crowd cheered as his mask changed quicker than a second.

He twirled around, raising his fan up, with seamless movement, and his dance continued. After another swift movement, his mask changed to black, with white outlines to show the features.

Afterward more dancing, it changed to blue.

Then to a mix between blue and red.

All of this, he did within the blink of an eye—if an eye could blink that fast at all.

Moving forward, with his fan placed in front of his face, the audience was waiting for another change.

Cheong-Jin lingered, taunting the audience, making them want more. Kaori told me that he responded to Cheong-Jin, Jin, or Cheong.

From behind the microphone, was where I stood. Although that was not where I stayed.

Rather, I found myself moving, despite being wholly unaware of doing so until long after the fact, closer to the stage to get a better view of the Face Changer.

Since I was along the curtain side, the audience could not see me at all, giving me the freedom to admire, and go unobserved.

To know.
    To see.
    Then to be unknown.
    And be unseen after.

Tour guide!

———

To tease.
    To tempt.
    And to triumph!
As the performer lowered his fan, there was no change! The morph that the audience was waiting for had not come.

We all assumed that his mask would change, but it did not. Rather, the Face Changer raised his arms to the side, saying 'yes, you didn't expect that, did you? Same mask!'

This led to people laughing.

However, a Face Changer requires more than just precision and incredible skill—there has to be something else within, that can be unleashed without, that can jump off the stage and latch onto the watcher.

This Changer went further than that.

Standing up, he raised his hand to his ear, asking the audience to let him hear them. To invite them to cheer for him. With us all, you didn't have to tell us twice. All too eager, the audience cheered for him actively.

All too willing to feel the excitement, to fall into the exhilaration that occurs when being swept up in the euphoria of the moment, I clapped for him as well.

I had seen Face Changers before, and now I would see

another, blending the familiar with something that I was surprised by—different. Because, what occurred next was surprising, and what I was wholly unprepared for.

The performer left the stage! He went down the steps, moved around the curtain, and he went in front of the crowd, on the ground.

I had never seen a Changer walk up to his audience and greet them, but it was so.

Due to the large size of the audience, there were adults and children sitting down on the ground, in front of the people who were on the benches.

He walked up to those families and people on the ground and proved once again how he was something all new to me. He greeted the people.

Overjoyed, everyone, especially the children, responded by slapping his hand as well, even going so far as other kids rushing forward to shake hands with the Changer. Even more-so, came an action that added even more to who was the man behind the material mask. One child came forward with his fist in the air, hoping the action would be reciprocated.

Leaning even more forward, I kept my eyes on the Changer, unable to look away. What would he do? Would he know? Would he return the gesture?

Amazed and satisfied, I smiled as I saw the Changer balled his fist as well and returned the gesture. On the child's face was exhilaration and joy. How could she have felt anything else but special? From out of the throng, she emerged, moving forward, hoping to be seen, and to desperately feel that this talented person spied her out of the corner of his eye.

Well, he did see her. He noticed.

She was given a moment, and she would never forget him. What child could do otherwise? What would I give to ask the Changer how did it look? When the children rushed forward, excited for him to notice them, to feel special from under and over the surface of their self-assurance, did he know? Did he know what he gave them?

Emblematic of a remarkable aspect of human nature and a quick willingness to understand, a Face Changer, from China, gave an American child—a moment. Never had I seen a Changer do such. In his costume, it was a true symbol of the culture and tradition that he upheld with every moment and every gesture. Moving fluidly, and passionately, he was what he symbolized. But, over and under, through the foreign, the familiar burst through. And, even with a mask over his face, his character was unfolding itself to the happy some, to the open some, to the band of viewers.

After he finished slapping the hands of those in the front, his dance continued, not on the stage, but on the ground, in front of them. As he danced and twirled, moving his fan seamlessly in the air, he spun around, and his mask was now a deep green. The expression on that mask gave an indication of a cynical/cunning aspect to his character.

Since he did it so close to people, they all cheered more exuberantly.

Moving to the other side of the crowd, he greeted more people, before he turned again and brought the crowd into a greater height of suspense. This time, it was a half mask. The top part of his face was still hidden, but it ended under his nose. Thus, his lips, chin, and cheeks were visible.

We only saw part of the hidden man. We would not be satisfied until we saw the whole man from underneath.

Once the cheering died down, he moved elegantly, back behind stage. Going back to the steps, he halted.

While I did not see his expression, because intention is all in the eyes, I felt the intention all over his body.

He didn't just take a moment to breathe—he was building up anticipation.

After a few seconds, he moved back onto the stage, with the same energy and execution that he began with. We had now come to the climax of his piece.

Dancing more around the stage, with flashes of black, gold, red, blue, moving fluidly and organically, he whipped around, the mask completely disappeared, and we were left seeing his face. The Face Changer finally showed us the man from underneath. His skin was a nice tan, his face was wide, his eyes were slanted, and his cheeks were full.

Upon seeing him, the crowd roared out, for their anticipation had been met and reached its culmination. And upon hearing their praise, the Face Changer smiled. A beautiful smile.

That was the *familiar* that I did remember from many years ago.

At the end of the performance, the Changer always revealed his face, and they knew—they always knew that it was the moment where they could show emotion, as well as elation. If doing their job correctly, they used the *grand* reveal as a chance to do a *grander* relatability.

It's their chance to reach across the stage and connect.

Despite myself, or ignorant of whatever I was supposed to believe I should be like, I felt the need to reach out and relate in return. And so, I gave in, not accepting the habit of the cynical snob, who finds it intelligent to thrive on the ability to disconnect and claim to be 'above it all'.

Well, I was not above it all. I found myself, without even

thinking first, but thriving on instinct, to be amongst it all. Or below it, call it what you will.

I related to him immediately. Drawn into the spell that he cast over the crowd, he enraptured all and held nothing back. Truly, there could be no other way for me to feel anything else but what he had asked of us.

———

Eventually his dance came to an end, he removed his headdress, turned back to the crowd and bowed.

His hair was short and traditionally black, but I had no time to admire his exit, because I had to return to my job.

Falling out of the fantasy that he placed over us all, I fell down to the present, rushed back to the microphone as Kaori lowered the music and gave me the 'you can talk now' signal.

"Wasn't that amazing?" I spoke into the microphone. The crowd shouted out in agreement. "Our next performance will be the Peacock Dance."

I explained to the audience that this was a folk dance that would be done in the style of the bird that it was named after.

"So," I said, "please welcome Tsai to the stage."

Kaori turned off the mic and began to play the music.

Tsai came onto the stage. With her black hair stylistically done up, Tsai was a very thin woman with a distinct and unique face.

She wore a white dress, with a few volumes to it that led to her flowing through the landscape on the stage.

When the music began, Tsai started her slow and elegant dance immediately.

With her hands, and turns, she gave you the distinct

image of if a peacock really had been morphed into a woman, with an organic transition.

With a different act, in comparison to the first act, there was still a cohesion, that was organic to have the show continue.

Standing to the side of the stage, my angle and view was drastically different from the audience's perspective, giving me the ignorance of knowing the image from the front, but only from another angle. Another lens.

Eventually, the Peacock Dance came to an end, Tsai bowed gracefully and exited the stage.

Kaori dimmed the music, turned my mic back on, I thanked Tsai for her performance, and then began to introduce the next act.

This time, it was the juggling act, and the juggler was Pierre, who was not Chinese at all. Indicative, once more, of how Philadelphia was struggling to come back, how this festival was scrounging around to have an act at all, I was quick, as well as eager, to accept and understand.

When it comes to talent that is willing to open its arms to us, beggars cannot be choosers.

Behind him was his assistant, Ally, who handed him whatever props that he would spin in the air. Pierre was not a child, but was a man in his late forties, which only added to his experience. Or rather, his age cemented his skill. With bleached blonde hair, he clearly had an inviting presence as he moved energetically on the stage. Ally had brown hair of a medium length, a lovely face, and a beautiful full figure. In her face was kindness, and openness.

The same could be said of Pierre.

They looked like good people.

Then again—they were performers. Behind the stage, in

the cold light of reality that does not happen when you are putting an act on, time would tell.

Once the act began, I would see the surprise of knowing that I was not watching hand-juggling, but foot juggling!

Eventually, the juggling turned to him juggling a very large playing card that was half his body size, which Ally had brought over, without there being one mistake occurring.

The fear of knowing that he could drop whatever fell from his feet and fall on his face. Of one wrong move made, one trick of the movement, and all could come crashing down.

Yet, how was I to know? Riding the high that comes from the audience cheering from every trick that you master and complete, the euphoria had fallen over the audience, and they were there with him—in the seats and on the stage, with him linking with them, and them becoming a part of him.

And all the while, Ally was there—to hand him his final juggling object: a very large hourglass.

My mouth widened, astonished, as I wondered how he could accomplish this.

Placing the table on Pierre's feet, he continued to juggle it, over and under, around and with incredible dexterity. With every trick, the audience was astonished and cheered at the proper times. Finishing after the climax of his act, Pierre embraced the receptive audience, before he and Ally went back off stage and I introduced the next act.

It was Tsai again, in what would be the fastest costume change ever. Her dance outfit was now a mixture of black, red, blues and whites, with a more modern kind of dance, that was inspired by Chinese Frescos.

While I was quite certain that the Peacock dance was

prettier from the front, for some reason, this dance was more appealing from the angle that I watched.

As she danced, I assumed about Tsai, based on her looks and appearance.

I made the guess, that as the summer wore on, she and I would never say one word to each other.

This supposition was wholly without foundation, and I do not know why I had that thought, but there it was, laying at the core of the irrational side of my brain that thrived on instinct rather than experience. After all, we had not even been introduced yet. So, what the hell was I talking about?

And then came the final performance: Cube Art.

Once more Pierre and Ally returned to the stage, with Pierre dressed differently. He had a giant cube-frame in his hand, that was a little over half his height, and he juggled it, with all the flair and panache that he had with his previous performance.

After a few minutes, the act ended, cementing the triumph of the show.

When Kaori lowered the music and turned the microphone again, I accidentally knocked into the pole, but luckily, I was backstage, and no one saw that foolhardy move.

"Let's welcome all of our wonderful performers back to the stage for one final round of applause: Jin!"

Now, with the outer costume off, Jin was just wearing his black performance pants, and the black tunic that was underneath his costume.

The Changer, of another world, had morphed back into the everyday man that he was.

"Tsai!" I called out.

Still wearing her full costume, Tsai walked gracefully onto the stage.

"Pierre and Ally!"

Pierre and Ally dashed energetically behind them and all four performers took their final bow.

I gave closing announcements, encouraging the audience to partake in the excellent food vendors as well as enjoying the beautiful lanterns.

After announcing the time of the next show, we had finished.

Kaori turned off the microphone, I changed the background of the stage, to indicate the 9:00 p.m. time for the next performance and turned to her.

"Fwehh!" I said, mopping my brow dramatically. "Was I pathetic for being so nervous about this?"

"I was nervous on my first day."

"How long did the nerves last?" I asked, lightheartedly.

"For me, it lasted the whole day. But for you, it might be longer."

I chuckled.

"You're funny."

"I try."

"And you're right too. I'll be nervous every time I come to work here."

Kaori picked up her bag and slung it over her shoulder.

"Really?"

I chuckled, taking out some throat spray, because I felt my voice getting sore. "Get to know me a little better and you will see why."

Rather than being disturbed by my cryptic behavior, Kaori shrugged, accepting it for what it was, and left to enjoy the festival.

Finishing coating my throat with the spray and a cough drop, I slung my bag over my shoulder and went back out the way that I came.

As I moved around backstage, it was as vacant as it had

been when I arrived. All the performers had gone back inside their tents, returning to solitude and safety.

After all, the epidemic was still a problem, and they could not afford to get sick. It was expected of them to perform every night, making illness or injury to avoid as much as possible.

When looking at the tents, and knowing the occupants in them, I wondered at Tsai—and especially Jin.

Two years ago, the COVID-19 disease was 'believed' to have originally sprung from China, and there were all kinds of rhetoric that was hostile in tone. Our politicians, at the time, were the worst about it as well.

And inside of the tents, Jin and Tsai were safely kept. It was for their own physical and health safety, yes. But as I folded over every political scenario in my mind, I could not help but wonder and worry of how we viewed them. Did they presume that we hated them? That we despised them for a plague that was beyond their control?

After all, these things just happen. Sadly, yes. But history has proven that plagues spread, especially when two nations are constantly trading with the other.

But where there are problems, humanity must always find someone to blame. Leading to the innocent people getting caught in the crossfire of that persecution.

Jin and Tsai were performers.

They had done nothing.

And if they did fear how they would be received, this was Philadelphia—all have claim here. Or all ought to be.

And perhaps, one day, they would not perceive me as a threat.

May I not be judged until I had done something stupid.

Sadly, eventually I always did something stupid.

I went back out to enjoy the lanterns.

———

With a swiftness, I raced through the darkness. I had just finished the last performance of the evening, and it was 10:45 pm. Quickly saying goodbye to Kaori, I changed the background to the stage, slung my bag over my shoulder, and went to make a hasty exit from backstage. When doing so, as I moved along the tents, I heard some scuffled movement.

Out of the side of my eye, I saw flashes of black, gold and red in the darkness. What was more was that I vaguely saw the half outline of a man, watching nothing—after all, what was I to anyone backstage?

Stopping slowly, I turned around, just in time to see the Face Changer's arm as he moved along his tent, and I saw him swiftly disappear.

Hearing a zipper, I was unable to see from the angle where I was. Yet, the sound of the tent's zipper closing gave every indication that he had gone back inside, and I was left looking into the empty night.

Such a little moment, that gave me no reason for pause —but I paused.

I had a train to run to.
Then a trolley to get on after.
To hopefully make it home before midnight.
And to wake up early the next day.

But I froze.

All kinds of reasons could explain this situation. After all, Jin had just got done the show and probably didn't want to close himself off in his tent. Perhaps he just wished to breathe and walk about a little. Or he was curious.

Or he merely wished to have a moment of nothingness, especially after finishing his performance. Often times, we humans have the inclination to, every now and again, fall away from everything. Our bodies and brains shut down, so that we can restart our systems and come back to life.

Yet, for a fleeting moment, I saw his eyes. His expression before he retreated back into his tent and shut out the night.

I could not help but wonder... But what was the point of doing that? Being a young woman, needing to get home, in hopes of surviving all that occurs after dark, should have been my main prerogative.

Adjusting my bag over my shoulder, I dashed from backstage, passed the large dragon lantern, and left the festival behind.

Since the event was over, many people were filing out, crossing the street with me. I was relieved in not being alone, because there was safety in numbers. As I walked past the National Constitution Center, my mind wandered to earlier that day when I had seen the Tibetans protesting for equal rights.

In the dark, there was nothing left to speak out for, as the sun had gone down on another day. Reaching the train's steps, I passed a homeless person who was dozing off by the light of the station. I walked down below, to avoid eye contact with the junkie who was shooting drugs into her veins, right there for anyone to see, took out my train pass, and got onto the train's platform.

With there being a few people already there, I remained close to them and had to acknowledge that I would be waiting for a while.

Looking down, I saw all the drug needles along the

tracks, discarded by the many addicts who haunted the public transportation locations. What about being in public made them want to show us their business? Did they want to be seen? Did they want notice? Or was it simply because they did not care about anything anymore?

Who knows?

Because we know not to ask.

Asking someone why they choose to give into the worst of themselves is the most dangerous thing to do.

Even though it's something that we all are curious about.

In due time, the Market-Frankford Line train arrived, I took it to 13th Street, where I would catch the trolley home. Due to the lateness of the hour, I knew that I would be in for a long wait.

Sitting next to two women, who clearly had returned from a fun party, I took out my copy of a book that I was reading, placed my bookmark to another page and began to read where I left off.

Or attempted to read, is more like it.

For, despite the book being a compelling read, I found myself going over the events of the day. Or rather, the events of the festival.

From the lanterns, and how they looked at night, to Kaori, Tsai, Pierre, Ally—and what of Cheong Jin!

My eyes widened at a sudden realization that was perplexing, to say the least.

In my mind, I saw Kaori. Her face, while somewhat generically lovely, I remembered all her beautiful features.

With Tsai, her face was more distinct, it stuck out to me, very prominently.

The same with Pierre and Ally. I recalled precisely how they looked and would never forget their appearance.

Although, there was Jin.

Between removing his mask when he had finished his act, and him walking on the stage, I saw his face, as clear as my own hand.

And yet, for the life of me, I could not remember what he looked like now.

His face was a blank.

Chapter 8
Another Public Transit Tale

December 1, 2024

From blue to blank.

That is what you do to your disposition whenever you have encountered a very awkward scenario.

Your mood is a color and then you reset yourself.

Or if you are smart, you do it.

You must reboot, or you will carry the anger around within yourself, and the next thing you know, you've unleashed your rage toward the wrong person. Thus, creating a vicious cycle of victimhood; where does it end?

It ends, in just more of the same.

Whatever that may be, to your definition of 'same'.

Leaving the cares of moments ago behind me, I focused on the 'more of the same' ahead.

That man who I disagreed with and ridiculed me for not marching in the protest to save Chinatown was gone, and I could move past him.

Riding into the busiest parts of the city soon, we reached City Hall. City Hall was a building that, for the longest time, was the tallest building in the city—until it wasn't.

"I heard that there was a curse about the building, or something like that," I heard someone near me say.

Turning, I looked at the two people who were sitting opposite of me, with their cameras out, eager to take a picture of the historic building. I never rolled my eyes, nor was judgy about people taking pictures of it, for why not? It was a beautiful structure, who, when you become used to it, you walk right past it, and it becomes just another part of the mundane scenery.

Then, occasionally, you look up at it, you know?

In the way that sometimes, you become super aware of your breathing, how the ground feels when you walk on it, the softness of when you touch another person's skin when they hold you, and it all feels new again.

Every now and again, you look up at City Hall, and you take in the entirety of the building. How incredible it was when it was first built.

How it still stands. And all the work to make it.

New!
It feels new again.
And so...

It brings you back to life.

"You are right," I said, marveling at the building that I had seen many times before. "You're referring to the Penn curse."

"The what?" the woman asked next to him. They both had the same accent.

"It's the Penn curse that you're talking about," I repeated.

The bus stopped at a red light, so I was able to talk about it in more detail, for them to take a picture.

"Look at the top of the building and you will see a statue of William Penn," I added, "he was the English Quaker who founded Philadelphia and Pennsylvania. He wasn't perfect, but he was darn well better than most people in his time. The King of England gave him this land, in the new world, to pay back a debt, but Penn quickly began to realize that this was not the King's land to give him. This land belonged to the Lenni Lenape tribe, so he paid them for the land. His statue was put on the top of City Hall, and it became the tallest building in the city. And here's where the curse began."

They leaned forward, interested.

"In Philadelphia, we had four main sports teams before we got the Union Soccer Team. Our baseball, football, hockey and basketball teams. Then, a few decades ago, another building was built that was taller than City Hall."

I shifted in my seat, crossing my legs to get more comfortable.

"It's called One Liberty Place. Because of that, City Hall was no longer the tallest building in downtown. That was when all our sports teams went through a slump. They never won any national championships. It was said that William Penn's spirit was very angry, so the sports teams were cursed. The superstition grew so popular that the taller building placed a small statue of William Penn on their roof. So, he went back to being the highest thing in the city. And here's where it gets fun. Just after that happened, our baseball team, the Phillies, won the World Series. Eventually, our football team, the Eagles, won the Superbowl.

William Penn's curse was lifted, and now our sports teams are not cursed."

"Do you believe that?" the man asked me.

I smiled with my eyes.

"Hell yeah. What's life without a little bit of irrational superstition?"

———

Since it was City Hall area, and it was about the time that everyone was getting off from work and out of school, the traffic was—well, you know, right?

Due to the large number of cars, and other buses, be it transit or touristy, even when the light turned green, it was slow-going. We barely moved more than a few feet, when the light turned red again, and we were stuck in traffic.

Red!

Traffic!

As if, with the turn of the mind meets the turning back of time, a series of unfortunate events rolled back upon me.

I found myself engulfed in a slew of bad memories— and bad histories, not often belonging to me, but still affecting me, as many of us can feel the effects of tragedies from generations ago.

The interior clearly began to meet the exterior, because I began to flinch, or made a face to show that I was not happy about something.

"You okay?" the woman asked.

"I'm fine," I assured them, "I'm not sick or anything. It's just that—you know how you are sitting down, nothing is wrong at the moment, and then suddenly, you remember something bad. As if, your mind just won't let you rest in peace. Like—your brain has to think about something to ruin the moment, because that moment of peace is not good enough for you?"

"Ah," the woman said, rolling her eyes, "yeah, the moment of self-hatred that comes out of nowhere, and just bites you in the ass. Yeah, what happened?"

"Well, it was three things. The first one is historical. The second one was something that I saw on the news, and it happened right when we are about to turn the corner. The third one happened to me."

"What was the first thing?"

"Look that way," I said, pointing to the left side of the building. Following where I gestured, they saw a statue, a short distance away, of an African American man. "That's the statue of Octavius Catto. He was a teacher in the 1800s, he was a civil rights leader, he was the first one to desegregate the trolleys in Philadelphia, and he also desegregated baseball here in the USA. The first time that a black and white team played against each other was in 1869. It was the Pythians versus the Olympics. Once that game was played, baseball teams, of different races, began to finally play each other. That led to baseball eventually being integrated within the teams."

The man looked at me, confused about what I had said earlier.

"So, why is that bad?"

"Because he also was the one who successfully got black men to vote in Philadelphia. When he was walking back from voting, for the very first time, he was killed by a group of men."

When hearing that, the bus grew quiet, still as a grave-yard that no one wishes to enter. Only was the traffic outside to be heard, moving everything along in its common course. And naturally, there was also the sound of the bus's engine below, rumbling underneath us, but it was not to interrupt the dead moment that hung in the air.

Rather, it served as a reminder, pushing us further and further down, reminding us of worse times that have gone passed. And of worse times that could lay ahead. The rumble continued, becoming that of a hum, letting us linger in what I said.

But we all felt it:
 The soft seats we were on.
 The floor beneath our feet.
 The air being pumped in.

The cars outside.
 The people who sat within.
 The outside world seeping.

Entering through our pores.
 Dragging us down.
 While also lifting us up.
 Through tragedy.
 And also, history.

Which becomes enlightenment.

But as is the way of all things, noise enters. For that is what signals a great change in atmosphere and vibe. The light turned green.

The bus's sound changed as we moved along, and souls moved along with it. It was time for us to shift away from this moment, and drive on, drifting to our next emotion, with the traffic taking us along with it.

Eagerly, I went with them.

The bus moved around the corner, and to our right was a historic building called the Masonic Temple. It was a classical structure that was in the Greek style. Like everything else, over the years, it is pretty to look at but is now rendered less of a location for a secret society and more of a footprint in history.

Especially since, right next to it, was the Water Revenue Building, where you went to pay your city taxes. Just a little dose of the reality of bill paying to bring you come crashing down to the present.

That helped my 'moving on to the second part' a lot!

"The Second thing happened right there," I said, pointing ahead. I was gesturing to the road up ahead, where people were waiting for different buses to take them somewhere.

Right behind it, was LOVE Park.

Love Park was a legendary part of the city, where there was a giant red sculpture that said the affectionate word, but written like this:

LO
VE

While the park itself was not very large, it was commissioned by a famous person, was a good meeting hub, and once more, giving green spaces in a modern city.

After all, that was what Philadelphia was initially intended to be.

A city with a slice of country, instead of being solely a concrete jungle, where you could easily lose yourself.

A concrete jungle is all well and good, as long as you want to get lost.

But as for the rest of us, who want to be found? Well then…it's best to get on with it, I suppose.

"It happened a year ago and it was all over the news," I continued. "A biker gang was riding through Center City. They had their faces covered up by their helmets."

I pointed to 15th and JFK Street, which was right up ahead.

"There was a woman driving the car, with her kids in the back seat. One of the bikers jumped off his bike, jumped on her car and kicked the back window in."

"Oh, yeah, I remember that," a woman in the first seats added, recalling the same moment. By the looks of her, she was not a tourist, but was a city resident, who was just taking the bus to get near where she needed to go. She was wearing pants with stylishly ripped holes in the knees, a thermal shirt with a red flannel shirt over it, and a puffy coat. "When the biker smashed her back window in, the mom jumped out of the car and faced the biker down."

"Seriously?" the man near me asked.

"Yeah," she continued, taking the narrative away from me, a task I was perfectly happy to relinquish. "She screamed at him, which shocked him. That pile of shit thought that she was honestly going to sit in the car and do nothing. She was screaming at him, about how she had kids in the back seat, and then he took out his gun, right."

"What?" another tourist asked.

"Yeah," I confirmed, remembering when he aimed the gun at the woman. "He did."

"Put the gun right up to her face, aiming it at her," the woman continued.

Everyone was alert in their seats, dying to know what happened, as well as worried.

"What happened next?" the woman near me uttered.

"She kept screaming at him and didn't show any fear at all. Then he put the gun away and bashed his head against hers. And remember he had a helmet on."

"Did the woman fall down?" the man asked.

"No," the woman said next to him, even though she didn't see it herself.

"That's right," I affirmed, "no, she didn't."

"How did you know?" her friend asked.

"Mom instinct," the woman surmised. "Since her kids were in the car, her protective gene kicked in, she didn't even feel pain and just kept going."

"Yup," I said, remembering everything else afterwards, "she just kept screaming at him. Then he got back on his bike—and she pushed him off it."

"She did that?" the man asked.

"Yup," the other Philadelphian added, "she did, and he fell on the ground. At some point, he got back on the bike and rode off. One of his other friends kicked her car, before the whole group rode off and left."

"Was this all recorded by security cameras, or something?"

"Yes, but not by security cameras," I clarified, "it was taped by a tourist."

The couple looked at each other and so did all the other tourists who were on the bus.

"A tourist was on a tour bus, like this one, but it was a double decker bus with the top open. Since he was sitting at the top, he was recording his ride on the camera. He was taping his journey when the gang rolled up right next to the bus and he taped it all. It was on the news in less than 24 hours. The mom was able to get her car fixed, because after the video went viral, many people donated money to her, so she could repair her car."

All the tourists exchanged glances, wishing to say anything, but unwilling to say everything. Nothing was needed, as it ought to be.

A tourist caught the whole thing.

When it comes to feeling a kindred spirit with bravery, through association of similar identity, you cannot help but see yourself in the shadow of their actions.

The link is there.

It comes.

It connects.

Then it leaves.

But it was there for a second.

"I'm still amazed that she did not flinch when she saw the gun," another male tourist said.

"I think," the woman near me said, "it's because she didn't see the gun."

"You're saying that her eyesight was bad?"

"No. I bet she could see fine, but her instincts kicked in and she did not—or could not—see the gun. All she saw was the man who almost hurt her kids, and how she had to stop it. She actually could not see the weapon, because in defensive mode, the gun was never there."

Focusing ahead, I recalled the video. I remember the mom's ferocity as she leapt out of the car, how she faced the man, how her eyes did not even move when he raised the gun to her head. How her entire face did not even flinch when he bashed his helmet-covered face against hers. How she did not stop berating him.

Such was the will to act.

For her, the gun did not matter.

Because the gun, in her mind, was not even there.

Courage often comes, not from long deliberation, but by the spur of the moment, and the power of pure instinct. We knew it. Even if we did not originally have the courage to do the same.

"And what about the third event?" the man, from the couple, asked me. "What was the third thing that happened?"

"Oh," I said, my tone turning casual, "Look over there."

They followed my hand, where I gestured to the street, 15th and Market, where there was a giant sculpture of a clothespin. Truly, it was a giant clothespin that was about three stories tall and was another Philadelphia landmark.

"It was right there where I got in the middle of a fight, and almost got my ass kicked," I answered casually.

"What!" Everyone on the bus shouted.

———

"What?" Everyone on the bus had shouted.

A natural response if I ever heard one. Although, I did not foresee that the bus driver had said the word right when everyone else had. What even triggered their astonishment further was how nonchalant I was about the announcement. And what's more? It was because I was nonchalant about the conflict soon after it had occurred.

"Yup," I said, as the Kite & Key bus was stopped behind three Septa buses that were picking up passengers who were waiting at the main bus stop at 15th and JFK Street. "Oh, that was a night. It happened when I was on a shuttle bus, trying to get home."

"Yeah," another Philadelphian said, losing all surprise and acknowledging that it was more of the same. After all, we both were public transit riders, so we had seen our share of 'all hell breaking loose over the dumbest of reasons'.

"I can see how that could play out. What happened?" she asked me. "Did you accidentally make eye contact with someone, and so they wanted to punch your lights out?"

"No, I wasn't the problem. I just joined the problem."

"What the hell? You don't get in the middle of fights that you don't belong in. What are you smoking?"

Rubbing my eyes, I had heard that lecture before. Self-preservation was never something that I was good at. But ONLY when I do it for something that has nothing to do with me. For, what are we humans if we do not sometimes have the strange knack of rushing into fights that are not the fights to rush into. And then occasionally not fight the fight that is worth fighting for?

To fight or not to fight? In modern times, that is the permanent question that hangs in the air, and we pretend does not exist. Even when the social undercurrent shoves it right into your eye.

"What was the fight about?" another tourist asked.

Closing my eyes, I dug up the memory...

Ten months ago...

———

My eyes had shot open when I heard a large announcement that was made on the train.

I took two modes of transportation to get home: the

Market Frankford line train (known to Philadelphians as the 'L'), and the 11 Trolley, which took me home. Usually, I would get off the L at 13th and Market and catch the 11. But that evening, after I had gotten finished from work, I joined the masses who, doing the same, had flooded the train stop at 2nd and Market Street.

Like the rest of them, the exhaustion of the day was telling, to the point where we were shutting down, internally. From the drooping of our posture, to our slow walking, it was like we were zombies from the movies 'Shawn of the Dead', or 'Warm Bodies'. The only activity that most people shared was the capability to remove their phones and lose themselves in any games or podcasts that they had on their devices. That literally was all that they could muster up, and I did not blame them. Because, when it comes to emotional resurrection, the best savior was the 'screens in our jeans'.

When waiting for a train, the first thing that you see is the light on the tracks, flashing ahead and letting you know that you will soon get home.

Then you hear the noise of the engine. Next, you finally see the train turn the corner. And you wake up again. You feel uplifted.

Once the L stopped at the platform, the doors opened, a couple of people got off, but the rest of us passengers came on in droves, got seats where we could or stood when there was no room.

The day had been long for me, and I had spent the last hour of work, with my eyes open, but my brain shutting down, and everything else inside of me was slipping away. Usually, falling asleep was hard for me to do, but this would prove to be the exception. The second that I sat down, the worst happened. I fell asleep immediately. Which was the worst thing that I needed, because I was getting off soon. Yet, by providence, once the train arrived at 13th Street, a voice came over the intercom.

"The trolleys are not operating underground!"

The announcement had made my eyes shoot open and wake up.

"No trolleys are underground!" the voice repeated, through the train cars, "All trolleys are on diversion at 15th Street. All trolleys are on diversion at 15th Street!"

There was a collective mood shift in the group throughout the car that I was on. Trolleys, even with their occasional setbacks of electrical issues, or it not getting by because some jerk just *had* to park their car on the tracks (seriously, if you see train tracks of any kind, don't park your car on them!) they were a comfortable way of public transit. There was something about a trolley, and its steady rocking, that put you in a Zen state, or made you drift off to sleep.

Shuttle buses were a good substitute. But they were not comfortable.

Also, since it was wintertime, it was cold, the sun had already set, and there was a tension in the air. It cannot be described, nor defined in any way. All I know is that we all felt it keenly, as we had got off the train. We all filed outside, up the steps, passed the clothespin, and saw a slew of buses that were filed along the street.

Out, in the night air, the feeling did not disappear. All of us were exhausted, somewhat grouchy, and disturbed from being inconvenienced. As the chill hung over us, and the darkness loomed above, we were quiet. But there was an anger that lay underneath.

Anger always begins with a silence, that would soon boil over. Without any evidence to why, I felt it; there was mischief in the air. Something bad was going to happen. And it did.

First, the 10-trolley shuttle bus came, then the 34, the 13, the 36—and finally, the 11-bus pulled up. Quickly people raced on, to get a seat, or a comfortable standing place.

I let others move forward, because I felt that the mischief was so close to waking up.

With it being filled up, with so many people, I contemplated on whether or not I should wait for the next bus. There was too much of a chance of being caught up in something. After all, all it took was for one person to accidentally shove someone here, or step on their toes there, and someone would take it the wrong way.

Looking up at the night sky, the clouds were thick, and you could see them against the black. Ignoring my superstitious side, I got on, chalking it all up to human hysteria.

How often we humans can be wrong and right all at once.

The fight did not begin on the shuttle bus.

Rather, it was brought on.

Once we packed into the bus, like sausages, we heard a commotion occurring. Before we knew it, a young man ran onto the bus, holding his hands over his head, in a protective position.

Three other young men charged at him, pushing past all the other people, and began to punch him. All four of them were in their late teens.

The mischief had presented itself.

Everyone on the bus had frozen, taking on the 'don't interfere, for nothing can be done' posture. On the other side of the fight, were a husband and wife, with a child in between them. Placing their arms over the child, they were shielding him from any blows that could accidentally strike him.

When it came to myself, I was quite the coward. But when it came to a fight where there was one against three, and the reason for attacking him was an overreaction, it was not a fair fight at all. Rushing forward, I grabbed at one of the men and began to pull at his arm.

"Hey!" I cried, "let him go! Stop it!"

Strength, they had. Compared to them, I was scarcely a weight on either of their arms. I was about to get myself beat up, over a cause that I was ignorant of.

The man who I took ahold of turned on me with a swift glance—that showed no animosity. The only thing that was in his expression was to make a quick retreat.

Dropping his arms, he moved away from the man he was attacking, raced off the bus and disappeared into the night.

The second man did the same thing, only he rushed out of the back doors of the bus and ran in the opposite direction.

The third man, however, was persistent. Being shorter than the other two, perhaps there was an anger fueled by a desire to show that he was larger than his height and how tough he was.

He continued to punch the cowering teenager, until another man rushed from the back of the bus.

Grabbing the man from the back, he raised his arms under the attacker's, immobilizing him, making it impossible for him to continue fighting.

"Come on, man!" the defender cried, at his wit's end, "It's late, and we gotta get home! I'm tired, goddamnit! We all gotta get home."

Restraining the teenager, he pulled him to the bus's front door and kicked him off the bus.

A minute later, a teenage girl had got on the bus, wearing sweatpants, a bra, and her shirt off.

The fight had been about a girl.

Walking to the young man who had been attacked, I touched his shoulder. "You okay?" I asked.

He did not respond.

It was like I was not there. The man who had forced the other teenager off the bus, returned where he was seated in the back, took out his phone, and it was like the incident had never happened.

Eventually the police came on, to get a report of what happened. However, since the situation had resolved itself, there was nothing to report, the victims were practically silent about what happened, and the police began to leave.

"Thank you, officers," I said to them as they passed me. I got barely an acknowledgement—in fact, they walked right past me, left the bus and that was an end to the whole affair.

The spirit of Mischief had run its course.

All went back to their lives, as if the moment did not happen, except for the couple who had been shielding their kid from any flyaway blows.

Naturally, since the little boy had watched a fight, the boy was shaken, and the mother was coaxing him. Looking at the boy, as his mother wiped his head, soothingly, he looked at me. Being not more than eight years old, at most, his eyes said everything, chronicling the entire conflict in his childlike mind. He could not unsee it and had a million words running through his brain. Thus, making him the only one worth speaking to.

"Well," I said to him and the parents, "didn't expect this, did you?"

"No," the man said, "and this is our first time to Philadelphia."

My eyebrows rose, as my attitude shifted from amusement to astonishment mixed with slight humiliation. This was their first time in our city, and thus, their first impression of us. The Mischief had not fully left just yet. I was an idiot to think otherwise. While the rest of the people on the bus wished to shut out the rest of the world, for obvious reasons, they could not shut out their ears.

The other people nearest to me blinked, as I didn't feel remorse for them. If I was to feel embarrassed, I preferred not to feel it alone. As they looked back and forth, between each other, they could not help but share the shame that comes with how we are perceived, and how we will be perceived.

Now that the fight was over, the conflict resolved, their social armor was torn down, and they were left to become vulnerable to the one thing that they could not afford to do on public transit: they had no choice but feel.

Emotion!

A dangerous thing to have when riding alongside others. Then they looked at the couple, the child, and quickly looked away again. For, when looking at the three of them, their feelings of shame, by association, had reached such a pitch that they could not bear it any longer. They practically hurled their attention back to their phones, to check messages, or watch some sensational news that the media released, and drown themselves in information that takes them away.

I could not be mad at them for that either.

But I was still a tour guide, whether I liked it in this moment or not.

"Where are you from?" I asked them.

"Mexico."

"Well," I said, raising my eyes and giving them a 'please still like us after that whole thing' look, "Welcome to Philadelphia."

The husband and wife laughed, while still protectively holding their little boy—safely away from what the world could throw at him...

———

"We're from Mexico!"

After I had finished telling the story to the tourists on the Kite & Key Bus, the exclamation came from the couple who were nearest to me. I was not surprised, because the Mexican accent was one of the few accents that I was familiar with. I had recognized it immediately.

"I know," I responded, "what part?"

"Mexico City."

"That's a beautiful city."

Having nothing else to say, I decided to mimic my words from the story.

"Welcome to Philadelphia."

Making the connection to the story, they chuckled.

"We were given a better first impression. What happened after the bus got moving?"

"Ah," I said, finishing the last of the story, "don't worry about there being any more problems. Once we got moving, no one was in the mood to do or say anything stupid, so peace reigned supreme. What was unique was the little boy."

"What about him?"

"Now that the problem was over, it stopped being terrifying to him and started being funny. He began to do a mock version of the fight and began throwing punches in the air. Soon he was laughing about it."

"Ah," the Mexican woman said, "it's the Displacement Condition."

"The what?" another tourist asked.

"Come again?" I added.

"I call it the Displacement Condition. This happens sometimes. Now that the danger was over, it was not real anymore. It's in their memory, and they forget the reality. Time either numbs a terrible moment, or it augments it. But when most of us experience something traumatic, we can easily forget the horror right afterwards, because our systems force us to become numb. It's like an emotional amnesia. Why do you think that a politician can be terrible, destroy lives and ruin this country, and they are seriously the worst! Then, a few years later, you forget what they did. Your emotions become displaced. The displacement condition."

We all looked at each other.

"I guess that it must be it," I agreed. "Because it all felt like it had faded away and felt very distant. Since the trolleys were not operating underground, all the buses were taking us to 40th Street, where we could catch any trolley there. Once we arrived, we got off, I led the Mexican family to where they were supposed to be, they thanked me, said goodbye, and that was the end of that."

Truly, that was *that.*

Come.

Connect.

Leave.

Finally, I could do my job.

"What was it like?" The Mexican woman asked me. "For them to have been the only ones to thank you."

"What do you mean?" I questioned.

"Well, think about it. The man who you protected from his attackers didn't thank you. The girl, that the fight was over, didn't thank you either. The police ignored you. Only the couple with the kid thanked you. You didn't notice that they were the only ones who thanked you?"

Biting my lip, I looked ahead, my face evidently screwed up, because I had to confess something that was not a big deal, but felt heavy, nonetheless.

"Yes," I said simply, "I think that I did notice."

When I looked at them again, they felt the tonal change in my voice and somehow knew that I felt a sort of pain. Even if they could not define the pain, nor understand it, they sensed it. Of that, I appreciated them immensely.

"Oh," she replied, hurriedly, "sorry."

"Don't be. I suppose someone had to say it out loud for me to realize something."

Either ignoring or being completely oblivious to the awkwardness that fell over us, the other Philadelphian uttered a truth, which broke the curse of tension and helped us all move on.

"In all seriousness," she continued, "if someone were to possess the storytelling skill, ride on a bus, trolley, or train for a month... you'll have all the writing material in the world to make a series."

We all laughed.

The couple got off at Love Park, and that was the last of me ever seeing them. Outside of the park, all around it were skyscraper buildings, and where us locals spent most of our days.

Clearly choosing to walk where the everyday Philadelphian went must have been a definitive choice of theirs.

They would take a picture in front of the LOVE sign and then be amongst the mundane in the city.

Leaning back, my mind flashed over to when the little boy on the bus was doing a mock version of the fight that he just witnessed.

The Displacement Condition, it was called.

In slow motion, I saw him punch the air, turning the serious into a joke.

Chapter 9
Young & Beautiful

July, 2022

Walking back to the festival after a long summer day where the weather was hot, I was exhausted from being overworked, and my voice was not at its best. Turning the corner to go past the Independence Visitor's Center, two boys were fake fighting each other. Because it was all pretend, they were not exchanging any real blows.

When seeing me, they stopped, raised their arms, indicating me to stop and said, 'Halt!'.

Playing along I raised up my arms, stopping in place.

"Permission to go forward?" I asked.

"Try and get past us," one of them said.

I shuffled back and forth, they mimicked my actions, then I did a fake move to the left, shifted to the right very fast, and rushed past them.

"You cheated!" one of them cried.

"Yup!" I said, raising my fist in the air triumphantly as I jogged past them. "I won!"

My victory was short-lived in their memory, because they turned around and did the same thing to the next person that crossed their path.

Walking back to Franklin Square, there was already a long line of people who wanted to get in. At this point, it was my fourth day working at the festival, and the ticket people at the front knew who I was. Moving through the lines, I walked along the pathway, under the long line of lanterns, found a seat by the fountain and sat down.

For some reason, I had the strange habit of arriving half an hour early. It must have been my fear of being late. After all, if you are there already, what's the worst that could happen?

After moving past the ticket collectors, I moved along the brick pathway with the lanterns overhead, went to the mini golf area to let Matthew know that I was there.

"Oh, and just to let you know," Matthew said, "if you want something cold to drink, I'll give you a wristband and you can get free cold drinks here."

"Seriously?" I asked, overjoyed. "Hot damn, hand it over. Thank you."

Ducking back into his office, Matthew re-emerged, with a paper wristband that I wrapped around my wrist.

"You are a saint," I said, walking away.

"I know!"

Walking near the park's carousel, I found one of the few benches that was empty, plopped my butt down, and began to knit a scarf for my mother. As I removed the needles from my bag, I took out the red yarn and continued my work.

Knitting, being an activity as much as part of the muscle as it is over the mind, is one of the few times when I was at peace and my brain stopped plaguing me.

That's the problem with thought: it's brilliant, until either it makes you overthink something that is simple, or it makes you rationalize the worst sort of behavior and inspires you to follow the worst kind of people.

Logic works, until you spend hours focused on excusing the illogical.

Wisdom gives you rest.

Sadly, I was still at an age when I was not wise half the time.

I was locked into stasis between enlightenment and irrationality. Day in and day out, I would often wonder, and worry, about which side of pendulum my personality would fall.

Don't worry. I was at the stage in my life where I stopped leaving emotional casualties behind.

But those failures are still in my past. Right now, I don't want to tell you about them.

When I tell you, it will come in due time.

But right now, the story is the thing!

Knitting away, I felt tranquility washing over me, giving a wave of dull serenity in its place. A restless person would have begged for anything to happen at this point, like a plane crash across the city, a car accident, or news of something stupid that our previous President had done, so we could laugh at it and assume that it would have no lasting repercussions.

When it comes to us Americans, we always make fun of our presidents, assuming that they would not return and do something horrible.

Well…that's what we thought at the time.

But that's another tale for another time.

Simply put, knitting protects you from the strange side of your brain looking for conflict. It makes you enjoy the peace of there being nothing wrong and also shields you from the other tendency of the brain to look for problems where there are none.

Life is filled with false prophets who get you to join their cults by making you think that everything around you is terrible, and they lure you in with fake promises of how they are the answer, how they will give you wealth, and a land flowing with milk and honey.

Everyone needs to watch an episode of the tv show, "Star Trek", 'The Way to Eden'. It leaves you with hope, while also showing you the dangers of falsely believing that...there ever was a 'Golden Age'. There was never a Golden Age. But, as my mother always told me, 'That's how false prophets get you, and keep you'.

Knitting cleared my head and saved me from many of those. For some reason, the constant application of applying yarn to needle, helped it all make sense.

I have never been deceived since.

I cannot say that it is an activity that can save you all from false prophets who talk well and do everything to make you believe that our lives are garbage, and they are the only ones that can save you. But find *something* to protect you from that.

For the love of Sociology! Find something!

One time, I was deceived.

In a big way.

May the world forgive me.

———

As I was knitting along, I looked up and I saw Cheong-Jin Chang! Freezing in place, I could not help but lower my needle and watch him.

The main thing that attracted my attention is the same thing that attracts so many of us when we see a performer: when they step off the stage and become just like the rest of us. Of course he was not wearing his costume. It was too ornate and beautiful to be worn anywhere else but on stage. Rather, he was wearing black shorts, a black shirt that said, Chinese Lantern Festival, and black sneakers.

He was walking from the stage, looking around slightly, but not very much. Despite that I was near him, he did not look my way at all, which gave me ample time to analyze him.

He walked awkwardly! That was the surprise of it all. On stage, he was elegant, and in control of his movements. He clearly knew how to dance, and to be smooth.

At first, I wondered if he had sprained his ankle or something, but that was not it. There was no limp involved. Then I looked at his face, took in his round cheeks, his beautiful eyes, his short black hair, and thin lips. Reading in between all the mystery that swirled around him, I realized that his walk was not customary.

That was how I soon came to see...he was young. He was a very young man, clearly at most being in his early twenties.

And that age breeds insecurity.

Now it all came together and made sense. On stage, it's his kingdom. He controls it all. But when you are just another face in the crowd, the roles change.

When you're young, sometimes, you can feel alone among strangers. Being used to it is often a skill that you grow into as you age. I didn't master it until I was in my late twenties.

Thus, I firmly believed that he was nervous. He was a little *nervous* being amongst the people. Instantly, I felt a strange worry for him. A concern that stems from wishing to say, 'it's okay, I've been there'.

For a moment, I almost stood up, to make a move to him, but I stopped.

A quick shiver shot through me, followed by a fear of me feeling like an unwanted person. What if he did not even remember me? We were not at the place where I could approach him, out of nowhere.

He would be uncomfortable around me!

All these sensations shot through me, like lightning, and came to my senses. I was not wanted, and so I remained sitting there, until Cheong-Jin walked past me, to another part of the festival, disappearing from my sight.

Between his awkward walk, his short height, and average looks, I should have thought nothing more. On the contrary, I thought of something else entirely.

Beautiful.

I found him to be young, and despite all ideas of what conventionally good-looking was, I thought he was the definition of 'Beautiful'.

Looking down, I was about to continue knitting, but I could not bring myself to resume.

Sitting there, I did not feel like knitting anymore.

I could not focus, and I was beginning to lose my bearings.

What was going on?

―――――

The time of the performance duly came; I made my way to the back of the stage and still did not see anyone else.

Once I got set up behind the microphone, Kaori entered, and said hi to me.

The show began and it progressed as usual.

Once more I saw Jin open the show, making the audience love him, for that was his way. Standing on the side, I cheered every time that his face switched masks, until his face was revealed at the end, leading to a grand applause. When lifting his headdress, to reveal a kind face, a *warm* face, the people liked him more.

Closer and closer, I directed my attention to his eyes, cheeks, nose and his mesmerizing hands. With every gesture, he wrapped the audience around him, bringing him closer to that thing called 'binding ties'.

I leaned more forward, determined to memorize every line on his face, to commit him to memory. After all, I would not see him until the curtain call.

Once I introduced Tsai, she was midperformance when I was in for a shock. Thirsty, I leaned forward, grabbing my water bottle. I was mid-drink, when I saw a figure appear from out of my peripheral vision. At first, I thought it was Matthew, or another technician who had come to check on the sound system, when I saw a swish of black pants. Practically choking on the water in my throat, my eyes widened in astonishment.

Cheong-Jin Chang!

Entering this side of backstage, he had removed his outer costume, to reveal a simple black tunic undergarment. The tunic had a collar with gold pattern around it.

Next to the sound system was a large fan, to keep it cool and from overheating. With it being an especially hot day, Cheong-Jin's costume must've made him sweat, so he stood behind the fan, to cool himself, talking in Chinese to Kaori.

Ignoring how rude it was to stare, I forgot, and could not resist. That was the first time that I had seen him up close before.

Until now, there was a stage to divide us, where I determined everything by distance, and by trying to find the familiar in the unfamiliar.

But there was no point now.

When coming near me, the unfamiliar had drawn so close. Thus, I could take in his appearance even more. He was skinny, but healthy.

His arms were a little pale and fit, while his face was slightly darker. There were some marks on his cheeks, like there were with mine. His lips were thin, but his smile was wide as he talked to Kaori.

Within me, my nerves had grown more awake, as if an electrical current had run right through them all. I felt the air grow close around my skin, and the bumps that were produced from it.

His voice was clear, animated, and with a gentle masculinity to it, as I listened to him, while not understanding a word.

Happy that he did not see me when he entered, I was able to feel relief at him being ignorant of my 'choking' moment.

Without thinking, I felt my posture straighten, me tuck my stomach in more (many of us women, without perfectly flat stomachs, often do), and wishing to put my best foot forward.

At first, I looked at him.

He only looked at Kaori.

Then I smiled at him.

He still spoke to Kaori.

I smiled more gently.

He looked everywhere else.

I kept smiling, out of pure instinct, hoping to give a first impression.

Occasionally, I would watch Tsai's performance, but then I would turn back to smile at Cheong-Jin again. Determined I was, to not be dismissive, or disrespectful. I want him to know that I came in peace.

I also did not want to give the impression of giving into any generalization that is placed on us Americans; that we are rude.

Eventually, Cheong-Jin stood up.

Leaning up straighter, I waited for him to notice me. Perhaps it would only be a nod, a blink, and dare I to hope —a smile back.

Turning everywhere but at me, he left that side of backstage, went back to his tent and disappeared.

I was ignored.

I felt my stomach sink.

I knew that I would have a hard time knitting anything between shows.

————

Walking quickly to catch the L Train, I let my mind wander over the series of the evening's events.

After the first show, I sat where there was no one on the bench, took some time to get reins back onto my attention, rope it in, and I continued to make a scarf.

The next show did not produce a close encounter with Jin. He never came back to that side of the stage to see us.

Or to see Kaori, to be more accurate.

Walking past the side of The National Constitution Center, I passed a couple who were holding hands, and it was like an image that was cemented in my memory.

Our minds, much like that of a camera, can create snap moments that have no connection to each other, but they all come together to capture the full scope of the human experience.

My eyes narrowed in on them holding hands, and it made me wonder. When was the last time that I held a man's hand? The simple act of intimacy that signified so much, even though the action be so little.

Blinking, I quickly dismissed that picture from my mental scrapbook. That moment belonged to the couple, not to me. Because the last time that I held a man's hand, with passion passing between us, was the last of a series of mistakes.

I failed at love.

Better to be alone, than to cause a mess.

Erasing the picture of their handholding out of my mind, and returning it back to them alone, I continued to walk to the train.

In the dark night, my mind wandered back to the black mask that Cheong-Jin begins with, and the black shirt that he wore when he was walking around the festival. Taking in his awkward moment, as he walked through the festival with a massive sense of uncertainty, it just occurred to me. As well as making sense of why he looked through me.

Yes, perhaps he had no desire to get to know me at all.

Or it was just that he was not comfortable being in a place where he did not understand anyone else around him.

And they could not understand him. He spoke Chinese.

I, like many people at the festival, only spoke English. A language divided us.

Him.

Me.

The more that I looked at his walk, his posture, was of a man who was amongst those who could not understand him, and it pressed in on him, that had no choice but to affect his movements.

After all, when seeing him move backstage, he walked confidently and gracefully.

Why would he look at me?

After all, when he looked at me, what would he see but the distance?

The foreign.

And what could never feel familiar.

He got nothing from the very idea of me.

Eventually, I got to the train stop, only to see the train close its doors just as I raced onto the platform.

On the other side of the doors, one of the passengers saw me staring through the window.

Our eyes locked as he saw my expression fall, disappointed that I would have to wait for another twenty minutes for the next train.

He looked at me, helpless, as I looked pained.

Standing back, I rolled my head down as the train went on its course, and I stood near the booth. There was no public transit worker in it, but it still was better to stay near the exit, in case a criminal came on the platform and attacked you.

But now that I was standing, alone, and at midnight, I realized once more.

I could not remember his face.

After all the times of seeing him, the Face Changer still was a mystery to me.

How much I was sick of it, you could not believe.

I didn't want it anymore. When reflecting on the events of the evening, I should have been dismayed.

Naturally, I would have realized that there was no point in me trying to get Cheong-Jin to notice me. And why would he? Kaori was beautiful. She was his fellow Chinese immigrant, so what was there to me?

It was natural and traditional of me to walk away...

But I was not going to do that!

Contrary to my natural habit, I didn't look at it as a resignation.

I saw it as a challenge.

Cheong-Jin Chang, I have seen you.

Now I want you to see me.

I have all summer. I will not stop until you notice me.

Because, when you do, finally I will be able to remember your face.

Eventually. The train came, I got on, and the doors closed behind me...

Chapter 10
Hero

December 1, 2024

The Kite & Key bus doors opened at the Comcast Center Campus, and two women got on.

"I don't know why you wanted to stop here," one woman said to the other, "it's just a building."

The other woman responded in a different language. This went back and forth for a little bit before the first woman began to speak English.

"We are supposed to be speaking English, remember? You're not going to learn the language if we keep speaking French. You must practice."

"French!" I blurted out, overjoyed. This made them both flinch as they turned to me. "You both are from France?"

"Yes," the second one said, casually. Neither one of them was upset at my interruption. In fact, I suspected that they had grown used to that happening to them. We Philadelphians always were flattered whenever the French came to visit us.

"That's brilliant!" I continued. Now I was about to shower them with praise, which would make them uncomfortable. But I had to.

I just had to. I wanted to let them know that we would never forget what the French did.

"I know that this is going to be annoying to you," I continued, "but thank you for saving our revolution."

Blushing, they both smiled and looked at their lap.

"I'm very well aware that, without France," I continued, "the United States of America would not exist."

Some other people on the bus looked at us. Outside of the two French women, the rest of the people on the bus were locals. I knew this, because they paid with their bus keycard.

"What?" one of the men seated behind me asked.

What was even more surprising was that he lowered his phone, curious. How many people lower their phones to just, you know, take a moment to be curious about something that is not 'scandalous'?

"Yes," I answered his question, "When the American Revolution began, we were a rag-tag army, savage, completely unprofessional and ill-qualified. George Washington, alongside other national and immigrant officers, had their hands full making us into soldiers, until other nations began to help us. The main one was France, who literally swooped in and saved us, along with the Haitians that they brought with them."

"Haitians?" A black woman said, a couple seats away from us. "You said Haitians?"

"Haiti was once apart of France," one of the French women said, "it was one of our colonies." She looked at me, in surprise. "I had no idea that we brought our Haitians with us when we came here."

"Yes," I compiled, "over five hundred Haitian soldiers came with you, and they fought for America's Independence."

The black woman leaned forward.

"My mother was Haitian."

The bus went silent.

I looked at her.

The French did so as well.

All cellphones remained on people's laps.

She knew what she was feeling.

We all knew it.

As shared emotions hung in the air, we all felt the awkward binding tie that presses against us.

The binding tie is beautiful but is also too powerful for many people who don't want to keep feeling.

Connection is daunting to most of us who just wish to pass along, because connection is too expensive for the modern person.

Caring has always cost much. How sad, isn't it?

But I was a tour guide. As everyone looked down, almost ashamed of feeling the link between us, I was what I was.

Connect!

It's all that I had to me.

"Your mom's people were one of our heroes," I furthered. "Those Haitians were a part of a regiment of Free Blacks who volunteered for our fight for independence. Your people were there when our country was created."

Her eyes widened from wonder, and despite herself, she had no choice but to do something that one tries to avoid when traveling on the bus: feel.

Unable to control herself, she began to weep uncontrollably.

Out of respect, we all looked away as she cried, covering her face.

"I," she said, fighting to hold back her tears, "I never thought we—it was us. It was also us. And…"

With the emotion swelling up within her so much, she stood up and rushed off the bus, wiping her eyes.

At first, the bus did not move. Now that she had gotten off the bus, we were able to stare at her, without being rude.

Standing on the sidewalk, the woman's eyes were closed as she was steadying her breathing. With her hands on her hips, she was trying to stabilize herself and returned to a state of calmness—or numbness. Whatever is needed to survive the day.

Eventually, the bus had no choice but to keep riding along, back on its course. Closing the door, it drove off, and she was left on the sidewalk, losing herself again.

———

"It's not her fault," the French woman said to me, tearing her eyes away from the half Haitian woman, "she had no choice but to react that way."

"Don't worry," I said, "I understood. Did I rub it in too much?"

"No!" she said, swiping the air, "I'm sure that she appreciated that. We French are different; we like it when you give us credit for saving your asses."

The bus laughed.

"I know that you must have hated us when we did not honor the alliance that we made with you guys when you were back at war with England again," I said. I was about to explain what happened, but she cut me off.

"We're not angry at that. First, you repaid us when you

came to help us in World War II, so it's all square. And also, for those of us who know how to open a history book, after the Reign of Terror, that literally ruined every alliance that you made with us."

I closed my eyes, relieved.

"Oh, thank goodness," I said, happy that she saw why the New United States had broken the alliance they had with their French saviors. "Not only were we broke, and no money or ability to help, but if we did—"

"You would have been helping the new regime that had just mass executed over 27,000 of its own people, including the French King who had made the alliance to save your revolution."

"Precisely. If we did not help you, we would be wrong. If we did help you, we would still be wrong. So, either choice we made, we ended up looking like the bad guys. And that's been our label ever since."

"Yes, that is so American."

We smiled at each other.

"If it helps, we don't hate you," she said, "We know that, last month, a lot of you made the right choice, and we know that you fought hard to do your best. I'm sorry that it didn't work out. Politics just brings out the worst in people."

I looked up at her, sad.

"I'm scared this time."

She put her arm on my shoulder.

"I know. But with what you are going through, France has been through this before, and we're still here." She looked at me, to get the message across. "France is still here."

———

The French couple got off at the next stop, wishing to walk through the most cosmopolitan part of the city, to get comfortably lost with the Philadelphians who were going about their daily lives.

I gave them one last look before I directed my attention ahead.

As I did so, out of the corner of my eye, through the views between the buildings, I saw One Liberty Place, the skyscraper that had eclipsed City Hall.

Softly! Softly! I thought, finding quiet amusement in the building that they had placed the small statue of William Penn on, bringing an end to the curse that had rested over Philadelphia...

Chapter 11
A Good Man

"I curse you!" A child said to another child as they were playing with fake wands.

Wearing one of my nicer dresses, I moved around the children, who were playing in front of the Christ Church Burial Ground, an old burial ground that existed before the USA was even born back in 1776.

Laughing, I dodged between them, heading to the Lantern Festival.

Once I got there, this time, I was not very early. Once I entered, there was only five minutes before the first performance began, so I dashed behind the stage.

Since it had rained earlier, the stage was being wiped down by Matthew, and some other stagehands.

"Hey!" I said to them.

"You look nice," Matthew said.

"Thanks. Hopefully, I can keep it up."

Moving backstage, I was so preoccupied with lifting my dress up over some dirt that I did not look where I was going.

At the last second, I looked up, to see myself about to collide with someone.

There was nothing for it as I walked right into him, and he closed his arms around me.

"Cheong!" I gasped.

With my hands pressed against his chest, I was looking right into Cheong-Jin's face!

I was thunderstruck as our eyes were so close to each other's that I saw every detail of his face.

From a mystery...to closeness...

And so close, with my hands pressed against his chest, I felt the warmth that radiated from him.

Each person has a definition to their face. Their features mean something. For him, his face still defined one word:

BEAUTIFUL

———

Revelation does not often take time to discover, but rather, it can be done in the blink of an eye.

Just as I was able to deduce everything about him, sensitive to the sensations of my body pressed against his, he had remembered himself and pushed his body off mine.

Immediately, I moved back as well, mimicking his action. "Sorry!" I said, despite that I was aware that he would not understand.

"Sorry!" he repeated. His voice was hurried, as mine was.

On both our sides, there was nothing to recommend us, by way of a first introduction. Immediately, I felt like a failure. This is not how I wanted us to start.

Flustered, I repeated the word 'sorry' again, before I

moved past him, practically jogging away from him as I moved to the other side of the stage.

Kaori was already there, by the sound system, as she saw me looking so flustered.

"You okay?" Kaori asked.

Putting down my bag, I bit my lip and held my hands on my hips.

"I'm fine," I answered, automatically, "I'm fine, I..."

"Oh," Kaori responded, not convinced, "okay."

At this point, I had learned to be comfortable around Kaori, and she had grown to be comfortable around me.

As such, I think she deserved an explanation.

"Cheong-Jin," I said, but I practically breathed the name. "I ran into him backstage."

"Ah," Kaori realized, "because you both can't understand each other, you didn't know what to say. If you just nodded, he wouldn't get offended, or anything."

"No, I literally collided into him."

"You did?" she asked, casually curious.

"Yes." Not looking at her, I stared around the curtain, at the many people in the audience. "Sorry. That was the first words that we ever said to each other. Sorry. That's not how I wanted us to begin."

Sorry! That really was how it all began for us. Our meeting was an apology.

At first, Kaori did not respond, but I was certain that it was mostly because she just didn't know what to say.

When she was finally about to open her mouth, she realized that it was 7:30.

"Oh, we're beginning!"

"Perfect."

I got behind the microphone, and the show began.

As the audience cheered, Cheong-Jin moved elegantly

onto the stage, and began his performance. With each mask that he changed on his face, I had more time to reflect on my first assessment of him. Being removed from the feeling of his body against mine, I could now be logical. At the time, in my mind, I had seen a man of superior looks, of impeccable beauty that he left me dumbfounded. But now that we had been separate, I could embrace objectivity.

He was thin, of a healthy skinny frame, that was normal for acrobats. His wide face was not symmetrical; that was very common. His body and his face were no more or less than average. And being 5 foot 5, the fact that our eyes met, indicated that he was practically my height as well.

A short man, thin, of no great superiority of hand-someness.

All along the stage, he moved, dancing and morphing, becoming one main thing: the Ballad of an average man. He was done, and then eventually Tsai took the stage, followed by Pierre and Ally.

When the show was over, it was natural to return to a state of lack of curiosity. Why should I care about him? It made no sense to me. Then I remembered feeling his hands pressed against my waist, the heat of his chest on my hands.

Now, there was no going back.

Sorry would not be the definition of how we would know each other. Our beginning, middle and end, will not be done through an apology!

I make the rules! Not fate.

By the end of the night, he would know me.

That, I promised.

———

The second show is different than the first one, in so much that the Face Changer performs at the end, with Pierre and Ally beginning the show with the juggling.

Before the show began, Pierre gave me a thumbs up from the other side of the stage, and Ally smiled at me.

'You both will be great', I mouthed to them.

'Thank you,' they both mouthed.

Introducing them both, the crowd met them, with interest, and they left the stage to thunderous applause.

Next, was Tsai's peacock dance again, and she was mesmerizing. While she was hypnotic, she would remain a mystery to me the entire summer. From a hot day to a cold one, we never spoke once, and she would be someone that I introduced on the stage and would never be introduced to her. Thus, rendering my initial judgment of her to be right.

Everything that I knew about her was the personality that she brought onto the stage, and when she left after she bowed to the audience, her personality left with her.

On the second show, the Face Changer came at the end, so there was no chance of Cheong-Jin coming to see Kaori throughout the show. He remained in his tent and only came out when I would announce him.

Patience is a virtue, but not to me. We humans like instant results, and instant acknowledgement.

Eventually, it was time for the third show.

Standing on the side of the stage, I had wrapped my shawl around my shoulders, worried that the mosquitoes would risk trying to get past the bug spray I had put on.

On the other side, by the steps leading onto the stage, stood Cheong-Jin. While he wore the rest of his costume, he did not have his mask on, or his headdress.

Now was the moment.

As he waited to go on, I was determined. Living on a

prayer, I took a step close to the stage, staring blatantly. Unable to do anything else, he turned and looked at me with his captivating stare.

Staring was not proper.

And a smile was not enough.

What could make him, through all the faces that he was met with, care for me.

Driven by an impulse that, to this day I still do not know where it came from, I filled my mouth up with air, and my cheeks puffed out. I looked like a marshmallow face.

Then, with my cheeks looking ugly and distorted, I poked my left cheek with my fingers, as if I was bursting a bubble, and my cheeks deflated. I had no time to reflect on it and realized that it might only create a further distance between us and bring about an unwillingness for him to even want to know me.

I had no time.

So, what would happen?

Cheong-Jin smiled.

He smiled at me.

And that's where it all began.

———

Beginnings are easy for some, but not for all of us.

For me, a relationship, be it great or small, has to begin in a gradual way. With Kaori, I also was a little bashful about asking her about him very much. Over the next few days, it was not remarkable for a grand sort of connection.

It was him finally looking at me, smiling at me, and me returning the gesture with making a face to have him laugh.

Language was, and would be, our great divider. I knew one word in Chinese, and he knew three words in English.

How amusing it was that I discovered that 'sorry' was one of those three words. That put an end to any worry that I had about our first meeting. As such, a connection could never be achieved through glances here and there.

From other sides of the stage, I would wave to him before he went on, he would wave in return, put on his headdress, and then begin his performance with his fan.

Of all the words that we never managed to say was goodbye. Therefore, each day was another hello, as we would glimpse each other in passing, knowing that our looks were all we had.

Our expressions were the only thing that we could share, and for my part, I would fall into his eyes, wondering about the man who was underneath it all.

Was he funny?

Was he serious?

Was he kind?

Or could he be mean?

The question of him finally came to an end one day, when I would have to ask something of him.

One night of the festival, after the first show finished, I always pick up my bag, walk out, sit down, knit, or walk around and see the lanterns. As I left backstage, I moved around some of the audience who just finished watching the show. To my surprise, when I had emerged, someone noticed me and approached me.

"Excuse me," the woman said, "you were backstage, right?"

"Yes," I said, "I was the M.C. Did you enjoy the show?"

"Yes, I really did. I was wondering if maybe you can get the Face Changer to sign my program?"

She handed me her festival program, hoping that she could get Cheong-Jin's signature. I was not surprised at Jin's popularity, because he was often the audience's favorite. For some reason, my stomach was filled with dread.

Looking up at the woman, with her family behind her, I immediately wished to oblige. Taking the brochure and pen from her, I breathed in heavily.

"I will ask him and do my best. But sorry if I can't get him to."

Turning around, I walked quickly backstage. After all, time was not on my side.

Kaori was still the only one who was bilingual. If she was not backstage anymore, I could not talk to Jin or ask him anything.

And that was the thing!

I had never asked anything of Jin before. And our communication was silent, where we were removed through language, but connected only through action.

This would be the first time that I spoke directly to him.

Moving past the tents, over the polls that held the stage up, I felt like my insides were squirming from this one simple request.

I was scared.

I do believe that I was willing to face a dragon, rather than do this simple and uncomplicated thing. My feet felt like lead, my legs were clumsy, and I wished to be on the other side of the world.

Give me coldness.

Indifference.

Inactivity.

Being removed.

But red-hot emotions? Oh dear.

Why are we humans so quick to get in the way of ourselves?

Eventually, I made it to Jin's tent, turned to where the

flap was open, and was met by Kaori standing in the opening, and Jin was sitting down.

I clearly had interrupted their conversation.

They both stopped talking, turned to me, and again, I wished that I was anywhere else but there.

My nerves were awake and attacking every single logical aspect of myself, as I felt hot and cold simultaneously.

"Sorry to interrupt," I extoled, practically breathing my words, out of nervousness. When I spoke, my words were rushed, anxious as hell. "Really, I am sorry. But there's a woman outside and she was hoping that she could get Jin to sign her program."

Kaori turned to Cheong-Jin and translated my words. As she did, he looked at me, and I felt even more frightened.

I could only imagine how I looked to him, standing there, shaking like a leaf in the wind. I am not very pretty, but my nervousness must have looked even less so.

Despite my better instincts, I could not look away from him.

Our eyes locked again, and I fell into the curiosity that he wove around me, and how inferior I felt in his presence.

'Please, don't hate me,' was what my eyes said, 'please don't be mad that I interrupted you'.

As he looked up at me, while Kaori continued to translate, my expression was still pleading.

"She loved you," I added, mesmerized by his refusal to look away from me, "she thought you were wonderful."

Eventually, Kaori finished translating for me. Jin looked at her and then looked back at me again.

Biting my lip, I looked down at the ground, worried that my cheeks were red.

When I looked back up at him again, he was still looking at me, without fear.

That made me proud of him.

He turned to Kaori, said something and Kaori translated for me.

"He's coming out to meet the woman."

———

He was?

Cheong-Jin meant that he was going to walk out and meet his fan.

You could have knocked me down with a feather!

"Thank you," I said to Jin, moving back.

Immediately, all the tension within me was released, and gave way to a bittersweet joy.

Jin stood up from his seat, I moved from the tent's flap, and I avoided eye contact with them as I led them from backstage, around the large dragon, and to the grass where the woman was.

When she and her family saw Cheong-Jin, their eyes lit up and I felt more comfortable now, and less nervous.

The show was over, but I was still Cheong-Jin's M.C. My job was to announce him.

"Everyone," I said, "this is Cheong-Jin. And this is Kaori."

The woman and her family immediately began to shower him with compliments, that Kaori was left to translate, and I stood back, becoming a spectator to this all.

Naturally, a small crowd gathered around the family and began to speak to Jin, inquiring about him and his life.

Quietly I remained there, overjoyed. This gave me the chance to know him, without me having to ask him about himself in an awkward conversation.

As they spoke to him, I also learned that he had been

learning his skills for five years, and that he was twenty-three years old. The discussion continued, and I watched Jin the whole time, as he listened to Kaori's translations, and he answered the questions, comfortably.

He could have just written his name down and sent me out with the signed program. Instead, he emerged to greet the people, and be amongst them, without prompting or request.

I could never talk to him, because of the language that divided us. But knowing this about him spoke volumes of the man that stood before me.

He was open to knowing more than just the sphere that he revolved in. Weaving things around him, he brought everything together, in mere conversation that confirmed what I believed him to be: a good man.

Eventually, greeting the Face Changer had come to an end, the people thanked him again, and I thanked Kaori for translating.

"Thank you," I said to Cheong-Jin, hoping that was one of the phrases that he learned.

Stopping in his tracks, he looked at me one last time, nodded to me, and continued to walk backstage, where he could rest until the next show.

Parting ways with them, I turned to the family who had spoken to Jin.

"I was so worried when I asked him for his autograph," I professed to them, amazed and impressed. "I had no idea that he was going to come out like that."

"I know. He was wonderful."

"Yes," I uttered, turning my head, and watching Jin as he walked away, talking to Kaori. "He is, isn't he?"

I felt my tone soften, as my stomach returned to a calmer state.

Turning back to the family, I felt that it was my duty to give some sort of farewell to them.

"Where do you come from?" I asked them.

"Vermont," the woman responded.

"Ah!" I replied, "our fourteenth state. Nice to meet you."

Her eyes lit up, along with the rest of her family.

"We're the fourteenth state?" she asked.

"Yes," I confirmed, "you're the first state that was created after the thirteen American colonies declared their independence. You're our fourteenth state."

The woman smiled.

"I didn't know that. Well, I'll be damned."

Smiling, I slung my bag over my shoulder.

"Thank you for coming to the festival, and welcome to Philadelphia."

They smiled at me as I walked away.

———

Being alone now, walking around all the other crowds, passed a set of lanterns that were composed of birds and flowers, I was able to reflect on the previous events.

All throughout the conversation, I was able to look at Cheong-Jin, as he did his best to speak to the people. His voice was clear, distinct, but was also lovely to listen to.

Now that he was off stage, he was no longer larger than life but was as human as the rest of us.

He walked out to his fans, knowing that he would need someone to translate for him.

Thus, I learned a larger aspect of his character: he was not afraid to walk up to what was foreign to him, or to ignore gratitude. He was not the kind to take those who liked him for granted. They mattered to him, and it brought to light what I could do no less than admire.

He came.

He connected.

And left no sooner or later than proper.

I was distracted as some children ran around me, and I moved down the pathway to the other side of the festival.

Many people had their cameras out, doing their best to get the best pictures with the flowers that hung everywhere, over us, like that of a colonnade.

Respectfully, I waited for them to get their pictures, so that I was not in the frame.

Once I moved along, I made it to the end of the park, where there was a large jellyfish lantern, that was the most unique aspect of the festival.

With it being over a story tall, its legs were many strands of lights, where you could walk along, and in between. With it being a lantern that could be touched, people would move around and under the many legs, weaving their way through lights that illuminated the night.

Passing under the fish, I began to weave my hands through its legs, while some couples were taking pictures together through it.

One of them asked me if I would take a picture for them, and I was happy to oblige. Taking three shots for them, they moved along, and I passed by them, through the many lights of the lantern.

When doing so, weaving my hands over and under the strands of blue illumination, my mind fell into the question that was Cheong-Jin.

Every time that I was near him, I was nervous. Hearing his voice brought a great uncertainty within me. When he was gone, I wanted to know where he was, and what it was like to see him. When he was there, I wished to be on the other side of the world.

I was speechless, even though there was much that I wanted to say.

He was beautiful at first. But when seeing him, off stage, he was as average as myself.

Time can be a great asset to understanding the loveliness of a person, and a great modifier as well.

You can meet someone, think they are beautiful, and then find them to be dull as a box of rocks.

Or you can meet someone who is plain. But over time, they become the most beautiful person in the world to you.

And so, time did its work.

What was beautiful had become average.

When seeing Jin come out to meet the people, smile and be friendly, the average unwound, and everything became pronounced and augmented.

His round cheeks were filled with animation.

His eyes had so much life in them that could not be extinguished.

His black hair was the same color as mine, with a smooth straightness.

The thinness of his body was agile and athletic.

The gentleness of his lips had a beautiful voice that rose from behind it.

In Jin's spirit, I saw light.

Gone were all previous assessments.

In its place, was affectionate awareness.

I had now faced what I felt, to be the ultimate trick.

Of my heart pushing itself to wake up and wonder.

There, in the blue light of the lanterns, I could not believe what was happening.

My mind was overpowered, I was losing my bearings, and I stumbled where I stood.

I was beginning to feel for him.

What was more alarming was that I felt like I was in the middle of it all, before I thought that I had even begun.

Inwardly, I was angry and bitter!

At this point in my life, I was resigned to never feel anything for a man again.

Yet, here I was, feeling every single emotion that begins with feeling a deep affection. A man who I was not suited for. Who I was not made for. And who would never care for me.

The emotions were rising up and could not be ignored.

How long it had been before I saw that there was no turning back.

I liked him, and so, sadly, all that I could do was go forward.

Truly, it was most inconvenient.

The last time that I liked a man was five years ago, and I ended up making one of the biggest mistakes of my life.

Why did this happen?

———

After my asking Cheong-Jin to give the Vermont family their autograph, our interactions between us changed from awkward to comfortable.

We could not speak with each other, because we could not understand the other.

But we could look, we could smile, laugh, and stand near each other amidst a comfortable silence.

That was the best that I could hope for and aspire to.

The rest of the summer at the Philadelphia Chinese Lantern Festival could be described in flashes.

Flash 1

After his performance, he came to our side of the back-stage, with his shirt off and chest out, so that he could cool off from the heat.

Flash 2

One time, he did a dance near me, I forgot my lines and had to scrounge around to correct myself on the micro-phone. When done, I threw my script at him. He caught it against his stomach. Rushing up to him, I grabbed the script and pinched his stomach in the process.

Flash 3

I screwed up one of my lines, and he said, 'it's okay'. He had learned two more English words. I smiled at him.

Flash 4

After one performance being done, he said 'good job' to me, and I curtsied.

Flash 5

When he came offstage, I said 'you were great' to him, but he did not understand. I hated myself for never learning any Chinese.

Now you ask, what of the other performers?

Throughout the summer, I had grown to bond with Pierre and Alley. Ally even hugged me sometimes.

Though they were not the main focus of my encounters, when at the festival, they were without doubt the ones that I had grown to be closest to.

And that's why their role in this story is sadly small.

Needless to say, because my friendship with them had never gone through anything else but casual pleasantness and no conflict, they could never be the beating heart of my story. Yet, let it not be forgotten their names, the time in my life where I met them, and grew to admire them.

———

The last week of the festival eventually came, and it was a series of highs and lows.

Three days before the festival ended, Tsai had to leave, because she had to return to China.

I wish that I could tell you that I would miss her, but there was nothing to miss. The entire summer, we never spoke once. In fact, I have no recollection of her ever being ten feet near me.

Cheong-Jin overcame our language barrier, but with Tsai, she was a mystery that came and went. But I was not that curious to unfold the mystery behind her. As such, her departure was casual and calmly felt. However, we needed another performer, or our show would be incomplete.

"We're getting a replacement," Matthew told me, when I had just finished giving a tour throughout Old City, "We've got another dancer."

"Great," I said, relieved, "what's her name?"

"Constance."

I raised an eyebrow. "Constance?" I asked, worried. "Nice name, but do we know if she is Chinese?"

"I know, right?" he asked, scared. "We're worried that she won't be Chinese too."

"Damn straight," I replied, sincere. "If she's not, then Jin would be the only Chinese performer for the festival. We can't have a performance where most of the performers are not actually Chinese. To quote Mark Twain, 'that dog won't hunt'."

Matthew laughed at my reference.

"Let's hope for the best."

Fortunately, we got the best.

Constance was from China, she was a little younger than Tsai, and her dances required more flexibility and range. Tsai's performances were more graceful and elegant, while Constance's dances were livelier and more varied.

Her first dance was one that she had with a musical instrument and showed how limber she was. The next dance was a fan dance, where she moved with youthful steps.

She was brilliant, and she came to the festival, right when we were closing.

What a strange arrangement.

Yet, I stray from the ending of the summer myself.

How much I wanted it to end on a grand moment, a gesture on my part to render the summer of having a climactic point.

No. Perfect endings are only ones that are written down.

Seldom do we humans end things correctly and give the grand finale that we wish we had made. We are too flawed for the happy ending to find its way to us.

My last day was not the last day of the festival.

Rather, it was two days before the festival ended.

On my last day, Constance had managed to say hello to me, which was more than what Tsai ever did, and I wore my best dress.

I had wanted Jin to remember me, at my best.

The first two shows went beautifully, and I found myself growing misty. For as the evening wound down, I was wholly aware that I spent a whole summer thinking about a man who I knew that I would not see for a year.

On his last performance of me seeing him, Jin stood on the other side of the stage, waiting for the show to begin and him to be introduced.

When his eyes fell on me, I did a little dance to show off my dress, unapologetic in what it did in the eyes of puritanical morons.

Lifting up the blank mask that was on his face, just enough for me to see his lips, he smiled and laughed.

Victories have every right to be gained where they may, and since my triumphs were little, I was content to bask in them.

His smile was like a hint of light in the dark of the evening.

His laugh was a melody that moved over the voices in the audience and reached my ears—even though my hearing was horrible.

If this was to be my last night in seeing him, then I would give him the best announcement of the summer.

After greeting the audience, I welcomed Jin to the stage.

"Friends, give a round of applause to our wonderful Face Changer, who is a true delight, Cheong-Jin!"

The audience cheered as Cheong moved passionately and elegantly onto the stage, moving to the center, where the audience was greeted by him: faceless.

As the dance progressed, with his masks changing

between fiery dance movements that placed a spell over people, I watched him jump off the stage, and the audience cheered as they thought he was done.

Their surprise when seeing him come amongst them, never ceased to amuse me, as he greeted the men, women, and children in the front rows.

Due to the season ending, this was the largest audience ever, and Jin was left to approach almost fifty people in the front row.

Leaning my head around the curtain, I wanted to see as many people rush to meet him as children scrambled to get a chance for him to notice them.

Over and under, around and through, was the way of his ability to reach them, to establish that he was the closest thing that they would ever meet to an ideal.

After changing his face to the half mask, where his lips and chin were exposed, he was met by cheers, as he dashed back onto the stage, for his finale.

After a few more dance moves, he turned around, revealing his face when facing the audience again.

That was the last thunderous applause that I would hear him receive, as he bowed to the people, and moved off the stage.

As he did so, he turned and looked at me, as I smiled at him, filled with gratitude.

Gratitude! Why did I feel that? I cannot explain to you why, but I felt it, nevertheless.

Constance was the next on the stage, where she waved to me again before she began, then Pierre and Ally did their juggling act, followed by Constance again with her fan dance.

Pierre and Ally were last on the stage with cube art, and I gave my final 'Let's welcome all of our incredible performers back onstage for a final round of applause', Cheong-Jin, Constance, Pierre and Ally!"

They all came, bowed, and left the stage. Except for Jin.

Being in quite the gaming mood, he did two backflips, as a bit of an encore.

Ever the showman.

Turning to Kaori, I picked up my bags and gave her a wistful look.

"It was nice meeting you, Ka."

"Huh?"

"Tonight's my last night for this. That's why I got dressed up. Was I going overboard?"

"No, you look nice."

Since we had developed comfort with each other, we hugged and said that I hoped to see her next year.

She moved behind the curtain, and I assumed that she left.

Our farewell was organic, well-organized and neat. There was nothing about it that left me to feel as if I had not done my part, so as I picked up my bag, I was shocked when I saw Kaori still backstage, standing next to Cheong-Jin.

He was wearing his stage pants, his shirt was off, and I saw his beautiful skin glowing in the night.

Unable to resist looking, I rested my eyes on his chest and dared to think—to feel...and see the rawness of his beauty.

Moving passed them both, I turned to them just as Cheong-Jin looked at me, with all the confidence in the world.

"See you tomorrow," he said, his voice clear.

I marveled at him, for it was evident that he had spent the whole summer trying to learn more English and had succeeded.

You see, it's not always the larger things in life that impress you, but the smaller moments. For without choosing to appreciate those things, life would be very dull. Very dull indeed.

I was proud of him.

As such, it was my turn to do something equally impressive, to return the gesture.

Letting the smile reach my eyes, I looked at him charmingly.

"Actually, today is my last day. It was nice to have met you, Jin."

Kaori translated for me, and I never stopped looking at him the entire time.

When Kaori finished translating for me, Cheong-Jin looked awkward, and bowed to me gracefully, but with no smile on his face.

Without thinking, I nodded my head slightly, then walked away, around the back of the stage, and to the exit.

My feelings of failure were immediate.

———

You have, I am sure, experienced that time when you realized that you had fallen short in some way. Wholly aware that you could have done better, you reflect, reflect more, and then conclude that you were your own worst enemy.

I did not bow back, because I was not used to doing such.

I nodded, yes, but I was not wholly ignorant that the Chinese custom was to bow back.

How could I have forgotten myself that much? How

much I wanted to give the best goodbye there was, the most heartfelt, to indicate that I would miss him.

I *would* miss him.

That much was certain, but I could not say that. We never developed a bond that made me able to say that. After all, how would he receive that sort of response? I would make him uncomfortable, and I would despise myself even more.

Yet, how was that when compared to how I felt at the moment? How much more I wanted to say!

I did not, for fear that I would say more than what was enough.

Walking down to the L, I saw the train leaving, after I had missed it.

Not angry, I lazily swiped my Septa card on the kiosk, walked through and felt the wind sweep over me, that comes whenever the train enters or leaves the station.

I deserved to be late, I felt, as I sat down on the bench.

Looking ahead, I saw the other side of the train tracks and saw a homeless person.

Forlorn, I watched every single move that she made, sitting lazily, her eyes drooping, her clothes dirty, and her shoulders were slackened.

You see, after you feel like you failed at something, your soul either gets restless, or very resigned. You become quiet, but your spirit is disturbed.

Either you get up, and start talking to yourself, going over everything that you wish that you had said.

Or you become sensitive to everything around you.

I felt the coldness of the bench that I was on, the grunginess of the platform's floor, all the trash that people throwed on the train tracks, the darkness in between each side of the terminal, and the homeless woman on the other side.

Everything about her, from her broken spirit to her defeated look, deflated even more as she tried to find something in the nearby trashcan, but was forced to give up.

Dirty searching for dirty, on top of more dirt.

All of it seemed to morph together, weaving around me and drowning me in all the sordidness that comes from disappointment and regret.

Eventually, the homeless woman sat back down, her energy completely spent.

Looking down, I had no choice but to realize that we were seated in the same way.

I thought I was shit.

Eventually, I heard the train come rolling in the other direction, going toward Frankford, which was not where I was heading.

As it rolled in, on the other side of the tracks, the last thing I saw was the homeless woman, in all her dirt, as she got on the train, heading for another place that she could not call home.

We were lost...

Chapter 12
Out of the Many, One

December 1, 2024

" ... I knew she wasn't homeless," an Australian man said, who was sitting behind me on the Kite & Key Bus. Hearing the world 'homeless' had quickly taken me back to the memory of the homeless woman who I remembered seeing on the L train platform, on my last night working at the festival. Two years ago, it had been, but the moment was seared into my brain.

As is the way with everyone else in the world, I could have a quick memory and maintain a conversation at the same time.

Turning more toward him, I put my knee on the seat, so that I could look at his face. He was a mature man, probably in his early sixties, with short white hair, and glasses. His white skin was the traditional tan that all the Australians had that I ever met. And the traditional disposition; Australians usually were great tourists. They had a natural friendly air, were not afraid of people, and were willing to like anyone who liked them. They also were willing to tell stories. Once he stepped into Philadelphia, this man did.

"So," I said, repeating his story, "you were walking along, and you found a woman on the ground, unconscious, and people were walking around her."

"Yes," he said, "It happened yesterday. We were coming from seeing the Declaration House, and there was a woman, passed out on the sidewalk. Her legs were completely open, and I thought that it was so unladylike. But since she was dressed properly, and there were some items next to her, I knew she wasn't homeless."

He leaned back in his bus seat, his tone becoming softer and more contemplative.

It was a truth, that I knew to be self-evident, that he was still affected by what he saw—and did not see.

"People moved around her," he said simply, but pained. "She was laying there, on the ground, and they just moved around her, completely ignoring that she was there."

There was an unnatural silence that rested inside of the bus. Whether it was because other people had nothing to say, or they were on their phones, the absence of sound made his simple words more pronounced.

In cities, sounds are comforting. The noise can remind us, even when we are lonely, that we are never fully alone.

Now, however, it would have been an intrusion, getting in the way of what I was hearing. And so, for the moment, thank the Spirit of the City, that the sounds were at rest.

"How did you know?" I asked him, horrified that people ignored her. "How did you know that she had suffered from a heatstroke?"

"I had seen it before, back home, in Australia," he explained. "I just got the sense, by the way that she was dressed, that she must've passed out. So, I nudged her, she

144

woke up, she looked around, her eyes were hazy, and she asked what happened? I told her that she had passed out. She looked around, embarrassed, and then she looked at me again. Do you know what she said next?"

"What?" I whispered.

"She said, 'I promise that I'm not on drugs'." He chuckled, but it was not a funny laugh. It was one soaked in sadness.

"People probably thought she was," I assumed, "but that was no excuse for ignoring her, not by a long shot."

"No," he said, "it was not. I got her something to drink and called the Park service. They came, gave her more to drink and cooled her down. She kept assuring me that she was not on drugs; she was afraid that I did not believe her. Eventually, I convinced her that I did know. When she finally cooled off, she remembered what happened.

She was carrying some things to her car. She was feeling hot and exhausted, and so she thought she would make it in time. But she didn't, eventually giving way and passing out on the sidewalk."

Rubbing my chin, my shoulders slackened as I let my weight rest even further on the seat.

Out of shame?

Out of embarrassment?

We all have the Spirit of Philadelphia in us.

And what did the people do...

... they moved around her.

The Spirit of the City was watching that.

———

Keeping my pain to myself, I let him continue the story.

"What happened next?" I asked.

"Get ready for something stupid," he labeled. "Once her body stopped shaking and she had control of her hands, she called her mother. Her mother did not pick up. Then she called her father. He picked up eventually. Soon after that, her mother called her back. Because she put the phone on speaker, I heard it all. She told her mother about what happened, and her mother responded by saying 'why didn't you call me first, instead of your father?'"

I sat bolt upright in my seat.

"What!" I asked.

"Yes. That was her response. After her daughter told her that she did call her first, her mother then said 'well, I'll put your dinner away for you'."

Every part of me turned red-hot, from anger.

"What?" I repeated.

"Yes," he said, heavy.

"Not 'oh my god, how are you'," I remarked, quoting what I thought any mother would naturally say when hearing her daughter passed out, "not 'I'm coming to get you', or 'do you need to go to the hospital?'. She didn't say any of that. She just said, 'I'll put your dinner away for you'?"

The Australian nodded.

"Yes," he said, bitter. "That's all she said."

Looking away from him, I looked ahead. I would say that I had been watching the scenery out of the window, but it was a blur.

The Australian let me sit there, reflecting on the coldness that this woman was faced with, from all directions, but his.

All those people who moved around her did not care. Did not see. Looking everywhere else, but at the truth that was right in front of them.

That would be the label of the United States of America in the year 2024: everyone was looking everywhere else, but at the reality that was right in front of them. Except for the few, who saw everything...while being grossly outnumbered by the rest, who would fail to act.

When finally looking at him again, he saw the pain in my eyes and how I was almost being brought to tears.

"She could have died," I uttered.

"Yes. She could have."

"I'll put your dinner away for you," I repeated the mother's words, 'I'll put your damn dinner away.'"

"I know," he said, rubbing his lips. "I know."

"Well," I said, trying to avoid crying, "you picked the right time to come from Australia, didn't you?"

He smiled gently.

"Happy to oblige."

"Oh!" I said, "your stop is coming!"

He turned and I showed him on the bus map.

"There it is!" I pointed out the window.

The bus had turned onto the Benjamin Franklin Parkway, we were passing the Barnes Foundation, and were coming up onto the Rodin Museum.

"The Barnes Foundation has some of the best Art collection in the city," I said, "and Art classes are still taught there. Up ahead is what you want, the Rodin Museum. I swear, the Rodin Museum has the largest collection of sculptures that Rodin made, outside of Paris."

"Where is The Thinker?"

"As you get closer, you will see it."

Passing the Barnes Foundation, soon, we came upon the Rodin Museum, and as he stood up, I stood up with him so that I could show him.

As we walked to the bus's doors, I gestured along the trees, near the Museum.

"There!" I said, "There it is."

Through the bus window, was the black sculpture of a well-built man, sitting down, leaning forward, with his arms on his knees and his hands under his chin.

"That's The Thinker," I said, which was the name of the sculpture. "It's a cast of the version that was made in 1902. Rodin made the original sculpture in 1880."

"Beautiful," he said, amazed, "even if it's not the original one."

"Thank you," I said, misty. "Right now, I feel like, everywhere I look, we have suffered from people who just don't care. And it's going to get worse."

Being taller, he looked down at me, confused for a split second. Then his expression shifted to understanding and was able to look past my words and see what was underneath.

"Yes," he responded, gently. "That's the one thing that you should learn from us Australians. Back home, you *have* to vote. It's illegal not to."

My mouth fell open, thunderstruck. How did he know? Truly, how did he know what I was feeling?

"It is?" I asked, surprised.

"Yes. Back home, you must vote every time and cannot just ignore it. If you don't vote, you must pay a fine. No one wants to pay a fine, so we all vote. You all should start doing that."

Sighing, my eyes were filled with tears, but I kept them from pouring forth.

"Many people fought and died so that my people could vote," I said. "Now it's like it doesn't matter to many of us."

"I know," he said, being aware of basic history. "That's the sad tendency; people don't *think*."

Tapping my shoulder was his version of a farewell.

I nodded to him, and silently, we parted ways as he got off, to go to the Rodin Museum and take a picture of the iconic sculpture.

———

Sitting back down in a different seat that was closest to the right window, I watched closely as the bus moved along.

Resting my eyes on The Thinker statue, I took in his black form, as he leaned over. When Rodin sculpted the original, I could not help but wonder what thoughts the model had, who Rodin chose.

The range of what could be, and should be, can dance across the mind in the blink of an eye, and the Thinker still sat there, reflecting all of us, at some time or another.

When we could not be distracted by everything in life that filled up our day, and we had no choice but to sit down for a minute, and just think:

Who am I?

What do I believe?

What do I fight for?

What should I follow?

Who should I not follow?

Who should I love?

How can I get more money?

But how do I not sacrifice my morals just to get the money?

Pulling all things together, The Thinker does that. Dragging us from every bit of excess to simple truth, to what makes sense, and what should not be.

What a piece of work he is! Truly masterful, as he shows that art can be the great dissembler.

For some strange reason, I removed my wallet from my bag, opened it and took out the one-dollar bill. Flipping it over, I looked at the eagle artwork on the back and saw the inscription.

E PLURIBUS UNUM

'Out of many, one'

William Shakespeare once quoted that 'All the world's a stage'.

All too true.

But also, the perception of the mind can turn the whole world to art; a form that is everywhere but can be overlooked.

Quickly the world turned to different hues of reds, blues, yellows, pinks, and the people around me were no longer three-dimensional. Rather they were brushes of artwork, moving against the terrain.

As they moved to and fro, one of them turned darker as it fell, passing out along the concrete jungle. Suddenly, all the colors grew stale, the figures became more rushed and frantic, their figures and faces turning ugly as they looked everywhere else, but at the black figure, who lay still on the ground.

There were so many of them! Rushing to get to where they were going, as well as rushing to ignore what was before them.

Then, through all the madness of the many, one emerged, moving quickly, risking looking down at the concrete, to waken the black figure, who moved again.

The brushwork stopped, and the many figures looked on the mover, who helped the black figure rise. The painting therefore was rendered less ugly now, less horrendous, and all the colors resumed as the black figure rose amongst them again.

He only had to come from a long distance away.

ONE

As the bus rode on, The Thinker grew smaller in the distance.

But I cannot help but wonder, as the sculpture sat there, frozen in time, constructed through art, how much he has seen over the years.

How long had he been watching us...

Chapter 13
The In-Between

June 1, 2023

"Watch!" Matthew said to me, as we were walking to Franklin Square to see how the lanterns were going to look. "2023 is going to be much better than last year."

Removing a few strands of hair that had fallen in front of my eyes, I squinted as the sunlight was really intense.

"I'll believe you," I said, "I'll believe you."

After the 2022 festival, the days turned into weeks, the weeks into months, and the months became almost a whole year.

The Fall season was the traditional one for Philadelphia: too short.

The Winter season was also traditional: cold, but not enough snow to kill enough insects so that our summers would not be too overrun.

Spring was always a toss-up, being the most unpredictable one. It was cold, it rained a lot, and you never knew what the temperature was going to be.

Then Summer was now upon us, and I was basking in the heat. Whereas other people can't stand sweating, I'm fine with it, because my body gets to breathe and not wear many layers. From one moment's end to the other, I hear someone wishing for colder weather. I'm too coldhearted to sympathize with them.

I thrive where others try to endure, as they thrive where I am miserable. It's all about give and take, isn't it?

In all those months after the festival, I wish that I could say that my mind left Cheong-Jin behind, in the summertime, as I moved forward and had many experiences that allowed me to forget.

However, at this point in my life, I had developed a habit of finding being static to be charming.

I worked.

Went home.

I brought groceries.

Went home.

Worked more.

Went home.

Occasionally I went shopping in a clothes store, or online, because of the eternally selfish habit of needing to buy something to feel satisfied. Is it the hunter-gene in us, where we need to search for things, to find fulfillment? Our ancestors used to hunt for their food, and now that many of us don't, we have to satisfy that aspect of us through shopping. I am certain that I do not know why. Someone better than me would have to answer that conundrum.

What I did know was undeniable; I never forgot him.

Secretly, I kept him deep within my thoughts, where I let

him dwell in my daydreams. Sometimes the purer side of me won out, and we had conversations that I always had wanted to have with him. Other times, the wanton side of myself was victorious and I fell into him, with our bodies pressed against each other, and he held me close, never to be parted.

The dream often grew too much, to the point where I was angry with myself. I had turned him from reality into a dream. When I saw him again, that would not be fair to him, or to myself for that matter. Thus, I was resolved, when I saw Jin again, I would be happy to see him but also understanding that I meant nothing to him. And I knew why. He was a performer who was cheered by millions of people.

I was a co-worker passing through on his way to everything that awaited him. He was always racing toward something. While I was always lying in wait for something good to happen.

Something to bring resolution to my past.

Or at least, a reason to justify what all those mistakes were about.

At last, Matthew and I reached the front of Franklin Square, as the workers were putting up different lanterns to contrast with the previous year gone, and the new summer rolling in.

The brick walkway into the festival was just as impressive as it had been last year.

Each summer, the Philadelphia Chinese Lantern Festival had to be re-built, with all new sets of lanterns.

A new year.

A new look.

As I looked up at it, I felt the inviting colors rush over me, as the world took on paint strokes on a canvas, washing itself over in hues of reds, golds, and blues.

It had been almost ten months since I saw this spectacle, and I felt the familiarity of it wash over me. I wondered how I went so long without it being here.

Philadelphia always had a Chinese community in it since before America's Civil War. Their existence was a part of the Spirit of the City. But the festival breathed more life into it. It resurrected everything about what made their *chi* a part of the living mechanism that belonged to the city...a city founded on many different nations who were screaming out for an identity that longed to keep more of the same or wanted to be unique to where they had run from, or where they had no choice but to come to.

Every city, town, and village are founded on many screams. The trick is turning those screams into conversations.

The Spirit of our city is the same spirit that runs through the country; it swings between both. And just when we thought we reached cordial conversation, the screams return, and we begin the process all over again.

Sadly, you never notice how we claim to be going forward, wishing for progressivism and the equality initiative to take full effect.

It's because we are plagued with a cyclical system, where people wanted to go back—to what? Honestly, what are these better times do they remember?

Newsflash! They never existed.

But this scene was different. When looking at the Chinese Lantern Festival, everything took on a better light, the view was warmer and gave prospects of feeling like a balm has been placed around you, making you feel safe.

'Home,' I felt. It felt like I was home again.

After being away from this for a whole year, I wondered how I could have been without it for so long. Yes, as you age, you learn to carry on, but when you are confined to one circle—nothing like the world coming to you. For as you learned, I cannot go to it.

Placing my arm around Matthew's, I felt elated.

"You might be right. This is the better year."

I could not wait, but I had to hide my exhilaration.

After a year of not seeing him, Cheong-Jin would return to Philadelphia.

My heart was awake again.

———

Last year had broken me, with how much I worked. All last summer, I was fighting back sickness, from exhaustion, as well as constantly losing my voice.

The Summer of 2023 would be different. I said that I would only work Saturdays, so that I would not run myself into the ground like I had done before.

When the Festival finally opened to the public, I was all pins and needles, waiting for the weekend, so that I could see old friends again, and have Kaori translate that I missed them all.

Except for Pierre and Ally.

Since they were not Chinese, I knew that I would never see them again. After all, they had been there as a replacement for the lack of performers we could get.

Instantly, I knew that I would miss them, since they had been so kind the entire summer. Yet now that COVID 19 was no longer a big threat to all of us, like it used to, Chinese performers were coming to Philadelphia, and we had enough talent.

As such, Pierre and Ally were in my past, and I had to accept that I would never see them again.

But Cheong-Jin!

Seeing him again would make it up for me not seeing the rest. His coming was enough. From Monday to Friday, my thoughts filled with his dancing, and his figure—but still, not of his face.

Another reason that made me crave the sight of him was because of another revelation that I had to deal with for the ten months that he was gone from my life.

His face had disappeared.

Whenever my mind would wonder over to him, I remembered his voice, his body and his movements, but his face vanished from my memory.

It was like some curse was placed over me and just as I got closer to remembering him, the image was snatched away.

My nerves were frantic and my craving for his presence grew more augmented by every hour.

Friday night, I could not sleep in anticipation of seeing him.

My mind did not want to rest, from excitement, and felt miserable and exhausted the next day.

After work, I rested my eyes just enough to look presentable and did something that I never did. I put on some makeup.

When it was finally time to go there, I thought it would be best to be at least a half-hour early.

This way, I would have time to see Kaori, talk to her again, and then maybe she would have more time to translate between Jin and me.

When walking to Franklin Square, I caught a glimpse of myself in the glass windows at the National Constitution Center.

Straightening my dress, I did my best to look

presentable. When I did so, I chuckled. During high school and college, I had no intention of looking nice. Content I was to wear baggy clothes that hid my figure, and I also treated pajamas like they were uniform; I was a staunch believer in not dressing to impress. By not trying, you felt cool.

As you age, you can easily do a complete 180 and go in the opposite direction. Learning to be lovely in your apparel has as much to do with confidence as it does have to do with work etiquette.

You look nice at work, to make yourself presentable.

But you also do it because you realize that there is nothing shallow about dressing as such. Where once before, I thought nice clothing indicated an obsession with looks, I learned that, in fact, I had been the snob for so long.

There is no shame in dressing up or dressing down. I just despised the wrong things for so long.

Misdirection, as I have learned, is a sickness. It goes around more than the common cold.

Once I felt that I was presentable, I continued to walk to the park, and very soon, I found myself looking on the sign:

PHILADELPHIA CHINESE LANTERN FESTIVAL

I felt the familiar wrap itself around me, overjoyed that I would see old acquaintances. Now I could continue what I had started a year ago. And what was abandoned for ten months could start up again.

When I checked in at the minigolf house, to announce that I was there, I was in for a surprise.

"Hey Bri," Matthew said, as he gestured to his right. "This is Michelle Ling, and she's going to be the one to do the music for you this year."

Internally, my posture felt like it stood up even straighter than ever.

What about Kaori?

Turning, I saw a Chinese woman, equally as beautiful as Kaori was, and probably around the same age, which was mid-twenties.

Like her, her black hair was straight, perfect, they both had the exact lean, thin, but shaped figure, and a well-framed face.

Hiding my disappointment, I smiled at this new person who had clearly taken Kaori's place.

"Hi," I said, "I'm Briseis. Briseis Cunningham."

"Hi," Michelle said, with clear English, but with a defined Chinese accent.

"It's nice to meet you," I responded.

She echoed the sentiment, and I felt the awkwardness that comes whenever you meet someone new.

"You look really pretty," was all that I mustered, with my voice a little fluttery.

"Thank you," she replied, back, equally as bashful. I felt comfortable in the fact that we were in the same boat; we didn't know what to say.

"Well," Matthew continued, "I'll take you backstage again, so you can re-learn everything."

"Great," I said, a little knocked about by the turn of events.

As we walked, Michelle got a phone call, so she had to excuse herself as we headed to the stage.

"I hope she didn't notice that I was surprised," I whispered to Matthew, "I thought that I was going to see Kaori again."

"That's usual. Every summer they have a different person doing the music. The job is usually done by temps."

"Temporary people?" I asked. "Then...is Kaori even working here at the festival?"

"No, she didn't come back. Like I said, it's usually a summer job for many people."

"Oh," I replied, a little filled with consternation. "Well, another one comes, connects, and leaves. Why am I surprised by anything anymore? Well, at least I get to see Cheong-Jin or Constance. Unless Tsai is back again."

"Oh, you didn't know?"

"Know what?"

"Every year the performers change. We have a whole new lineup of people."

"A new lineup!" I gasped.

When seeing my shock, Matthew looked at me queerly.

"Yes. You thought that there would be the same people from last year?"

"Yes," I responded, astounded, "I did. I thought we would get them back again, with some more new performers to make up for Pierre and Ally being gone."

"No. We get new performers every year."

"So, the ones from last year are not coming back at all."

"Mostly likely, no."

Outwardly, I looked only surprised, but internally, I was devastated.

Cheong-Jin was not coming back. I was choking from within on the grim reality.

I would never see him again.

Michelle had finished her phone call and rejoined us.

―――――

When going backstage, I saw the long red dragon on the

green, where people were already taking selfies next to, despite that it was still daylight.

"But we have a good lineup this year," Matthew added, "all the performers are women."

"Really?" I asked, both proud and equally disappointed.

A whole demonstration where female performers do all the routines, is inspiring and signaled a wonderful message.

But Cheong-Jin would not be there. The pride one has in their own gender is proper and ought to always be so. However, if we feel for the opposite sex, romantically, that is —then there will always be a fascination with them.

There is nothing wrong with men and women being drawn to each other, in the same way that there is no error in the same gender having connections. *Both* dreams are correct.

For many months, I had a dream—a dream I waited to happen, and it left me with expectations, and something to wait for. We humans long for things, but oftentimes, the wanting is more satisfying than the having.

This time, I refused to be caught in that trap. When seeing Cheong-Jin again, I would accept that there might be awkwardness and inability to communicate everything to each other. Although I also would accept that seeing him was better than waiting for him.

Now, I would not even get to put that to the test and see if I was correct in my resolutions.

How much I wanted to see him!

But that is life, isn't it? A series of personal disappointments that mean nothing, in the grand scheme of things, but so much to us at the moment.

And the moment is everything. Because it has a right to be. We have a right to stand there, feel the heartache, let it make us turn into statues, where we shut out the emotion.

Afterwards, a moment later, we turn into a Banshee, our feelings spill out all over the place, then we shout and scream.

We break. Because we have the right to break!

No one tells you that little fact of life. It's okay to break sometimes.

Feel disappointment.

Feel betrayal.

Feel despair.

Be sad.

It's only when you don't repair yourself, after the proper time of grieving ends, that makes you unforgiveable.

For me, the proper time of grieving could only be for a few seconds. After all, I was meeting new people.

I would cry later.

When going backstage, there were five Chinese women of various ages. Most of them were young, but one of them looked like she was in her forties.

"Hello!" I said, waving, "I'm Briseis. It's nice to meet you all. You can call me Bri."

Assuming her role as a translator fast, Michelle introduced me.

One of them spoke.

"They are happy to meet you as well," Michelle explained, which left me smiling.

"You all look lovely," I complimented them. And it was true. All of them, in their unique way, were various forms of gorgeous.

"This one is Gong," Michelle said and gestured to the older one in her forties. Though she was older, and had wrinkles, she was very handsome.

"That is Zhang and Youki," Michelle pointed to Gong's left. Both women were clearly in their twenties. Zhang was traditionally beautiful. There was nothing incorrect about her features.

The other woman, Youki, had less perfect features by far. While that should have rendered her as being not as pretty, it was the opposite. Sometimes, the flawed diamond has a more comfortable look to it, thus making it easier to warm up to.

"And that is Lucille and Lee."

Sitting down on their phones, Lucille and Lee looked up at me and nodded. While their names began with 'L', their looks were entirely different.

Lucille was tall and built, indicating that she had to be the more muscular side of the acrobat's act. Her features were strong and striking.

Lee was short and slight. Like Zhang, her face was conventionally perfect.

When each woman acknowledged me, I could not help but mark the difference than last summer.

In 2022, that summer, meeting the performers was a random free-for-all kind of situation. I was never formally introduced, and I met them over the course of the summer.

This time, it was different. I was formally introduced now, and they knew my name.

When going to the other side of the backstage, I saw the familiar sound system that Michelle had to regulate. When going back there, we put our bags down as Matthew showed me how to change the stage screen from showing the times of the show, to the Chinese temple image.

"By the way," I said, "I forgot to mention. Your name is my mother's middle name."

Michelle looked at me.

"My mother's middle name is Michelle," I said.

"Oh." Michelle smiled. "Cool."

"Did your mom name you that because she liked the name, or is that her name too?"

"She liked it, yes, but she wanted me to have a more common name. She was hoping, that if I ever went to a different country, especially America, a more common name would help me be more accepted."

"Oh," I responded, a little embarrassed at me not making that deduction before, "I never would have thought of that. Is that a real thing?"

Shutting my eyes, I realized that was a personal question.

"Sorry," I said, "you do not have to answer that."

"It's fine," Michelle assured me, "I'm not afraid of you asking me something like that. Personally, I think it has helped me."

"Did she ever want to name you anything else?" I asked, picking up the script. "Or was Michelle exactly what she always wanted?"

"She really did like the name and was probably always going to go for it. But my middle name is my grandmother's name. I think she did like the name just as much but chose what could help me the most." Michelle looked directly at me. "Leerong. My grandmother's name was Leerong."

I nodded.

"Either name works," I said, "but Leerong is brilliant."

"Yes, it is."

Matthew finished instructing me, so I started to practice by changing the background on the stage.

"Is your name Briseis, because it runs in the family?" Michelle inquired.

"No, my mother's name is Botswana. Like the African country. And my grandmother's names are Judy and Edith.

I'm named from a character in Greek mythology. Have you ever read the epic poem called *The Iliad*?"

"No, sorry."

"It's fine. Most people know about it, but don't read it. No judgment. It's about the Trojan War, between the Ancient Greeks and the Trojans."

"Oh, I know about that! That was the war that began when the Prince of Troy ran off with a Greek king's wife, Helen. She was said to be very beautiful."

"Yup, she was. The war lasted ten years, and the main fighters on both sides was Achilles, who fought for the Greeks, and Hector, who fought for the Trojans."

"From what I remember, Hector was great."

"He totally was. In the ninth year, the war stopped going well for the Greeks, because the lead King Agammemnon, was the worst of the worst. To make up for losing a Trojan woman that he liked, he took Achilles's lover, Briseis. When he took her, Achilles stopped fighting in the war, withdrew, and the Greeks suffered for it. Literally, if Achilles did not fight again, the Greeks would have lost."

"So, that's what you're named after?"

"Yeah. My mom read the poem, liked the name, and here I am." I raised my arms out to the side, showing how resigned I was to the idea. "I'm named after a man's lover, who was taken by another man. I love the name, but it kind of was like a bad omen."

"Being named after a woman that a man stopped fighting a war for?"

Blinking, I looked at Michelle, as she gazed at me with her innocent eyes.

"I never thought about it that way before," I considered. No, really, never had I thought of it, from that direction." Chuckling in a bittersweet way, I tried to explain. "I always looked at my name as a beautiful curse. It was lovely, but it put me on the wrong path."

"Names don't control our actions," Michelle said, "they just give us history."

Eventually it was time for the show.

I changed the background of the stage, so that it showed a red temple on the back, and then I made the announcement.

"Good evening! Welcome to the Philadelphia Chinese Lantern Festival at Franklin Square!"

The audience cheered passionately, giving the indication that we had a large crowd.

Enthusiastically, I introduced the first act, which was carpet juggling. It stared Gong and Lucille, where Gong would juggle small carpets with her feet and hands, while she did acrobatic moves. I told the audience to give them both a round of applause.

When I finished talking, across the stage, Gong shouted something, smiling at me.

Sadly, because of my inability to hear things over distances and over music, I didn't understand. Looking at her, confused, I would feel even worse when Michelle translated to me what Gong said.

"She said that you introduced them well, building up the audience and making them excited," Michelle explained.

"Oh!" I responded, mortified that I didn't smile and nodded back to Gong, showing her that I appreciated her kind words.

Gong and Lucille took to the stage, and Lucille really showed that she was the 'muscle' of the group. She was the one to hold Gong, and support her as Gong did flips, splits, handstands and other incredible moves, while literally juggling carpet with her feet and hands.

Long story short, they were both incredible in every way. And for Gong to still be that awesome in her forties, showed that she was all about her craft.

The next up was, and always would be, my favorite.

After all, what is a Chinese festival without a Face Changer?

Last summer we had one... we had Cheong-Jin.

Now we had two: Zhang and Youki.

Where Cheong had a black ensemble with flashes of red and gold, with bold prints, Zhang and Youki had white robes. Where both of them matched in that regard, with many equally ostentatious prints and also being vibrant, Zhang had a white and blue theme, with a fan. Youki had a white and pink theme, along with a pink cape.

While the Face Changers had always been my favorite part of the festival, I had high expectations and set it by a standard.

Zhang and Youki met them in spades. Since there were two of them, it allowed the routine to not get tired. Sometimes, they danced in unison, and other times they did different movements, or stopped while the other could do a routine. My favorite part was when Youki's mask turned into a monkey, and she moved her hands like one, and did a brief jig.

Reaching the climax of their act, they stood back to back and changed their masks at the same time. With it being well-synchronized, they turned their heads and changed to a new face in the exact same split second.

Once they were finished, I cheered for them on the side of the stage, and then had to introduce the next act, which was ribbons and dancing.

With rainbow attire, Lee came on the stage and twirled ribbons as she did a dance. She was lovely in her movements, and from the side of the stage, I liked how she made the ribbons twirl around her as she turned and flipped them.

From the front, I confess that I was not certain how it looked, so I believe that I had the best seat in the house when it came to her act.

The fourth act was, for the audience, the highlight of the show: jar juggling. Though it's not jars that she juggles. Lucille came on the stage, in a different outfit, that usually is worn on circus tight rope walkers. A chair was put in the front of the stage, and she would juggle laying on her back, and with her feet.

Like it had been with Pierre, she juggled a few items. The last two things that she juggled was a picture frame, which led to the audience cheering merrily, thinking that was the end.

Then Gong and Zhang came out, carrying a table!

"What!" I gasped, thunderstruck. I looked at Michelle, astounded. "What!"

"Yup," Michelle nodded. "Yup."

My reaction mirrored the audience. When seeing that table come out, the audience extoled a collected 'whoa!' and they could not believe what was about to happen.

Holding my breath, I watched as Lucille juggled the table, and sometimes with one foot.

Yeah, she tore the house down.

The fifth act was one that I liked, which was a tea-pouring ceremony. Dressed in nice costumes, Lee and Youki did a tea pouring dance, where they did dances and movements as they poured tea into a cup.

This worked well, probably usually, but there was a—

CRASH!

I heard glass smash against something, and I jolted forward, wondering what happened.

"Michelle!" I exclaimed, turning to her. "Did you hear something break?"

"Yes, I did," Michelle said, going forward. The dance continued, but it was a stall, as Michelle assessed the situation. "She dropped the cup, and so it broke. She needs something to pour the tea in."

Michelle rushed backstage, as I stood on the side, helpless. Watching the very subtle panic in Youki's face, they still continued, as if nothing happened.

Eventually, Michelle found a red plastic cup and managed to hand it to Youki from offstage, so that the dance could resume.

Sadly, the plastic cup was no substitute for a real teacup, but they continued. When Michelle came back to the sound system, I appealed to her immediately.

"Do we have any more teacups somewhere else?" I questioned.

"No, we don't," Michelle replied, taking out her phone, equally as dismayed as I was, "we have to order more."

The act resumed, and while Lucille's performance could not be rivalled, I still liked Youki and Lee a lot.

Telling the audience to give them a round of applause for their skill, I concluded the evening.

"And for our final performance," I declared, "is the wonderful art of plate-spinning."

All the performers came out for the final performance, except for Youki, who could not do the costume change in time.

They wore white and orange ensembles with some green design on a small part of the pants.

Gong and Zhang literally did rolls and slow backflips while still spinning the plates.

There was no way around it; whatever my personal feelings, this would be a better summer. There was just something about these performers that gave every indication that we were going forward, instead of going back. We must *not* go back.

———

By the next week, I had grown comfortable with the women and acknowledged that they were my superior in every way. What made them superior was not their talent, but one true factor: that *they* didn't think they were superior to me.

I didn't have anything like their talent.

They would smile every time that they would see me.

They had skills that I could try for years and not ever do.

They would acknowledge my presence.

They were the stars of the festival.

When I wore something nice, they noticed.

I existed. To them, I existed.

That's all that we ever ask for, isn't it?

———

The summer began and ended in the same fashion. Every Saturday, I would show up, enjoy myself, and then worry as I went home, about what could happen to me.

You see, what must be understood about the Lantern Festival is not only beauty, but the sense of safety. Everyone who came there, no matter what their background, or who they were told and ordered to hate, the baggage that wore them down as they had trudged through the day—they left it at the entrance.

And there it would remain, when they left again.

But inside the walls of the event, we felt safe, like a collected sort of individuals who could leave the mistakes of the world outside and know that we could all just be one.

Of course, I was being naïve. There is always going to be someone who ruins it for everyone else. This is the flow and ebb of the human experience, which cannot be avoided, sadly.

There must always be a stain to ruin an image of beauty. Sometimes, I think, it's because we want the stain. Despite that it ruins the view for everyone else around you.

But in the confines of the festival's walls, no one wants the stain. They don't want their vision to smear, or to care about what mistakes they made, or horrors they suffered under. At the festival, there were no villains or victims. They are simply living.

I think, despite missing what was gone, I was happy.

Eventually I accepted that Cheong-Jin, Pierre, Ally, and Kaori were gone.

Quickly, I forgave Zhang and Youki for not being Jin. I know that it was irrational to have ever been secretly angry with them for him not being there, and them being the replacements. There is nothing rational about that thought process, but I never said there was. It's wrong to not forgive someone because they aren't the original that you are used to. But that is a traditional response to change.

You hate it.

Even when it's good for you.

In sad fact, sometimes the better it is for you, the more you resist it.

For a week, I gave into that horrible habit.

But only for a week, thank goodness.

Two years ago, if you had seen me, I would have been evil about it for a lot longer.

Now, karma had bitch-slapped me enough around to know what's what.

Due to my comfort with them, I had thought to make a special gift for each of them.

On my last day seeing the show, I asked Michelle if she would stay backstage, for the second performance, so that she could translate something for me.

When going backstage, after they finished, all six women were assembled there. Michelle had done well in telling them to stay together, rather than separating to go to whatever part of the festival that they needed to find a break at.

As they looked at me, I shuddered, nervous. Looking into their faces, I worried that I was presumptuous to have given them anything, but I was already in the deep now.

"Since it's your last night here," I said, breathy, "I made you this."

First, I took out a bag I had knitted, then I took five small clutch purses that I also had knit. All six bags were red, with five stars on them, with the design of the Chinese flag.

When seeing them, I felt the immediate release of a gift not being unwelcome.

Smiling, they each took their bag, demanded to have a picture with me—and they hugged me.

Feeling their kind embrace, I found the joy of knowing that I was not an oversight to them.

You see, that is the blessings and trappings of society. It can be overbearing to us, to the point where we are constantly suffering the mishaps it brings. But then there are moments when all that works in the world comes through the society, balls it all up together, to find something glorious.

They cared about me.

As I cared about them.

Hot damn.

———

When I got home, around 12:00 a.m. (to have to wake up five hours later) I was still wide awake when I fell into my bed.

Dragging at the annoying tendency to need to sleep, but your mind won't let you, you lay there, doing everything you can to make yourself drowsy. The pain of not being able to come down!

While lying under the covers, watching episodes of the comedy show 'Gimme a Break', I felt the heaviness of another summer, another year, come and gone.

More importantly, I still was not fully adjusted to what I had not considered before: the importance of staying put through change, but also how to walk away when it's time to go. Oftentimes those are regarded as two very different things that ought not to mix.

How foolish a notion.

Every situation and action do not require the same response, or reaction.

Sometimes *this* worked. Other times, *that* worked.

This summer, I learned to love the new performers, and not be weighed down by what was.

As such, I also accepted what is.

Cheong-Jin was gone.

Pierre and Ally could never come back.

Kaori and Michelle would also be gone.

And now, so would Gong, Zhang, Lucille, Lee, and Youki.

Everything that had tied me down to the festival was gone. The familiar, the link, was nice, but was naturally temporary.

I knew this and marked it.

But I knew that I was not perfect. Never would be, as a point of fact. If I agreed to work as the M.C. for next year, I would not be happy. Places are brilliant, but it's also people that tie you down to a place.

The people that I cared about would move along to another city or country, spreading their lives, and their skills, and leaving when the wind changes.

Was the power to adjust more or less powerful than the ability to stay put?

I'm sure that I do not know.

What I did know was that it was time to walk away.

Taking out my laptop, I opened my Gmail account, and began writing to my supervisor:

> Hey! This summer was a blast, and I had a great
> Time working at the festival. But, due to it
> being so late at night It's gotten too dangerous for
> Me to be travelling on the train. Sadly, I cannot work
> at the Chinese Lantern Festival Next summer. Sorry
> to be A bother. But you'll find other people.
>
> Cheers,
> Briseis

Closing the book on my life, I had made my choice. That was the end of my summer in 2023.

Chapter 14
Orange, White and Green

December 1, 2024

"It's coming," I said to a little girl who was sitting behind me on the Kite & Key Bus. Her name was Shannon, and she was from Ireland. Her father, who was a U.S. Citizen, with Irish ancestry, had been living in Ireland for the last fifteen years.

Shannon was one of those bold children, age 8, who knew that, when her parents were around, she would talk to any adult with the same confidence as the most self-assured grown-up.

Quickly, she became comfortable around me. When discovering where she was from, I was all too eager to show her where the Irish flag was.

In Philadelphia, there is a long stretch of road that is called the Benjamin Franklin Parkway. Along that road, there are many flag poles erected, displaying the flags of many different nations all around the world.

As a child growing up, I would play in the fountain that

was near that area. When we finished, our parents would drive my brother and I down the parkway, where we would see the plethora of flags before us, waving in the air above, as a symbol.

A symbol of everything that we had become... that we had striven to be like. Those flags marked a journey of the USA, and how it had achieved respectability among the many nations that came before us.

Our flag flew as well, with the colors molding into the others, through respectability and through example.

It used to be like that, until this year.

Now, it was shown that the American flag did not stand for morals but only held up along the winds of money.

This year, the American flag was bought and sold.

"There!" I said, gesturing out of the window. "There is the Irish flag."

Shannon followed where I pointed, and her eyes widened as she saw her nation's banner, flapping in the wind.

"I see it!" the little girl said, eagerly. "Dad!"

"Come on," her dad said, putting her on his lap so that she could get closer to the glass and see it better. "There she blows."

The girl pressed her hand against the glass, taking in the simple but effective event.

"We're there!" she cried, a little loud, but no one was of the mind or mood to tell her to lower her voice. "We're there."

Her head turned as the bus drove down the parkway, until the Irish flag was no longer in sight.

Eventually, Shannon turned back to me.

"Did you ever hear of our Declaration of Independence?"

"A little," she said.

"I'm teaching her about it," her dad explained. "And about how the American Revolution has ties to the Irish Revolution."

"Good," I said, "because there is a connection. And here's another one. Fifty-six people signed the U.S.A.'s 'Declaration of Independence'. But three of those signers were from Ireland."

"What?" they both said together, astonished.

"Yes," I laughed, "three of the signers of our fight for independence were from Ireland."

The dad looked more pointedly at me.

"I never knew that."

"A little-known fact," I replied, charmingly. I loved this bit of trivia. Afterwards, I turned to the little girl. "Also, did you know that one of the best spies, during the American Revolution, was an Irishwoman who lived here Philadelphia."

"No way!" the girl exclaimed, her eyes widening even more as she leaned into me. "Is that true?"

"Oh, yes. Her name was Lydia. She spied on the British who were in her house and sent the information to the American Continental army. If it were not for her, we might have lost the war."

"I never..." the father began, "I never..."

"Heard of her?" I finished his sentence. "It's not your fault. After the war was done, her daughter and descendants told her story. But because of bias and the fact that espionage is all about leaving no evidence, historians refuted her story. But, once we looked at all the facts surrounding how secrets were getting out of the city when it was occupied by the British, it all points back to her." Looking at the girl directly, I wanted to drive the point home. "History is littered by girls and women doing much but being overlooked by many people—including being cast aside by our own kind. But the page turns, and then people remember us, even though it was long after the fight."

With adults, I would be ridiculed for being sappy or melodramatic, but with kids, it was always better.

Adults justify villains.

Kids prefer heroes.

Right now, at the end of this year, kids need heroes more than anything else.

To counteract the villains who won.

I could be cheesy—because for kids, cheesy was cool. It's sad when that instinct dies in them. But right now, I had her at the age where morality mattered before malignity became fashionable.

"But one loss does not make a defeat," I continued, trying to help her understand to the best of my ability. "The first different person to try and change things, for the better, never gets credit or always loses. But their fight is the beginning of a larger fight. Most losses are not a permanent one; it's just step one to a delayed victory."

Instinctively, the girl wrapped her fingers around her father.

"I try to tell her that," her father said. His expression was not what I expected. Rather than hopeful, it was listless.

Or, to put it better, he looked sad.

"You must understand, though," he continued, his voice a little weary, probably from feeling like a failure. "I thought this time it would be different. I thought, this time, the right choice would have been made. I thought that we were better than this. And so, I told her that, this time, prepare for a something good."

My mouth dropped open as I looked between the dad

and the girl. Oftentimes, we empathize with another perspective than our own, but we don't always know how to fully relate. Until someone surprises us by making us feel their emotions.

Here you had a father, with a daughter he clearly loved, wanting to protect her at all costs, but also make her believe that she was capable of achieving anything, and never allowing her to be sent back to a time in history where her rights would be stripped from her.

He told her that the right cause would win.

Sadly, that's not how history works. And we are living history now.

"You were in Ireland when you heard the news," I deduced, my voice shaken—because I was shaken. "You were there when you saw that we failed."

The father nodded slowly and gravely.

"And you had to tell her," I whispered, gesturing to his daughter. "You had to tell her what happened."

Slowly, the father looked down at Shannon.

"Honey," he said, "I just need you to not hear something for a second. You know what I mean."

Shannon nodded as her father placed his hands over her ears. When he knew that she could not hear him, he continued.

"I gave her so much hope," he continued, "and she woke up the next day, excited for the good news. Then I had to tell her. I had to tell her about the loss."

Looking down at Shannon, she could not hear, but she was looking into my eyes, making it easier to fall into them. How was her father able to do it? To look into her eyes and tell his daughter that all had fallen apart.

All his promises were for nothing.

"When you had to tell her, you must have felt like the loneliest person in the world." I realized.

He didn't speak, but he nodded.

"I hated us," he said, "It was like a thousand beautiful glass windows being crashed together at one time. I hated us all. And I had to watch the world see what we did."

"How we failed."

"Yes."

Once more, I felt the pit in my stomach, recalling a mistake that I made eight years ago. When looking at the girl, red grew up within me of the great wrong that still haunted me.

I just met her today, but it didn't matter. Eight years ago, I let her down as well.

"You have every right to hate us," I said, "because we did. Now all that I have left is my anger."

"Then fight," he said. "I'm too far away. I know that you are tired and feel like so many other people betrayed you. You're right. You were betrayed. But after your rest, I still need you to fight."

Silently, I nodded. "I don't know how."

His voice was heavy.

"Do you know why I hold my hands over my daughter's ears? Because it's bad enough that I was wrong about our democracy, how you didn't elect her as president, and how our courts failed. The country had one job, and it failed so bad at it."

He narrowed his gaze on me, while referring to his daughter.

"As her father, I told her that she could become anything, and that belief was taken from me! I felt betrayed by my own people," he said, pointing to his white skin. "So, all that I have left is that I don't want her to see me break," he said, tears in his eyes. "I'm her father. I don't ever want her to see me be anything else than her hero. It's all that I have left."

He leaned more towards me.

"Find a way to fight," he urged me. "Because if you don't, we've got nothing left to believe in. And I will never forgive any of you."

————

When hearing those words, I nodded as Shannon's father removed his hands from her ears.

As he looked down at her, he shook his head. Within the blink of an eye, all pained emotion was gone, and he was back to being 'Dad, the Invincible'.

Leaning away from them, I realized that the conversation was over. As it ought to be.

Looking backwards, out of the window, I saw the three colors of Orange, White, and Green, flowing in the wind, as the Irish flag flew further and further away...

Chapter 15
What Hope May Come

June 1, 2024

"Your hair," I said, as I was walking to Franklin Square, "it's lovely."

I had been walking to the premiere night (okay, I'm not actually sure it was even called that), of the 2024 Philadelphia Chinese Lantern Festival. While I was walking, I had been next to two women, who were clearly a mother and daughter. The daughter was in her twenties, and her hair was dyed with orange, white and green.

"Thank you!" the daughter said.

"Is it symbolic of a team or a flag? Ireland has those colors."

"Oh, this one I'm doing because it's also the colors of India's flag. We are from India."

Immediately I turned into the penitent woman, embarrassed at my own ignorance. I had seen the Indian flag many times. How could I not have made the connection, especially considering they obviously looked Indian.

"Sorry!" I rushed out, "I was being stupid. I know the Indian flag, and even like it."

"It's okay," the mother assured me, "Both flags have the same colors. It's natural."

"Thank you," I said, still a little humbled, "Actually, when it came to the American Revolution, the last shots fired connected to the war, happened just outside of India."

Quickly, their expression changed to curiosity.

"What?" the mother asked.

"Yes," I continued. "In the USA, the main battle was the Battle of Yorktown. It was decisive, and it ended the fighting in the American colonies. But since it was the French who were the main heroes that helped us win, it didn't end there."

I steadied my words, to make sure that I enunciated everything correctly.

"The French and the Brits continued to fight, because of our war. Well, the French had colonies in India, and so wherever they went, they would recruit colonists from that area to fight in their battles. So, the French would have brought Indians from their colonies to help their side, because of us. So, the people of India ended up being drawn into the closing act of the American Revolution, making India connected to USA's independence. The first shots of the American Revolution began in Lexington, Connecticut. But the last official shot concluding the global impact of the American Revolution, was right on the coast of India."

When hearing that, both were amazed at the connection.

"I never knew," the daughter said.

"History is too deep an ocean for anyone to know much. That's why I like telling it; it helps me be interesting, because without it, I have nothing else to talk about."

They laughed at my joke-non joke. After all, behind my humor was the truth. Deep down, the best joke comes from a pathetic reality.

"Is this your first time in Philadelphia?" I asked, returning to casual talk.

"Yes. We are actually here for a wedding," she said.

"Oh! Who are the lucky couple?"

"My sister," the daughter said, "she went to the University of Pennsylvania, and got engaged there. We came to Philadelphia for the wedding."

"That explains why you are dressed so nice. Congratulations to your sister. And please, don't get mad at me, because I would advise you not to do that whole 'my sister is getting married, so when is it my turn' kind of thing?"

They laughed when I said that.

"Love is not a race," I continued, "or you'll quickly get married to the wrong person before you even had time to live a little."

"Don't worry," she responded, "Mom has told me all about that trap."

"I made that mistake when growing up," the mom explained, "when you grow up, you're told get married and have kids. That led to me almost marrying the wrong man at a young age. Luckily, he hit the road, I cried for a little and then managed to get a job. I didn't get married until I was in my thirties, when everyone had given up on me."

"I am in my thirties too, and am not on the lookout, really," I said, "if the right guy comes. But if not, then it is what it is."

"That's how I feel," the daughter responded. "At first, I was thinking about coming here, because my ex-boyfriend got accepted to NYU, and I was looking at colleges too. But we broke up, and while I like Philadelphia, but I kind of don't think that this is a good time to live in America."

"Asha," her mother reprimanded her, "that was rude."

"I'm sorry," the daughter responded, apologetic, "I didn't mean to—"

"It's okay," I assured them both, "I think I understand. You're worried about November, aren't you?"

"Yeah," Asha responded.

"So am I," I replied, heavily, "unless a miracle happens, we might start going backwards. Our justice system is corrupt, our main media outlets are sane-washing evil, and every day it's becoming clear that, most likely, no one is coming to save us from what might happen. I'm hoping that it won't come to that. Come and live here when we begin to make sense. When we get things right, welcome back."

At last, I reached Franklin Square and smiled when I saw the Dragon and words 'Philadelphia Chinese Lantern Festival' again.

Even though it had been a year since I last cast eyes on the event, it still did not feel like a long stretch of time.

This was amazing, considering that the rest of 2023 was uneventful, to say the least.

I liked uneventful, because it made me feel like life was running smoothly.

Sometimes when life is eventful, it can easily mean that something is going terribly wrong.

Yes, occasionally it can also mean that things are going right...but still!

The year 2024 rolled in and so did my worries. Subtle anxiety was brought in along with it, and I was right to feel that.

The political and social climate had reached an all-time high, and this was the 'eventfulness' that I had dreaded.

So, when looking at the festival sign, I felt an immediate relief.

Even though I was just going there for that one night, it was enough to give me a calm and vibrant distraction from all the mania that was going on.

When going to the front, I explained to the ticket-teller that I was there for the grand opening event—or whatever it was called.

When let in, I looked for my supervisor, Matthew. After wandering around, I found him, surprised to see me.

"Bri, what are you doing here?"

I blinked, surprised by this.

"You don't remember? Remember your email when you asked me if I could work on June 18th? I said that I could, so," I raised out my arms, "present!"

He closed his eyes, and I knew what that meant.

"Ah," I teased, "what did you do?"

"Screwed up."

"Welcome to humanity. How much did you screw up?"

"I thought that you meant that you were open to working today, as a supervisor for a walking tour. I didn't know that you meant that you wanted to work this fundraiser/premiere."

I closed my eyes as comprehension dawned on me.

"Ah, that makes sense. I got a call today from Jess, asking me why I was not there, and I told her that I was not scheduled. Now, it all makes sense. You thought that I meant that I was free to work today, and I had meant that I wanted to work this gig tonight."

Matthew looked sheepish.

"Whoops."

"You have a lot to learn, young Jedi," I joked.

"I don't watch 'Star Wars'. I'm more of a 'Babylon 5' kind of guy. What is a Jedi again?"

I raised an eyebrow.

"For your safety, I'm going to pretend like you didn't ask that question."

"Fair enough. Don't worry, we'll find some place for you."

"So, this is a fundraiser? I thought it was a premiere?"

"It is kind of."

"Help me out with your kind ofs. They have more meanings than one."

"It's where a lot of people come here, where they give out refreshments, it's a party, people bet on things, and we try to get donations to pay for this summer season. It's closed to the public, but we're going to have the Face Changer perform his act."

"The Face Changer is performing?" I asked, not with much enthusiasm.

"Yeah. After the fundraiser is done, he will give a performance, as a teaser for the festival."

"Well," I said, casually, "whoever the changer is, I'm sure that they will be great."

"You don't sound that excited. What happened to you, by the way? You only agreed to work this night, and that's it."

"I'm tired of getting home late," I lied. White lies are fine as long as they stay there. Then try not to use them again. And if you can, tell someone, afterwards, sorry, 'that was a white lie'. "Things never were safe. Now they are even less safe than ever."

"True."

"Do you know what's sad?" I asked.

"What?"

"Despite it all, we are still living in the better times. I'll be damned."

"Yes, you will be damned."

Since I was an add on for the fundraiser part of the evening, there was really no place for me.

Seizing the bull by the horns, I stood at the end of the brick walkway, right in front of the water fountain, to tell people where the tables are to bet on things, what time the fundraiser begins, where the bathroom was and so forth. Simply put, I made myself into the greeter for the event.

Where there's a will...

The event progressed easily. Since it was a hot day, we handed them free fans, to keep themselves cool.

All around the park, there were tents with things that people could bid on, fancy finger food being brought on trays, and the elite (or socially elite) were betting on what they wanted.

Those items ranged from a bottle of scotch that was over twenty years old, to a fancy night at a restaurant, or four tickets to the football game.

During this all, I was finally able to eat something— much to the chagrin of my food belly. Before that, I was able to suck my stomach in and look like it was flat, making it appear that I was fit. We've all been there, haven't we?

Until we eat something.

And then we can't suck our stomach in anymore, try as we might. Welcome to being in your thirties!

Once I accepted and digested that first-world problem, I looked forward to the Face Changer after the next part of the fundraising event.

We walked back to the stage and had to sit through another request for donations to help fund the park.

This is all well and good, in theory, but people can only

give but so much before they feel like they are being bled dry. Some of the people began to get up and leave, and we were losing our audience.

Drastic measures had to be taken, so the main organizer for our touring company intervened, put an end to it, so that we could get on with the Face Changer's performance.

I sighed, relieved, because the last thing that I wanted was for the Face Changer to come out, and there would be nobody there to cheer for them.

Saved by 'reading' the room!

The Face Changer was announced, and I moved to the front row, to get the best view of the performer.

Since I was resolved to only see the show for this night, and maybe only see it again, at the end of the summer, I was going to take every opportunity I could to enjoy this.

While there was the initial excitement of seeing a Face Changer again, I was only mildly enthusiastic about it.

After all, what was I about to see that I had not already seen, that was better?

I had seen the best, so what could this performer show that had never been seen before?

The familiar music struck up, that was the Changer's anthem, practically, as I folded my legs in front of me.

There was a flash of movement as the performer came onto the stage with a natural energy and master of movement.

There were flashes of Black.

Of Reds.

Of Gold.

And a red fan!

A fan remained in front of his face as he moved to center stage.

It couldn't be!

Like I said before, when you watch a Face Changer so many times, you know who it is, even before they remove the mask at the end and show their face.

Their movement is their signature.

Their skill is their identity.

Just as the Face Changer placed himself centerstage, flourishing his fan in front of his face, he stood in place.

At last, he lowered his fan, to remove the black cloth over his features.

I knew that form of facelessness.

He was back.

Jin Chang had come back!

———

The trolley ride home had me practically overcome.

I thought I would never see him again. Truly, I had resigned myself to that reality.

I had been met with all the pitfalls that come with losing hope in seeing something again, then ending with acceptance that I had to move on—and he was here.

At the end of his performance, he removed his headdress, confirming that I was right.

From the beauty of his smile to the self-assurance of his ability that led to the natural grace that he exuded when he was on stage.

There was no misstep on his part. He was resolved to be as good as he ever was.

When a delightful surprise falls back into your life after you have moved on, is nothing short of believing that the story does not always have to end.

Rather, it can flow in different ways and then arrive again

at the very same place that you had begun. Sometimes retreading good beginnings can be nothing short of scorching cold. Your body is on fire, but your brain is frozen at the idea of it ever being as good as you imagined it would be.

How I missed him. Never could I tell you what attachment took hold of me when I was near him, but such is the rules of attraction; there are no rules.

It happens. Before You even know it comes.

But when it comes...

Prepare for the emotional thunderstorm!

Come thunder!

Come lightning!

Let it all collide.

Let it all come crashing down.

I came to realize that is what I wanted.

That was what I needed.

I needed to collide into something that was lovely. Maybe even crash into it.

To understand what it meant to feel something again.

In the two years since seeing him, I never felt anything romantic. When growing up, crushes were my bane. I despised liking someone, because it was such a distraction. It got in the way of me thinking of other things.

But now, I realized that, when we become comfortably numb, that's when the real mischief begins. That's when you open the door and listen to the vampire as he gives a compelling case to let them enter. It's when, in a rush to feel something, you support the wrong cause.

This was not me being numb now. I felt my heart patter and so, making me sensitive to everything around me.

Being aware of the air I breathe in my lungs. Knowing how heavy the ground beneath my feet felt.

It was raw truth in my life again.

What am immense magnitude of gratitude that I felt.

You see, once you let one emotion in again, all the emotions come in.

I was not sleeping through life anymore.

I was awake.

Thus, I decided. I would tell my supervisor that I had changed my mind.

I would work at the festival. I would agree to be a substitute; I would work there any night that other people could not do.

Finally, I came to my senses.

―――

The first day of getting to work at the festival was slow-going. Many people wanted that job, so I had to wait at least a month before someone needed me to cover their shift.

At last, in mid-July, I was given the opportunity, and I jumped on it, eagerly.

When the day arrived, I was so nervous that I didn't sleep the night before.

Yes, there was the excitement that comes with something to look forward to.

Then there comes the dread.

Just because you look forward to something, does not mean that it will work out.

As a result, I was regretting the dress that I was wearing, the broken Chinese that I was attempting to learn, the fact that this festival had a whole new set of performers that I had to become acquainted with.

Cheong-Jin was the only one that I would know, and what if he didn't remember me at all?

These were the hysterical thoughts of someone who clearly didn't have much going on in her life; every uncertain element felt like a mountain.

Ah, the drawbacks of privilege!

It's those many complaints about the small things that now have led us down a path where we might be presided over by a violent conman who makes false promises. Privileged people who feel like they deserve more, and whine about so much, are often duped by those people.

But I still had blind hope that we would get lucky. That we would wizen up. Even though all was falling apart.

Hopefully 2024 would be the year of a miracle, and everything would come together, bringing order again, and saving us from the '*pit* and the *pendulum*'.

It turned out that I could not have been more wrong.

Bracing myself, I left my work, stepping up my game by wearing make-up again. (While I was *so* not a makeup girl, I respected the habit of wearing it.)

Eventually, I made my way to the festival, wearing a lanyard around my neck this time, to show that I worked there, and entered.

Since I had worked there the previous two summers, I knew the routine and made my way to the stage immediately.

When I went back there, I was met with two lovely Chinese women, who were sitting down, looking at their phones.

There was a man sitting opposite them, dressed in a white costume, who also was on his phone.

Nervous, my voice cracked a little, as I opened my mouth to greet them.

"Nihao," I uttered, which was the Chinese version of 'hello' and 'you good?'.

The Chinese man nodded, and the two women lowered their phones, but didn't say anything.

I felt like my life was over. I must have looked like a fruitcake.

And what was worse was that no one backstage could speak English. Simply put, I was screwed.

Accepting the fact that I was, quite possibly, going to have a bumpy summer, I quickly moved to the other side of the stage, where the sound system was.

To my surprise, I saw a familiar face.

"Michelle!"

Turning to me was Michelle, from last summer.

"Briseis!"

Happy to see a familiar face, I hugged her a little rashly. Not minding it, she returned the gesture.

"How have you been?" I exclaimed, so over-excited. "And you look great."

"Thanks. So do you. I've been good."

"I didn't know that you were still a part of the festival."

I gave her a shrewd look.

"You like it, don't you?"

"Yeah," Michelle replied, gurgling, "it was supposed to be a summer job, but I found that I like it a lot."

"I never thought that I would see you again. This is great. You can introduce me to the performers and translate for me."

Her face shifted from pleasant to disappointing.

"Oh, sorry, I'm not going to be working the backstage anymore."

"You're not?" I asked, deflating, "but—don't you have to do the music?"

"The performers change music and do all that stuff on their own."

"Oh," I replied, "well, okay."

Michelle gave me a sympathetic look. Truly, I must've looked so pathetic.

"You're not happy about that, are you?" she asked.

"No. Not really."

"Wow." She grinned. "You must've missed me."

We were interrupted by a man walking to the sound system.

Thank goodness that Michelle was there for that one moment, because she could translate for me. If I was not to see her for the rest of the summer, at least, I got lucky that she was there at the time.

The man she introduced me to was Karl, who was an acrobat.

Another man entered, and he was *young*. Like nineteen years old young. He did an act called Space Walking. His black hair was wavy and was cut down to his ears, whereas Karl's black hair was shorter and straighter.

"This is Ling," Michelle referenced him. I smiled at Ling, and he nodded to me, looking me up and down, to size me up.

"And they," Michelle said, pointing to the man and two women who I said my broken Chinese greeting to, "Are Ken, Lily, and Zoe."

As I looked around the corner to look at them again, there was the familiar tent backstage so that the performers could change their clothes.

Slowly, from inside the tent, emerged a male figure.

Cheong-Jin was staring at me.

He was back in my life.

A second can feel like an eternity.

That is the case when you are either enraptured, or when you are humiliated.

For me, the second felt like a visual intoxication of rapture.

In that quick second, I took in his straight black hair, his round face, beautiful smile, his thin but strong body, and the confidence that radiated from him.

It follows, as is natural, for me to stand, transfixed, my eyes lit up with the passions that erupt when you waited two years to see the last person that had stirred something within you. Then you smile and feel as if you walked into a fairy tale.

But this is me that you are talking with.

The romantic, staring, and longing approach never worked for Jin.

Falling back onto my instincts, I did what I recalled working: make funny faces at him.

Smiling, I kept opening my mouth, then closing it suddenly, and puffed out my cheeks.

Jin returned the gesture, by mimicking my expressions. Afterwards, he smiled and waved to me.

My heart felt like it was pounding in my chest, ready to burst forth at the idea that all my worries were for nothing. He was happy to see me.

Or pretending to be happy.

Like a drowning woman clinging to a raft, I was okay with either.

I was given the script to perform with, said goodbye to Michelle, who left the backstage area, and I was left to the devices of Karl, who controlled the music, for the most part.

When Karl was performing, though, he would switch it over to Ling, who only performed his act for the second show.

When Karl lowered the music that plays at the end, he turned on the mic, I nodded if it was okay, he nodded back to confirm, and I began:

"Good evening! Welcome to the Philadelphia Chinese Lantern Festival here at Franklin Square!"

The crowd cheered.

I gave the traditional information for the history of the festival and how it is celebrated in China.

Before I had begun to speak, I had gone over the script, to make certain that I would not trip over my words. Nothing is more humiliating than stumbling on words like 'beautiful' and 'tradition', in which you regret all the lack of attention you paid to your own diction, and makes you wish to run to the hills, trying to escape your own stupidity.

Cheong-Jin was back; I didn't want to stumble on my first day in seeing him.

And Jin was first!

"We begin our performance with the wonderful art of Face Changing, where the performer changes his mask quicker than the blink of an eye in this three-hundred-year tradition of the Szechuan Opera, expressing the many thoughts and emotions of the Face Changer. Let's welcome him to the stage!"

The crowd cheered again, and the familiar music struck up as Cheong-Jin appeared on the other side of the stage, wearing the same costume that he did two years ago.

My heart danced when observing him in the familiar attire that I had grown accustomed to seeing him with.

He moved gracefully and passionately onto the stage, made his way to the center, with his face covered by the red fan.

Fluttering it in front of his mask, he eventually lowered it to reveal the blank black face that he began with.

Now I felt like everything was falling back into place again.

Refusing to take my eyes off him for one second, I cheered for him every time that he changed masks within the wink of a second.

Even more I became enraptured as he did his signature habit of jumping down from the stage and greeting the audience.

Despite that I could not see very well, I knew that children were scrambling forward to see him. He could not fail at impressing the crowd, who were eager to know and love him.

I never stopped caring for him—feeling a deep attachment for him—and longing for him as well.

Call it pathetic.

Call it being drawn to the untouchable.

Call it what you will.

I do not blame you. Have not and never shall. But it is reality, all the same.

Attraction and desire, I have learned, is sadly meant to be nonsensical, and maybe, to be a bit of a mess. For if we loved in a practical and objective sort of fashion, who loved us in return easily, and without the mishaps that usually plague us on the bumpy road to affection, then it would follow that mother nature would look on us and render us dull and tedious to observe. We had to keep her amused, at the expense of driving ourselves mad.

I may not be the most fascinating person that you have met, but even occasionally, I do surprise myself and give her something to watch.

The second act in the show, was the artist art of hula hoop.

It was performed by Zoe. She had a pink and yellow attire, with white dance shoes. Her hair was pulled up, in a ponytail.

At first, she started with three hula hoops, with one on her hand, the other on her body, and then on her feet.

Then she picked up at least three more hula-hoops and began to turn while spinning around.

The last part of her act was when Ling came out, with at least twenty hoops in his hand.

The crowd awed when seeing it, as Zoe put the many hoops over her, then she flipped them over herself, and it looked like she was right in the middle of the 'Slinky' toy.

The crowd cheered as she turned, then she began to spin around as she hula-hooped the whole set around her body.

This was the first time that I had seen that kind of performance.

The next performance was a folk dance done by Lily. Her dance was in three acts. While she danced, it was rhythmic and lovely, but it also required her being very expressive in her face.

While the first two acts of her dance were lovely, my favorite was the third. It was upbeat and required the most amusing expressions on her face. Like Zoe, Lily also was very beautiful.

The fourth act brought Zoe back to the stage for her teeter-totter performance. Karl remained onstage, to assist her, as she had to stand on a board that was placed over a rolling teeter-tot. She did this in three levels, which scared the hell out of me. Although, she made it through it each time, without falling once.

The final act for the first show was Ken, who was a chair

walker. That meant that he would stack chairs on top of each other and do acrobatics on them each time.

Once he reached his balancing act on the fourth chair, he sat down on the top seat, folded his legs, placed his hands on his lap, and began to massage his hands.

The audience went wild as he had them eating out of the palm of his hands.

Once he finished, Ling jumped onto the stage to help him get the chairs down.

He bowed, and then I shouted through the microphone:

"Let's bring our performers on the stage for one final round of applause!"

They all ran back onstage, bowed and left.

I gave my final speech into the mic, telling everyone that we hoped they enjoyed the rest of the festival, inviting them to eat at the food vendors that were there, and wished them a good evening.

Once I finished, Karl turned the music down, we gave each other a very nervous quick nod (Karl didn't know any English at all, and I still could not hear Chinese, so we had no choice but to be awkward about it), and he left to go and talk to the others.

Suddenly, I grew anxious, and a little bashful. No, scratch that! I felt *very* bashful. For reasons that I could not explain, I didn't want to walk backstage and see them. I felt —embarrassed, though I could not explain why.

All that I could assume is that... you know that feeling when you see someone, you walk away and then see them again very soon after.

You don't know what to say to them.

You said everything already, and don't know how to strike up the conversation again.

Or they are embarrassed to see you so soon.

This, much to my ever-loving tendency to overanalyze the trivial, and under-analyze the larger things in life (I am human after all) was my conclusion.

But I couldn't stay back there.

That would be even more awkward.

So, I placed my shawl on the side of the stage, raised myself on it, so that I got no dirt on my dress, stood up, walked to the front, jumped off it, walked along the grass, fell in line with the rest of the festival visitors, and disappeared into the crowd.

Once I got safely away, with the stage far behind me, I could breathe.

What was all that about?

"I'm not ready," I said to myself, "after all this time, I still don't know how to face him again. I don't know what to say."

Meanwhile, I didn't notice that three people were near enough to me, to hear me talking to myself.

They laughed and walked away before I even had the chance to make an explanation.

Closing my eyes, I laid my shawl down on a nearby chair, sat down on it, and reclined backwards.

When doing so, I searched through the photo album that was stored in my brain, to see Cheong-Jin's face.

Just as much as fear of being speechless again had dissolved, my joy of seeing him again had risen.

And as I had set out to work diligently on how to approach him when I saw him again, I was met with the most annoying provocation ever; I couldn't see his face.

Every time that I conjured him up in my thoughts, the image slipped away.

I practically stomped my foot against the ground, enraged.

Why was I not allowed to remember him!

For the second show, there was a slight variation.

Cheong-Jin began it, as usual, for the first performance.

As he stood on the other side of the stage, waiting to go on, he was dressed in his costume, his face covered, and I was determined to exert myself more.

I waved to him, smiling. Returning the gesture, he waved back.

Before then, I had a whole forty minutes to wonder how we could communicate, and working on my Chinese. After all, we were from two different worlds, and two different languages along with it. Life, in its many fashions, was not on our side.

Long story short, I was still nothing short of terrible as Jin took to the stage and cast a spell over everyone who was seated.

While the second act was the hula-hoop, the third act was different. Ken and Karl performed a two-man acrobatic act to the song 'Conquest of Paradise', from the movie 1492.

Karl did all the lifting as Ken performed most of the acrobatic moves.

Taking in Karl's strong body frame, it all made sense: he was the lifter. The support system to Ken. Judging by their seamless movements between each other, it was apparent that they had been doing this together for a long time; they trusted each other.

The fourth act was Lily's Chinese folk dance again.

And the fifth act was Ling's Space Walker performance. A large apparatus was brought center stage and Ling performed acrobatic movements along it, while also using his muscle to make it look like he was walking on air sometimes.

Despite all his incredible flexibility, it was when it

looked like he was walking on an invisible line that stuck out the most.

And at nineteen years old?

Good gracious! What was it like to be touring at that age? That's when your emotions, passions and hormones are still on fire. Touring did not give him time to have a steady girlfriend—or boyfriend. Between that, and the insecurity that plagues a person during their teenage years— and mind you, that insecurity does not end when you reach eighteen. No! Unless you are the sort who is born with a natural confidence, that level of insecurity continues well into your twenties. And when you are a performer, I don't think it ever ends.

Cheong-Jin was different. His very aura oozed confidence. His smile was the proof of it, for it was a cheerful aspect that made many women feel a swift comfort around him.

When the third show was about to begin, I was backstage, in my usual spot, drinking water, popping a cough drop in my throat to help my voice even more, when I heard a voice behind me.

"Hi."

Turning around, I was not prepared for who it was.

It was Cheong-Jin.

While I felt like my body had turned to lead, my mind did not have time to be so overwhelmed to get my tongue stuck in my throat. His sudden arrival rendered it impossible for me to get tongue-tied, forcing me to jump right in.

"Jin!" I exclaimed, feeling the heat rise in my skin as I knew that my face must have lit up. It was made evident by how he looked even kinder when he approached me.

Like a moth to a flame, I felt my feet move of their own

accord and I drew close to him. When seeing me open to our re-re-meeting, Cheong-Jin did the same.

Eagerly, we both drew close to one another, and without thinking, or knowing what I was even about, I fell into his eyes as I pressed my body against the side of his, gently. And how much happier I was that he did not recoil or jump back. Rather, he accepted that I felt compelled to rest in between the joys of seeing him, and the forgetfulness that comes with recollecting oneself. When feeling part of his body pressed ever so softly against mine, I lost myself even more than before.

"You came back," was all that I could muster. Looking down at him, he was wearing fitted black pants that came up to his waist, a white button-down shirt, and black suspenders. Simply dressed, in every way, but I found him to be simply intoxicating. Then, realizing that he probably did not understand me, I said 'I'm sorry' in Mandarin Chinese. Again, *broken* Chinese.

"It's okay," he responded, slower, "it's nice to see you."

"It's nice to see you too," I responded, "I did not think that I would see you again."

"Yes, it has been a year since I saw you," he said, "it has been a year since we saw each other."

"Two years," I said, raising up two fingers. "It has been two years since I saw you."

"Yes," he flinched, agreeing to my correction, "two years." At last, I lifted my eyes to stare directly into his, which was easy to do. When in the presence of someone who you care deeply for, they appear as larger than life. But, in truth, they are human and as small as the rest of us. And like us, every now and again, they must stand naked in the face of their imperfections. I was not at the place where I saw Jin's flaws, so I completely forgot that Cheong-Jin and I were around the same height.

Yet, when falling into the depths of his brown eyes, I felt as if I was falling into the deep caverns of the Earth, with her folding her arms around me and saying, 'rest now, my warrior. Rest!'

"You see?" he declared, referencing recalling me, "I remembered."

Without thinking, I reached over, pulled at his suspenders and released them as they smacked against his chest. He let out a reaction, chuckled nervously, and then walked away.

By all accounts, I should have felt presumptuous and immediately regretting my forwardness. Yet, I did not.

Instead, I felt a strange elation at my rash behavior.

I had done something. That was everything to make me satisfied. I had done something!

And now, I could go forward.

It was the beginning of everything again...

Chapter 16
The Prison

December 1, 2024

"Everything is wrong!" the Kite & Key bus driver yelled into his radio at the dispatcher.

Dazed and confused, those of us on the bus had to organize ourselves.

Up ahead, there had been a terrible car accident, and we had driven right into it, slamming into the truck ahead of us.

All of us felt a jolt. While some of us had only slammed against the seat in front of us, others of us sitting had experienced a stronger force.

I was one of the three people who had fallen on the tour bus floor. While the fall was not bad, I was not prepared, so I hit my head against the hard surface.

Rubbing my head, I had looked over to see a mature-looking man also in the same situation. His knock against the floor had only impacted his arm, but he flexed it as he rose to his knees.

In situations like this, it's interesting how quick a link can be formed. When struggling to rise, we looked at each other, and our eyes locked gazes.

"Are you okay?" I asked, my voice a little hoarse, from the shock.

"I'll be fine?" he responded. "You?"

"I'll live."

"But your head?"

"I know a concussion when I feel it," I had responded, still holding my head, "this just requires some ice, painkillers, and I'll be like my old self."

Just as I said this, the bus driver was shouting, "Everything is wrong!" over the radio.

Around the same time, the other man and I managed to stand up, while the other passengers were checking their bags, to make sure that nothing fell out of their purses.

As I managed to rise to my feet, I heard the driver say, "Oh no!"

Taking action, (yeah, I had a way of always rushing to help anyone else, other than myself. Seriously, when it came to self-defense, I was such a wimp) I moved down the aisle and looked out of the front window.

"How bad is it?" I asked, then my eyes widened. "Oh, god!"

A truck had skipped a light, and flipped a car over, and the Kite & Key bus drove into the back of the truck. Between the collision, and it being on a common street, it led to confusion, much alarm over what to do, many people rushing along, and traffic being backed up. The world is the world, but when you are walking about, in your everyday life, the streets you walk in, and the neighborhood you revolve your life around, is your world. And when everything comes grinding to a halt, when an alarm and hell come rushing in, ravaging the order and chaos that you thought you had, you lower your phone. You stop reading your book. You stop talking about trivial stuff with your friends.

You look up, see the horror, and either of these three things happen:

You freeze, out of terror.

You assume someone else will solve the issue.

Or you pause for a moment, then rush in, remember your morality, on pure daring instinct.

"In case an ambulance has not already been called," the bus driver said, "I've called a septa ambulance and paramedics."

"There's gas leaking," I said, squinting through the window. "The people aren't getting out of the car."

"And I don't see movement," said a voice next to me. I turned and it had been spoken by the same man who had fallen down on the bus's floor near me. "No one in the car is moving. They're unconscious!"

"We can't wait for a damn ambulance!" I rushed out, horrified.

"Open the door," the man ordered the driver, pushing at the door.

"Opening it, damn!" The driver declared, opening the door. Next to the man, I stumbled off the bus, and we ran to the flipped-over car. At this point, there were two women near the car, who were checking the passengers and driver.

"Both are unconscious," the first woman said, "we can't get the window down."

"But we don't have anything to break it open," the second woman said.

The man and I leaned over and saw that there was a driver and a passenger in the front seat.

"If we bash it open," the man said, the glass will hit them."

"We have to break the back windows open and get them out that way." I flexed my hands as I realized what to do. "The driver! The bus driver always has to have a crowbar with them, to pry something open on the bus if there is a problem, or if there is a trolley ahead of them who can't change lanes. Get the crowbar from the driver!"

The man raced back as I eyed the gas that was spilling on the road. My body froze over, despite that I could still talk.

"Get far away from here," I said to the women. I felt the stillness in my face, as well as heard the staleness in my voice. "Get to the corner, tell everyone to move far away, and stay there. Then call the fire department and explain the gas."

The women saw the gas leaking as well and didn't need to be told twice. Obeying, they rushed away, doing as I ordered, as the man ran up to me again, with the bus driver's crowbar.

Instinctively, I stood back as he raised up the bar and brought it crashing down on the back windows of the car. After three whacks, the window fully shattered.

"Give me your coat," I ordered him, while removing mine and my scarf. After he gave it to me, I laid all our outerwear down, in the car window, so that I didn't scratch myself on the shattered glass.

Being the smaller one, I was the ablest as I crawled through the glass and reached the two unconscious people.

"Oh shit," I whispered as I saw that the one in the passenger's seat was a boy, who could not be older than ten. When I tried to unclasp their seatbelts, the mother's worked fine, but the boy was stuck.

My mind was amazed at the spirit of chance as I reached into my shoulder bag, pulled out the scissors, along with a copy of my book, 'It Can't Happen Here', that were next to the project that I was knitting. Putting the book back in my bag but keeping out the scissors, quickly, I cut the seat belt and pulled out the little boy first.

Thin in build, he was not heavy, but there was blood on the side of his face, and it was rolling down to his neck.

"Here!" I said, as I handed the boy to the man. He took it as I began to pull the mother from the driver's seat. Fortunate that she was not heavy, I managed to get her through the window, the man picked her up, I lifted the boy, and we quickly moved to the end of the road, away from any explosion that could erupt at any moment.

Once we joined the rest of the people who were huddled at the end of the corner, our adrenaline had been exhausted. Now that the situation had come to an end, our energy was spent as we slunk to the ground.

Breathing out and in heavily as I wished to fall into a deep sleep, I was still holding the boy in my arms as I looked at the man who still held the mother.

Before I fully succumbed to being tired, I looked below me and saw that the little boy was wearing a uniform that I was familiar with. When I looked at the mother, she was wearing similar attire.

"Tibet," I uttered.

"What?" the man asked.

"They are from Tibet. That's the robes that the protestors wear when they are giving their liberty speeches in front of Independence Hall. They are Tibetan freedom fighters."

The man looked down at the woman in his arms.

"I should have known," he uttered.

I didn't hold it against him, because it was the heat of the moment, and it was also natural for him not to notice.

"I'm Briseis," I said, not knowing why I thought that was the correct time to introduce myself. "My name is Briseis."

"John. I'm John."

"Nice to meet you, John."

Our eyes closed, relaxing as we heard firetruck sirens getting closer.

———

Once the firemen arrived, along with the paramedics, John and I sat on the sidewalk, watching the scene. To the left of us passengers, were locals who were still curious and compassionate for what happened.

The firemen had neutralized the gas, the problem had been solved, the truck and the Kite & Key bus was moved out of the way so that traffic could move around the flipped over car.

As we watched the mother and the son being taken into the ambulance, our bus driver approached John and me.

"Because the front of my bus is dented," she explained, "we can't go anywhere. But another bus is coming soon, you'll be able to get on that one, free of charge."

"Thank you," John and I spoke.

She looked past us, and at the mother and son as the paramedics closed the door to the back of the ambulance and were about to take them to the hospital.

"Will they be okay?" she asked us.

"Yes," John answered. "I overheard the paramedics. They said that they are both stable and will recover eventually."

"Thank god for that," she said, as the ambulance turned away. Then she looked at us. "You both okay?"

"Yes," I said, "we're fine."

"Right."

Having nothing else to say, the driver walked away, got back on her bus, sat down in the driver's seat and took out her phone. I think she was quick to do it so that it could drown out the world.

Right now,
    I do believe
    that I needed the world.
    Even the worst parts of it.
    I just needed to bleed...
    ...to know that I was alive.

"Can you believe it?" John asked.

Hearing his voice took me out of my thoughts.

"Believe what?" I returned.

"They were at a protest, and now this happened to them," he elaborated, referring to the mother and son, "it just goes to show you that—"

"When it rains, it pours?"

"How did you know that I was going to say that?"

"I didn't," I answered, truthfully, "I don't know how I managed to do that. And it poured alright."

"Yes, it poured hard."

"Another marker on the road to show what's going to happen over the next few months."

"Ah," he said, understanding what I was referring to. "Yes. I hope everything will be okay for you all."

"Thank you. Because I am scared."

"You should be, and it's okay to be. By the way, it was lucky for you to have your scissors on you."

"I wish that I could say that it was coincidental, but it's not." I raised up my bag, opened it up and showed him my knitting project. "I always have scissors on me because I knit all the time."

"I see now. What are you working on this time?"

"It's for a friend. I'm not a good knitter, even though I like doing it a lot. I just know one stitch and only how to knit things that are straight lines. Right now, I am making a scarf for a friend from South America. I'm making a scarf from the country's flag colors. South American countries have some amazing flag designs."

"Don't tell me which nation," he said, looking at what I was knitting, "let me guess."

He looked at it, and his eyes brightened when he saw the answer.

"Columbia. Or Venezuela. Or Ecuador."

"Yup," I said. All those flags had the same color scheme. "It's Columbia."

"If you work hard enough, are you ever going to do the Brazilian design?"

"I want to," I professed, eagerly. "I really, really, really do. But there's a problem. I can't do it."

"Let me guess. It's too hard."

"Yes!"

John laughed.

"The Brazilian flag is as cool as the others," I added, "but like the Tibetan flag, it's too hard for me to make."

My laughter died down as I grew reflective. I thought it was subtle, and that John would not notice, but he did.

"You're remembering the mother and child now, aren't you?"

"Yes," I answered, slowly, "but it's also something else." Rubbing my face, I closed my eyes for a moment as I contemplated what I was going to say. After all, John and I didn't know each other, so why would he care about the foibles that were attached to the pitfalls of my character?

"Earlier today, on the bus ride, before you got on," I explained, "I had an argument with a local."

"What was it about, if you don't mind my asking?" He furthered.

I wondered why he wanted to know.

"I'm surprised that you even care," I admitted, raising my eyebrows at him, "We really are living on the edge, conversation wise, aren't we?"

"Why do you say that?"

"Because you are curious about the little things," I deduced, "when people care about the little things, it's just when it begins to sink in that you almost died. We both did."

John looked ahead.

"I guess that makes sense."

"We need to speak," I said, "or we'll bleed." I knew that I sounded like I was spewing nonsense, but there was nothing for it. "I work in Old City, so I see the Tibetan protestors often. But I also know about how one of Philadelphia's sports teams wants to put a stadium right next to Chinatown."

I told him all about how I cared for the Tibetans cause, but I also worry about Chinatown being uprooted because of the stadium that might go so close to the historic neighborhood.

About my confusion of how I could love the Chinese

people, but also deeply empathized with Tibetans who wanted their freedom from China and all the oppression that has occurred.

Afterwards, I told him about the man who scoffed at me for not joining the Chinese during their peaceful protest to preserve Chinatown.

It all just came pouring forth, like as if, if I did not speak about all these occurrences, that had nothing to do with him, and everything to do with me, I would go mad. Tumbling forth, the truth did, in a rush of narratives that would seem trivial towards anyone else other than myself.

Especially after what we had just survived.

When I finished telling him everything, to my surprise, he listened attentively.

What's more, he leaned forward as I spoke, which always gives the indication that you are engrossed in the narrative.

"So," John summarized, "basically you like the Chinese people, and the Tibetans, but you know that if you were to show respect for both, then both sides would hate you, for not choosing one. Correct me if I made the bad deduction, but you know that if you showed respect for the Tibetans, some of them would expect you to not like the Chinese. And if you like the Chinese, some of them would expect you to not like the Tibetans. But if you empathized with both, you would be called fake."

I felt my body slacken, while my energy also rose.

"You knew what I meant?" I asked.

"Yes."

"That's exactly what I feel. So, I can't talk about it to either one of them, and now I don't know what to do."

"It's fine not to do anything, in this case," John answered. "You see, when it comes to other nations, it's best to differentiate their politics, from the people. But that's not what you are told to do. You're in a world where you are told that you have to be for someone, or against them. Everything that I say now is in the general sense, and I'm not speaking specifically. If you are an ally to one, then you must be the enemy to their enemy. That's NOT what must be done. Ever. If both sides say that you can respect each of us, at the same time, then choose both."

John leaned forward, making his intent more pertinent and direct.

"*But* if either side tells you that you must love us, at the expense of hating the other side, out of blind obedience, never choose *that side*. For that's how evil characters rise. They build their platform through 'division'. They feed you on the narrative of us vs. them... rather than the one defining aspect of humanity, that is the very best of us: *We*, the People."

When hearing those three words, my eyes began to grow watery of the concept of all that it signified. Those three words, when revealed and acknowledged, represented all that was best in us.

And now, those words were being forgotten, laid to waste, and thrown to the wayside, under the concept of:

Me

Me

Me!

While it also always ought to be: Us!

"Yes," I whispered, "that's all I wanted. That's all that I ever wanted."

"Precisely. And 'We, the People' should always be as it is."

———

When arriving at that conclusion, I looked ahead at the bus driver who was still speaking with headquarters over the walkie-talkie.

Biting my lip, I looked down.

"Now," I whispered, "I wonder what happens now. We didn't think about what was good for *all* of us."

"And that comes to the second part of it, I guess," John explained, "which is what happened last month. You're thinking of November 5th."

I looked at him, surprised.

"That's where your mind was going, wasn't it?" he furthered.

I nodded.

"I don't want you to use the exact words," I said, "because I don't want you to get attacked if someone over-hears you. But yes."

"Thank you for worrying about me, but I'm not afraid. I've seen some hard things in my time, so it makes one numb to intimidation. And, as you can see, I'm not from the United States, so I am an outside observer."

"That probably makes it easier for you, when talking about it."

"Oh, yes," he said, "it does." He looked ahead. "I was able to lean back and see it all unfold, objectively. I'm assuming you voted for the side that lost."

"Yes," I answered simply, still ignoring the mistake from my distant past. "I was. I remember going to sleep early that night, and then I woke up suddenly. It must've been around two in the morning. The sky was still pitch black, and I woke up with a jolt. It was like some horrible force pushed me to wake up. My body was sweating as I felt like every-thing was crashing down around me. Even before I turned on the television and watched the news, I knew. I knew that we had lost. And the most horrible thing was beginning. Before that, I never cared if the person that I voted for won or lost. But this time, it mattered. It mattered so much. I could have done more."

"You did all that you could," he assured me, "you voted the right way, and that is all. Everything else was left to decisions made by others, who thought of themselves, and not of you all, as a collective. I have a question, if you don't mind me asking."

"I've reached a point where I stopped being afraid of questions," I acknowledged, "Go ahead."

"I know that most African Americans voted one way. Some voted the wrong way, but most of you understood the assignment and voted for her. So, when the next day came, and you saw how a large amount of other nationalities did not do the same... did you feel betrayed? Did you feel like many people abandoned you, after all these years of you all supporting them?"

Surprised at his brave inquiry, I looked at him directly. Not out of anger, but astonishment. How did he know that we had undergone that sensation?

"You knew?" I asked. "You knew how we felt."

"Of course," he said, "if I were in the same situation, I would have felt the same."

Looking between us, I noted his light skin versus my dark brown complexion.

Suddenly, all the tension released within me, as the kindred spirit came rushing in.

"I'm so afraid to talk about it," I uttered, "because I didn't think that anyone would care."

"Many of us care," he added, "just not the majority. You see, the reason that I come to this country is because I have a lot of friends here. I talk to them, and through them, I have made more friends online. For every person of a different race than yours, who voted for something better than what is happening now, had to watch their own people support something that was against what was the best option for *everyone*. Including people who look like me. You see, you blacks were not the only ones who were betrayed. White people, Latinos, Asian Americans, Arab Americans, Indian Americans, women, or anyone outside of the status quo, watched as they were let down by their own kind. And after they made the moral choice, they had to watch themselves get grouped into the side that made the mistake and betrayed you all."

———

Truly, the world had been turned upside down.

Between my guilt of a mistake that I had made long ago —and the pain of being disappointed from finally making the right decision, my mind was transfixed to this moment. For we all know, when going back into the real world, you will be met with denial, resistance to the truth, anger at you pointing out what really happened, and to ask people to no longer be blind. You will be met with a much more vengeful version of denial, resistance to the truth, and red-hot anger.

That is what happens when you choose to care about something; you get burned.

And when you care about something because you have seen the horrors of what happens when people don't care about the things to care about properly for, the flame burns you the most.

You spend much of your time being in the ring of fire.

And when knowing that you will be placed in social and environmental hell, you do two things: you run and compromise. Or you tighten your belt, and say, "Come what may, and do your worst. I will not duck and run, for I am already here!"

And then you take comfort in those soft moments.

Those moments where, out of the corner of the *eye* of *Time,* you hear someone say, 'It's okay, I understand'. You keep those fleeting moments of peace stored in your memory, locked in a safe that cannot be touched.

Because you know, each day, another tide of anger will come your way, so you use those memories to serve as a balm that soothes the scars that you will receive because of your human desire to always 'speak up and speak out'.

May this moment serve me well and be the tourniquet that saves me for what is to come.

"You've heard that," I uttered, my voice low from emotional exhaustion. "You've heard people say that?"

"Oh yeah." John rubbed his lips as he looked ahead, gazing casually at a post-accident scene. "Neither side was perfect, because neither side can ever be perfect. Everyone will always be human working through an imperfect system. And that imperfect system is set up by an old guard who, sometimes, can choke the next generation with its outdated strictures that gets in the way of us moving on for the better. Every new set of people who step in suffers from previous alliances that do not age well, or from people who have grown too lazy to do their jobs properly or courageously and sometimes can take a turn for the worst. Of course, some traditions do work and must be preserved."

"Respect the old, but move forward," I summed up.

"Exactly. I've seen that happen, time and time again, and so have you. But this time, the right choice was obvious. And sadly, what's happened has now happened. And here you all are...you're scared now, aren't you?"

"Yes," I whispered. "I'm scared all the time."

"Don't be...because that's what they want. But if you are still feeling betrayed by those who ought to have known better, go ahead. Be angry. You were reminded, once again, that the unity that you thought others felt with you all was not real. You were even betrayed by some in your own race. Feel let down. Feel disgruntled. Because if you forget it, then you will always be walked over and be used." John looked out of the side of his eyes. "I know how alone you feel."

"How?" I asked. "How did you know?"

"I don't know. Maybe it's because we both easily could have died just now. I don't know."

I smiled at him as I looked at the ground. That answer made sense to me, even if it would confuse others. Gently, I tapped my foot against the concrete for a moment.

"I was talking with a woman once," I explained, "and she said, 'chin up, we are living history'. At this moment. I try and tell myself that we are living history right now, but that doesn't mean that I have to like it. Because I don't like it. After all, so many of us thought that the worst was behind us. But now we must figure out where do we go from here." Once more, I looked at John again, taking in his strong, but comfortable presence. "You're a foreigner. What must the world be thinking of us now?"

He sighed.

"Never mind," I rushed out. "I don't want to know what they think of us."

"Some of us thought you were better than this, it's true. But many also feel sorry for you."

"They do?" I asked, hopefully.

"Yes," he replied, gently. "They...empathize. They see all the foolishness that is happening, but they also know that you are a young country. And that a lot of you wanted a better way. We do see you all."

"Thanks. God knows what the Germans think of us right now," I chuckled.

"Yes," he replied, gurgling too.

"It must be like they were watching us walking to the edge of a cliff, and them shouting, 'don't fall. Turn around!'"

We both had a good laugh over that.

Once our laughter subsided, a sudden thought came to me. At first, I didn't think to ask it, because I wondered why I even had that thought.

But did I even want the answer? There was a strange foreboding about what response I would get. Yet, I was so driven by curiosity that the question fell out of me.

"If you were born here, in the USA, what side would you have been on?" I asked. Licking his lips, John looked down at the ground.

"I've learned to accept either answer," I said, "even if I don't agree with the answer—or even if I don't like the answer." When seeing that my question caused him distress, I realized that I was being too forward about it. "Sorry, I should not have asked. I was being a jerk."

"It's okay," he replied smoothly. "I'm just taking my time here, because I have to weigh it all out."

Internally I fortified myself. I knew it; he might say something that would upset me. But I promised myself that I would respect anything that he said, even if it hurt.

"Go on," I said, "I'm ready."

When John finally spoke, he was choosing his words carefully and slowly.

"Being a foreigner," he said, "it's easy for me to know who the right person was to choose. Especially since I was raised on a very basic idea of right and wrong. Of respecting the law and punishing criminals. The answer is simple. But that's me, as an outsider, who can be more objective.

"But if I was born here, and I was raised in a family that was taught different things and never learned anything else... add that to all the subtle lessons of racism and sexism that *we are all taught* and has affected us permanently, as well as sometimes, we are only exposed to one narrative, based on the News we are looking at.

"Honestly, I don't think I would have known who to believe in, and who to choose." John did not look at me as he answered the question. "I don't know. I don't know if I would have stood with you."

Closing my eyes, I looked down. How much I wanted to hate him for being honest! I remained motionless, sitting there, frozen inside as I decidedly refused to look at him.

Just like he did not look at me.

"Yes," he replied, slowly, "yes. I get it. It's okay to hate me for saying that. I just want you to understand what another side of humanity thinks like. But yeah, definitely hate me now. It's okay. It's okay."

My anger was so loud that I had to remain quiet. With much exertion on my part, it took me all my collected sense to utter two words.

"Thank you," I whispered. That was all that I could muster up.

Soon, the next Kite & Key Bus arrived. Since his confession, John and I did not speak. The conversation had grown too heavy for either of us.

He gave me a simple and honest answer.

I gave him a simple and silent reaction.

I know that I should have been more objective, but I could not help but hate him in that second.

I was a tour guide, not a saint.

Once the next bus arrived, silently, John and I stood up, got back on the bus again and we continued to drive along to the next location.

Internally, I was going through a state of incredible unrest as I was losing my bearings. It's easy to hate, as it is easy to love. But it's the hardest thing to understand what you cannot understand.

Everything was crying out, and I wanted to cry out with it. Deliberately ignoring John, I took out the bus's map, to show where we were heading to next. At first, I was reading without paying attention, so I did not recognize the words.

Eventually, I focused and saw that our next stop was the Eastern State Penitentiary.

Lowering the map, I looked ahead, out of the window, as we drove along streets, passing people who were walking along, some with their dogs, and children coming out of convenient stores with their candy.

They looked happy.

Because they were.

With the adults, it is naïve to assume that they all were filled with joy. After all, it is not right to wear one's heart on one's sleeve. So, whatever troubles they were feeling, they kept it concealed. Especially since we are in a world that makes us all dwell on what makes us angry. And who we should be angry with.

But regarding the children!

They were a different matter. Kids were better at being unafraid to show what they were really feeling.

So, when seeing them run through the streets, looking happy, I could believe it.

I wanted to be that way myself.

Yet, being older, and more aware of what is going on all the time, has now rendered that impossible. That's the product of being informed; you can't ever go back to innocent happiness. You have outgrown it...which is tragic.

But as the bus rolled on, I focused on the children, letting myself rest on their freedom, and not caring for the trials that we adults must endure.

Their lives were simple. When they were right, they got praise. When they were wrong, they got punished.

When did we stop punishing the worst of us? When we got older and started saying the words: 'it's complicated', to justify things that have no justification.

Is that the rule of adulthood: compromise?

When turning a corner, my eyes widened as I was met with a clear view of the Eastern State Penitentiary up ahead, on Fairmount Street.

There it was.

After so many years of living my life, working and then going home, I didn't stray from the same old route. As a result, it never put me in the way of seeing the Penitentiary at all.

So, I wasn't just playing the tourist; now I had fully become one.

Right in the heart of North Philadelphia, stood a castle that looked like it had been removed from Europe and dropped right amidst urban life.

Only the castle was a prison.

The Eastern State Penitentiary was America's most historic, and expensive, prison. It was one of the things in our city that was worthy of being described as 'iconic'.

It was based on the idea that solitary confinement would encourage reformation and inner reflection. The prison's radical philosophy and grand architecture made it a model for prison design worldwide.

The prison opened in 1829 and remained open for 147 years. In that time, it held nearly 85,000 people.

It closed down in 1971, due to riots, it was not large enough to store more prisoners, and it was too expensive to maintain. The City of Philadelphia bought it in 1980, but that was after it fell into disrepair.

Somehow, the disrepair became part of the appeal that has drawn people to visit this prison ever since it was open to the public.

The most famous prisoner to be held there was Al Capone, the legendary gangster during Prohibition, when alcohol was illegal.

As the bus pulled up to the stop in front of the prison, I sensed motion to my right.

John was standing up.

This was his stop. The Eastern State Penitentiary was his destination.

Slinging his bag over his shoulder, he moved down the aisle, to get off.

The bus driver opened the door, and John slowly got off. He was a man whose actions seemed to be very deliberate in everything he does.

When looking at his departing form, I was stricken with a sudden burst of resolution. It was nothing to do with me compromising, because I was not in the mood to compromise.

No, I was going to do it, because it made sense.

I stood up as the door closed, rushed to it and turned to the bus driver.

"Please," I said, "open the door."

The driver obeyed. Standing in the doorway, I poked my head out.

"John!" I called to his back.

Standing still, at first, John remained. After a couple of seconds, John finally turned around.

When looking at me, his face was like a stone, obviously preparing to hear me shout at him.

"I..." I began.

"Yes?" John responded.

"I don't hate you," was all that I could say. "I will never agree, and I want to believe you would always have done the right thing. Either way, I do not hate you for telling me the reality."

When hearing that, his shoulders relaxed and his eyes softened, even though the rest of his face was expressionless. But I knew, just as he knew. He was happy.

"Thank you," he said, "but you would have every right to hate me. I will not take that from you, because even I'm not stronger than prejudice."

"No one is. That's why I accepted my prejudice a long time ago. By acknowledging it, was the only way that I could kill it."

"Never walk away from your better judgment. Always remember, because it is true: We, the people."

I smiled gently.

"Good luck, John."

"Don't break, Briseis. Don't break."

I moved out of the doorway, the bus door closed, as it drove away.

Eventually, John and I tore our eyes away from each other as I sat back down, and he walked into the penitentiary.

The life of a tour guide:

Come.

Connect.

And leave.

I did my job again.

I was satisfied.

Leaning my head back, I rested my eyes on the grandiosity of the prison that was another artery in the fabric of our city.

I had not been inside of the penitentiary in ten years, but the interior of the building was imprinted in my brain.

What was once an epic place of confinement giving way to time, and it fell to ruin. The inside fell into another definition; it was a haunting place of crumbling cellblocks and abandoned guard towers.

There was not one part of the prison that was not designed deliberately, and with extreme care. When it was opened, over a century before I was born, the cells were designed so that they were one-person cells. Unlike prisons today, you had no cellmate. This was done out of a controversial movement to change the behavior of people convicted of crimes through confinement in solitude with labor.

If you were alone a lot, it led you to not being corrupted by other prisoners, made you philosophize about your life, and what steps you could have taken.

We all have evil in us.

But when evil is constantly in the company of other evil, they can join. There is no cure. So, the problem spreads and we, the people, are their victims.

When looking on the prison, and recalling all the ruined rooms, the castle walls, the narrow corridors, and the cots and chairs that once were used frequently by the prisoners, I remembered.

Those empty rooms did not seem to be merely void. But rather, I felt like there was an after-effect, a remnant of every prisoner who remained there.

A part of each prisoner, a bit of his soul, was left behind as he left.

Whether it was one of the cots he slept in, a chair he sat in, or he did cheap labor in, his thoughts remained behind as he reflected on his life.

Moments of reflection must have come.

Then the self-hatred.
Then the acceptance.
Next was the understanding.
Then the shame.
And lastly, enlightenment.

And on the day of his release, all his bad and good intentions were left to remain in the many stones and parts that held it all together.

That was when I knew how many of them arrived at the conclusion that they would shape their lives.

They realized that, at some point, they had been wrong.

A powerful revelation.

I found comfort in that possibility, because of the desire for order.

Every prisoner was there because of the law. Because of the concept of justice. I knew that, in life, there would always be corruption and inequality, but this prison still served to tell us that, at some point, justice was served.

For it stood to acknowledge what our second president, John Adams had said. He was a man of great ideals, and great mistakes. Like all the rest.

But he was right when he said this about our nation:

A government of laws, not of men.

The penitentiary stood there, shouting at us to be a government of laws.

But now, going forward, we are becoming a government of men.

The Penitentiary would fall into further disrepair now, where the rust would fold over, and become even more knurled as the ghosts of the prisoners' revelations fade with it.

The bus drove down the street, the penitentiary disappearing from my view, as I looked away, recalling better times, back to the summer.

Back then, laws being lost was not something to worry about, because life was beautiful.

Life had order, because it had nothing to do with what was now going on...

Chapter 17
Freedom

August 22, 2024

"The day is over," I cried, to my co-worker, Shelby, "freedom! To quote William Wallace."

We were at the office, and we had just finished working.

"I thought you had to work at the Chinese Festival tonight," Shelby recalled.

"Oh, I do, I do, I do," I replied, merrily and giddy. "But I don't call that work anymore. At this point, I'd face being out after dark, if I get to work there."

Shelby gave me a look.

"You like someone," she deduced. "You're glowing."

"Glowing?" I said, pointing to myself, as I practically skipped out of the room. "What? Me? I have no idea what you are talking about."

Shelby laughed at me as I went to the bathroom, to get changed into a nice dress.

I was going to see Cheong-Jin tonight.

I still had no idea what I was going to say to him...but I

for damn sure was going to give it everything that I had in me.

———

The first person that I always saw was Karl, who organized the music.

His nervous laughter around me was endearing enough, because I could tell that he was good-natured. I reached that point where I would touch him, without his permission, which never made him or Ling mad.

Since I could not communicate with them very well, all that we had was physical communication. As a result, I had no choice but to touch them.

With Karl, he knew that I was just doing my best to show that I was friendly.

But Ling, being so young, didn't know what to do with my outwardness, and could easily get turned around.

He was at the age where he craved the attention that I gave him but also was shy under it. It was not his fault, because I was the same way once. Ah, the trappings of being a teenager; you both want and didn't want the same thing. I do not care what anyone else says, but that time of your life is the hardest.

Though, while he was sitting down, behind me during one performance, we had begun to try and understand each other.

"Can you teach me English?" he asked.

I replied with the Chinese word for yes, but only if he would give me the Chinese word for whatever I said. Ling nodded.

I pointed to my eyes.

"Eyes."

He repeated the word and gave me the Chinese version.

I pointed to my nose.

"Nose."

"Nose."

He gave me the Chinese version.

We did the same thing for lips, cheek, face, neck, and hair.

Then I pointed to my skin.

"Black." Then I touched his black hair, pulling at a few strands, so that he made the connection. "Black."

When seeing me pull his hair, Ling smiled, and his eyes became gentler. I think he was happy. "Ah! Black."

"Yes," I said, "black!"

Then I tapped my skin again, to reaffirm.

He started speaking in Chinese, but somehow, I was able to understand what he meant as he tapped his own skin. Knowing what he meant, I was too afraid to say it, for fear of being offensive. But after he scrounged around for the right word, I gave in, for the sake of helping him on.

"Yellow." I said, pointing to his skin color, "Yellow."

"Yes!" he said, happy that I understood him, pointing to his skin color. "Yellow."

Instinctively, I relaxed, relieved that I did not say anything offensive. So often, we humans spend, not communicating, because we fear that we are impertinent. But we end up walking on eggshells for nothing; because people understand labels that come from description.

He described himself as yellow, while I identified as black.

When looking at each other, our eyes locked, and I saw that we had found a link. It was an awkward one that sprung from our desire to know each other better, but the language barrier was too much.

All we had, most of the time, was our looking at each other. And as a nineteen-year-old who was transitioning from being a boy to being a man, he was torn in every direction, emotionally.

"Boo!"

Just as I was about to teach Ling how to say 'stomach', we were interrupted by a man who jumped from around the curtain, from being done his performance.

I jumped, from the shock, and only was left to scold the man who spooked me.

I looked up to see Cheong-Jin, smiling at his triumph.

My scolding immediately transitioned to teasing.

"You!" I cried, merrily, as I play-punched him in the stomach. Of course, it was another fake punch that did not hurt really, and he recoiled playfully.

"Scaring me now," I replied, rushing up to him, wrapping my hands around his waist. Yes, I really was free-falling now, without a parachute, and hoping that I would land on friendly shores.

Thankfully, Jin did not recoil.

"How are you?" he asked.

"Tired," I said, "but I try not to show it. How are you?"

"Okay."

"Good." My eyes turned gentle, as I kept his stare. "I know, you will be great again."

Smiling he looked down.

"Oh, and can you tell me the Chinese version of good luck?" I asked.

He told me the words. It was nothing like how I heard it said online. I groaned, realizing I had been given the wrong translation. I asked if he could repeat it. He repeated it.

I tried it and I failed at it.

"Oh!" I groaned. "Where is Kaori when you need her!"

Cheong-Jin laughed as he walked away. I watched his retreating form, perhaps with a hungry expression on my face. My desire for him had already reached an incredible pitch, as it pounded within my brain and under my breasts.

He was smart to walk away from me sometimes, as I was smart to do the same.

In his presence, I could not control any part of myself as I found myself falling into a downward spiral of craving and wantonness.

His mere existence intoxicated me, filling up every moment with an excitement in the air that did not extinguish when he walked away.

Eventually, I turned around to see Ling still sitting there. Instantly, I remembered myself and straightened up.

He continued to look at me.

"Shen-ma!" I cried, which was the Chinese version of 'what!'

Smirking a little, he looked at the ground.

I rolled my eyes; must I be so transparent? My intentions must have been as clear as a plain glass window.

"Back to our lesson," I said, walking up to him and tapping his chin. Ling smiled again.

We went back to our Chinese English lesson.

———

Four days later, I was back at the festival again. The second performance was already done, and I was walking along the lanterns. Since it was nightfall, I was able to see the illumination from each lantern in full.

While I was surrounded by beauty, and also by crowds of people who were moving along, either enraptured by the spectacle, or looking at their phones—I do not judge much, but at such a festival, why are you on your phone?—I felt the comfort of walking away from a scene that had been totally out of my element.

Externally, I looked as casual and complacent as ever.

But internally, I felt like a trainwreck.

When passing the cherry blossoms tree lanterns, my mind wondered over to what just happened in the second show...

I had just finished announcing the third act, which was Ken and Karl's acrobatic number—I'm still amazed at how Ken would perform all those incredible stunts, while still wearing rings on his fingers. Well, style is style.

Ling had just gotten done turning off my microphone and turning on the music so that the performance could commence. Sadly, Ling, through no fault of his own, had a tendency to turn off my microphone before I finished talking. It was awkward, to say the least, but I really think he just didn't know that I was not done yet.

Oh well!

Just as Ling walked away, back to the tents to sit down, I would still watch the performance from the wings.

Just as Karl lifted Ken up, where they locked hands, and Ken did a handstand in the air, I heard shuffling behind me.

Turning around, I saw Jin standing there, wearing the tunic he always wore under his face changer outfit.

I let my heart jump into my throat for only a second, before I found my voice again.

"You thought you could scare me again?" I smiled. "Cheeky!"

Cheong-Jin smiled as he came forward, slowly.

He might as well have been walking in slow motion, in my mind.

Standing up, I found myself walking towards him, so

that I could hear him better. Because of the music, I had a hard time understanding people when they talked to me, so I had to get close to him. By the will of kismet, I was thankful that I had a reason to be so close to him.

Once I reached him, I felt the heat of his figure, even though we did not fully touch.

"What do you do for a living?" he asked me. "When you do not do this?"

While he had learned to speak English beautifully, I worried that he could not hear it very well. That's the disconnect between the tongue and the ear: you can speak something, but you cannot always understand it when you hear it.

"I am a tour guide!" I began. "Do you know what that means?"

"Yes."

"Yes, I lead people around, and I show them Philadelphia."

"Then...you could lead me around?"

I smiled.

"Yes, I can lead you around. I would take you anywhere that you like."

When saying this, I never stopped staring into his eyes, despite that we were extremely close to each other.

Blushing, he looked down at the ground.

"Have you always lived here in Philadelphia?"

"Yes. Where do you live?"

"Now," he furthered, "I live in Washington."

"You do?" I asked, my eyes growing large, "all the way on the other side of the States. I have never been to Washington."

"You haven't?"

Turning more toward him, I became more interested in his history.

"What states have you gone to?" I asked.

"I've been to Washington, Texas, Pennsylvania, New York, Massachusetts, New Jersey, Georgia, New Mexico, Arizona, and Michigan."

"You've been to more US States than I have, and I live here," I said, laughing.

"You have?"

"Yeah. Jin, I don't go anywhere very much. Also, I have something to tell you."

"What?"

"I don't even know how to drive."

His eyes enlarged when hearing that.

"You don't?"

"No," I responded, "I live in the city, so I never needed to have to worry about driving. And I've always been too scared to drive."

"What are you talking about? Driving is easy." He mimicked driving, "It's fun too."

"Until an accident happens," I responded, "and I have a way of causing accidents."

"How can you cause an accident, when you don't drive?" Cheong-Jin wondered, turning more into me. Despite not asking, I placed my hand on his hip and was relieved when he did not remove it. I suppose we reached a point where nothing I did intimidated him anymore. My constant invasion of his personal space and acceptance of the unspoken yearning of desire to embrace him had become easily accepted.

That was all that I could hope for.

"Sorry," I apologized, "I was not speaking in a general sense. And I just realized that you don't know what I mean by that. I mean that I have a way of knocking into things and causing accidents just because I have bad luck."

"What does that mean?"

"It's regarding my life, and when it comes to romance."

"Romance? What? Are you married?"

"No."

"Have a boyfriend?"

"No," I added, "I don't date, because of what happened five years ago. Jin, I made a bad mistake."

"What did you do?" he asked, his voice lowering.

Intrigue! That's what we all need, every now and again. Intrigue. And the only way that it can happen is, through the wheel of time, at some point, one of us made a grave mistake. And thus, they had a story to tell, for those who needed to hear a story.

And so, I began to tell the story that I have hidden from you, through all this time. A story that I was not proud of, by any means. However, that is the only redeeming quality that I had; I was not proud.

"It began about ten years ago," I explained. "When I was in my early twenties, I realized that I had terrible taste in men. I'm not saying that men are bad. They are not even the full problem. Rather, it was that I had a way of walking past all the nice men and ran into the wrong ones. So, I stopped dating for at least three years. Then I got involved with a guy, who I knew. We worked together. It didn't work out, because it turned out he had a wife."

When hearing that, Cheong-Jin, due to his youth, reacted as a good man naturally would. Color drained out of his face, and he knocked his head backwards, against the curtain behind him. Astonishment and alarm were etched across his features.

He was looking into the face of someone who was 'the other woman'.

———

There, Jin stood, looking at me, transfixed to the spot. Since he was done performing, he had all the time in the world to hear my tale. Since he did not walk away immediately, I found comfort in that.

After all, he could have thrown my words to the wayside, walked away, and ignored me for the rest of the summer—which was only ten days away.

Ten days!

That was all that I had left to be with him.

"I," I began, then I shut my mouth for a second. I had to do my best to form my sentences perfectly, to get the point across. But at the same time, I had to be honest about everything and let him know that I was not the person that I used to be.

"They were not married yet," I explained, "but they were engaged. He never told me about her. And since we were friends, he knew my history. You see. When I get physically romantic with someone, I feel a deep connection. I have a hard time letting the person go. What I mean is, when I start to like them a lot, I keep liking them. And it takes me a long time to let go."

"Did he know that?"

"Yes. Since we were friends first, I told him that about me."

"So, he waited till after you both kissed, to tell you that he was engaged."

"He said that he assumed that I knew."

"He assumed!" Cheong-Jin repeated, bitter.

"Yes. I told him that we never talked about it, and he said that he thought that everyone knew."

Slowly, Cheong-Jin shook his head.

"It does not matter what he assumed. Before you ever kissed, he should have asked you if you were okay with kissing someone who was engaged to someone else. He should have been clear about that. Especially since he knew that you get attached fast. And you…"

Looking at him with a wistful expression, I placed my hands behind his back.

"Yes? What were you about to say?"

Cheong-Jin shrugged. I could tell, from his posture, that he was afraid of saying something that might hurt me.

"What's wrong?"

"I—I should not say it."

His eyes and his body were evidently filled with uncertainty and apprehension. I knew that, deep down, I would be fine with him supporting me or chastising me. As long as he spoke, that was all that I cared about. After all, he was a good person; I can take harsh advice from a good person. Because they are the only ones who are worth hearing such advice from.

"I'm not afraid," I assured him. "I'm not afraid of you."

His eyes rose to me, and comprehension dawned. Even though my words were not clear, he understood me.

"Are you sure?" he asked.

"Yes," I replied, evenly. "I am sure."

"You—you were lonely, weren't you?" he suggested. "Were you lonely?"

My heart melted.

How did he know? Truly, how did he know?

Slowly, I nodded.

"Yes," I whispered, "I think I was. I was very lonely."

He smiled when he saw that I was not offended by him observing what was within me. Sometimes, people feel bad for reading into another person's soul, and then saying that person's secrets out loud. As they ought to. And when that happens to you, if it is done for the sake of giving you catharsis and closure, then you must show appreciation to the person who gave you the moment you needed to move on.

"He knew that," Cheong-Jin elaborated. That's how they get to people like you. I talk about bad people. They know that you are lonely, so they give you that moment of connection, no matter what it will cost you. Because they know that you want to be loved, so much, that you will take what they offer. Even if what they offer you is poison."

"It gets worse," I said, emotionally and pathetically. "I didn't hate him afterwards. I forgave him. And I still liked him. That's why I don't date. Because I realize that I am weak. I am afraid that I will become like that again. And I don't want to be. I don't want to be!"

Instantly, my body began to shake, and it was like I could not control the spasms. Immediately I began to feel the weight of my mistake coming crashing down all around me as it pressed against my person, pulling me to the ground into a grave of my own making.

Ignoring any way that he was raised to not be too intimate with a person who you barely knew, Jin wrapped his arms around me, to steady me.

My spirit deflated and it all lay still as I fell into his embrace. Collapsing against his chest, I felt cradled. All speech left and only remaining was the desire to be comforted. To be accepted.

"I don't know how it happened," I wept, resting my face against his neck. "I should have hated him. Maybe if I met his wife, or at least knew her name, she would have felt real to me, and I could have despised him for her sake."

"You never met her either?"

"Not once."

"So, she didn't feel real. People have a way of not being real until you meet them. Then, one day, you realize that they are...and their pain is your pain. And you see it all for the first time. Is that what happened?"

Slowly, I nodded. "I was wrong," I said, "And earlier on, I could..."

"What? Could have what?"

"I could have said 'no more'."

"But you said it eventually."

"Yes."

"Then that's it. You said it eventually. Not everyone says it at all."

He did no more and no less than the most casual and also grand of gestures; he offered me his hand.

I stared at it, as it lingered there.

Though my glance could not have lasted more than two seconds, a whirlwind of revelations washed over me.

In his hand stood the ability to move on.

To accept.

And be accepted.

To feel anew.

To believe.

And to leave the world outside.

For that was it!

To leave the world behind.

Here, in the confines of the festival, on the borders that surrounded the event, we could get away from it all. The walls were not holding it in. It kept the trappings, cares and worries of the outside world from reaching us.

In the outside world, there is freedom—that cannot be denied. The freedom to do whatever you wish. But freedom is also like a weight that leads to you needing to care for everything, from the most trivial to the most tumultuous. And when you choose the freedom to *not care* for what goes on around you, you let a demon in. Demonic behavior thrives on indifference, because no one is there to care to stop it from happening.

Thus, freedom is a release, but it is also a weight. You must care for yourself, but of others.

You must care about:
Education
Poverty
National continuance
Morality
The lack of morality
Crime
Chaos
Children
How everyone's problems must be yours!
How your problems mean nothing to those who ask you to care for theirs, at the expense of your welfare!
Horror
Abuse
And politics.

But inside of the festival, there we do not have to worry about freedom to care for those things.

Rather, we are free *from* having to worry about all that.

We were all safe, for a little while.

Thus, we could wear our hearts on our sleeves.

We could put our guard down.

We could revel in the innocence of being among a haven.

Together, we would all walk around each other, along with each other, and pass each other, wearing the same mask.

I took Cheong-Jin's hand.

"There, you see?" he assured me. "You did not stay stuck there. You got out."

"I did?" I asked, hopefully.

"Yes. You got out."

———

On the walk back to the train, I felt light as a feather. I had finally told one of my secrets out loud, and the world was still spinning.

Of course, the turn of the globe did not rest on my personal failures and revelations—as it should not, for anyone's vain sake.

The *Grand Release* was finding *her* way into my life, and there was such exhilaration on my part. To reach a new height, that can sometimes happen when you have a grand experience is everything you would wish.

Until you remember another shame.

Another mistake.

Because that's what the mind does sometimes. Even when there is nothing wrong, and you are on the right path, your brain remembers the other problem.

It reminds you of your other failure.

That large failure in your life that you did your best to outrun. The one that you, if you were taught morality and how to apply it, feel a deep regret for. That you learn from. It's the mistake that is like a foil, that is the complement of your virtues, that tells you to *never* repeat that again.

The problem is that *that* memory loves to come back to you at the oddest of moments.

Like a ghost of the long past, it rises like a phantom and swallows your happy mood.

It did that just now.

From the caverns from the depths of my history, it came back, like a vengeance.

My brow furrowed as I sat there, on the train, near midnight, and I fell back into myself.

Gone was the good moment.

Gone was the closure that I had just experienced.

And in its place, came the shame and guilt.

Thank goodness that there were not many people on the train, since it was so late.

Now, I could sit there, letting the blackness of the sky find its way into my psyche.

Eventually, the train reached 40th and Market Street, where I got off, and went down the steps, where my brother was there to pick me up.

And so, I was back where I had always been.

Back to being locked in wretched stasis.

Chapter 18
A Charming Refrain

The cheering of the crowd was immense as the performers took their bow on stage.

Two days later, I had been working the festival again, and the first show had gone by brilliantly.

Once I gave the closing speech, thanking the audience, I got my bag ready, and was just about to sling it over my shoulder, when I sensed a presence behind me.

"Jin?" I asked, not turning around.

"How did you know that it was me?" he asked.

"I've gotten used to your shadow."

At last, I turned back to him.

In his speed, he had changed out of his costume and was now wearing regular clothes. Looking at him, up and down, I just realized something.

"What?" he questioned, noticing me looking at him, up and down.

"Nothing, it's just... I never saw you in regular clothes until now. Like, casually."

"Oh," he said, looking up and down at himself. "Yes, that's true."

"It's just so...strange."

I laughed, and he echoed the sentiment.

"Strange?" he repeated, "to know that I'm like everybody else."

"In look, yeah, but," my voice faltered a little, "you'll never be like everybody else. It's not your way."

Grinning bashfully, he looked at the ground.

"Are you going to walk around the festival?"

"Actually, I was going to take a quick walk to Chinatown."

"Oh." I was pathetic. I didn't know how to be subtle, charmingly. Rather I felt like I was a bull, bashing full ahead. "I haven't been to Chinatown in a while."

Without saying anything, Cheong-Jin offered me his arm.

Maybe it was okay to be a bull about it! Sometimes, subtlety perhaps is not the solution to the problem.

Slinging my bag over my shoulder, I placed my arm in his, and we walked down the brick path that led to the exit.

Once we were shown out of the gate, and were walking toward 8th Street, I found my footing with conversation.

"So," I began, "you've learned a lot about me, which is not really a lot. You've learned that I was born here, have always lived in the same house my entire life, that I don't know how to drive, have not gone to nearly as many US states as you have, and just work and go home... am I boring to talk to?"

Cheong-Jin chuckled. "I can talk to boring."

"Good. Because that gives me the excuse to ask you anything, and everything. If you don't mind."

"I don't mind."

"What made you want to be a Face Changer? Why that life? Mind you, it's a beautiful life. But what drove you?"

"There's more to it than you think. I like what I do, but in truth, I was more-so told to do it. It had to do with where I was from."

"What city?"

"I was born in Guizhou."

"Is that a place that is good for training?"

"It's a city that you are sent from, to go to training."

When hearing this, I was confused.

"What do you mean?"

"Guizhou is a poor town. It's one of the western towns in China. Guizhou is like Yunnan, Xinjiang, Qinghai, Tibet, and others."

When hearing the name Tibet, I flinched. But I didn't say anything.

We were still coming from the grounds of the Lantern Festival; we were safe from the trappings and failures of the world outside. Here, all was free. All was equal. Your politics did not matter, nor did your pain. All that mattered... was the people.

"The western part of China is less developed, and there are more poor people there."

"So East is considered...richer?" I inquired.

"Yes. With Guizhou, when you grow up there, people work hard, because life is—hard. Life hurts sometimes. I have a brother, and it would be easier for the family if I was sent away, to acrobatics school. Some of us are sent there, because our families are too poor to look after us. It's our only chance to have a life."

"You are sent there even before you know that's what you want to do with your life?" I asked.

"We do it even before we are old enough to learn if we even want to do something else. Since we do it since we are little, it becomes who we are. Does that make any sense?"

"Yes," I responded, rolling my tongue behind my teeth, surprised at what I was learning. "It does. I'm just—I just can't believe it. To go somewhere and become something before you're even—wait, how old were you when you were sent off to acrobatics school?"

He raised his hand to show me the number.

"You were six?" I questioned, alarmed. "You were six years old!"

"Yes," Cheong-Jin affirmed. "I was."

I could not believe it. Of course, I was under the clear understanding that Jin's skill would have taken years to accomplish, but...

Six years old!

"You can't believe it, can you?" Jin asked.

"I know that I should, but I admit that I'm still trying to wrap my brain around it all." I leaned into him a little more. "What about being around your family? Of making friends? Of going to regular school?"

Cheong-Jin shook his head as we reached Chinatown.

"For some of us, that is not our fate. It is our life, and we live it."

———

"It's true," Michelle told me. "It is their life. And they accept it."

The next day, before the performances had begun, I had been walking around Franklin Square and ran into Michelle. When she joined me, I immediately began to appeal to her about what Jin had told me.

"It's the way of many of those in the festival. They start young. You know Ken?"

"The chair walker, yeah. We never talk, but he smiles at me whenever we walk past each other."

"It's understandable that he doesn't talk much to you, and I'm happy that you don't get offended by it. He was taken to acrobatic school when he was four years old."

I stopped walking in my place, turning to her, shocked.

"What! At four?"

"Yes."

"But what about elementary school? Did he get a basic education."

"Not really. He was not taught any basic education for many years. Now he can read and write, but he couldn't do much for a while."

I continued to walk along with her, past the beehive lanterns, which gave off a buzzing sound and had one of the combs in the hive open. Flashes of Ken danced across my mind, as I would watch him finish his act by standing on the chairs, like he had just climbed a mountain.

"I can see how his skill took many years," I gathered, "but I'm still trying to adjust to the idea of something I never thought about. It's a culture shock, but I guess that he was fine with it. There is probably something fun about being able to spend your childhood being physical and learning that sort of stuff."

"Yes, and no. I think, at some point, Ken began to wonder about what it was like to go to school like the rest of us. After all, he is educating himself now. And he has also really gotten into Taoism. Do you know much about Taoism?"

"No, to be honest. When I was in school, I mostly learned about Confucianism, but even then I don't remember that much."

"Confucianism and Taoism began during the same dynasty."

———

"I do," Cheong-Jin translated for me.

In between performances, I had the courage to ask Jin about Ken, who offered to be a translator for me to Ken. At first, I was a little anxious to interrupt Ken, who preferred to spend his time between shows to sit there, silently, on his phone.

But once Jin assured me that he would not be upset if I imposed myself on him, Jin spoke to Ken, who was all too happy to lower his phone, and speak about Taoist beliefs.

"I began to start studying Taoism three years ago," Jin continued to translate. As Ken kept talking, the more Jin would interpret to the best of his ability.

"What dynasty did they both begin in?" I asked.

"It was during the Spring and Autumn period," Jin continued to translate. "Which was the first half of the Eastern Zhou Dynasty. A lot of Chinese philosophers came during that time of Chinese history. There was Confucius and there was Lao, who was the master of Taoism."

"I was told that," I explained, "Confucianism talked about constantly applying personal and governmental morality."

"Yes," Jin informed me, "that is most of it. His teachings were also about peaceful social relationships, righteousness, truth, and also about leaders. He believed that a ruler's responsibilities had to also be about leadership through virtue."

"Which leaders often never do, sadly," I put in, cynical.

"Pretty much. There is more to it. Confucius was about

bringing back the values from earlier times in Chinese history that had been forgotten about. There were a lot of problems during the Spring and Autumn period. There was a lot of fights for political power, lords were fighting each other a lot, the royalty was losing its influence—lots of conflicts were going on."

"Like now?" I parallelled.

"Yes. Like now."

We both chuckled.

"So, Confucius wanted to return to the older ways. He was all about family loyalty, respect your ancestors, your elders by their children. And wives must respect the husband."

I gave Jin and Ken a look.

"I know," Jin said, raising up his arms in a 'I get it' kind of way. "The husband should respect the wife too. Those were different times. You know that."

My *expression* relaxed.

Jin translated my 'mood' to Ken and Ken chuckled, nodding to appease me.

My *mood* relaxed.

"Confucianism believed that these things would create an ideal government. For if there is no respect among a family, how can there be respect in society?"

I nodded gently. After all, it was true.

"And Confucius was a staunch believer in the Silver Rule, instead of the Golden Rule."

"What is the Silver Rule?" I asked.

Cheong-Jin tilted his head closer to me.

"Do not do unto others what you do not want done to yourself."

"Oh," I uttered, falling into his eyes as our faces were

closer than ever. "That is what the Silver Rule is. That's where that philosophy comes from."

"Yes."

"Now I know."

As quickly as I was giving way to my sensibilities, driven by the desire that I felt for him, I gathered my sense. Blinking, I looked away from Cheong-Jin and back to Ken.

"And Lao?" I asked Ken. "What does Taoism focus on?"

Ken spoke and Cheong-Jin translated.

"Taoism was founded by the Chinese philosopher Laozi. In some sects of the Taoism there is Chinese Buddhism, Confucianism and Chinese Folk Religion. One of the foundational texts to Taoism is 'Tao Te Ching', which Laozi wrote."

Jin leaned into me again, and I felt my body slacken as his arm accidentally pressed against my side.

"I know the core parts of the philosophy, but I know that Ken wants to talk about it, so here we go," he whispered, conspiratorially.

"Fire away," I whispered back.

Ken continued to explain things, with Jin translating, as I allowed myself to lean against Jin's side, casually. What was more was the joy I found in knowing that he did not recoil but had no fear in me enjoying the closeness that I desired of each other.

"Taoism has a few main principles. The first is to have harmony with the Tao."

"What is the Tao?"

"The universe. Taoism is to believe that humans and nature should live in harmony with the Tao, or the universe. This harmony will allow them to merge with it, free their souls, and become immortal. When you die, the spirit of the body joins the universe.

"Another principle is yin and yang. That's where those terms come from. The philosophy is that the universe is made up of opposing forces that are connected and complement each other. And so, that is the Yin and Yang. And Taoism is also focused on moral wisdom. Taoists believe in being simple, sensitive, flexible, and independent, and in having few desires."

I looked at Ken.

"Is that what you focus on between performances?" I inquired.

Cheong-Jin translated my question.

Ken nodded and said yes in Chinese. 'Yes' was one of the few Chinese words that I knew.

———

"Another way to become a performer is if a teacher takes you on," Michelle elaborated as we were eating dinner, next to one of the Chinese food vendors.

It was the next night, and I met up with Michelle between shows. She elaborated more about how acrobats were chosen. Each time that I asked, I worried that I was imposing on a world that was secret and was not my right to know. But the more that I gathered my courage, and asked questions, the more I found out that they liked us knowing about their lives, the choices they made, or the choices that were made for them.

"There are two ways to get a teacher," Michelle explained to me, between bites. "First, the teacher has to have a connection with the student. When they meet, the teacher must feel a bond, a link to their pupil."

"Really?"

"But also, it is best to also have the student's family give the teacher gifts."

I wiped my mouth as I felt some food hanging from the side of my lips.

"Gifts?" I asked, surprised. "What kind of gifts?"

"Things like special tea and wine. That sort of stuff."

"So," I repeated, for my memory, "for a teacher to want to take on a student, where they become experts, is if the teacher feels a connection to the student, and if the family gives the teacher special gifts."

"Yes," Michelle said, taking a drink from her cup. "Remember the face changers from last summer?"

"Yes, I remember Zhang and Youki."

"They both were taught their trade by teachers, who felt a connection to them. And then there are people who become performers because it's a family tradition. The jar juggler last year, Lucille. Her mother and grandmother were also foot jugglers. So, it ran in the family."

"That explains why she was so damn good," I responded. However, being the talentless soul that I was, my mind naturally wondered to the less fortunate—the less loved. What of those unlucky ones who were not as preferred as the others? What about the ones who were not chosen at all?

"But if a student never finds a teacher who feels a connection to them, and the family cannot afford to give a teacher gifts, then they cannot be chosen?"

Michelle nodded simply, but heavily.

"And also, in acrobatic school," Michelle elaborated, "a student is given more attention if they are considered better. They get more opportunities to perform more in festivals and special events."

"And if a student is not considered as good, then they are given less opportunities, or none?"

"Yup."

Biting my lip, I leaned back in my seat.

"Well, that's not fun at all. If you are not as good, then you are given less and no chances, so that must hurt your pride and self-confidence. And when you are a teenager, like Ling, and you are being passed over, that must feel like the worst."

"It's the way of the world when it comes to being a performer," Michelle summed up, "all your morals and principles don't matter if you aren't good enough in other people's eyes."

"But even if you are good, there is always personal prejudices," I said. "Like, you can be great, but if your teacher does not like you, or you are not as popular as someone else, you get passed over. I've seen that happen before, where someone is really good at something, but because people take a natural dislike to them, they don't choose them."

"That can happen too. You can easily be the right person for the job, but get passed over, because of human error."

Taking a drink from my water, I found joy in knowing that someone felt a connection to Cheong-Jin.

"Do you know how old Jin was when a teacher taught him?" I asked.

"He never had a teacher."

In my seat, I did a double take.

"What!"

———

"It's true," Cheong-Jin confirmed as I was following him backstage.

The first performance was over. I had sought Cheong-Jin out and he was bashful about explaining his self-education but also inviting in divulging the story.

"You taught yourself Face-changing?" I questioned, astonished. "How?"

"I watched other people do it, I studied them, and I figured it out."

"But—but—but," I stuttered, which led to Jin laughing at me. "I just can't understand how. It's hard to do, and you taught yourself. You didn't have a teacher at all?"

Jin shook his head.

"Not at all. I went to acrobatics school, and that's it."

In my mind, I was quoting Shakespeare, as many of us have the inclination to do, every now and then.

What a piece of work is man!

How noble in reason, how infinite in faculty, in form and moving how express and admirable, in action how like an angel, in apprehension how like a god!

"What?" Jin said.

Closing my eyes, I rubbed my cheek.

"Was I staring at you again?"

"Yes," Jin responded, "you were. It's fine. I am not afraid."

"Good."

Gathering my courage, I looked at him.

"I will tell you what I was thinking, in a minute," I said, looking at the ground, "But not right now."

"Okay," he said. "I will accept that."

"And I am being awkward."

"It's okay," he assured me.

"No, I am being unfair to you. If I made this awkward, it's my job to get us back on track. I never—you are a very good performer. I never got the chance to tell you. I would have thought that you would have had a teacher."

"Thank you," Jin replied, bashfully, as he looked at the ground now.

"Did you teach yourself because you know how to teach yourself things? Why would you not have been chosen? You know how to make people love you. You—"

"Are poor," he said. "My family could never give presents to a teacher, and I never found a teacher who chooses a student based on feeling a connection with them."

"Were you different back then than you are now?" I asked, leaning against a desk that was backstage.

"I don't know."

"Well, they were wrong," I stated, "people can be wrong a lot, and not choose the right person."

Smiling, he sat down at the desk, right next to me.

I fell into the joy of having him so close to me again so that our fingers touched ever so slightly.

"You are nice to me."

"You are worth being nice to," I assured him.

Both him and I were, once more, at a loss for words.

The knife of kindness!

It can slice you...

In the strangest of ways...

Because compliments are given...

And you don't know how to repay it.

Jin had all the talent.

I had no talent at all.

He had no choice but to have nothing nice to say back to me, as repayment. Because there was nothing to report.

How hard it is for talented people and non-talented people to converse, sometimes; there can be an imbalance of conversation. Even when both sides understand equality so thoroughly.

"Thank you for thinking I had a teacher," he said.

"You are welcome, even though you clearly did not need one." Gently, I knocked my head against his shoulder, and he did not retract it.

When doing so, I glanced over his shoulder and saw all the masks that he used on the desk.

"Man of many faces," I joked.

"Do you want to know what each mask means?" he inquired.

"They have different meanings?"

"Yes."

Tugging at my dress, I turned around with him, and he laid out all the masks on the desks. Pointing to each mask, he showed me its definition.

"Face-Changing in the Sichuan Opera is also known as Bian Lian. Each mask depicts a different emotion, mainly through the mask's color."

He pointed to the red mask.

"This mask means bravery. But a red mask can also mean anger or loyalty."

Next came the black mask.

"Sometimes black means righteousness, but the black of my mask means—"

"Fury?"

Jin blinked, surprised.

"You knew that?"

"Yes," I responded, equally as amazed at my own deduction. "I didn't know how, but I could tell by the way it's made." My focus was directed solely at the black mask, and I felt a deep connection to it. "I think…it's because I understand it better than any of the others." As quickly as I had fallen into my reflections, I had fallen out of them. "Go on, though. Keep explaining them to me."

"This white mask."

"The panda-like one?"

"Yes. It suggests cunning. And the green mask means fear or being desperate."

When he finished explaining the other masks to me, I looked them all over.

"When we change the masks so fast," Jin said, "we show how us characters' rapidly shift emotions within a story."

"In the same way that a person can shift how they feel quicker than the blink of an eye," I said.

"Yes."

Once more, our eyes met, and we fell into each other's gaze.

There was no way around it.

I was in love with him.

———

From his black hair.

To his kind eyes.

He wove everything together.

Outside of his presence, the world seemed to be spinning into chaos.

But, when standing next to him, it all made sense.

Everything was Sense!

Before him, love and attraction had all been insane and chaotic for me.

Yet, when near him, my adoration was that of logic and reason. I loved him, because he was a good man. How often we do not choose those we care for, *because of their virtue.* But, for the first time in my life, I had done so.

How liberating!

For the first time in my life, I could say that, under the cloud of romantic affection, I felt—free. And as if the cracks of sunlight were peeking through.

Such a piece of work was man!

"Now I can tell you," I said, "about why I kept looking at you before."

"Yes," he said, "why?"

"I just realized something."

"What?"

"You're sexy."

Jin blushed as he smiled.

We were interrupted by a sound.

Cheong-Jin and I literally were knocked off our rocker, as we were pushed out of the bubble that we had fallen into, and felt reality rushing in.

Karl and Ling had entered and said something, in Chinese, to Jin.

Jin responded, stood up and turned to me. "Since you want to know about student and teacher, those are them."

"What?"

"Karl. He's Ling's teacher."

"Oh," I said, looking at the two men, "They are?"

"Yes."

I analyzed both men, one younger and the other older.

"That makes sense. They both act like brothers. I see what you mean by the teacher needs to have a bond with their student." I gestured to Ling. "He looks up to you, you know?"

"He does?" Jin asked, perplexed by this.

"He's nineteen years old and is insecure. You remember that age. It's a scary time. And his heart and body are constantly thinking about romance, but he doesn't know where to find it."

"That's true," Jin said, "when I was that age, I thought about girls all the time."

"And so does he. And you are confident. He likes your confidence, because he wants to be like that too."

"That's true, especially since his skin is darker."

"Darker?" I asked, tilting my head. Looking at him, I took in Ling's complexion.

"In Asia, it's like everywhere else," Cheong-Jin explained, "lighter skinned Asians are sometimes treated better than darker-skinned ones. Since Ling has darker skin, he was happy to get a teacher like him. Because you see that Karl has darker skin too."

That was true. Both men were not very dark, but still there was a distinct difference than Jin's fairer complexion.

"Wait," I realized, "if some Asians are not treated as well because their skin is a little darker, then what do some Asians think about us?" I gestured to my black skin. Then I raised up my hand and chose the whole 'ignorance is bliss' route. "Never mind! I don't want to know."

"No," Cheong-Jin said, "I do think that you do."

Grabbing my hand affectionately, then releasing it, Jin walked off to speak to Karl and Ling.

I didn't take the time to tell him. Tomorrow was my last night working at the festival.

It would be the last night that I saw him.

———

The next day, I was all anxiety and anxious as I rode the L train down to 5th and Market Street.

You know how, when sitting on public transit, there is

always someone who is talking loudly on the phone, so that the whole car can hear their conversation?

It cannot be ignored, and you don't want to ask them to lower their voice, because you know that it will do no good.

As such, all you can do is accept it as part of the charm of public transit, along with the habit of never sitting in the back of any bus, trolley, or train, because that's where everyone wants to be weird and engage you in the most bizarre conversations of your life.

Honestly! Sometimes being in the back of a bus or trolley is like riding on the equivalent of the scariest moments from the animated movies from the 1990s (back when kids movies were not afraid to be bizarre...and very unsettling). Or it's like being on that strange ferry ride in the movie 'Willy Wonka and the Chocolate Factory'.

Seriously, the one (and only time) that I sat in the back of the bus was such an emotionally jarring experience! Trust me...it was terror time.

Trust me...it was terror time.

Luckily, I was sitting in the middle of the car, in the idle part of the train, so at most, all I had to worry over was overhearing a conversation where a passenger was complaining about News consumption.

"How many times must I tell you to never watch FOX News Media?" a guy wailed into the phone. "Each time you do that, I have to bring in an exorcist to save your butt from the hellfire of misinformation. And you're watching it while eating dinner? It's like 'how about a daily dose of evil grem-lins selling your soul to the traitorous scum-buckets who dish out fake news with your steak and potatoes'? Turn off FOX and watch something to purify you from the demons that are dragging your soul into the abyss of lava that wants to burn off your manhood."

Everyone on the train could not help but laugh. Me included.

When realizing that we all heard him, the guy lowered his phone. "I'm right and you know it!" he wailed to all of us. "We're being led to the cliff, like lemmings, and taking our country with it."

No one was arguing with him, because we knew he was right. If we lose our country, it's only if we do it by sleep-walking towards our destruction, which is helped by corrupt mainstream media who was selling us all out, with their constant lies—to get more ratings. It's like what our 16th President, Abraham Lincoln said: 'As a nation of freemen, we must live through all time or die by suicide.'

And there were a lot of people sleeping instead of being awake. I thought, in a couple of months, more people would wake up. I had no idea that I would be so entirely wrong.

But I am getting ahead of myself.

————

Eventually I reached 5th and Market, got off the train, having been entertained the whole time by the passenger who was still talking loudly on his phone.

As I emerged from the bus stop, I encountered two people who were studying the map.

"Need help on where to go or are you lost?" I offered. Usually when people look at me, they can give me a strange look, but they were not discomforted by me approaching them. Still, I thought it was best to explain myself.

"I'm not weird, I promise. I work in this area."

"Splendid," they said, "we were looking for the best place to eat."

"Thank you for making it easy," I said. I offered them to go to the Lucha Cartel restaurant on 2nd and Chestnut Street, if they liked Mexican, or to Nick's, or the Irish Pub if they wanted something equally as nuanced. After showing them where to find it on the map, I asked where they were from.

"Canada," they said, "we're visiting from Canada."

With their open expressions, I felt a sudden rush of connection and desire to be respected. I didn't know why, but I felt like I would not be happy unless they knew that I wanted to show that we were worth being liked. And that we liked them, in turn.

I reached out my hand for them to take, which they did, and we clasped hands.

"You have a fantastic flag," was all that I could say.

"Thank you."

"Thank you for coming to see us again. It's nice when you come."

"We're getting that," they said, understanding me, and not thinking me to be on the wrong side of 'weird'. "Literally, we've been feeling that vibe all day from you guys. Your city is pretty."

"Thanks. Coming from you guys, that means a lot. Enjoy the food. I think you will like it."

"Thank you, and where are you headed?"

"The Chinese Lantern Festival," I said, as I was walking away. "It's my last day. Guess what?"

"What?"

"I don't like endings," I said, wistful.

Instead of wondering why I confessed that, they understood.

"Many people don't."

"Yeah."

I continued walking away to work, as they walked towards a good meal.

———

The walk to Franklin Square was very heavy. For my feet, at least.

As well as for my mind.

This was the last day that I was going to see him, and I didn't know what to make of it all.

When I arrived there and saw the large line of people who were waiting to get in, I held my hands to my side, steadying myself. Oh well! It's life and life only, eh?

Walking in, I decided to make it my mission to pay particular attention to the lanterns as the night fell. Even though it was still summer, the nights were growing colder, and I shivered a little as I walked to the stage.

The stage! There it was. Never will I pretend that much of my life was wrapped around the few times that I got to work there.

So much of my life was work and rest. Rest and work.

But here, I could say, beyond the shadow of a doubt, that I lived. That I was free. Going backstage, I greeted the performers, but Cheong-Jin was not there.

He was in the tent, getting his vibrant costume on.

Determined to give the best announcements that I would, I welcomed the audience and gave the usual description. When doing so, Cheong-Jin appeared on the other side, faceless as usual.

"Let's give our face changer a round of applause!" I spoke into the microphone and cheered for him.

He gave me the thumbs up, as the music played, and he went onstage.

Since this was my last performance to do, I was going to be focused on every routine, and easily, choosing to enjoy it if I had seen it all for the very first time.

Novelty is what people look for and find interesting.

But if you tell yourself that whatever is old can feel new again, then you begin to smile more. Everyday life becomes fascinating again—unless you never found everyday life interesting to begin with.

By the time that I got to the end of the first performance, the crowd gave their final applause, and I waited for a couple of minutes, until Cheong-Jin finished changing into regular clothes.

Once I gave him that time, I went back to the tent and put on a brave face.

Up until this point, every interaction that I had with Cheong-Jin was reactive. But never had I gone out of my way to be proactive and seek him out.

Courage, Briseis!

"Cheong-Jin!" I called.

"Jin?" Karl uttered, looking at something on his phone. "Bri calls you."

Jin emerged from the tent, putting on his flannel t-shirt.

"Hey," Cheong-Jin said, buttoning up his shirt. "What's up?"

"You are," I said, trying to sound charming. Understanding my joke, Jin smiled. "I was...wondering if you are doing anything before the next show?"

"You want to take me somewhere?"

"Not too far," I said, "the festival is all that we have. Do you want to take a walk along the lanterns for a bit?"

Cheong-Jin turned his head to the side, and I mimicked his action.

"Well?" I asked. "Are you going to tell me no?"

Jin moved his head back up straight, I did the same, and I was still left in limbo.

Finally, Jin raised his arm and offered me his hand.

"Let's walk as far as we can walk," he uttered.

Laughing, I took his hand as we walked out from backstage and passed the large red dragon that guarded the entrance.

Inwardly, I was in a state of ecstasy as well as great anxiety. Cheong-Jin said yes. He agreed to take time with me.

I was at ease. But since he said yes, now I had to think about what to say

What comes next?

ANXIETY.

"Are you hungry?" I asked him, "because I can buy you some food."

"Are you hungry?" he asked, as I lowered my eyes and focused on our hands holding.

I shook my head.

"No. I just want to walk."

"Then we can walk."

At last, I looked at him, taking in his kind eyes.

"Why did you have to do that?"

"Do what?"

"Be kind again. When I first met you, I had a feeling that you were nice. But now I know it, and you did it again."

Jin chuckled.

"You are being nice again."

"You make it easy."

We reached the part of the festival where there was another very large blue dragon that surrounded a temple.

This one was a moving lantern. The dragon's face moved from side to side, growling a little.

"I know that there are naturally no blue temples in Leshan," I said, gesturing to the lantern, "but what else is there?"

"You remember that I lived there for a bit?"

"Yes."

"You should go there. Let me show you."

Jin moved me to two benches that were nearby, we sat down, and he began to look Leshan up on his phone.

Accidentally, our foreheads knocked against each other, as we slowly parted, Jin began to show me the pictures. The first was a large statue that was carved out of the side of a sienna mountain.

"That is the Leshan Giant Buddha," he said, as my eyes widened at the scale of the sculpture.

"It's beautiful."

"So is the Emei Mountain," Jin said, showing me the mountain from another angle. "It has other sculptures and inscriptions along it." He showed me the other images of the incredible monument that blended nature and human invention.

"Mount Emei is a place of historical significance as one of the four holy lands of Chinese Buddhism," Jin explained. "Buddhism was introduced into China in the 1st century, through the Silk Road from India to Mount Emei, and it was on Mount Emei that the first Buddhist temple in China was built."

"I never learned much about the Silk Road," I admitted, unafraid of my ignorance. "Was it like a trade route?"

"The Silk Road was everything. It was a trade system that lasted for centuries," Cheong-Jin explained. While he did so, being a tour guide, I let the words turn into actions.

The festival and Philadelphia melted, as we both moved through time, and I saw a whole system of roads and activity moved around us.

"The Silk Road was a network of trade routes that connected the Eastern and Western worlds for over two thousand years."

Over and around us, I saw the roads, and the country that rested around us. I saw the network of land and sea routes. A road connecting the Roman Empire and China. Then later, stretching to the Medieval European Kingdoms.

It was a link that connected many civilizations. Through the exchange of goods, ideas, and religion. I saw traders moving their many vehicles filled with silk, cotton, wool, glass, gold, silver, salt, spices, tea, herbal medicines, and more along these pathways, food, and much more. It was a form of global economy that not only conveyed objects, but also ideas. Ideas!

With those ideas came great demand, and high prices—life has not been or ever would be financially easy. But again—ideas! After all, that's what a road does, doesn't it? It connects. Rather than divide. Walls must be built, sometimes, but a road—oh, a road!

All around us, I saw merchant caravans that covered specific sections of the route. I saw every good day. And every bad day. The spreading of culture. But also, the spreading of disease. After all, with us humans come an equal share of life...and death.

One cannot separate the first from the second, now can we? That is why we will always look forward to, and equally dread, a new road being built. They have no choice but to, sadly.

How strange we are...to hate what we love, at the same time.

"I want to show you the Jinding Mountain and the Baoguo Temple," Jin continued. "Do you want to see?"

The Silk Road dissolved around me, the festival had returned, and I was back to being in Franklin Square, Philadelphia, in late August 2024.

Looking at Cheong-Jin, I found the comfort of feeling like I had not been forlorn, of falling out of my dreams and landing onto reality, harshly. For, when being hurled out of our daydreams, where everyday life feels like a cold rock that we slam into, is the usual wake-up experience.

But not this time. This time, with Cheong next to me, I had landed softly, happy to be where I was, rather than somewhere else.

"I'm still here," I assured him, "I'm not going anywhere."

That was permission enough.

———

Jin showed me the Jinding Mountain, and the Baoguo Temple. Afterwards, he showed me other places that he had lived, including Chengdu. He showed me the Temple of Wenshu, Prosper China Park, and other places. We had grown so engulfed in him telling me about China, that we lost track of time. We found ourselves walking very briskly back to the stage, so that he could get in costume.

"Good luck," I said, as he was about to go into the tent, "I know that you will be great."

Moving his head out of the flap of the tent, he studied me. "You want to go to China, don't you?" he questioned.

Placing his hand behind my back, I thought about it.

I wanted to see the world, and China was among those places. However, there was one thing that stopped me from going—besides being too poor. It was the one thing that stopped me from going to many places:

Prejudice.

Hatred.

Bigotry.

Is there discrimination in the USA?

Of course! All those sad qualities exist everywhere. Humans, despite our best efforts, cannot avoid the rest of humanity.

But your home is familiar!

So, you know where the danger is, and not to go there. You know how to avoid biasing of difference. And in Philadelphia, we had the power to combat it very often. In my city, there is a road—a bronze one, that achieves connection from everywhere.

Hatred may rest here for a bit, and find temporary accommodations, but it cannot last. Philadelphia cannot, nor ever be, a permanent place for regression and bigotry.

Because we were born over many roads crossing over and under, and causing such a great overlap, that having one identity is an allergy to us.

Intolerance of other cultures, or of other ways, is a poison that will eventually kill us, because it violates what we wish to be. We may give into intolerance, from time to time, because we are a city of humans—but our waking is swift, quick, and cannot be ignored.

Hatred—come!

Bigotry—enter.

You will win a few battles. But eventually, you will ultimately lose the war. But what of other nations? Of other lands? Does a Silk Road run through them? That was what I was afraid of? How could I know? I had reason to be afraid.

So, I had only one answer: to not give a full answer.

"Yes," I answered truthfully, "I do. But if I would go, would I find you there?"

Jin smiled. "Yes, you would."

"Then, when I am brave enough, I will go."

I started to walk to the other side of the stage, when I remembered what I had to tell him. I had been so wrapped up in the joy of being beside him that I did not tell him.

"Jin!" I called.

"What?" he asked, joy in his eyes.

"I forgot to tell you—tonight is my last night."

What a stark transformation!

And a scary change.

Cheong-Jin's eyes changed from pleasant to cold.

"What?"

"Yes. Um…this is my last night working the festival."

"What!" he hissed. Gone was the joy. His expression was a subtle anger. "But tomorrow?"

"Someone else got the shift. I wanted to work. But someone beat me to it. This is the last time that I will see you here."

Without noticing, Cheong-Jin stepped back. In his eyes was discomfort, then disappointment, then dissatisfaction, and finally disdain.

Angry, he turned away from me and went back to the tent, to get changed.

———

My walk to the microphone was cold and I felt dead inside. I didn't know what to do. Truly, I didn't know what to do. I didn't know anything. I never knew anything!

Standing there, I waited for Karl to come and turn the music on. He made to acknowledge me, but he was no fool.

Seeing my wistful expression, he knew that there was something wrong.

He understood. This was the end. There are no good words for it.

Nodding, he turned down the music, turned on the microphone, and I began to narrate the final show of the summer for me.

———

When coming to the end of something that you like, it is always fast. Fleeting.

All throughout the show, Cheong-Jin never came to see me after his performance. The loss of his company was felt hard and understood harshly. I knew what he meant and felt.

He was angry with me and understood why. Having just come to a point where we grew to consider speaking to each other when he left, had never been fully reached.

There was tension between us, that could not be explained. It could only be felt.

I was going through the motions as I was losing my bearings again. Nothing felt safe anymore. My heart was not safe. I felt the great unwinding as time moved on. Because time does not wait for you, or even for itself. It just goes.

The show came to an end. The performers gave their final bow, the audience cheered, and the show was over.

It was all over.

Slowly, I gathered my things and looked at the empty stage. Where was I going next?

Sighing, I walked backstage, as the performers were getting their things, to leave. Their casual behavior was a little antagonistic for me. For me, it was final. For them, it was just another show.

As I started walking to the other side backstage, I halted.

Without even looking, I felt a sensation of eyes on me. Turning around, I saw Cheong-Jin standing there, his shirt off, because he was still getting changed.

Our eyes locked gazes. I was resigned and wistful. His was a subtle resentment. Both wanted to ask the other if we could still stay connected, through calling each other, or writing.

Why were we both so afraid? It was like—we did not know how to do it. Sadly, I raised my arm up, with this being the last goodbye. Mimicking the action, he did the same. I knew, deep down, that we would never see each other again.

———

Crying, I rushed out of the festival's entrance, running down the sidewalk and disappearing into the darkness. I was a coward! Such a coward! Why was I afraid of asking if we could call each other or talk over the computer? Why didn't I do that? After all this time, what was I so scared of? I had chosen isolation over love. Love! Why did I turn away from that chance?

But I did. That's what I did. And thus, I belonged to an ancient race of humanity: the kind that did not choose what was in their best interest.

I reached the L train and waited for it to come on its platform. Eventually it came driving down the tracks. Between the light coming from the train, and the sound of the engines, I felt all that visual and loud sound crashing onto my brain and ears.

Love is artwork that stretches out onto a canvas, illuminating everything. But to do it, you must be brave enough for it first. Again, I was not. After all this time, I was still a coward—and a coward I would always be.

As such, the final show of the Philadelphia Chinese Lantern Festival came to an end. As it took its leave, so did my chances on seeing a new dawn to a new way of life.

Trying to grab ahold of all the precious memories that I had for the summer brought another daunting reality. I could not see his face. Cheong-Jin.

All the experiences I had for the entire summer rushed through my mind, with perfect clarity. I remembered Michelle, Karl, Ling, Ken, and the others. I saw them. But every time that my mind reverted back to the Face Changer —he was a blank to me. It was like he was being removed from my memory again.

I could not see his face.

I could not see the art.

It was taken from me.

Chapter 19
The Steps that Became the Stuff of Legend

December 1, 2024

"The Art Museum steps!" the bus driver announced. Leaning forward, I looked through the window of the Kite and Key bus, and around the corner, the Philadelphia Museum of Art appeared. The Kite & Key bus always circles around the museum first, to drop people off at one of the entrances.

The second stop around the building was in the very front. Due to movies, film, and legendary marathons, the Art Museum's front steps have become famous.

At last, I had reached my destination.

Standing up, I slung my bag over my shoulder and walked to the front door. At this point, I was the last person on the bus. That was strange, because this was one of the most popular tourist sites in the city.

At this point, all that I suppose was that, between it being later in the day, and because December has never been a peak time for tourists, naturally it would be empty.

"Thank you," I said to the driver as I got off the bus and stepped on ground again.

The bus driver nodded to me but didn't say anything else as she closed the doors behind me and drove off.

There I was, standing at 29th Street at the Benjamin Franklin Parkway, and looking up at the legendary museum. A prime example of the architectural being in the style of the Greek Revival, the museum was large, impressive, expansive, and inspired by the Greek and Roman temples, from cultures that were far older than ours.

Behind me was an island, in between the streets, that had a round fountain in it, with an impressive set of black statues to adorn the structure.

It was followed by a long stretch of trees that gave nature's elegance to the urban area. Thus, behind me was the successful execution of the Philadelphia promise that William Penn believed in when he founded the city in 1682; the idea of having parks and lots of green spaces, to give people the feeling of country life in a modern city.

Thus, I was returned to the parkway with all the different national flags, in the short distance away, waving in the wind.

Turning around, facing me were the legendary steps— the steps to the Art Museum.

From concept to construction, those steps would become immortalized in film and television. From all over the world, people came to run and walk up those steps.

Once you reach the top, you turn around and you see the most impressive view of the city before you. On the early morning, if you were to take a jog down the parkway, walk up them and turn around, you saw an old city, before a swift sunrise.

And behind you was a young building (young in the eyes of history), but with an old and classical design.

There she was: Philadelphia Museum of Art.

Raised before me.

The New.

And also the old.

Buildings drip of the souls that built it, hanging on to the edges of each piece of architecture, filling up the place. But a beautiful building, unlike the humans that make it, do not have the flaws that we possess.

No, fortunately. All the building represents is the better parts of us. The very best in us.

Feeling the perfection of every part of the museum, I found the joy of seeing something that fear, flaws, and failure could not touch.

I approached the steps.

———

With each step, came a flash of memory.

Flash 1

I took the first step.

I remembered when I fell down while giving a tour.

Flash 2

I took another step.

I recalled when I got an 'F' on my history exam in high school.

Flash 3

I took another step

When I was taking dance classes, the other girls were making fun of me.

Flash 4

I took another step.

In college, when I was in a class, all the students, my fellow classmates, hated me. I never said anything mean to them, but since I was the least talented one, I was easy to bully.

Flash 5

I took another step.

I re-lived when my first boyfriend in college broke up with me.

Flash 6

I took another step.

When I realized that I would never be the best at anything. Or good enough for anyone.

Flash 7

I took another step.

The moment came when I realized that the world did not want true heroes anymore. It all came down to money and power.

Flash 8

I took another step.

I forgot Cheong-Jin's face. The hardest loss of all.

Flash 9

I took another step.

When I learned that there was no law anymore. What will go on to happen will be at the hands of the corrupt. Justice was dead.

With each step I took, I felt my limbs grow heavier and heavier. As if I was being dragged down into an abyss of all my revelations and realizations. Of when I knew that all was falling apart.

Both myself and the world around me. All was coming undone.

Coming to the last step, the last flash came to me, like a tornado swirling around my vision.

Flash 10

I took the last step.

I remembered, in early November, when I went to my local voting location, and cast my vote, for *her*, in the election. The next morning, I literally jumped up from a nightmare that I had been having. Leaning forward, I clutched my chest, feeling as if I was at the foundation of a panic attack. My whole body shuddered, and every part of me felt like it was going to die.

How did my body know? How did it know what had happened, and that the worst choice was made...

I fell on the concrete, my face crashing against the hard surface of the art museum steps.

Groaning out, I was amazed that I was not in more pain. All that I experienced was a slight ache in my jaw, but that was it. Placing my hands on the ground, I limped as I stood up and looked upward. To my right, I saw the Philadelphia flag, with the blue and yellow colors, harkening back to when we were originally part of Sweden.

To my left, was the USA flag, as it lay limp against the flagpole. The red, white, and blue, hung still, motionless, with no direction on where it wished to go.

How it was so much in accordance with how everything had turned out. I was so terrified and felt the pain that seemed to never leave. It was a pain that millions of people in the USA felt, because we knew the bleak fate that lay ahead of us.

We knew that there would be chaos ahead, as well as scandal, drama, injustice, persecution, witch hunts, bigotry being allowed, tolerated misogyny, discrimination going unchecked, lies becoming the truth, losing our friendship with other nations, dictatorship winning, and death. People are going to die. It will happen, I knew, deep down.

Over, across the ocean, Germans are looking on us, knowing what is to come. After all, they were the ones who warned us. They tried to protect us from the worst side of history repeating itself, and—we failed.

Teenagers and kids, younger than 18 years old, are watching us now, and thinking how could we adults be so stupid, consumed by hate, or uneducated?

This is the nation that we gave them.

I knew, as I know now more than ever—that in the future, they will hate us for the choice that we made. Whatever happens, I felt that any good that occurs in the next couple of years would be followed by many worse days, worse actions, and worse crimes. In fact, the decision made earlier this month in November, by its very nature, is humiliating. We are an embarrassment to any young person who was taught basic right and wrong.

Nothing permanently good can come when our nation chose lawlessness over law.

They will know that millions of us brought about a world that pushed our land backwards, instead of progressing on, like they are taught to do.

We took them back.

And thought us right.

Some adults will try to brainwash them.

But the truth will come out.

They will know that we lied to them.

They will know that we sold their future.

For money. And Immorality.

It is decided.

They *will* find out.

They will never forgive us.

———

As the wind picked up, I looked away from the flags and turned around.

There she was: Philadelphia! In all her glory.

The Philadelphia Museum of Art is known for many things. Among them is that, when you walk up the steps, you turn around, and you get the best view of Center City. There are no words for it. Nothing can be fully described. It can only be felt. This view has to be felt.

Usually, whenever I look out, and I see the sun casting its gaze over my city—I feel alive. I often saw my whole life in front of me and explaining what it all was meant for.

But this time, I didn't feel it.

All that I saw...

Were senseless mistakes.

And my mistakes.

Once more, I was losing my bearings and not understanding how did we get here? I still cry out, in the depths of my soul!

And what was worse was all the people who did not get involved—who did not choose to protect our democracy because of their purity politics. I was enraged at those, on my political side, who did not vote, and could have saved us from what is going to happen. This was important to our country continuing. And they did not get involved. What has to happen for people to get up and care?

To see the bigger picture and that our continuance and respectability in the eyes of the world was at stake! To understand that nothing is perfect... but that doesn't mean that you should just not cast your ballot. Because perfection does not exist! It's about *'imperfection trying to be better'* versus pure evil. Too many did not show up, to protect our country—and by extension, the world—because they chose their 'purity and ideals' over *actual* human lives, preserving our democracy, our constitution, and helping us find a way back to being a government of laws, *not* of men. Not voting, while being of a liberal mindset, was not going to help, and only worsened things. Your beliefs don't matter, if it leads to inaction, and gets people killed/degraded. It is *not* the road to heaven that is paved with good intentions.

I can protest and petition against an imperfect administration that still follows our laws and respects our rights. I cannot protest and successfully petition one that is fascist and does not care about our rights at all—and plans to remove those rights.

Always vote to get the 'flawed but infinitely better' administration to serve in one's government and then rant and rave out its shortcomings afterwards. You can always put out small fires, after extinguishing the larger fire. But if you allow the larger fire to spread, putting out the smaller fires will not matter. Because it will be too late. Whenever you allow a criminal to rise to prominence, giving them dominion over others, and granting them the ability to access unlimited power, it is like that of watching an arsonist lighting a match to burn everything, and not wrestling the match away from them.

Your inaction, by definition, makes you an aid to the crime.

However, when firemen do come to extinguish the fire, you don't let them have your house burn just because you don't agree with the views of some of the firemen. You let them put the fire out and then argue their views on Tuesday.

I, like millions of others, cast our ballot to get someone to put out the fire, and then we'd argue with them later. But we never got the chance. So now, all must burn, because some thought the argument was more important than keeping the house from going up in flames.

Now all burns!

At my wit's end, I looked out over the city, raised my arms and roared into the wind. "Is anybody there? Does anybody care!" Inwardly, I wept as I collapsed on the step, in agony.

Did anyone see what I was seeing? I saw the end of our democracy and how we would now look in the eyes of the world. I saw how far we had come…and how far we fell backwards. I didn't want to go back.

Suddenly, I felt the world return to me as I heard a sound.

Standing up quickly, I turned around to see a man standing there, embarrassed.

Wearing traditional clothing for a man in his mid-thirties, who clearly was going for the scholarly look—jeans, corduroy jacket that came down to his knees, a golf cap, nice glasses, with a warm sweater, homemade scarf, and fingerless gloves, he started.

"Sorry!" he said with an accent. "Very sorry."

Immediately, I began to shift around, humiliated.

"I was—I was—I was," I stuttered, but then I stopped the stammer. Accepting defeat, I stood still and let my shoulders sink. "You heard that, didn't you?"

"Begging your pardon, but it was hard not to."

"In my defense," I said, raising my arms fully out to the side, "I really did think that I was alone."

"I get it. First, everyone talks to themselves like that. Second, this was evidently a clear case of you needing to get something off your chest."

"I don't think I'll ever fully stop getting this off my chest, not to sound vulgar."

"You don't. I get why you thought that you were alone. I just came out of the museum a little while ago. I was doing research for a project that I'm doing back home."

I detected his accent.

"Where are you from?"

"The U.K. I'm from Britain."

My eyes widened. Of course! How did I not know that from before.

"Britain," I repeated, warmly. Britain! The last mother of

the Pennsylvania commonwealth, before we declared our independence. Before we separated ourselves from Britain, for a freedom that led to the world being turned upside down. I said the only thing that I felt made sense. "Well, welcome back home."

"Thank you," he said, fully at ease, as he looked past me, and out at the city that was before us. "It's nice to be back again."

―――――

The Brit approached me slowly as he faced outward again, looking at the most impressive view of the city that there would ever be.

"It's a beautiful city," he began.

"Thank you for liking it. We really do appreciate that. We want to think that you find us worth being noticed."

"Well, I do. Do you want to hear a terrible secret?"

"What?"

"A part of me wishes that you never separated from us. I wished that we still had this place. Do you hate me for that?"

I shook my head.

"Not at all," I assured him. "I get it. To be honest, neither side was wrong. Britain and the American colonies were both right. We were just on two sides of an argument."

"I like that."

"After making every mistake, I've learned to look at history objectively. Mind you, let's be honest, this land belonged to the native tribes. This is their land and everyone else were immigrants, by choice or by force. And we're descended from those immigrants."

"True," he accepted. "I don't deny that."

"I think that's part of our large problem today. We don't want to accept that about ourselves, so we run from it."

"And we stopped running from how we created you lot," he continued, "that's why I am not angry that we lost you, even though it would be nice to still have you. When we lost you all, that was the beginning of us losing our colonies around the world. It must've sucked at the time, but now it's nice to no longer be a nation that is known as being colonizers."

"I know, right?" I agreed. "It's 2024. Why do people still think colonizing other nations is a good idea?"

"I don't know!" he declared. "We should be past all this."

"Exactly! And then there is that whole 'let's colonize neighboring countries, or countries we were friendly with before' attitude? What's up with that?"

"I know!"

"And I'm pretty damn sure that this mistake will continue into next year," I wondered.

"Usually, I'm not a pessimist, but I agree. Unless something incredible happens to stop it all but the whole world still seems to be on fire now. I think you might be right."

At last, the Brit looked at me.

"So, let's get back to what you shouted before. Let me guess? Bad day?"

"Bad previous month."

"Bad previous month? What? You got fired from your job, someone broke up with you, or parents died?"

"My job is fine. I don't have the courage to date. And I still have both my parents."

"Then what could…" his words trailed off as he began to deduce what I was feeling. He understood me. "Ah…"

"Yeah."

———

Resigned, I sat back down on the step.

"I'm sorry for how it all turned out," he offered.

"Thank you," I said, resting my elbows on my knees. "I knew that we might lose, but I was still not fully prepared."

"That makes sense." He sat down beside me, as we looked out, over Philadelphia. "Well, the good news is you believed in the better choice. No one is perfect, especially politicians. Politics gives people no choice but to make vicious decisions sometimes, and what's scary is when there is no right choice to be made. But with this...no. The choice was simple. And now, millions of Americans have now endangered your democracy, and your lives."

"It's harder than that," I said, "with this month, I was hoping that it would wipe away a mistake that I made eight years ago."

"Eight years ago," he said, trying to do the math, "eight years ago was 2016."

"Yes," I whispered, to the point where I was surprised if he could hear me.

Now it came down to the moment.

One of the largest mistakes of my life was now crying out inside of me, wishing to be revealed.

I had done so good a job of hiding it and leaving it behind me.

But it never left me as I felt the weight of many yesterdays press in upon me.

Why now?

When looking at this man, who came from the nation that we fought to be free of—why did I feel as if I had to tell the truth? As if my secret must come now or I would burst.

Any explanation I had—I did not know why, and so the reason must be consigned to oblivion.

But now, I knew. I just had to tell him.

"Eight years ago," I uttered, "that's when it began for me. That was the year that I made the wrong choice."

"I think I get it," he said, "eight years ago, you voted for the wrong person."

I nodded, looking away from him.

"Yes. And that choice cost me so much. When I did that, I became part of a problem that never left. It led to so many mistakes, and the problems never died. It got worse and worse. Eight years ago, the choice was evil."

Unable to control myself, my body began to shake.

"I told myself if I did not go back, it would all be okay. But I helped make that problem. By choosing it, it has choked everything that we are. I helped create this mistake. I helped cause it. I was evil that day, and I don't know where to go. I don't know where to go!"

As my body began to shake more violently, it was halted by the feeling of something on my skin.

Looking down, I saw fingers wrapped around mine.

The Brit held my hand.

———

When feeling his skin on mine, I looked into his eyes. There was no anger, or confusion, or perplexity. There was something that I did not expect: sympathy.

Sympathy, compassion, equality, and kindness!

When will humanity understand that those habits are the most masculine things in the world?

To preach the opposite to men is destructive, perverts their nature, and encourages them to be tyrannical. Thus, they become robbed of their true selves and spend the last minutes of their lives trying to get it back. How painful it is that it easily happens too late.

They were taught to fear, to seek strength through division, and to go through life believing in the us vs. them maxim. Thus, they become victims of a cycle that turns them into wheels. They spin but never escape the rotation. They are made into devices, but not human.

My hand was being held by a human. By a man who knew. I needed kindness. My body stopped shuddering and relaxed. Closing my fingers around his, I let it remain there, happy that he did not release his either. Once more, we looked out ahead of us, at all the roads that lay ahead.

All those roads felt like it was one large labyrinth that I would get lost in.

"Forgive," he uttered.

I turned to him. "What?" I asked.

"Did you ever forgive yourself?" he uttered, "for what you did years ago?"

"No," I managed to answer, "I did not. And I never can."

"You can't?"

"No, I can't forgive myself. And I don't want to."

"So," he said, "you'll forever be fighting yourself. And this spot seems like the perfect spot for that to end."

Releasing my hand, he stood up, removed his scarf from around his neck and began to wrap it around his hands.

"Stand up," he ordered me.

"What are you doing?"

"I don't know. It depends on if you cooperate. Come on, stand up."

Removing my bag from off my back, I stood up.

The Brit raised up his arms, like boxing trainers do when they are coaching their students on how to jab.

"Start punching. Not too hard, but even if not, I won't feel a thing. Go on."

"How will that—"

"It will help. Believe me, I've been there myself. Now, throw a punch."

It would make sense that I should have been hesitant to give in...but I was a tour guide. Many of us learn, through experience, not to reject people whose instinct is to help you.

Raising my arms, I breathed out as I threw the first punch.

At first, it was a gentle jab.

Then the second, I threw it harder.

The third time, my heart was rising to the occasion as I fell into a fight that I didn't know that I had.

"Again," the Brit said, "to the willfully ignorant."

I punched harder.

"To the bigoted ones."

I punched harder.

"To those who attacked your democracy!"

Angered at remembering the violent mob of many people who marched and attacked our nation's capital in an act of domestic terrorism, on January 6th, 2021, I punched harder.

"To those who try to re-write history with their agendas!" the Brit said, more spirited.

I punched again, feeling the hatred rise in me. He continued giving instructions.

"To those who had no right to call themselves people in the courts of justice. And are corrupt."

I knew that my face was screwed up from violent rage as I punched his hand.

"To those who should have executed the law and then did nothing to protect you all from what has happened."

Seeing the face of every judge, court, attorney, and politician who stood back and did nothing to execute justice, I punched harder.

"To forgetting that you were supposed to be a government of laws, NOT a government of men!"

Remembering that quote, I punched harder as my cheeks burned.

"To fascism rising under the pretense of patriotism!"

I punched again.

"To suppression of freedom of speech!"

I punched twice.

"To people who want to be dictators!"

I punched twice again.

"To those who sold your government and democracy to the highest bidder and used you all!"

I punched three times.

"To those who normalized insanity and cruelty!"

I punched again.

"To running campaigns on hatred, gaining power by dividing people!"

My eyes were on fire from fuming as I punched again.

"Who breeds you all to turn against each other, for their own benefit!"

I punched twice again.

"Who replaces truth with constant lies! For destroying reality!"

I punched three times.

"Who forget that you are the *UNITED* States, who should respect each other, and be there to support each other, through calm or crisis, and not expect anything in return. It doesn't matter what you believe—you all should help each other."

I punched harder.

"For those who ignore and disrespect your Constitution!"

Another punch came.

"For those on the left who did *not* vote or wasted their vote on third parties who were just there to take votes away from the better candidate. They caused this too!"

I threw another punch.

"For those who used foreign influence to override your basic rights to choose who you want to lead you!"

I punched four times.

"Now, for all the mistakes you made when you were once a part of it!"

Now I was punching freely and wildly.

All the self-hatred had come to the surface and was boiling forth. And it felt like every particle of me was on fire. The honest savage had taken over as I confronted every evil in myself and took it on.

I saw the monster
That I was before.
It was staring me in the face.
Laughing at me.

What a fool it was.
To laugh!
Expecting me to go back.
I was not going back.
Ever!

The creature rushed towards me, expecting me to give in and let it encompass me once more.

But I punched harder.

Harder, and harder.

Then, with one last blow, I knocked it far away, in the air and out of my existence.

It was gone.

"Stop!" the Brit cried. "It's done."

———

At first, I could not stop throwing my fists in the air.

The battle was over, but I still felt the warrior in me not ceasing yet.

Eventually, the Brit lowered his hands, grabbed my face and placed his forehead against mine. While I was grunting, like the wounded animal who was lashing out at anything and everything, he remained steady.

"It's okay. The fight is done. You won. Now come back. Wake up. Wake up!"

Feeling our foreheads pressed together, and his eyes so close, he was able to push his rationality and sanity back in me.

The fighter that had taken hold of me was taking so long to stop, but slowly, my hands fell to my sides, as the Brit closed his arms around me and held me as I fell against his chest, resting my head on his neck, hugging him.

"Rest now," he said, "It's gone. The worst parts of yourself are dead."

"It is," I wept, "I felt it go. It's gone."

"Yes, it's over. It's over."

I let him hold me like a child who, for the first time, had to be told by her parents that life is not fair.

"No one came to save us!" I cried when I thought of all the people, in our legal system, our Supreme Court, who could have stepped in and prevented what was happening. "No one came to save us!"

"I know. And around the world, we had to watch your laws die around you."

"Nobody was there!" I cried. "Our government, under that criminal, was empty. And people chose this! They voted for this or did not vote to prevent it! After all that has happened, this was what we chose? Violence against police officers, and they don't even care! Did anybody care? Did anyone see, what many of us saw?"

"That's why your fight with yourself is gone," he declared, "This November, you voted in the right way. You got out. You decided, of your own choosing, to see where you had gone wrong, and change course. Many people never chose to get out. You *got out.*"

"I did."

"Yes, you fought yourself, and now the fight is done. So, you can fight in another direction."

"What do you mean?" I asked.

"Terrible moments in history happen because of bad men, and the indifference of good men. If you keep fighting yourself, nothing will ever change, and you won't make any difference at all. Accept your failures and get back in the ring. Evil characters rely upon moral people doing nothing."

Letting me go, he moved back so that he could look directly at me.

"I am British. I love everything about *us—monarch, parliament and all...* and I'm saying this: I am proud of what you all became. Until now. Because the American Experiment has a right to exist. But if you don't fight, through constant peaceful protests, then the American

Experiment will die. You will forget everything that *you fought us* to create for *yourselves*. Don't forget who you are. And if you do not fight back, then you all die, by suicide."

He held my hands tightly in his.

"Every nation has been where you are now, and we are still here. But I'm not in the mood to see this have a lasting effect." He looked deeply into my eyes. "Don't die. Live! And if you don't fight, you'll feel as if you let us down. Because you *did* let us down before. Don't let us down now."

"We don't know how to fight anymore," I said. "We forgot what to do."

"Look to your history. Change always happened because of people who didn't know what to do at first. They knew they made mistakes, but they also knew that their community would not benefit from them walking the halls hating themselves. They kept you going forward, by understanding that your nation was more important than their lives and their pain."

Over his shoulder, he saw the Kite and Key bus coming.

Turning to me, he released my hand.

"I have to get back."

At first, I could not release his hand. I just wanted him to stay with me.

"I have to go," he urged.

As hard as it was, I released his hand, as he slung his bag over his shoulder. On it, I saw a symbol with a white and green background with a red dragon in the middle.

"I know that symbol!" I recalled.

"It's in honor of my mum," he said, "she was Welsh."

He gave me one last empathetic look.

"One day, we'll make you proud of us again," I assured him.

"If you fight, then yes, you will. We're an ocean away.

From across the water, make a loud noise, so that we can hear you. And we will hear you."

"When we do fight it, will you come back?"

He rubbed his cheek. "Yes. I daresay that we will."

He took a few steps down, then he turned to me and yelled.

"If it helps, I have been you!" he cried.

"How?"

"I supported our Prime Minister in 2019 and the one after that! And, at first, I thought Brexit was a good idea."

I felt the joy rise in me as I felt a kindred spirit. From the USA to Britain, him and I supported the wrong movement, once upon a time. I had read articles about that current time in Britain's political spectrum, all the hell it caused in Parliament, and how there were political problems up and down, and from front to back. Just like what we had been going through.

"Really?" I yelled.

"Yes," he roared. "Originally, I supported those sots!"

"Then we are both the same!"

"I know!"

Laughing immensely, I raised my arms out.

Laughing as well, he waved goodbye to me as he dashed down the steps and got onto the Kite Key bus.

Mistakes and misery really do love company.

Sitting down on the steps of the museum, I recalled a quote that I had forgotten about after mid-November. It was a post written online on a forum. It said:

It's okay, America. Right now, all over the world, there are dark men who are emerging with dark money, to take over society and ruin it. You are not alone.

--Alice, from Romania

She was right. We were not alone.
But we must not die.
No, we must not.

———

Despite the cold, I did not want to leave the museum just yet.

Now there was the first step. The wind was changing. And so, I had time to reflect. The monster in me is gone. With that great release, being willing to forgive, and then get rid of my demons, the scenery was changing before my very eyes.

The roads lay ahead, not for us to get lost, but for us to connect to every other aspect of ourselves. The sun was setting on us, but it was temporary. It would rise on us again. The architecture symbolized the history that kept us grounded.

Philadelphia! The blue dot that was in a sea of Red that was Pennsylvania. A state that was founded by an immigrant who was thrown out of college and thrown in prison for speaking up against vicious authoritarianism, and created a colony founded on freedom of religion, freedom of speech, fair trails and a government for the people. Those were the droplets that were supposed to make up Pennsylvania.

And now we are a raft in the middle of a red ocean. Refusing to drown, we must live, to realize who we were. We were a city where our Declaration was born. Where our Constitution was made.

We were the East. We crawled. So that the Middle could walk. The Middle walked, so that the West could run.

One day, we would remember that we were the place of the Revolution, after many attempts of making peace first. Thus, we became a place of laws. Laws that must be kept. But law cannot speak for itself. Humans must be there to enforce them.

Now I understood. I had to go back to the beginning.

Standing up, I looked ahead, seeing the skyway properly for the first time.

If you come to Philadelphia, do many things! Meet us— the people. Eat at our restaurants—the food. Take in our sites—relive who we were. But come here. Come to the steps of the Art Museum, and you will see everything.

All will be explained. You will not see merely us. You will see yourself and where you came from.

To connect—not to divide. That is what the steps deliver to you. Eventually, the Kite Key bus came once more. Rushing down the steps, I got on the bus and sat down as it rode off.

As the bus drove down the parkway, the museum grew smaller in the distance.

But it was there.

It was still there.

Chapter 20
The Beginning

The will!

That is what I thought as the bus rode along. The will to act. That is what we all have, but mostly, we don't know where to proceed.

The Brit was correct. By not taking action, the American Experiment would die, and we would die along with it.

'Look to your history,' he said. Yes, I recall now, that's what he said.

On the bus ride back into the heart of Old City, I passed the Franklin Institute, named after the most famous American in our history, who did live up to his name, and was worthy of his fame. He was the self-made genius, the self-aware imperfect man, who rose from poverty to prosperity, who was hell bent on being an individual, who still had a moral code, who tried to solve the crisis before he was pushed to the wayside, and became the reluctant patriot.

The reluctant patriot—a title that is both fitting and proper for those who always know to think first, then join the fight when the fight must happen.

Words must always be spent first before strife is.

Discussion must reign before war.

Be a loyalist, until revolution must happen.

And even before that, there must be talks and joint councils on both sides, on equal footing. Yet if one side is abiding by the rules, and the other side is not, then the talks will do nothing. Actions must be taken in its stead. But the taking a stand must be worth it—the fight must be about the loss of rights of the many—not just because of the wounded pride of one.

Ben Franklin knew.

His wife knew.

His daughter knew.

Eventually, the bus passed the Liberty Bell Center and Independence Hall, it rode down to the Museum of the American Revolution, that premiered George Washington's tent that he stayed in during our War for Independence.

Eventually we reached the bus's final stop, since it was his last shift. We were at 2nd and Market Street, near where the city first started.

The last stop was very convenient for me, as it stopped right where I caught the L train.

With a new sense of purpose, I felt refreshed as I stood up from my seat, feeling a light way about me. Thanking the driver, I stepped off the bus and watched as it closed its doors behind me.

The light turned green, and the bus turned, with its pink and familiar design disappearing around the corner. At last, I appeared to have now reached the end of my time as a tourist. As I waited for the light to change so that I could cross the street, to go down to the train stop, a sudden thought had struck through me, slicing into my current course. I froze in place, considering that my journey was unfinished.

History was what the Brit had talked about.

History.

Shifting my course, I did not finish crossing the street. 2nd and Market have a small island that separates the street from the road that will lead to the Benjamin Franklin bridge.

Along that small island, there was a walkway which had a series of brick arches that you passed under. They served as a framework for you entering the very front of the city: Penn's Landing.

Penn's Landing was the river front that ran along the Delaware River, or as the Lenni Lenape called it for thousands of years, the River of Human Beings.

When walking under the brick archways, I felt the weight of time being unwound, of the need to go back.

All the way to the beginning.

At last, I reached the edge of the walk and looked up to find the statue that was often overlooked and not often visited:

TAMANEND

When William Penn sailed to his 'colony' in 1682, having practically been pushed out of England by the king, he understood that this was not the king's land to give him.

As such, he set out to pay the Lenape people, and made a peace treaty with their chief, Tamanend. Extending his hand as well, both men, peacefully made an alliance with the other, where the newly found colony would co-exist with the people who had always been there.

The statue had Chief Tamanend standing atop a great turtle, and with an eagle on his shoulder.

Before my eyes, the image of both men, one of fair skin, the other bronze, taking hands with each other, attempting to find a moment of order and compassion in a world where morality counted for nothing and the world was spinning out of control.

Instantly, I felt a flood of memories wash over me, as I fell even further back into my past.

Here I was, at the beginning again, to when I was a little girl, driving in a Philadelphia neighborhood, with my mother...

———

"Mom," I said, with my American girl doll in my lap, "where are we going?"

"To a carpet store," my mother responded, driving onto a main street. "I know the owner and I'm thinking about buying a carpet for our living room."

"But Binxy might pee on it," I said, putting a coat on the doll. Binxy was our dog.

"Don't let those things in life stop you from getting what you want."

"Okay," I said, not understanding.

Eventually we arrived at the carpet store, I unclipped my seat belt, left the doll on the seat, got out of the car and followed her.

Together, we entered the store, and we overheard someone speaking in Chinese.

"Hello!" my mom called.

We heard a phone hang up, and a man entered from an office behind the register.

"Hello, Quay," he said, greeting my mother warmly, with a thick Chinese accent. My mother was named Quay.

"Hey Chow," my mom greeted him, as he came around the corner.

"You came to look at the new collection?"

"Definitely. And don't worry, this time, I definitely come to buy. My paycheck came in this week."

"That's what I like to hear." The man looked down at me.

"Hi," I said, waving nervously.

"Chow, this is my daughter," my mom said, "her name is Briseis."

"I'm named from a Greek woman," I explained, trying to sound adult-like.

"Nice to meet you, Briseis," Chow said.

"Nice to meet you too," I said, again trying to be clear and look professional.

"Briseis is six years old," my mom explained.

When hearing my age, Chow's eyes brightened.

"Oh, my son is six too."

"He is?" I asked, eagerly. "Where is he?"

"Xiang!" he called, "come! A child is here to play with you."

A boy literally ran down the steps. He had black straight hair that stuck out at all sides. When seeing me, he raced forward.

Happy to see a kid my age, I ran up to him and he took my hand even before saying hi.

"Come!" he cried.

"Okay," I said, nodding enthusiastically, as he pulled me along and into the other room.

When we entered it, my eyes enlarged as I took everything in.

"Whoa!" I spoke.

It was a large room, and the space was full of beautiful

carpets, that stretched as far as I could see. They were on the floor and against the walls, hanging up and also draped in unique ways.

"It's...it's...pretty," was all that I could say.

"Yes," he urged, pulling at my arm. Despite not knowing why, I liked him tugging at me a lot. I think it's because I was awkward, and he was not. His confidence that I have seen other kids have, but not me, was precisely what I needed. They had no fear, but in the right kind of way. They were not afraid of rushing up to us other kids and telling us to join them. All I needed was for children to invite me to things. I never knew how to ask them to let me in.

As such, when kids came up to me, so boldly, I saw them as the best thing that could happen.

"Now take off your shoes."

I did so, without even stopping to ask why. Then I realized it.

"Are we going to jump?" I questioned.

Smiling, he nodded. "Yes. We jump!"

"Cool!"

At last, we took off our shoes, and I stood next to him as we prepared to jump.

"Now, jump!" Xiang cried.

Laughing, together we began jumping across the room of carpets.

Skipping over the beautiful collection, it felt as if we were no longer on earth, but soaring over the clouds, that had decided to solidify just enough for two children to skip over it.

After we leapt on each cloud of reds, blues, yellows, greens, pinks, purples, oranges and blacks, intricately woven, Xiang tugged at my arm.

"I want to show you something," Xiang said.

"Alright," I agreed, following him.

"My dad made it for me."

He led me behind the carpets that had been placed on the walls.

Behind them was a strange and small pathway that we had to crawl up. The wall was on our right as I followed Xiang, on my knees.

"Where are you taking me?" I asked.

"It is a surprise."

Accepting that answer, I felt that we were moving upwards, when at last we came to an opening.

"See," Xiang said, as I looked out over his shoulder.

"A slide!" I cried.

"Yes."

Chow had made his son a slide out of the carpets.

"Here we go!" Xiang slid down the slide, and I followed him.

Once I reached the bottom, I jumped up immediately.

"Let's do that again!" I cried, taking his arm as he jumped up.

"I know, I know!"

Tugging at his shirt as he led me back behind the carpets, he let me hold onto him as we went through it all again.

Repeatedly, we slid down the carpet slide.

Eventually, on our last time, we accidentally slid down at the same time.

This led to us falling over each other, around each other, as we rolled down to the bottom of the carpet that rested at the end of the room.

Laughing, like I had never laughed before, I ended up with my head resting on Xiang's stomach, facing the ceiling as we lay there, resting.

"What school do you go to?" I asked.

"I do not start yet," Xiang explained. It was the summer-time. "But my dad is getting me to go to some school in the city."

"I wish you would go to my school," I urged him, "we would all be nice to you. I know that everyone would like you."

Rolling my head, I looked at his face.

He looked down at me.

"And I would be your friend," I assured him.

"I know," he replied.

When staring into his eyes, looking at his beautiful black hair, I think I knew, even as a child, what beauty was.

The world was in his face.

Xiang was beauty.

Instinctively, I raised my arm, moving it across the carpet that we laid on to get my hand closer to his.

Understanding what I meant, he moved his hand closer, and our brown and yellow fingers became intertwined.

With our fingers touching, I felt something new.

I felt peace...

———

Peace!

Standing there, before the statue of Tamanend, who had a moment of peace between him and our founder, William Penn, I understood.

Like revelations often do, I was overpowered as a wave of realities overcame me, moving across my mind at top speed.

Cheong-Jin Chang.
> But first, there was Xiang.
> I recalled Xiang
> holding my hand.
> I remember Cheong-Jin
> clasping my hand in his.

And I began to see everything.

In my mind's eye, was the rush of images that only the brain could make out. When I saw Cheong-Jin take to the stage, beginning as he always does: faceless.

His eyes, mouth, nose, and lips—formless. I was no longer seeing him from the side, but from the front as his image enlarged. All I saw was him—and the world that he brought to himself.

His face changed.

In his mask, I saw our entire American Revolution.

His mask changed again.

Across in the expression, I saw Wu Zetian, the first and only female Chinese Emperor, from the Wu Zhou Dynasty.

Hi mask changed again.

Along the red of the mask, I saw the Haitian Revolution in South America, the successful anti-slavery and anti-colonization rebellion.

Again.

I saw the Union Conflict of 1856-1905, which was between Norway and Sweden.

Again.

Along his split mask, I saw the many liberation movements and massacres in Africa, from the Church massacre, to the one in Zimbabwe.

His face changed again.

I saw the Battle of Dien Bien in Vietnam, where they were fighting for freedom.

The mask changed to black, of anger.

I saw the 1989 Tiananmen Square protests and massacre, where student protestors were killed in China. And how that gets overlooked due to oppressive censorship.

The mask turned green.

I saw World War 1

World War 2

The bombing of Pearl Harbor.

The Japanese internment camps.

The concentration camps all along Germany, Poland, and other areas.

I saw the Holocaust.

Then I saw the New Zealand Bastion Point protests.

The mask changed again.

I saw Francisco de Miranda who led the Wars of Independence in Spanish America

And again

I saw the End of the Samurai class in Feudal Japan during the Meiji Restoration

Again.

I saw France's Reign of Terror

Another mask appeared.

I saw the millions of slave ships that were sent to the Americas, from colonizing nations, filled with enslaved Africans, and sometimes, Irish. And the horror that is stamped across history.

And America's Civil War which was the darkest hour of our union splitting apart.

The mask changed again.

I saw when AIDS began to spread, and the government did nothing, at first, considering it as a punishment on the homosexual community. And the protests to get the government to listen.

Suddenly, I felt Xiang's hand holding mine.

The turmoil stopped.

I remembered Cheong-Jin's hand on mine.

The tragedies came to a grinding halt. They were not forgotten, as they should not have been. No, they simply gave way to the conclusion. That, at some point, all bad times end.

Cheong-Jin changed his mask again.

I saw Sojourner Truth give her 'Ain't I a Woman' Speech. Again.

I saw Woodstock and the Harlem Summer Festival.

Another mask appeared...

After the World Wars came to an end, I saw Germany and Japan rise again.

I saw the Japanese ending torturing American prisoners of war, and the ending concentration camps emptied, both in the USA and around the world.

Another mask took its place.

I saw Scottish born American John Muir found our national parks.

Another one.

When Ireland gained its independence.

Again.

When the Tsavo maneaters in Kenya were killed. Those were lions who were attacking Kenyan workers.

Again.

When during the Holocaust, Paul Gruninger was illegally bringing Jews into Switzerland, saving them from the concentration camps where death was waiting for them. It led to him being fired, and his life being ruined. Only in death was he declared a Swiss hero.

Again.

When the Eiffel Tower was built.

Again.

When the Statue of Liberty was given to the USA, by France. And there she stands, for FREEDOMS that ought to belong to all.

Again.

I saw Deborah Sampson, the woman who dressed up like a man and fought in America's revolution. Then I saw Caray Williams, the woman who dressed up like a man and fought in the black regiment of America's Civil War.

I also saw Harriet Tubman as she was serving as a General, in our Civil War, scouting the area for the Union Troops.

Again.

I saw the creation of Australia.

Again.

I saw the constant fights of women and blacks to ensure that all had the right to vote and to safeguard all rights. From William Still, the leader of the underground railroad, to Ruby Bridges—to Lucretia Mott, Marilla Marks Ricker, and Two Kettles Together, the American Indian woman who fought in America's revolution.

Another mask.

I saw the Moracco Flag, which was the first nation that had acknowledged the USA as being independent. Then I saw Ghana, where my ancestors were from.

Another mask.

I saw the end of the American revolution, and how we began a new nation.

Another mask.

Of when George Washington, after peacefully stepping

down as president, *peacefully* handing over the presidency to his successor, John Adams.

That was who we are!

We peacefully hand over power to the next person!

That is what made us American.

A transition of Peace.

The peace that our Founder, William Penn, offered when he took hands with Tamanend.

That is who we are supposed to be.

Anything less, is *not* American.

Anything less, is the actions of someone who betrays the fabric of who we are.

Finally, the last mask was removed.

I saw it!

Not just saw it, but I remembered it.

His face.

I saw Cheong-Jin's face.

And so, I now can never forget it.

I almost cried from happiness.

I had started at the beginning.

It gave me clarity as I saw the path ahead and now can see where it had come undone. Now I knew what to do.

From our nation's birth to now.

From Xiang to Cheong-Jin.

History! The many voices who cried out from the books that their actions were written on, cry out now.

They knew their mistakes, their failures, their successes and their achievements. And they all had one thing, and one mission statement to give:

You must go forward.

I am *not* going back.

Our ancestors did not give us history books for us to relive their lives.

They gave it to us for us to escape it.

Because if we go back, then we fail them.

For if we do go back, then we never see them clearly. They never wanted us to go back. They died, hoping there would be something better for us than the hell they had to live through.

As such, we were never acceptable to them, until we have proven to be acceptable unto ourselves.

Chapter 21

Home

With one last look at the Tamanend Statue, I gave him a nod.

"Wish me luck," I said to him, "that's all I will ever ask of you."

Turning around, I walked back the way that I came, went to the L Train stop, and waited for it to arrive. Once it did, I rode it to 13th Street, got off for the free interchange, walked down the steps and waited for the trolley. Very soon, it came, I got on and after two stops, every seat was filled with people.

As I looked around, at my fellow Philadelphians, of those who were born here, came here, or is just passing by, I know you. I mark you. We were here.

We come from a city that was a part of a revolution that began with one shot that was heard around the world. We are the place that the Declaration of Independence was born, with a phrase that related to all, not just Americans. We endured a revolution against a superior force and came out of it, not in chaos, like revolutions usually result in, but with a government.

We are a nation with a bell that, when it was silent, was louder than before.

We survived a destructive civil war and came out alive, in the end.

We have a constitution that many refuse to let die—for we know that may all our acts be to preserve and maintain our constitution or be nothing worth!

We were a nation born on slavery, misogyny, bigotry, and bloodshed. And we have spent every decade trying to realize the liberties that we were not raised on. Others still try to take us back but will ultimately be defeated. You see, time and history are more powerful than any human. They continue as we fade.

Humans die. But ideals are immortal.

A few seats down from me, I saw a group of five children as they were talking animatedly with each other. They were at the beginning of their life, while we adults were in the middle. We were not giving them a world of heroes now. But they deserved us to give them one. Now I know what I must do. Even if it leads to me losing everything. Even if it leads to my destruction.

I am a Philadelphian...cowardice is not who we were meant to be. But until that day, I shall lean back on the trolley, wondering about all the work that I have ahead of me, as I am surrounded by everyone who all have the same wishes as I do:

Life.

Liberty.

And the pursuit of happiness.

All those things being acquired, we look for more. Prosperity. Love. Thrills. To be beautiful. To have everything that you have ever wanted. To have peace, riding along the back of righteousness. To not be hated. To suffer no injustice. To have romance that is the stuff of legend. And somewhere there is a Face Changer who is taking you away from your worries and giving you a moment of beauty.

But until then, we settle for the one thing we hopefully all have: a comfortable ride as we find our way back home.

The End

Acknowledgments

I wish to give a special thanks to the Philadelphia Sports team, the 76ers, which after I finished this book, I learned that they turned down building the new stadium in center city. Out of respect for how that would affect the historic community that was nearby, they will remain at the South Philadelphia Sports Complex.

Thank you for caring for our city.

That's a form of heroism, for respecting the community.

Now please, enjoy the Afterword behind this acknowledgement.

Cheers!

Afterword

"Education makes people easy to lead, but difficult to drive; easy to govern, but impossible to enslave."

— Peter Brougham

Hello Reader, thank you for reading this novel. Since I am not a popular writer, I am aware that this book will not be read for many years since it was published in the year 2025. I am all too aware of the risks I took in writing this book, considering the times that we are living in.

However, with my life, from what I have often researched in history, is that times were always risky for those who dared to speak up, in general.

Due to my lack of popularity in the present, to any readers in the future who pick this up, I appeal to you.

Studying history, in *certain* respects, gives you a *certain* perspective. It leads to you always knowing how events and actions are remembered.

Most people think in the moment and base their choices on what they believe will satisfy them at present. Or at least, what entertains them, at present. This is a human tendency of ours.

But when you spend so much time looking up historical facts, you end up living in the past, seeing the patterns in the present, and you wonder about "how history will remember this moment in the future?"

As such, I am all too aware that the years 2024 and 2025 might be much talked of generations later in American History classes, and it will not be remembered happily.

It will be a time that had been the result of much misinformation, disinformation, lies, re-visionist history, the sane-washing of insanity, the moral-washing of true horror, where courts and justice systems were filled with corrupt people, discrimination, bigotry, the attempt to suppress free speech that does not adhere to an authoritarian mentality, and the media became a propaganda machine for *one* narrative to a *two*-fold system.

Simply put, these two years taught us that, whoever controls the media, controls the narrative flow of what we learn, and whoever controls that narrative, can control people.

While I want to believe that, whenever you read this in a future time, that our political system remains and that our history has not been re-written by those who wish to spew out a false narrative, I have to entertain the possibility that our government might be fully changed when this book gets read.

This book was indeed, split in half, between a social world, without politics, and the other half was a journey that the heroine undertook, that morphed from an emotional one, to a political one. Both parts of the story work together, to display that both aspects can exist in one narrative.

This led to the heroine having different journeys yet having the same growth through each.

From an emotional standpoint, Briseis Cunningham was a hero who was running from the mistakes of her past.

If you make a mistake, own it.

Briseis, like you, makes mistakes. Of course you will, because you are human. Failure and flaws are inevitable. But, if you confronted the flaw, failures, and mistakes (mainly how you saw your actions hurt others, rather than just care about how it affected you), you can be redeemed.

Sometimes, when we like something, we can be blind when we discover that we were wrong to ever like something, or someone. So, we make excuses. This is also natural. But when that thing we liked proves to be terrible in every way, we still look for reasons to justify why we are loyal to it. In this book, once Briseis realizes that she was wrong supporting the wrong candidate, she immediately realized that she was wrong and chose to wake up. But she did it because she researched the subject, and saw how her choices hurt others, rather than waiting to be affected by herself, to finally do something about it. Her wake-up was immediate, and was done through selfless reasons, rather than selfish ones.

She showed that she had the ability to 'change her mind,' rather than to remain willfully blind.

And if people get mad at you, after you did something terrible, that led to people getting hurt—let people be mad at you. They are grieving and are heartbroken; you owe them time to feel what they feel.

———

Now here comes the second aspect to this story:

For those who deem to silence the social aspects of this work, it is only proving that this tale is needed more than ever.

Indeed, I would be amazed if this book survives, because in 2025, I live at a time where false reports are flagrant, fact-checking is being removed, and there are threats to eliminate journalists, or persecute anyone who does not obey a certain regime.

The warning of people's basic rights being trampled on, by a vicious few, is not new to my time. It is an ancient problem. The best way that it was confronted and phrased was by the 32nd President of the USA, Franklin Roosevelt:

'We must especially beware of that small group of selfish men who would clip the wings of the American Eagle in order to feather their own nests.'

— Franklin D. Roosevelt, Four Freedoms
Speech

In the United States of America, our government's leader, our first president was elected in 1789, and the current one for me, is January of 2025. Since I do not know what the future holds, I do hope that tradition continues, and the American Experiment prevails after my time.

But at the end of the year 2024, freedom of speech experienced a large threat, after the Presidential Election, where there was widespread support for the belief of suppressing any news network that did not adhere to propaganda that was being spewed out by those who recently gained power.

This suppression of freedom of speech is often done through threats of lawsuits, slander, and negative rhetoric that is used to become the source to attack one organization, by another.

That 'another' is often shielded by a corrupt political official or lawmaker who is bought and paid for.

This is the same rhetoric that is often used to enable one faction of a nation, fueled by their hatred towards a certain type of people, be it race, gender, background or belief, to commit bullying or violent action against another set of people, and call it justified.

What's even worse is when someone fights back against them, the first set of individuals, who spewed the violent rhetoric, (or committed the first terrorist attack) act offended and cry out 'victimhood'. That's what villains do: cry out 'I am the victim' against anyone who stands up to them. And for some reason, the side that started the problem gets the most attention and invokes the most empathy. This was another problem with what ruined the 2024 presidential election: misplaced victimhood.

———

Thus, I shall begin with a document that was created in my home city, Philadelphia, in the year 1787, after the birth of our nation: The US Constitution.

After the United States of America had succeeded in becoming independent, the aftermath was chaos, people who served and helped the war was in debt, and the country felt as if their future was unknown.

Truly, we were a new nation that feared it would not last.

So, it led to a rush to look on previous societies and nations that would help us move forward in the founding of our nation, rather than moving back. A chief inspiration was the democracy and republic ideals of the Ancient Greeks.

Thus, coming together, between that, the concepts of William Penn's ideals of governance, and other elements, they formed the United States Government.

The new country was floundering when a collection of individuals met in Philadelphia and drafted the constitution of the people of the United States. The preamble of the document reads as follows:

'We the People of the United States, in Order to form a more perfect Union, establish Justice, ensure domestic Tranquility, provide for the common defense, promote the general Welfare, and secure the Blessings of Liberty to ourselves and our Posterity, do ordain and establish this Constitution for the United States of America.'

Each listing in that opening is vital to the nation's survival, from the establishment of justice to promoting the general welfare of the people. The constitution then goes on to explain the setup of the government, its separate branches and how they function in sections, articles and then came the amendments.

The Amendments, which were a set of laws to protect the people and the government from oppressive forces, could be added to, over the years, to cover everyone who was still not included originally. Suffice it to say, our Constitution was a 'living' document.

The first Amendment states as followed:

Congress shall make no law respecting an establishment of religion or prohibiting the free exercise
thereof; or abridging the freedom of speech, or of the
press; or the right of the people peaceably to assem-
ble, and to petition the Government for a redress of
grievances.

This is the foundation of the USA Democratic Republic.
Freedom of speech, freedom of religion, of the press, and to
peacefully protest against the government when rights are
being taken away. This is confirmed and set in stone.

However, in the year 2024, we experienced a threat to
these truths, by the very same people who claim to wish to
uphold it. They did so, under the image of a 34-count
convicted felon.

Our constitution also stresses that concept of separation
of religion and the state. Thus, meaning that religion should
be free for anyone to practice whatever faith they wish, but
no religion has a place in the political spectrum.

This was a deliberate choice, made by the founders of
our nation, for obvious reasons. First, the founding fathers
of the USA were educated, and knew the history of societies
that mixed church and state: it always ended badly and with
many atrocities occurring, in the name of religious faith.

In 2024, part of what led to a great disaster was the rise
of religious fanatism. Particularly the rise of Christian
Nationalism, and how it began to find its way into our political spectrum.

As a person whose faith is Christianity, not only did I
see the dangers of this, but I have always believed that
church and state should never, EVER, mix. To start linking
religious fanatism, including Christianity, to our govern-

ment, is wholly Anti-American. Not only is this stressed in our constitution, but also it is consistent with our history.

First, Christianity, or any religion that was imported to the USA, was not the original faith. The original faith of North America were the religions set up by Native Americans/First Nations. Those are the original faiths. Thus, to say that Christianity ought to return into our political arena, because it was the foundation of our land, well, it was not.

I say this as a person whose faith is Christianity: all other religions, including mine, are immigrant faiths.

Practically every founder, without fail either *happily accepted* or *did not* want Christianity to be in the political arena.

If people during my time read this, and are of the Christian Nationalistic mentality, I can tell you that they will quickly try to have this book banned, in some form or another. Many of them might call me a liar.

And they might even brand me as a socialist, communist, Marxist, or any other word that they use, but clearly don't know the definition of.

Well, here is where I offer you that pesky thing called FACTS.

Here are quotes from four men who were among the founders of the USA.

The first is Thomas Paine, the Englishman who wrote 'Common Sense' and inspired American Independence:

'All national institutions of churches, whether Jewish, Christian, or Turkish, appear to me no other than human inventions set up to terrify and enslave mankind, and monopolize power and profit.'

— Thomas Paine

Here comes the quotes from our 2nd, 3rd, and 4th Presidents of the United States of America:

'The government of the United States is not in any sense founded on the Christian religion.'

— John Adams, 2nd President of the USA

'Christianity neither is, nor ever was, a part of the common law. Christianity is the most perverted system that ever shone on man.'

— Thomas Jefferson, 3rd President of the USA

'Religion and government will both exist in greater purity the less they are mixed together.'

— James Madison, 4th President of the USA

Yes, these are facts. But in 2025, there is a threat to suppress facts and re-write history, or where certain individuals rely upon others to be uneducated, in hopes that they can use that ignorance to fill those 'uneducated' with their own agenda.

Most of the founding fathers knew that their faith gave them a sense of morality, and stability, but they left it in the church. While others began to reject organized faith or heavily questioned Christianity.

The best, and last, way of it can be summed up by the 18th President of the USA, Ulysses S. Grant:

'Keep the church and state forever separate.'

— Ulysses S. Grant, Sept. 29, 1875

And with *ALL* religions, people abuse it, and many suffer under that abuse.

Do not think one religion is more suitable for politics than another. All religions must not influence politics.

Religion can often become a tool for how Fascist or Authoritarian regimes rise and have large influence; they gain power through division and use religion to justify their right to divide. This leads to all sorts of atrocities—atrocities the founding fathers were trying to avoid happening in their new nation. When religion enters politics, it creates division.

The division begins as follows:

One party gets one part of a nation to hate the other, despise the other, and view those 'others' as the problem, as the cancer to our 'great nation'. Their words weaponize the first party, they commit violence against the 'others' they are told to hate, and so, the regime gets other people to do their dirty work for them, and their hands remain clean.

They are still guilty but not held accountable in a court. Thus, the only way to defeat this regime is simple: do not support them. Do not vote for them.

This should be simple.

There is only one problem: we are humans.

And humans, sometimes, will support what is against their interest. Because they like the hateful rhetoric— because of their inner hatred of themselves, or another.

And most people who have bigotry within them are wholly unaware of it. Prejudice rests in both the conscious and unconscious states.

As such, some people know that the best way to sucker people into supporting them is to gain access to what they hate, who they hate, and play on that hatred. They get them stirred up into a frenzy, and you have a following, who will love you unconditionally... even if/when the regime betrays them, which always happens.

There is no better way to say this than what the USA Vice President Johnson said, after he had to take over the presidency when the previous president, John F. Kennedy, was assassinated:

"If you can convince the lowest white man he's better than the best colored man, he won't notice you're picking his pocket. Hell, give him somebody to look down on, and he'll empty his pockets for you."

— Lyndon B. Johnson, the 36th President of the USA

Yup, this statement could not be truer, and showed itself, in the year 2024. This was prevalent among a large portion of the white population. But it was not just limited to white people; this was a mistake that members in practically EVERY nationality made in that year. Millions of Americans were thinking only of themselves, and their own sense of superiority led to a big mistake being made. Too many people, both US-born, or immigrants even, thought this.

And here comes the next factor that affects everything: money.

A successful conman knows a fool when he sees them, and how to play on their hatred to get what he wants—and all the while, all they want is money, or power, or to be above the law. Then there is the other problem: falling for the conman's promise of giving you instant wealth.

Money is on everyone's mind, and what everyone wants, so people will sacrifice all their morality, all their compassion for their fellow man, for the pursuit of wealth.

And that's another way to lure you in. But when that happens, you end up making a choice that not only does not trickle down to you, but it also ends up hurting the community as a whole.

But many people don't think about community—about the big picture. They see the little picture and think 'if I choose what satisfies this little picture', it will satisfy everyone's little picture'.

Yet it never does. That mentality never works out.

But it's a pitfall that many stumble into. And so, they sold out our country, for 'gain'.

Again, back to history. Constant researching history, both modern and classical, will teach you one thing:

NEVER listen to anyone who says that they can make you rich while giving you *no* plans on how to make it so— and give you no concrete plans on how to make it happen. That is the *oldest* and most *successful* conman's scheme in the book. They know that money is the 'bottom line' for you. So, they play on that.

You can only trust people who have policies, who can *show* you how they can help you financially. Even if those policies take some time. Wealth does not happen overnight. It's not a form of magic. It's often acquired through time, effort, and through joint councils working together for the working class.

And if you are of the working class, when choosing someone to lead you, try to choose someone who was *from* the working class. Because they know what you are going through. They know economics and how money is handled.

If you elect *super* wealthy people, who have always been such and have never experienced financial problems, they don't know what you are going through and will continue to support those who are like them, because it's all they know.

They don't understand your issues. Wealthy people are phenomenal for anthropological purposes and charities. But wealthy people and politics must never coincide. Because it leads to politicians being bought. That was another problem in our government. On high levels, politicians were bought through organizations that were funding them. The politicians were owned by corporations.

As such, set aside your bigotry and choose who understands your struggle the best, through experience and empathy. And who has actual plans on how to proceed by understanding core facts.

With facts, no matter how boring those facts may be— you have to look at them.

And if you find yourself supporting someone, because they can guarantee that you will have money, you have to care about their principles, their respect for the political office, their compassion for others, their ability to realize their own imperfections, must have a sense of loyalty, and their acceptance of those who do not agree with them, especially when they have made a mistake. If they have no concrete plans on how to keep your society going forward, no sense of honesty, no respect for allies, no moral beliefs, no respect for your fellow citizens' basic rights, and is disrespectful to others at every turn, then you only took money, to sell out your country later. How can you expect to have a future when you lose your nation?

The conman knows this. They know to say precisely

what you want to hear and will say everything that you want there to be said. But their words weren't real. It's all a lie. Trust the person who says 'I will help you, and fight to make this right, but here is also the reality of what is occurring now and the time it might take...'

———

In the year 2024, there were many people who saw the problems, and tried to warn others. They were often ignored, or people said that they were overreacting.

This is the common reaction that occurs; before many mistakes happen, the warnings are real.

Germans warned other Germans about the evil that was coming, when Hitler was rising to power. People did not listen to them.

Russians warned other Russians about the fascism of Stalin. They were overlooked.

Many people warned others about plagues like AIDS, and Covid-19. They were told that it was not real and that they were overreacting.

All who warned the people were pushed to the wayside, called alarmists, and were ignored. Then the problem becomes colossal, and people get surprised that the warnings were real. But, at that point, it is too late. And you can't stop the storm from coming, because it's already there.

All that you can do, afterwards, is then create a resistance against the oppressive force that is coming.

These are all comments that can appeal to anyone, anywhere, and at any time.

However, since I do not know what is in store for my country, in the future, the United States of America, might be a history that gets forgotten. As such, people might not know what I refer to, or the history of our government, in this time period. Maybe I was getting ahead of myself.

After our successful revolution in 1783, the United States of America was fractured.

Many individuals came forward, created a government, and we would not have a king, but a president who served terms in office.

At the time, there was a two-party system:

Federalists and Democratic Republicans. Both political parties had slave-owners in their party.

The role of the Vice president was chosen and morphed over time.

The role of Vice President (VP) is mostly to be aware of everything going on politically, supporting the president, fulfilling ambassadorial duties, giving advice, breaking ties, etc. but actually having no power to make, dictate, or eliminate any policy. Whether they agree or disagree with the president or other government departments, the VP can't do much. The VP holds no real power, until they step into the role of president.

It was declared, eventually, that a president can serve only two terms. When doing so, they cannot run again. But they can run for one term and not be re-elected.

Either way, whenever a president's term comes to an end, they *peacefully* hand over the presidential position to the next person. This is a tradition that is special to many of us Americans. That is part of what makes us proud of who we are.

To ignore that tradition is terrible, and is detrimental to the continuance of our nation, and who we are as a Democratic Republic. We should peacefully hand over power, not violently try to take it.

———

This pertains to what led up to the year 2024.

In case a propaganda movement succeeds, and this horrible moment gets re-written, I will give the blunt answer and tell you the truth about what happened, without delicacy.

In 2020, our president lost re-election, for obvious reasons to anyone who tells the truth about his time in office. He was terrible.

Rather than respect our American tradition of handing the presidency over to the next incoming elected official, the loser did the most Anti-American and viciously violent thing ever: he refused to acknowledge the new president, lied about his losing, said the election was stolen from him, and kept repeating this lie.

He encouraged his followers to reject our new president, Joseph Biden, stirred them up with falsities, got them into a frenzy, assembled them into a mob, and encouraged them to march onto the nation's Capital and fight.

They did that, attacking our nation's Capital, violently assaulted police officers, killing one and brutally injuring many, rushing into the building, to violently attack and kill other politicians, in the name of 'their president'.

Meanwhile, the president who sent them there, did not join them, remained inside, watching the riot from a tv, doing nothing to stop the insurrection while his mob got their hands dirty for him. And he could get away with it.

The insurrection failed, naturally, but the country was devastated. The insurrectionists went to prison, there were trials, and so it should have led to the president being held accountable for his actions. Right?

No.

The courts/attorney general were filled with corrupt or cowardly people, who sided with the president who betrayed our democracy, our corrupt Supreme Court gave him immunity and stalled on the major trials, and the fake-republican (I refuse to call them real republicans) party failed to impeach the insurrectionist president. And the new administration's attorney general also was terrible. It reached a point where no punishment was enacted.

This led to the previous president now being above the law. That was the beginning of everything falling apart, and our democracy being perverted and beginning to fail.

Then, to gain power, billionaires rallied behind the 'insurrectionist-felon president' and led smear campaigns against the current president. The previous president began the long road of re-writing history of saying the January 6th insurrection was not that, but a day of peaceful protests and the insurrectionists were victims, as well as build his campaign on obviously false information.

You would think that, after that, the country would never rally behind such a person...

Right?

And here is the part that you might have learned in your history books—many Americans were entirely wrong about our fellow citizens.

Soon, January 6th's tragedy was re-written by selected groups, the lies were believed and accepted by many, and people began to seize power through 'divide and conquer'.

Among that came the spread of fearmongering, particularly aimed at the immigrant population, subtle but effective acts of racism, misogyny, and played on people's fear and animosities.

And through all that malignance and despicable behavior, the people chose it. Even immigrants chose it. We regressed as a culture, rather than progressing.

That is what you, perhaps, learned about in your history books. Thus, marking another dark time in our political arena. Footage and many recordings will show you the most absurd and vile behavior in the history of a presidential campaign/early presidency, and I am aware that you will look upon us and wonder 'Why? What did you do that for? Why did you make that choice?'

The answer is simple: hate. Deception. And ignorance.

The root of many of these problems also goes back to lack of education. A large portion of the USA citizens did not do any large research before they made their choice (or did not make a choice at all). Voting is important for the flow of any democratic society, especially for a nation where many people died so all could have the right to vote. But, in 2024, casting a ballot, for the best option of president was vital!

Mind you, some did not cast a ballot because they were pressured and literally harassed, forcing them to not vote. It was a time of election interference from foreign nations who had a specific desire for one candidate to win (the felon-president). Voting boxes were blown up, there were bomb threats at voting centers, etc.

But there were those who did not cast a ballot for other reasons, and that refusal to partake in a situation that was very important to the continuance of our national stability and international relations, led to a mistake made through inaction, and the price of their 'hold out', cost too high. And the cost was a complete threat to our democracy and the freedoms and civility that each state ought to have for the other.

The best way to describe it was put by our 34th president, Eisenhower:

"Some politician, some years ago said that bad officials are elected by good voters who do not vote."

— *Eisenhower, September 10, 1955*

This is a prime example of what occurred in November 2024.

However, whatever reasons that able voters did not vote, be the reason out of indifference, loss of faith in the system, or because they were taking a stand, out of support for a cause, I foresee that it will prove to be the worst course of action. Because it led to a criminal and insurrectionist, who causes chaos everywhere, getting elected. It also showed that those non-voters, chose their supposed 'principles' over the actual lives of American citizens, our neighboring countries, our allies and the world. They put their 'ideals' before preserving the safety of our people.

If this has lasting effects on our democracy, and it leads to dire consequences to the time period that the reader finds themselves in, all I can say is that I regret the choices, or lack thereof, of a significant portion of the USA citizenry.

As for Eisenhower's remark, history is littered by those who predict the future, based on mistakes made in the past.

So far back to the foundations of our republic, where the American Experiment began...

———

A Tale of Two Presidents

In 1789, the first president of the United States was inaugurated.

It was General George Washington, who was Commander-in-chief to the continental army that, through national audacity and international assistance, succeeded at gaining the country's independence.

Like his military appointment to lead the continental army, Washington did not accept the role of US president because he asked to do it, but because it was asked of him. He chose to become president, refusing to be a king, out of civic duty.

He did not want the USA to EVER become monarchal in nature and did NOT want us to be ruled by an ambitious dictator.

A false leader wants to rule and dictate. A true leader chooses not to lead people, but to serve them.

Our first president's administration was fraught with a country being wholly in debt from war, a plague, tensions between political parties, geographical bigotry, politicians who refused to get along, drama, and half the country being pro-slavery, the other half was anti-slavery, one half supported the new American government, another section preferred the government of other nations.

The USA was a new country that he had to do everything to hold together, against a global stage that wanted connections to the young country, through political interference.

Needless to say, Washington felt like he was in a living hell for a great portion of his two terms as president.

He was also trying to satisfy part of the nation that wanted to move forward, being progressive, and the other part of the nation that wanted things to remain the same or wanted to move backwards. This led to him making choices that were both very progressive and insanely regressive. He had achievements and failures. He took part in passing good laws and bad ones. He had many virtues and many flaws.

After serving two terms, he gleefully stepped down.

Among his last acts in the presidential position, was to give a Farewell Address to the American People.

This goes back to the central point of the quote from the top of the page: education.

Education, and knowledge of how things work, from an everyday perspective to how your nation's political system works, are vital aspects.

That's why I say that, when Civics was taken out of each school's basic education, it was one of the worst things to ever happen. Kids left their educational institutions having no idea how our government functions. So, I recommend to you, to fight to require that every student, when leaving secondary education, knows how our government works.

But along with that, is our first President's Farewell Address. Every American student should know, by the age 18, the key things in the first Farewell Address we ever had since the founding of our nation.

In the Address, Washington offers advice, love for his people, and also warnings to the American people of what you should be worried about.

Some of Washington's Address are dated, because he wrote it in 1796, but I will give you quotes that are timeless.

Please read on and see what should be learned by every citizen, be you American or of another nation.

Washington's Farewell Address to the people of the United States

'These will be offered to you with the more freedom as you can only see in them the disinterested warnings of a parting friend, who can possibly have no personal motive to bias his counsel...

The unity of government which constitutes you one people is also now dear to you. It is justly so; for it is a main pillar in the edifice of your real independence, the support of your tranquility at home, your peace abroad, of your safety, of your prosperity, of that very liberty which you so highly prize.

But as it is easy to foresee that, from different causes and from different quarters, much pains will be taken, many artifices employed, to weaken in your minds the conviction of this truth; as this is the point in your political fortress against which the batteries of internal and external enemies will be most constantly and actively (though often covertly and insidiously) directed, it is of infinite moment that you should properly estimate the immense value of your national Union to your collective and individual happiness...'

Because George Washington was stepping down, he could now tell the American people every truth he felt, without anyone persuading him.

As a result, he had no reason to lie.

In this passage, he shows his love for the citizens that he presided over (which is what every leader should possess).

But he immediately tells the American people to always care about the unity of your government, which was a testament to the unity that they achieved when gaining their national independence. Our unity, at all times, must always be a definite. It must always be a truth.

Then he goes on to warn you that there will be people

who will use arts and hateful rhetoric to weaken your belief in that, to make you either not trust the unity between your fellow citizens, or government, by people who want to tear it apart out of their own self-interests. Be it foreign or domestic.

That is what happened between the years 2020 and 2024, maybe even going back earlier. In fact, you could successfully argue that this has been building up in our culture over the last 40 years. Many of us did not know that it was growing to be such a destructive force.

Although, these last four (or eight) years brought about a successful political movement that was driven by convincing the American people to not trust the government, calling them the 'deep state', disastrously effective uncommitted movements, and a vengeful and vicious political figure rising again by convincing the American people that 'I will be the only one to protect you from them'.

It also was fueled by attacking other political officials, cities and states, demeaning and criticizing them, to ruin the unity that we have as Americans. No matter what part of America that we are from.

George Washington also mentions our union through collective and individual happiness—

That is the idea of always considering your happiness, but also the happiness of the community, as a whole.

That was another problem in the year 2024.

On November 5th, 2024, was when we voted for the next US President.

A large portion of the country voted considering themselves AND considering the country as a collective whole/our democracy/considering our allies.

But a larger portion of the country voted, not considering how the rest of the community would be affected.

They were focusing on themselves, either because of money, or purity politics (single issue voters). Their perspective stemmed of 'The Little Picture' complex, which I discussed before. This concept was put best by civil rights activist, Martin Luther King Jr.:

"Every man must decide whether he will walk in the light of creative altruism or in the darkness of destructive selfishness."

— Martin Luther King, Jr.

You must always consider, when voting, about both the 'Little Picture and Large Picture'.

It's governing dynamics in its simplest form: vote for what is good for you—and the whole group. And the continuance of our nation. This practice should be adopted in every nation: vote to preserve everyone in your country but do it in YOUR COUNTRY. Don't vote to help a nation while, at the same time, killing the nation you live in. Both are what I call 'indirect terrorism'.

Feel for other nations, fight for them, but never at the expense of killing your nation, and its respectability.

Or how we would regard our neighboring countries, or how we would be viewed in the eyes of the rest of the world. If you are wondering how the other countries viewed us, from November 6, 2024, to onward, I will tell you.

All the propaganda in the universe was never going to deceive how the USA would look, from the world's perspective.

We became one of the biggest jokes ever. The world was laughing at how wrong we were. What was even worse was how many Americans had no idea that we were embarrassments in the global scene. And that brings us to...

Here comes another passage from Washington's address to the American People, about alienation, and villains who play on that.

> '...discountenancing whatever may suggest even a suspicion that it can in any event be abandoned and indignantly frowning upon the first dawning of every attempt to alienate any portion of our country from the rest, or to enfeeble the sacred ties which now link together the various parts.
>
> For this you have every inducement of sympathy and interest. Citizens by birth or choice, of a common country, that country has a right to concentrate your affections. The name of American, which belongs to you, in your national capacity, must always exalt the just pride of patriotism more than any appellation derived from local discriminations.
>
> With slight shades of difference, you have the same religion, manners, habits, and political principles. You have in a common cause fought and triumphed together.'

And again, comes a warning that is timeless, and should always be followed, no matter what country you are from.

Wherever you are, NEVER trust or follow anyone who tries to viciously gain power in this manner. Power over the country, or you individually, by alienating you from the community, or your fellow countrymen, and to weaken the ties you have with them, because of their machinations and bigotry toward differences. Be it from regional differences, or social ones.

He did not want the US citizens to fall victim to anyone who played on discrimination to alienate individual states from each other, when they should all feel connected.

George Washington was right.

In late 2024 and 2025, the successful presidential campaign was one that was achieved on Washington's fears. Many Americans cast their ballot for someone who enfeebled the sacred ties we have to each other, through various acts of discriminations. Immigrants were another target.

Washington understood the importance of immigrant regulation, but he was NOT anti-immigrant.

This was self-evident, because of his time as commander during the American Revolution. As I said before, many foreigners either helped, or fought for the American side.

Because Washington knew this, while he despised foreign interference politically, he did not despise the individual immigrant.

Again, regulations were made during his terms, with there being border customs, but it was not about using immigrants as scapegoats to our problems.

He says this when he says citizens by birth 'or choice'. He understood moderation and regulating the immigrant crisis, but also understood that immigrants, especially ones who came to contribute to our society, had a right to be in the USA.

During his time, the idea of forced mass deportations of immigrants would have been met with a flat out 'What the hell?'.

In this particular circumstance, we are talking about the United States of America, which I know is what you are still curious about. So again, we shall focus on that.

If you have researched the year 2024 and saw that there were immigrants who voted for the anti-immigrant presidential candidate... you are right.

I wish I could understand why those people thought that voting against their own interests was a good plan. In truth, I never understood it. Many believed that they were only going to touch the criminal immigrants, but most of us easily read between the lines and knew that there were not enough immigrant criminals to be deported. As such, we knew it was going to get ugly, immoral, and violent.

But going off of what *other* immigrants have told me about why other immigrants voted against themselves is for these reasons:

Language barrier. There are some immigrants who never grasped the whole English language, so it was easy for them to get tricked.

Self-hatred was a factor. Next was racism and sexism. A contributing factor why the other presidential candidate of the 2024 election lost, was because there is a portion of the country that, consciously, or subconsciously, would never vote for a woman, especially not a woman of color. Some in the Latinx community have been very outspoken about the fact that many, in the different Latinx cultures, there is much misogyny and anti-blackness. This gender and racial discrimination was not limited to the immigrant, but across the nation. As a common person, I've had many conversations with quite a few immigrants of the Latinx, Asian, and Arab communities who have no problem with secretly (and publicly) telling me about the fact that a sizeable portion of their own culture do not believe in voting for women. And definitely not black women. And so, many will always find a reason not to vote for them.

And some immigrants will do everything in their power

to be accepted by the status quo: white. Here's where it's funny. A white person that I know said it best to me one day, regarding non-white people: 'those people are not white. They will never be white. They need to stop trying to be something that they are not and learn to vote for their own interests, and everyone else's. Many rich ambitious white people rarely care about the rights of your brown butt. They don't care about you; they just want your vote. For God sakes, where is your pride?'.

In 2024, both white people and people of color tried to warn Latinos and other cultures. Their own people tried to warn them. But... it is what it is.

They try to re-write it because it's not pleasant to talk about. The best way to explain the good and bad of our culture is said best by Ken Burns:

> "As some question how to teach American history to our children—and even question the history itself—I urge us to confront the hard truth, and to trust our children with it... the dark parts of American history are important to teach, and that ignoring them is dangerous. A great nation is one that can acknowledge its failures."

Right now, in January of 2025, many of us are trying to confront this failure of ours. While we do so, we are moving forward, attempting to correct the wrong, but not losing faith in our institutions. But many are not trying and are normalizing this terrible time in our history. Talks of racial and gender inequality get pushed to the side, and no one, in the mainstream media, or within the political parties, want to address the obvious elephant in the room: Bigotry helped win the 2024 election.

This brings us to another quote from George Washington about ignoring geographical discriminations:

'Here every portion of our country finds the most commanding motives for carefully guarding and preserving the Union of the whole. The North, in an unrestrained intercourse with the South, protected by the equal laws of a common government, finds in the productions of the latter great additional resources of maritime and commercial enterprise and precious materials of manufacturing industry. The South in the same intercourse, benefitting by the agency of the North, sees its agriculture grow and its commerce expand...

The East, in a like intercourse with the West, already finds, and in the progressive improvement of interior communications by land and water will more and more find a valuable vent for the commodities which it brings from abroad, or manufactures at home. The West derives from the East supplies requisite to its growth and comfort—and what is perhaps of still greater consequence, it must of necessity owe the secure enjoyment of indispensable outlets for its own productions to the weight, influence, and the future maritime strength of the Atlantic side of the Union, directed by an indissoluble community of interest as one nation.'

THIS is vital to every person, no matter what country you are from, to feel.

And none more-so than for the US Citizen, no matter what time period you are in.

Washington was a Southerner, who was asked to fight a

conflict that began in the North, and ran his presidency from the North, and had a Secretary of Treasury, Alexander Hamilton, who was a foreigner.

What's even scarier is that not only was Washington right, but when his words were *not* listened to, it led to America's Civil War. That led to a great split in our nation that had lasting effects on our *union*, the death or injury of over 860,000 men who fought, and destruction of the union so many people died to create in the 1700s.

And this rang true again in 2024. With the new president elect being chosen, brought about another breach in our union that had been built over the last eight years.

One of the scariest elements in the upcoming presidential administration is an echo of the horrible 2017 administration: not helping states that did not vote for you.

This is something that I cannot stress enough: whatever country you are from, and what time period you are in, my future American, DO NOT EVER allow yourself to be led, socially and politically, by someone who only will help those who voted for them/always agrees with them.

A true leader supports the whole community.

The best way of defining this principle is what the 49th Vice President, Kamala Harris said, when she had to step in and run for President.

'Our unity is our strength, and our diversity is our power. We reject the myth of "us" vs. "them." We are in this together.'

— Kamala Harris, 2024

With the USA, if we still exist when you read this, put aside your discrimination with other states that people tell you to hate. Love and support each other, no matter the difference.

Right now, in 2025, we have a leader who does not believe in supporting states that did not support him. This is not only Un-American, but also of course, is inhuman.

On top of that, it presents an Orwellian universe, where, if 'you don't adhere to everything that we say and do, we will not help you'.

This is how Fascism rises. Through blind conformity.

The dangers of this were cemented in the words of our 35th president, John F. Kennedy:

"Conformity is the jailer of freedom and the enemy of growth."

— JFK

Looking ahead, I do so hope that all 50 US states will band together, maintaining binding ties, independent of the federal government. It does not and should not matter what the political leanings of each state are. As Washington said, we are connected by a common cause; to stand with each other. If our government forgets its purpose, it is up to us 'We, the people' to remember this.

First, all fifty states are united from the Native tribes that occupied the land. That is our common history. It may be hard but can easily be nourishing to learn of the original people that your state belonged to.

And look at it this way:

The thirteen original colonies on the Betsy Ross Flag were at a time when the USA was born and had to come together, unite, or we'd all fall down.

It was an experiment that was well worth a try, but it

was not easy. The thirteen colonies had to struggle to maintain this alliance, and survive as a new, fragile, and weak nation, at first. Our history, as being of the 13 first US states, is the entire nation's history. Feel our connection to you, as we hope you feel it to us. And let us always keep that connection, which builds community between states, rather than just inside of one. Each state has its own identity, as it ought to. But it must be a bridge to all the rest, at the same time.

When our nation has suffered natural disasters, other countries came to our aid, making themselves superior to the mentality of the new dominating political party in the government. As such, if any country who helped us, in my present time, does read this, I will tell you what a sizeable portion of the USA feels:

Gratitude and much appreciation.

And a request to maintain your identity and do not give into any bullies that threatens your independence, your self-confidence, and do not ever bend the knee. By standing for your own and standing up to anyone that threatens your personal liberty, be it our country or another, stand up to us and them.

In the 21st century, colonization is absurd and atrocious. Build alliances but never bow to a tyrant.

And if the USA ever turns into that, you do not hurt us by resisting. You are right to.

It goes back to a quote said by Civil Rights Activist Malcolm X about black and white relations:

'Whites can help us, but they can't join us. There can't be black-white unity until there's first some black unity. We cannot think of uniting with others until we have first learned to unite amongst ourselves. We cannot think of being acceptable to others until we have first proven acceptable to ourselves.'

This quote is true for black Americans. But when you take that quote and extend it to the whole USA, or any country that you are in, place your country's name in the quote and it will become even more apparent. Being from America, I will apply it to our present course in 2025:

'Other nations can help us, but they can't join us. There can't be American-foreign unity, until there is first some American unity. We cannot think of uniting with others until we have first learned to unite amongst ourselves.

We cannot think of being acceptable to others, until we have first proven to be acceptable to ourselves.'

Right now, Americans have not proven to unite amongst ourselves, and not to be acceptable to ourselves, because we are listening to people who want to reap the benefits from our division. By dividing us, they've conquered us, and so, simply by all states uniting with each other, by building communities and extending warm respect and mutual assistance, we can win and get ourselves back.

And for other nations, thank you for helping us when we need help, but do not join with us until we have proven worthy.

But no matter what—resist colonization. Keep your identity, because you will always want your original self back anyway.

That brings us to another quote from George Washington regarding such nefarious people who prey upon the public in such a way. He says:

'One of the expedients of party to acquire influence within particular districts is to misrepresent the opinions and aims of other districts. You cannot shield yourselves too much against the jealousies and heart burnings which spring from these misrepresentations. They tend to render alien to each other those who ought to be bound together by fraternal affection.'

This was the largest political plague that ran through the United States of America from December 2020 all the way to 2024.

Misrepresentation and misinformation!

When the president lost re-election in 2020, as you recall, he refused to accept the defeat, declared the election was fraudulent, spread that lie, leading to the misrepresentation that caused jealousies and heart burnings across the nation, stirring up the American people, as if their rights were taken just because one man lost.

This rhetoric was repeated until many people, out of willful ignorance, chose to believe it. This led to a cult being formed and took the country by storm. This led to the 46th president of the United States, Biden, not being accepted by a large portion of the country.

What made this worse was the media. Eager for a story, they chose sensationalism and popularity over substance, news, and morality. A particular news station emerged over the others, was clearly fueled by a propaganda campaign of falsities and lies, making the infamous insurrection-inciting president the main focus, and popular again.

This is the very definition of misrepresentation that springs from jealousy and fills the void for those who are looking for a reason to be angry and who could blame for their worries.

This led to people forgetting the horrible January 6th insurrection, despite that it was only a couple years ago. Even though it should have mattered to everyone.

And like I said before, sole consideration for money kills morality very fast.

Since Washington warned the American people of this in 1796, he clearly was familiar with this tactic.

The negative side effects were not isolated to 2020, and the four years that followed.

Rather, history was simply repeating itself from the Civil War that occurred in the 1860s, when Abraham Lincoln became our 16th president.

People often say that American's Civil War was not over the issue of slavery. That is a lie. Slavery was a main part of the war, as well as other contributing factors.

Among those were the fact that the Southern States' politicians were angry that they felt they didn't have enough say when Republican, Abraham Lincoln, was chosen as president. They were angry at the Northern states, for their rights being 'trampled upon'. Simply put, Lincoln was not who they would have chosen—who, by the way, was from Kentucky.

Objections flew up immediately after his election, and several weeks into his presidency, Civil War broke out, and the Southern Confederate states chose another man, Jefferson Davis, to be their president.

Not only did the 16th president have to endure a Civil War weeks into his administration, he had to endure the country rejecting him as their leader, because of hurt feelings. Then another president was put forward, as the final rejection. We were a nation of two presidents.

And the cost of this rejection of Lincoln's inauguration proved to be too high.

There was NOTHING good about that time except that the Confederacy's defeat led to the abolition of slavery. But it led to the USA lying in ruins, and much destruction of the confederate states. It also led to a terrible time, where there was a horribly failed reconstruction, (a failure on the Republican party's part, as well as not holding the traitors accountable for their crimes against the union) and the South took their frustration out on the black community, attacking and murdering many of them. The republican party may have freed the slaves but only caused another great problem by not protecting the enslaved blacks, after the war. Evil crimes continued. There may have been good intentions, but no follow through.

In the future, if you compare the 1861 administration, to the 2021 administration, you will see a shocking similarity in that both presidents had to endure being rejected by their own countrymen, through jealousies and misrepresentation, it caused violence, and a break in tradition of accepting the new president.

Here's the large difference:

Our 16th president was a Republican.

Our 46th president was a Democrat.

This showed how, over time, both parties flipped their ideologies.

The Democratic party of 2021 was very similar to the Republican party of 1861.

In its early years, the Republican Party was considered quite liberal, while the Democrats were known for staunch conservatism. This is the exact opposite of how each party would be described today, in January 2025.

The Democrats have more liberal views nowadays, going for more progressive principles, attempting to go.

This change of the democrats turning into the liberal

ones, that the republicans originally were, did not happen overnight, however. It took time. But it actually makes sense, because here's a shocking truth. For a long time, some bad faith characters in the republican party were constantly painting the democrats as the villains, who must be eradicated, but here's where it gets ironic: republicans are actually another form of democrats.

When the republican party was formed in the 1850s, it was formed primarily by three groups: former Whigs, Free Soilers, and anti-slavery Democrats.

The foundations of the republican party were democrats! Yes! That is the secret they don't want to tell you. Republicans are the descendants of democrats.

And there were some republicans, in the South, who still did own slaves before the republican party fully formed.

But there is no way around it. If the republicans from 1861 were to meet the republicans in 2024, they would not only not recognize them as republicans, but would speak out against them, based on their own viewpoints.

So, for those in my time who cannot see the parallel, I will show it to you:

Both 1861 and 2021 presidential administration had to endure being rejected and dismissed as presidents. Both had to deal with violence triggered at them, and anyone who certified them as president. They would spend the next years suffering either a physical war, or an information media war, where both suffered a lot.

With the first, it resulted in his assassination and him dying.

With the second, it led to him being so much slandered, that he was forced to step down and drop out of re-election.

Both men suffered under misrepresentation and misinformation spreading about them constantly.

But here is the thing.

Abraham Lincoln would go on to become one of the most iconic presidents. Mind you, he was not perfect, but he is still a legend. The president who tried to usurp him, Jefferson Davis, has fallen into obscurity. In fact, many people don't even know about who he is. Yeah, his legacy will never age well.

So, for those living in 2025, you will find that we are reliving history, and many do not even see that they were backing the wrong horse—until it's too late. Until more people suffer because of the voter's choice.

And this harkens back to an Abraham Lincoln quote that I used in the book:

'As a nation of freemen, we must live through all time, or die by suicide.'

— Abraham Lincoln

I am giving you 'facts' about the explanation of this quote.

Lincoln warned that the United States could not be destroyed from abroad, but rather from within. He believed that mob violence would damage the rule of law and democracy. Lincoln feared that mobs would replace the executive ministers of justice and that this would lead to the rise of a tyrannical leader.

Reader, not only is there a similarity to what the 16th and 46th president went through with rejection, but Lincoln's worries were fully realized in both administrations.

When researching our history, from the violent January 6th, 2021, insurrection against the US Capital, and the rise of the insurrectionist felon president who encouraged that behavior, to my present time of January 25, 2025, it was the path that Lincoln predicted.

Mob rule became accepted, undermining executive ministers of justice, a tyrannical leader would be chosen, who said that he would be a 'dictator on day 1'.

Lincoln, a republican president, accurately predicted the rise of American's 47th president, and knew that it was not the path that the USA ought to tread.

That is something that many don't want the average American to know, in 2025. Because that would affect their control over the misinformation system they have erected. Even though it's history. They will slander this fact and call me every horrible name they can think of, for pointing it out.

In consideration of respect for our system and the law, Washington gave another warning and advice that needs to be always remembered by every American citizen, while also being exercised by them. Washington believed whole-heartedly in our US Constitution. He said:

'The basis of our political systems is the right of the people to make and to alter their constitutions of government. But the Constitution, which at any time exists, until changed by an explicit and authentic act of the whole people, is sacredly obligatory upon all.

The very idea of the power and the right of the people to establish government presupposes the duty of every individual to obey the established government.

All obstructions to the execution of the laws, all combinations and associations under whatever plausible character, with the real design to direct, control, counteract, or awe the regular deliberation and action of the constituted authorities, are destructive of this fundamental principle and of fatal tendency. They serve to organize faction, to give it an artificial and extraordinary force—to put in the place of the delegated will of the nation the will of a party; often a small but artful and enterprising minority of the community...

, to make the public administration the mirror of the ill concerted and incongruous projects of faction, rather than the organ of consistent and wholesome plans digested by common councils and modified by mutual interests...of the above description may now and then answer popular ends, they are likely, in the course of time and things, to become potent engines by which cunning, ambitious, and unprincipled men will be enabled to subvert the power of the people and to usurp for themselves the reins of government, destroying afterwards the very engines which have lifted them to unjust dominion.'

Reader, this is precisely what happened with the 45th president, from the year 2020-2025, and perhaps onward.

Literally, Washington described every horrible thing that led to the rise of a disgusting authoritarian machine that overtook our government. Here in January 2025, those 'unprincipled men', who had been lifted to unjust dominion, through their cunningness and ambition, because of forces that allowed them to subvert the power of the people.

Earlier, Washington mentioned the Constitution, because he was a strong supporter of it.

He knew, over time, that the Constitution would have to be changed, because it had to be. It was always supposed to be. In his time, there was still much injustice.

He was raised on injustice, being born in a slave colony,

that illegalized someone freeing their own slaves, on a plantation to a slave-holding family.

Washington was never given any exposure to the abolition movement at a young age. As a slave owner, even he knew that he passed some laws that were terrible.

So, Washington knew that the Constitution must be changed over time, but ONLY by the requests and actions of the whole people, for their freedoms, but *not* because of the whims of a few who want to change it for their own greed or selfish desires.

That being said, as he pointed out, whatever the US Constitution is, at the time, everyone has to honor and obey. It is not a set of guidelines that you can dismiss at your whim. It is *obligatory*.

For example, here is section 3 of the 14th Amendment of the Constitution. It states that:

No person shall be a Senator or Representative in Congress, or elector of President and Vice President, or hold any office, civil or military, under the United States, or under any state, who, having previously taken an oath, as a member of Congress, or as an officer of the United States, or as a member of any state legislature, or as an executive or judicial officer of any state, to support the Constitution of the United States, shall have engaged in insurrection or rebellion against the same, or given aid or comfort to the enemies thereof. But Congress may by a vote of two-thirds of each House, remove such disability.

Basically, if you are engaged in insurrection or rebellion against the government, you are not allowed to run for any political office.

And if it gets overruled, it has to be passed by two-thirds of Congress, but that would most likely be if the insurrectionist was fighting against an unjust law, or the rights of the people were being suppressed.

None of that applied to the January 6th insurrection in 2021. By the law, no one should be allowed to hold office who incited an insurrection, and it should have been fought for and debated.

But it was not debated to the extent of the law! Yet, it should have been. It was not because of the failure of the American experiment.

It was not that our judicial system was incorrectly designed. It failed because of corrupt or incompetent people who either did not care to execute the law or were bought by other people. Those sorts should not be in any court.

It was *not* the system that let us down.

It was the greed and evil of people.

The Constitution works, but the people who were supposed to enforce it did not.

A law cannot enact itself. Others must fight to maintain it. In 2021-2024, there were many in power who did nothing. So, the law became a joke.

And now to add to how Washington further cemented his warning of what led to 2024, he says:

'I have already intimated to you the danger of parties in the state, with particular reference to the founding of them on geographical discriminations. Let me now take a more comprehensive view and warn you in the most solemn manner against the baneful effects of the spirit of party, generally...

The alternate domination of one faction over another, sharpened by the spirit of revenge natural to party dissension, which in different ages and countries has perpetrated the most horrid enormities, is itself a frightful despotism. But this leads at length to a more formal and permanent despotism. The disorders and miseries which result gradually incline the minds of men to seek security and repose in the absolute power of an individual; and sooner or later the chief of some prevailing faction, more able or more fortunate than his competitors, turns this disposition to the purposes of his own elevation on the ruins of public liberty...

It serves always to distract the public councils and enfeeble the public administration. It agitates the community with ill-founded jealousies and false alarms, kindles the animosity of one part against another, foments occasionally riot and insurrection.'

Reader, that's literally what happened on January 6th, 2021, during the insurrection on our Capital, and onwards for the next four years.

To this day, I cannot fathom how our first president, in 1796, predicted everything that happened over two hundred years later. But it happened all the same.

The most iconic quote of 'those who ignore history are doomed to repeat it' is often overstated, because it happens so much.

We have reached a turning point in our history. People, because of their personal problems, their *disorders and miseries* led to them thinking that the grass was greener on the other side. Or rather that, the grass was greener four years ago, when it was not the case.

Playing upon those miseries, a dictator-type, who was fueled by the spirit of revenge from his loss, was able to regain his footing by assuring the people that he was their savior. False promises were made, and anything was said that the people wanted to hear, no matter how empty those statements were.

The oldest con in the book happened.

To add to all that, the 46th president's administration (Biden) did not have the understanding on how to combat all the lies that were being spread about them. His competitor was *'more able or more fortunate'* than him.

The democrats lost the election, and soon into the republicans' rise, the new administration, and current president, *'turns this disposition to the purposes of his own elevation on the ruins of public liberty'.*

All has unfolded, the way that we were warned about centuries ago.

Don't forget history, or you will be forever destroying yourself.

To add to the list of other things that George Washington predicted that have come to pass is this next exert:

> *'It is important, likewise, that the habits of thinking in a free country should inspire caution in those entrusted with its administration, to confine themselves within their respective constitutional spheres, avoiding in the exercise of the powers of one department to encroach upon another. The spirit of encroachment tends to consolidate the powers of all the departments in one and thus to create, whatever the form of government, a real despotism. A just estimate of that love of power and proneness to abuse it which predominates in the human heart is sufficient to satisfy us of the truth of this position. The necessity of reciprocal checks in the exercise of political power, by*

dividing and distributing it into different depositories and constituting each the guardian of the public weal against invasions by the others, has been evinced by experiments ancient and modern, some of them in our country and under our own eyes. To preserve them must be as necessary as to institute them.'

Simply put, the American government is meant to be the size it is to provide a proper system of checks and balances.

As such, no part of the government, from the presidency to any particular branch, has the right to step in and take power over another branch or agency. Washington knew that, if anyone tries to start encroaching their influence on a part of the government that they are *not* a part of, it will lead to despotism, which is the exercise of absolute power, especially in a cruel and oppressive way.

He knew that, if someone were to act like a dictator, be it on 'day 1' or any day, and start trying to do this, it would ruin our government and how it functions.

That's why Washington says that the continued separation of each governmental division, must remain separate and no one can intrude on them. That branch of the government must always control itself.

This was supported by what our 34th president, Eisenhower, who said:

'We've become, now, an oligarchy instead of a democracy. I think that's been the worst damage to the basic moral and ethical standards to the American political system that I've ever seen in my life.'

— Eisenhower, 1961

Both describe, in exact detail, what is happening in early 2025. The country is now under the influence of an oligarchy masquerading as a democracy.

People are being chosen to head certain offices in the government, not because they are qualified or right for the job. In fact, they are the worst people chosen for the job.

But they are being chosen because they answer to 'an individual' who will do their bidding at all times.

This is how you gain absolute power.

It also leads to the individual, or the oligarchy who now has consolidated that power, to dispose of anyone who disagrees with them, and hire those who always agree with them, no matter how unqualified they are.

Washington knew this, because he had seen it before, through personal experience and through the history he learned in his education.

And that again brings us to the most vital thing about the human experience: education. We must always educate ourselves, even when we are no longer in school. As we continue to learn, our knowledge makes us less easy to fool.

Tyrants love the uneducated.

Washington advised to avoid the accumulation of debt, and in times of peace, try to pay off the expenses that come from unavoidable wars. When the USA was born, we couldn't even pay back many soldiers who fought in the war, or the benefactors who helped pay for our war. Being unable to pay back debts weighed on Washington heavily.

Debt is something that haunts every society. When it comes to choosing a leader, take a good look at that leader's history on how they deal with finances. Especially if they ran businesses, how they have compensated workers, do they pay those who have worked for them, etc. Also, in the USA, consider the financial situation that the president had when they enter the presidency. If they enter their administration with the nation in debt, then it will take a while for that president to help our economy rise.

But if a president were to enter their administration with the nation not in debt, but is in debt when they leave, then they cannot be trusted with the nation's finances, and plan to spend the money on selfish pursuits.

Washington later on goes to say:

> 'Observe good faith and justice towards all nations; cultivate peace and harmony with all...'

In a world where war was happening left, right and center, Washington really just wanted peace and to build up the United States, and have it be respectful and respectable regarding the nations that were all clearly much older than the USA.

That's what our first instinct is to cultivate. When it comes to other nations, there should always be a constant effort to establish accordance and friendliness with them, be them your ally or a mere acquaintance. But if they choose to offend you/attack you, then it is perfectly right to respond with equal force.

All countries work best in that manner. Regarding leadership, to even mention a nation disrespectfully, for no reason at all, benefits no one, and makes things worse. *Words* of disrespect can turn into *actions* of disrespect, and right now, the government is in control of a leader who does not understand that.

To be respectful, and respectable, regarding other nations who come in peace, is not the actions of weakness.

Rather, it is logical, and I say to my countrymen, it is very American.

Love other nations *but* also love yours equally. Respect their culture, but respect yours, and don't throw yours away, out of love for another.

As Americans, when we fail to live up to our goals, dreams, and standards, do not run from who you are, but stay and continue to build who we ought to be. The grass is never greener on the other side.

For as Washington said:

> 'Against the insidious wiles of foreign influence (I conjure you to believe me, fellow citizens) the jealousy of a free people ought to be constantly awake, since history and experience prove that foreign influence is one of the most baneful foes of republican government.'

In the 21st century, this was proven true, and there was no greater evidence of this than the 2024 presidential election.

Other foreign nations not only were interfering in our election cycles, but in 2025, an oligarchy had found its way into our government, because the people in power had not only shown mutual respect for foreign governments that were averse to ours, contradicted our system, but also talked about how we should be like them. In 2025, our government had, through many subtle and overt means, been infiltrated by the negative kind of foreign influence.

What was even more amazing was the people who voted for the new 2025 presidential administration, were all for America!

While, at the same time, casting their ballot for someone

who preferred totalitarian governments over our own. If you are wondering, how can you wrap your brain around that idea, at the time, even *we* did not understand that mentality.

As Washington urged his nation, he heavily encouraged to have a great rule of conduct to other nations, and dealing with them commercially a lot, but have as little political connection as possible, to any of them.

That brought him to another topic, concerning the USA, that will always be a constant problem: alliances with other countries and nations.

In the 2024 presidential election, alliances with other nations were contributing factors for who voters wondered who they should and should not vote for. While I wish that this had not occurred, because it easily steered people into making the wrong choice, Washington expounds on the topic, to help give the reader clarity:

'It is our true policy to steer clear of permanent alliances with any portion of the foreign world—so far, I mean, as we are now at liberty to do it—for let me not be understood as capable of patronizing infidelity to existing engagements...

Taking care always to keep ourselves, by suitable establishments, on a respectably defensive posture, we may safely trust to temporary alliances for extraordinary emergencies.'

This here shows the difficulties and the complications of the American Experiment.

Washington knew that the best thing for the USA was to not make permanent alliances. He saw the danger of those, because you can easily get dragged into a conflict that is not only against what is best for the country, but the nation you are allies with, are not worth having the alliance with.

However, Washington also knew that alliances could be necessary, especially temporary ones. He knew that in extreme emergencies, you have to enter alliances.

He also knew that, if you have a treaty with a nation, you *have to* honor it.

This made sense because Washington had to deal with not honoring a treaty and suffered the backlash of that.

The French literally were the driving force that helped save the American revolution.

Then, in 1793, the same time that the Yellow Fever had hit the USA, the Reign of Terror happened in France. The French king, who made a treaty with the Americans and provided them with so much, was beheaded by the French Revolution. His queen was beheaded, and over 27,000 French people either were executed or died in prison.

It was pure savage massacre, ending with the death of Robespierre, the main revolutionary who led the bloody movement. Yes, take notes! If you plan to be tyrannical, what goes around comes around.

Then, a couple years later, France is at war with England, which was frequently, and they called the US to honor the treaty.

Washington, as president, did not honor the treaty. It was for both moral reasons and practical. Not only was the USA too poor and too weak to help France at all, but since the French beheaded the French king who helped the Americans, they were not going to honor this treaty. Because they were also appalled.

This led to what is timelessly known as the 'damned if you do, damned if you don't' scenario.

If George Washington helped France, he was helping a

nation who oversaw massacres and killed the king who saved his war. So, we would be terrible.

But if he did not help them, then the USA would be breaking the treaty, showing the world that we will break an alliance, and that we are terrible.

No matter what, Washington was going to lose, so he chose self-preservation for the nation.

He dropped a statement of neutrality and broke the treaty. This led to the French hating the US, and caused the Quasi War, which was an undeclared naval war between the USA and France.

This would go on to haunt Washington's time in office, where some were enraged with him over this, and he had to know that no matter what he did, he would be wrong.

As such, when it came to the USA's alliances with other cultures, Washington gave no concrete answer, because he knew that there was not one.

As such, all that he could advise was to try not to get into permanent alliances, but emergencies led to us having to make them, and if you do have an alliance with a nation, you have to honor it.

This complication, again, influenced voters' decisions in 2024.

The current administration had been stuck in a pre-existing alliance with a nation, who started off a war as victims of terrorism.

On October 7th, 2023, a group committed an act of terrorism to a foreign nation. They murdered 1200 people to its neighboring nation, wounded over 800 others, and took hostages. It was a horrible crime, and it sparked a war between those two nations. This conflict was between Israel and Palestinians.

Of course, there were other aspects that built up to this

crisis for many years, with evils committed on the opposing side.

The USA, naturally, honored our treaty with Israel, from a pre-existing alliance with them.

Then that nation's leader, Netanyahu, turned around, became genocidal, and it turned out that he was the worst war criminal. Truly, the man was pure evil.

That put the USA into a terrible position where, through the memorandum, had to keep supporting their ally.

While attempting to make a ceasefire between nations, the USA hoped the crisis would end, but the damage had been done. Genocide occurred and it was nothing short of terrible.

I always hate mass-murder. For obvious reasons. So, I was angry at the USA's inability to break away from the alliance when it turned sour. But my real anger was directed to two subjects:

1. Toward the terrorist group, HAMAS, that started the problem and hid behind their people which led to so many of their own people dying, who were innocent.
2. Toward Netanyahu, who retaliated by committing acts of genocide, out of revenge. And it turned out that he had been terrible even before that.

The USA ended up being pulled into a situation where they became guilty, by association. Due to an alliance gone horribly wrong, US citizens were angry about this, and it led to them voting against the current administration, out of resentment.

This was painfully erroneous, because the alliance was a

bipartisan one. It did not matter which political power was in office. Be it democrat or republican, they were always going to honor the treaty. The USA had no control over those nations' choices, and all that was in its power to do was to constantly attempt to negotiate a ceasefire. But that choice depended on the two nations that were at war with each other.

But many people did not think about that fact. They didn't keep focus on the two forces that were the source of the war going on, and the crimes continuing. They looked to the left and blamed the ally: the USA.

Remember what I said before, how attitudes can shift? Well, due to the successful echo chamber that circulated throughout American society, this became so, it led to mass division, and they blamed the current administration.

But it was not a democratic mistake.

It was an American government mistake. We had an alliance with a nation that was not in accordance with the Leahy Law. The Leahy Law is a U.S. law that prohibits the US government from providing aid to foreign security forces that have committed human rights violations. The law is named after Senator Patrick Leahy, who sponsored the legislation in the 1990s. Readers, this American mistake was not new in 2024.

The USA made this mistake before, where we followed through with an alliance, our allies turned around, started committing genocide, and we ended up being culprits by grim association. So, the Leahy Law applied to EVERY nation that we are allies with...except the nation who we helped in 2024, Israel.

That was a government error that should have been corrected many years ago... especially since those two nations, Israel and Palestine, have a history of being at violent odds with each other. This is a prime example of the USA not learning from their mistakes.

As such, I label that war as being a war of two villains and a failure.

The factions who fought on either side of the war were the villains. The first was a villain by committing the first action and later inaction, and the second was a villain by the way of eventual reaction (and for being the worst piece of crap I have ever seen).

The USA was the failure by not executing the Leahy law and getting the hell out of there, when genocide became an option. Our nation was wrong, and I do not fear saying it.

We failed, point blank. We aided genocide.

But all the blame got placed on the ally: the USA. Because it was easier for everyone to do that.

For people, it was focus on the ally, not the source. If you are reading this, in the future, you are wondering about how that was not going to work out well. You are right.

People jumped onto the bandwagon, a movement began telling people to either not vote, vote for a third party that would never win (and were not serious and ran just to split the vote), or vote for the convicted felon who displays a history of betraying anyone who crosses him.

And people jumped on that wagon hard. Many people voted for a criminal or did not vote at all. All, for the sake of...morals.

Not only was it short-sighted and incorrect, it may prove to be irrevocably detrimental to our country, countries we help, and those we are allies with. The well-being, stability and steadiness of the USA is like many countries: we affect more than just ourselves.

Hate genocide. Be enraged that we aided in genocide.

Protest it, as our constitution gives us that natural right.

But the solution should never be 'no solution', or 'a blatantly worse solution'.

And so, I advise this to everyone, no matter where you are from:

Research things for yourself. See all sides to a situation. Be both objective as well as patriotic.

Bravely face the failures of your country but never lose your desire to preserve it.

Never blindly listen to a movement that tells you to be uncommitted, and to not vote. Not voting, a right that so many men and women died for us to have today, is counter-productive, leads to no change happening, creates a stall in the progression of democracy, and is, by outcome, a form of national destruction.

Be knowledgeable of what is happening in the rest of the world. Be compassionate about their problems. But get all the facts. See both sides of a scenario. And look at the history of both sides, to find out what were the causes that led to an effect. Because you can easily be duped into destroying yourself, by giving into the ambitions of 'one'.

I wish I could phrase it better, but actually I'm going to add a quote from someone, who I never met, but said this on the computer in a comment forum, regarding those who voted, spitefully, in 2024:

'I have a problem with American "citizens" voting because of their issues with a foreign country knowing it would throw this one into disarray.'

This was spot on.

How can we help any nation, especially ones that our society took part in screwing up, at the expense of destroying our own, by voting out of spite? Or not voting, which is as bad as still voting in the wrong direction? We can't and must never do so. Because, if I predict the future correctly, here in January 2025, things are going to get way worse.

Another reason to not listen to others, of foreign nations, who urge you to vote for their own ends, but not yours, leads to three eventualities.

a. You will vote for the wrong person.
b. You will not vote at all, which is throwing away your voice.
c. If your choice, or lack thereof, leads to things falling apart, that influencer was willing to sacrifice *your* nation, for theirs. That's you giving everything for them. And them giving you hell, in return. You were a means to an end.

Only be there for foreigners and born citizens who care about other nations, but at the same time caring about the preservation of ourselves.

We can't help others when we are helpless.

We can't fix our mistakes, if we are constantly broken.

A foreigner, who desires the preservation of their native land, but also of the preservation of your own and respect of your culture, is the one you want as your friend.

When it comes to personal and national continuance, safety, and identity, it should never be:

You or me.

Us or them.

But it should always be:

You and me.

Us and them.

Because if you don't, and you don't vote, or vote as they say, you are taking the power from yourself and giving it to them. You showed that you can be manipulated. And so, they now know that they, through movements, can hold our government at ransom and get what they want, even if it hurts you. You gave away your independence.

It was not worth it.

So, in the future, if you ever find yourself in this situation, I hope this message helps.

Protest injustice and atrocities committed.

Protect the innocent to the best of your ability.

But stay patriotic.

Preserve the national institutions that keep your nation alive, respectable, and healthy. And call them out when they do not live up to the principles that we stand for. But do not destroy them. Use the system to correct the errors. If not, we will fall into chaos.

Don't let anyone force you out of that last piece of advice, trying to guilt you.

Thus, 2024 brought back the Washington reality: damned if you do, damned if you do not.

All I can do is look back with regret that the USA's alliance with a foreign war between two nations caused a great schism among the American people, which would hurt our future.

And that if that war had influenced my fellow US citizens to not cast a ballot in the year 2024, I am heartily sorry for it, because the preservation of our democracy was at stake, and it was vital that we should all have voted to preserve our nation and choose the candidate who respected our Constitution.

To stand against one atrocity, millions of Americans ended up creating many more.

Every day, I wish that the terror attack on October 7, 2023, never happened.

It was a crime and a tragedy that led to more tragedy,

and it solved nothing. It just led to the death of many innocent people, which I cannot forget.

If anyone reads this section during my time, this last
part will be heavily criticized. Many will denounce it, say it
is wrong, and they will declare that I should never have said
anything at all.

It's because they do not respect our institutions of these
sorts of freedoms, of my right to speak of it... and because I
said precisely what happened.

The world is full of people who will throw away everything written here, because it does not justify their
narrative.

When it comes to this history, do not solely take my
word for it, because I have no problem admitting that we
do not know all the details to every moment of the last
two years. Research it all yourself by objective historians
who refuse to be swayed by political preference. But if I
find out, years later, that the oval office tried to enact the
Leahy Law, and it got rejected, then I will accept that I was
too hard on the 46th president's administration and
apologize.

But I will not shy from the part we played. It happened.
We are your history. Don't fear the truth. Learn from us.

Again, with the war going on between Israel and Palestinians, from Gaza, the best thing to occur was for the USA
to withdraw from this conflict, but it did not occur.

This led to the Muslim community becoming enraged
over our involvement in the genocide, sparked by revenge,
and it led to three sects cropping up, in response to this
slaughter that we had now taken part of, through an
alliance gone wrong. It was the Arabs for MAGA, Uncommitted Movement, and the Abandon Harris 2024 movement, which all had a mission to influence as many of the

American people to not vote for Kamala Harris, the democratic candidate.

This movement was tragically effective, Kamala Harris lost the election, and these three movements took excessive pride in announcing the part they played in the republican candidate winning and put us onto the path that we are on now.

Despite the fact that the 47th president has not been inaugurated yet, I predict that path will be the worst path for us ever to be on. I acknowledge that I could be mistaken, but I feel like it will lead to our destruction. And more Palestinians will die. But I could be wrong.

While majority of the Arab and Muslim community, in 2024, felt elated for getting the 34-count convicted felon and adjudicated rapist, racist republican candidate into office—which is precisely what the 47th president was—not everyone was on the same agenda.

I have stumbled on older posts, online, by four different Arabs/Muslims who had a different opinion and outlook than a mass number of Arabs/Uncommitted movement supporters.

I wanted to write these four comments, to shed another light on a different angle, to show the Arabs/Muslims who voted blue, or wished to touch on the attitude that other Arabs projected onto the black community, who experienced prejudice and bigotry by the Arabic/Somali community.

When history unfolds, there will be documentaries on this time, the Arab/Somali movements of Pro-Palestine will be examined, and the devastating results that it led to, that were harmful to both Gaza, the USA, and other places.

I wish to show these voices, to show that there were some in the Arabic community who made the better decision for the country, on November 5th, and voted Blue, *or* who were not afraid to call out the Arabs who spewed hatred at the black community, who had supported VP Harris.

During the genocide occurring in Gaza, the Pro-Palestinian movement stirred in the USA, and Arab Americans started protesting for their fallen brethren in Gaza. But they needed help getting their platform up and running.

Many in the Black community came to help. They used their platforms to spread the word, helped the Pro-Palestinian movement rise, which it did. It became a phenomenon of speaking out against the USA's involvement in the war. It led to the democratic president being asked to step down, (though this was a bipartisan failure, and the blame should have been spread around more equally) and his VP taking his place, Kamala Harris.

When this change occurred, many people rallied at the idea of a new candidate, and a woman as well. Many in the black community embraced her (sadly, not all) and began to get behind her as a candidate. The black community, who had embraced the Pro-Palestinian movement and helped bring it to life, assumed that the Arabic community would return this 'alliance' by supporting this new candidate.

Sadly, they could not have been more wrong and were met with immediate disappointment.

The Arabic community eventually condemned her, angered at her not representing their movement enough, and blamed the democratic candidate for a war that she did not create, and had no power to stop.

They railed at the black community for supporting her, and the racism that was projected at the ally who had helped their movement rise, was agonizing.

Feeling betrayed, many in the black community (the

ones who refused to be guilted into backing down for believing in the Vice President) realized that they had been used. The alliance was broken.

The MAGA Arabs, Uncommitted Movement (those who would not vote at all), Abandon Harris 2024 movement, and third-party voters in the Arab community stirred up just enough to influence other Americans and contributed to the outcome of VP Harris not winning the popular vote.

The republican candidate won, and that might very well be the biggest mistake of the USA in the 2020s.

So, here are four online posts of people in the Arabic/Muslim community that either voted for VP Harris, or who wanted to acknowledge the harm the Arabic community inflicted on the black community, rather than sweeping it under the rug, like many others will attempt to do after they read this. Literally, I know that people are going to deceitfully deny the racism inflicted on the black community—but what else is new?

The First two posts are by Arabic women –

First Post:

'I understand why many people in the black community are angry with us, after this election. After all, without the black community behind us, our movement will be practically dead. So, I understand why they are angry with us for how we treated them.

— December 2024

Second Post:

'Stop saying that All of us Arabs did not vote for Harris! I did vote for her! So please stop hating all of us Arab Muslims. Try to see each of us as different. I showed up for her, and I am happy that I did.'

— December 2024

This third post was from a Muslim male:

'I understand why African Americans don't trust us now. You showed up for us, supported us, and we betrayed you. We literally broke our alliance with you, and we weren't there for you when you needed us. Don't trust us until we show that we are trustworthy.'

This fourth post, by his description, is an Arab Immigrant. It's very lengthy, but I had to post it because it delivers so many aspects of this situation that I was amazed by. I had to admire the boldness of it:

'I am a Palestinian Immigrant, who voted for the Vice President. If anyone responds to this post with anger, and calling me a traitor, I don't care. You who voted for that Orange Dictator, who is sadly, again our... president... I will never forgive you. You, in the Uncommitted Movement, also brought this about... and I will never forgive you. You, who voted for third party, out of spite, I will never forgive you. You have put this country, and Gaza, on a collision course that will lead to one outcome: the potential destruction of both.

First, I want to make it very clear that I am Pro-Palestine, but I am anti-terrorist. I despise terrorists with every fiber of my being. Not only for the fact that they mass-murder and take innocent lives, but it often always results in leading to wars where there is no end in sight and leads to more innocent people dying.

But with acts of terrorism the result is always the same: a conflict that will go on for years, die down, then resurface, and where there are NO heroes, by the end. Because each side had to commit evil atrocities to solve the conflict.

So, again, I am anti-terrorist. That means that on October 7th, 2023, I hated HAMAS. I admit, they have done some good things over the years. But I'm not excusing this. After what they did, I was outraged, from both the Israelis they killed, and the many Palestinians that I knew was going to die, in retaliation. HAMAS's actions signed a death warrant to so many of my people that day. Yes, this was an ongoing conflict between my nation and Israel that had spanned back for many decades. This is an ancient feud. So, I don't like acts of terrorism to resurface that feud, on either side.

That also means that I am, naturally, Anti-Netanyahu, who I will never speak his name after this. For now, I call him the devil. And rightly so. The man is pure evil and what he has done, (even before this war) I hope he burns for all eternity.

And since I am so anti-terrorist, the 2024 USA presidential election gave me only one choice: I had to do everything in my power to keep the 45th president from returning to power, because he is a domestic terrorist. On January 6th, 2021, he incited an insurrection on our nation's capital, and people died. As both an Arab, and an American, I could not protect my people from HAMAS and the Devil. But with my vote, I could protect Americans from being ruled by a terrorist, and help my people as well, with the better of the two main candidates.

Because SHE was infinitely better than HIM.

That is something many in the Pro-Palestinian movement failed to understand. And before you call me a traitor, go to hell. I am going to give every reason why she was the *only* candidate that was worth my vote.

For some reason, Americans blamed VP Harris for the genocide in Gaza. This confirmed just how stupid and misinformed everyone was. First, she did not start that war; it was Arabs, when they mass murdered 1200 Israelis and took hostages. Of course, there were problems and evils, already, from Israel's government's part—but I will not let that be an excuse for mass murdering 1200 Israelis.

Then it was continued by the Devil that reigns over Israel. He murdered many of my people!

And second, Vice Presidents CANNOT stop wars, or control treaties. Vice Presidents are, without doubt, one of the most powerless positions in the government. They honestly can't do a damn thing. VP Harris was in an administration that got dragged into a war through an alliance that was made before her president's administration ever entered office.

No one could predict October 7th.

Did I hate the US government for not getting out of that treaty when the Israeli Devil abused our treaty? Hell yes. I hated them for that, but no more or less than I hated the Arab Nations for being useless, and mostly HAMAS for not surrendering soon after the genocide began, handed over the hostages and saved Palestinians lives. HAMAS was wrong. The Israeli devil was wrong. The Arab Nations were wrong.

I held everyone accountable. Thus, in failure, we were all equal. But since I would never turn my back on protecting my people, I would not turn my back on protecting the USA. I despised the terrorists back home, so I would not elect a terrorist to the presidency. Because, by voting for the 45th president, I was enabling a terrorist. As an Arab American, what would that say about me? I didn't want to be known for that.

And since I knew who was to blame, as an Arab American, why would I ever blame a woman, in this country, for a war that men started, overseas, and is *their* fault? Why would I be such a failure that I would blame a woman, knowing she was in a powerless position, for what men, including men in my own race, has done? Thus, I overcame the misogyny that I was raised on—a misogyny that is very existent in the Arab community, as it is in all other nationalities—and knew to give the vice president a chance.

Also, I'm not a worthless idiot. When it comes to choosing between a 34-count felon, adjudicated rapist, failed businessman, racist that flaunts white supremacy in their cabinet—that banned my people in his first administration—who incited an insurrection, or choosing a highly-qualified prosecutor, who respects our constitution, and worked in all three branches of the government... why would I fail so hard that I would not choose the prosecutor?

I want to make it very clear that I still very much

support Palestinians. I am only talking of the Arab movement in the USA—that's what I left behind. The answer was simple; the pro-Palestinian movement was a phenomenal movement that exists because of the American democracy and its setup... but it was run by the worst people imaginable. They were racist, misogynistic, ignorant, uniformed, easily-misled, lacked vision, lacked solutions, and only created more problems. Everything that they were aiming for, I promise you, is going to lead to one inevitable outcome: the destruction of the USA, the American experiment, and the potential ruin of Gaza and Palestinians. The reason why is because this movement is led by people who are fueled by anger and revenge. A movement cannot survive from those things, because you end up creating a new reign of terror.

Also, I firmly believed that there were those in our community who were being bought off. I think they were grifters, who were being paid to swing our movement in the wrong direction. Also, there were white liberals, in our movement, who seemed to be racist. It made me wonder if our Muslim brother, Malcolm X, was right about them.

For those who were angry about Gaza, trust me, I am angry too! But their methods were not going to produce anything else but a worse outcome, because they aimed their wrath at the wrong people: the black community.

Before I get into the racism that I witnessed among my own people, which others will come forward and deny, saying that anti-blackness was non-existent in the Pro-Palestinian movement, you are lying! I do not suffer lies to pass anymore, because so many of you ruined our relationship with our black brethren, which I found to be intolerable.

For those Arabs who voted for the Felon-in-chief, you are the worst of us, by far. You voted for a man who hates our people, used us, and conned us. He was just promising anything to stay out of prison! You idiots! And, behind the scenes, it was the Felon-in-Chief who was secretly making deals with the Israeli Devil, prolonging the war, so that he could use that as leverage to convince you all that he was the solution. He also was the one who moved the embassy, helping create the problem. You were used! When will you see that?

I wish to touch on another of the worst by-products of the movement: the Uncommitted Movement.

I was approached, on a few occasions about how I should not vote back in November, and I despised that they would approach me about that. I came here...happy to have the right TO VOTE! For those in the Uncommitted Movement, and refused to vote at all, to you I speak to...your movement was the dumbest and most toxic movement that was, what I call, a movement that should die a fast death.

By withholding your vote, and telling others to, it was you telling yourself and others, to have no voice! What was that going to solve? Oh, that's right. Nothing! Everyone, in the future, don't ever listen to anyone who tells you not to vote! They are sabotaging your rights, and your voice, for their own agenda.

This was an election where there was going to be a definite outcome. Not voting held the American

Democracy for ransom, and we Arabs need the American democracy to be preserved. Without it, we have no platform!

We Arabs literally need a president who respects the laws of the constitution. Without that, we have no movement.

For you third party voters...this is another case of 'play stupid games, win stupid prizes'. You voted third party, out of spite, and look what happened. Not only was the third party not going to win, but the main candidate dropped out of the race on election night. As such, your votes were not counted, and it showed all of you that the candidate had never intended to protect Palestinians. It was all a sham. You got played.

I got complaints from people, saying that they were angry with the Vice President for not letting them represent us Palestinians at rallies. This was a no-win scenario for her. The fact is that both sides of the war were fought through two factions of terrorists. Then she would have been attacked and abandoned by those in the government for taking a side that they did not like.

But she vowed to protect the innocent lives in Gaza and have a two-state system. Don't believe me? Actually, watch her speak.

She was caught between a rock and a hard place.

Also, I felt like she would keep us safe, in the USA.

The third and final reason has to do with my experience with the black community. The fact is that the black community was the main reason our movement got a lot of notice. I appreciated them for that. Also, the ONLY reason we have any rights, at all, is because of the black community fighting for equal rights for centuries. We rode the wave of over three centuries of successful progressive movements. Sadly, I was of the minority of Arabs who remembered that. Put simply, when the logical side of the black community (not Black MAGA, who are straight up atrocities and embarrassments to the black community), told us that VP Harris was the better option, I was willing to hear them out. Once I spoke to them, I realized that they were right. Also, we Arabs enslaved black people for 1300 years, and committed so many atrocities against them, that it was hailed as a genocide. I will not pretend that my ancestors were not a part of that genocide that we committed. The Arab slave trade, that we committed on black people, was the worst slave trade ever. My people let them down before and our crimes were unforgiveable. I was not about to make the mistake again. I wanted to be there for the black community, which so many love to overlook. And all you who want to come at me with your bulls**t, for once *shut up* and *listen*. Because, to quote our fellow Muslim, Malcolm X, 'the chickens have come home to roost'.

Our president elect, the Felon-in-chief, is a white man, who has shown to be able to get away with the worst crimes and has immunity. He is lawless. Harris is a black-Asian American woman who adheres to the constitution. That means that she has to always be flawless. Impossible as that might be, but that's the double standard in life, when it comes to us people of color. That means that she has no choice but to be the best president ever, when he has the ability to be the worst, which I believe he will go on to be. If this new president betrays us, (which he will!) he will be able to get away with it. If she were to go back on her word, and betray us, the country would run her through the mud and get her impeached. She was the one who we could reason with, whether by her own choice, or by our strength. We would have held her accountable, which we have no power to hold him on. We are powerless, because we gave our power away.

Also, her words and actions show a woman who understands freedom of speech, and the right to protest the government without being attacked. I could protest her, without fear. We Arabs need that.

And this next argument made all the sense in the world: whenever black people get more rights, WE ALL get more rights. It's a direct correlation. So, if we had a black-Asian American female president, the Palestinian movement would have skyrocketed, because there would be a space for our platform. When many in the black community explained this to me, it made sense. I didn't come up with this idea myself, I admit, but I understood it.

Also, I knew that, by voting for Harris, I would be on the right side of history. I was hoping we Arabs, in the USA, would have wizened up and been able to say that.

But sadly, no. Many of us (not all) just couldn't do it, could we? We just couldn't be the solution. For that, my heart has broken.

On top of all of that, gratitude was compiled with it all. The black community had gone to bat for us, and I was determined to return the favor. And what did I get? Not only did I watch my fellow Arab Americans turn our back on the black community, but we straight up were racist/misogynistic to them. I had to hear those in my community call black people 'colonizers', and racist slurs. And then you told them to keep our names out of their f**king mouths! It was you who were the pieces of s**t. No, I don't want to hear your arguments and lies about it. Because every time you try to justify your behavior, you sound worse.

The truth is many Arabs were never going to vote for a black woman; Gaza gave them a good excuse not to. Don't believe anyone who tells you otherwise. They are lying.

Again, the fact of the matter is, you betrayed our black brethren. And betrayal leads to more betrayal. As such, eventually, we will be betrayed. And we will not have as strong a support system as we would have originally had.

And now we have a domestic terrorist back in the white house. I know what's going to happen. More Palestinians in Gaza will die. Other Americans will die. People that we help, in other nations, will die. Because we elected the worst administration ever, without thinking about ALL the other problems that we had, as a country. Even if there is a ceasefire, and Gaza is saved, don't celebrate. Believe me, we saved it at the expense of another nation getting slaughtered. We traded one evil for another.

I hate the USA's alliance with Israel. I hate that so many of my people are dead.

But I would never, EVER, elect a terrorist to the

White House, where I knew that would lead to more death. I was about reckoning, NOT revenge.

Going forward, to my fellow Americans, you live here! You can't help other nations, if you can't help yourselves. We were too divided, and as such, you played right into this new regime's hands.

And don't you dare call me ungrateful, because what is being solved? No really, how did your non-vote help anything? How did your vote for the convicted felon help? How did your vote for third party help? Don't pat yourself on the back. Trust me, I know terrorists. I know them well. Your actions got the domestic terrorist elected, and I know how this is going to end. The USA will be thrown into chaos repeatedly, and people will die for stupid reasons. Your non-vote, third party vote, and vote for that cretin will cause death. Believe me, the problems will still persist in Gaza. You simply brought the problem here.

Why did you have to go and kill yourselves?

— January 2025

This last comment was a quick add on, because it was posted online, after this book was written. Eager to have another Muslim perspective to the bunch, this person was responding to another Muslim who said that the current president (the felon) had lied to them:

'No, he didn't. His actions showed you who he was from day one. As a Muslim, I saw this 10 years ago. Unfortunately, my Arab Muslim brothers and sisters can't admit that their racism and misogyny led them

to vote against their best interest. For the life of
them, they could not vote for a black/East Asian
woman, emphasis on the black and woman part.'

— July 2025

Anyone from the distant future, who might pick up this
tale, do not just solely take my word for it, but research all
that happened. You will hear many perspectives of the
Israelis-Gaza war, but I am happy when I discovered these
five different perspectives, and some who were unafraid to
share their insight on the black community's history with
the pro-Palestinian movement. In my time, I already see
no one talking about it, in a mainstream sense, and I fear
that it will be swept under the rug and forgotten. Some, in
my time, will dismiss or discredit these five points of view.
But they were here. They exist and have a right to be
remembered. This showed the pitfalls of what George
Washington feared about establishing permanent alliances.
But we do have international alliances, which have
worked, and once more, explaining why Washington
understood that sometimes those types of alliances are
needed.

Now you know a tragedy of life: sometimes, nothing is
foolproof. Life is just complicated, and what is right can
turn wrong very quickly, in a different direction.

Having finished offering council, Washington gave
farewell to the American people:

'In offering to you, my countrymen, these counsels
of an old and affectionate friend...

Though in reviewing the incidents of my administration I am unconscious of intentional error, I am

nevertheless too sensible of my defects not to think it probable that I may have committed many errors...

I anticipate with pleasing expectation that retreat in which I promise myself to realize without alloy the sweet enjoyment of partaking, in the midst of my fellow citizens, the benign influence of good laws under a free government—the ever favorite object of my heart, and the happy reward, as I trust, of our mutual cares, labors, and dangers.'

— George Washington,19th September 1796

And so, Washington stepped down and peacefully gave the presidential powers to his successor, John Adams.

———

The Rise and Fall of John Adams

I shall not give long details of the Second USA's president's administration but only give the quick things that show what applies to the 21st century, and to the readers' time period.

George Washington and John Adams were two entirely different types of men.

Washington was a soldier and farmer. Adams was an attorney. Washington was a Southerner. Adams was from the North. Washington was known for being very courteous in public. Adams was known for being wise and then obnoxious. Washington knew how not to be affected greatly by criticism. Adams took criticism personally.

Washington was a slave owner.

Adams was a staunch abolitionist.

But with the Adams administration, it was a matter of the sins of previous administrations falling onto him.

Adams, too, despised the Reign of Terror and was accepting of breaking ties with France after that, but that led to so many problems during his time.

France, feeling betrayed, began to attack American ships, and led to the Quasi War between both nations.

This led to Adams being damned if he did, and damned if he didn't. Naturally, the newspapers criticized him (but they criticized Washington often as well), to the point where Adams could not take it anymore.

Between that, along with his hatred of his political opponents, his distrust over immigrants, and his deep recognition that anti-American sentiments were cropping up, in support of foreign preferences, he did something that proved to be his undoing:

The Alien & Sedition Acts of 1798

The Alien and Sedition Acts were a set of four laws passed by Congress in 1798 that restricted immigration and free speech. The laws were passed by the Federalists (John Adams was a Federalist), who believed that criticism of the government was disloyal. The acts were a direct attack on the Democratic-Republicans, the other political party.

In simple speech, these acts were a direct threat to the immigrants, making acquiring citizenship difficult. It also led to journalists getting arrested and jailed, led to the first efforts to reject the US Constitution, and was also done to weaken John Adam's foes in the other political party, who overall, was open to immigrants.

Guess what the reaction was?

If it was well-received, that reception did not last long.

The backlash was immense and that helped bring about the downfall of Adam's presidency.

Not only did the Alien and Sedition Acts not work back then, but almost all of them were repealed by the next president, Thomas Jefferson.

Sound familiar to the 47th president's incoming administration? Good. Because it is.

In 1798, the American people also spoke against it, showing the power of a movement.

When it comes to journalists publishing false statements about the government, it is a natural concern to be upset about.

This was one of the problems that we have suffered in the last four years. A couple of news stations, from 2020 onwards, thrived off false information, for the sake of being popular and increasing viewership. The truth stopped mattering. The winning campaign ran solely on lies.

This was not new, however. It was a problem when one of our charismatic/terrible presidential administrations, Ronald Reagan's era, got rid of the Fairness Doctrine, which mandated broadcast networks to devote time to contrasting views on issues of public importance.

The Fairness Doctrine, enforced by the Federal Communications Council, was rooted in the media world of 1949. Lawmakers became concerned that the monopoly audience control of the three main networks, NBC, ABC and CBS, could misuse their broadcast licenses to set a biased public agenda. So the doctrine was established.

It was effective, until the Reagan Administration fought to get rid of the doctrine, and eventually President Reagan successfully did so. This has led to a news network becoming biased, and one network became so biased, in the 2020s, that they pumped so many lies into supporting one presidential candidate to the point where it could not even be construed as 'News' anymore. It was just propaganda.

Fake news is frustrating, I know, but it cannot be met with violence or imprisonment.

It violates the first amendment of the Constitution.

Also, arresting journalists for printing news leads to one outcome: the government being able to arrest anyone just because they print or say something that they disagree with. This can become corrupt very fast, because it creates censorship. Where do you draw the line?

The best way that it could be said was through our 44th US President, Barack Obama:

"Censorship, in my opinion, is a stupid and shallow way of approaching the solution to any problem. Though sometimes necessary, as witness a professional and technical secret that may have a bearing upon the welfare and very safety of this country, we should be very careful in the way we apply it, because in censorship always lurks the very great danger of working to the disadvantage of the American nation."

— Barack Obama

Fake news can only be combatted by having another news outlet to combat those lies with constant truths, bring back the Fairness Doctrine, and the government keeping the public well-informed. That's how you kill fake news. Mind you, the American people have to be open to listening too, which is not a guarantee.

And that brings another reason why 2024 ended the way that it did. The public was being fed fake news and hateful rhetoric for the past four years (four decades in some cases), and there was not enough done to combat these lies by the government. President Biden's administration was terrible at informing the world of what they achieved and confront false news. It allowed lies to spread. Simply put, the democrats were terrible at getting their message out there.

It led to the people being easily deceived.

But one shining aspect emerged in 2024: left-wing independent media. Independent media is something that every country needs. Independent media are often compiled of individuals who are very passionate about getting real news to the public, researching everything through Ground News, and will keep you informed about everything, cover stories that mainstream media sometimes are not allowed to cover, and often do it with lessons in morality.

Because independent journalists and reporters are not a part of mainstream media, are not paid and are not working under someone, they have the freedom to convey the truth, are not easily intimidated by people and often cannot be bribed. They tell you the news, come what may. There are some mainstream media journalists who are trying to get the truth out, in our time, but there are few left.

When you do find those sincere indie networks, who are most committed to giving you the truth, constantly, you can't be tricked into voting for the wrong person. As a result, they were the best ones at maintaining morality in the news and were among the strongest voices in the pro-democracy movement.

When looking back at our times, I hope that you do have access to those videos, on independent media, and all they recorded. They were the valiant warriors on the front lines who did not normalize evil and represented those who were in the fight to preserve the American Experiment.

But sadly, in 2025, history might repeat itself.

If I were to predict what might happen, going forward, I foresee disease awareness not being reported, like it had done so before, massive losses to the working class, scandal, cheating, fraud, and maybe even many people dying, and it will go unnoticed. And people will lose their rights, and a lot of them won't even see it. I hope it does not happen, and that I am wrong.

But, with any hope, people will wake up.

John Adams, like Washington, was like every president: a combination of good and bad.

Adam's failure was a part of his legacy, I will not deny. But his virtue, of standing fast to despise slavery, is also in his legacy.

Welcome to the human race, eh?

———

The Echo Chamber

I always found it remarkable about how so many Americans were content to live in their bubble, their echo chamber, without being curious about the rest of the world, and how we would be viewed in it. After November 2024, we returned to being, not just a joke, but a very violent joke. We were now an infection to national and global spheres.

Here are two among the *thousands upon thousands* of comments that foreigners made in 2025.

This comment was a person who was bravely unafraid to acknowledge what politicians, corporate media, and many Americans do not want to acknowledge. But it's true:

'[The reasons] America didn't vote for Harris was because she was a woman and black. About half of the USA do not want either to be in any position of power: full stop. All the rest are lame excuses to cover that fact up.'

This next comment was from another foreigner, about why so many didn't vote/voted for the republican candidate in the 2024 election:

'Mate, I was watching the election and thinking they've got a choice between, let's put it lightly: medium steak with peppercorn sauce & broccoli, or pureed catshit served on a bed of catshit with catshit sauce. And most people voted for the catshit because the steak wasn't perfectly the way they want it, or they don't like broccoli, or they wanted a different sauce. Or they wanted a 100% vegan option. It might not be 100% perfect but anyone with a functioning brain would pick the steak over the catshit. And America chose to eat catshit.'

Extremism

Yes! That was part of our downfall: the dangers of the extreme left. The dangers of the extreme left also were a contributing factor that ruined us. While the right-wing extremists were willing to overlook every evil to get their candidate elected, a portion of left wing-extremists, also killed us, because of their outrageous purity.

Nothing is perfect, ever! No political candidate is perfect and runs the perfect campaign! Ever! Because it is impossible. So, the average person, who is realistic and cares about their country, chooses the candidate who is, morally and objectively, better for the country, and how we look on the world stage. They go off facts, logic, and consideration for the law, and do not vote on their emotions. They understand that 'purity politics' and single-issue voting is nothing short of destructive. Single-issue voting and purity politics is a way of saying 'that if the candidate does not align with every viewpoint of mine, or has this one habit that I don't like, then that's it! I'm not voting at all, or I'm voting third-party, although the third-party candidate will not win, and also does not align with everything that I feel as well'. It's an *all or nothing* concept; If you don't agree with me, always, then I won't vote for you.' That mentality is equally as destructive as right-wing extremism. While the right often gives way to religious extremism, the left does not show up, because of liberal extremism.

It's good to have liberal values, as well as religious values, but you must not let it consume you, to the extent where you make the obviously wrong choice. I have encountered leftists, who did not vote/blindly voted third party, and did not see the harm they have brought on their fellow citizens. And they don't seem to connect their actions/inactions to the result, which was national destruction. On both sides, of right and left extremism, they vote/don't vote, not caring about the effects that they have on the rest of the community. On both sides was carelessness and selfishness that was so destructive, showing how both sides cared more about their ideas/ideals than the people. Again, it may be January, but I already feel like there is a lot that spells disaster.

I don't care how much anyone rants and raves about what I just said and hates me for it. For those who still do not want to learn, I will not let their emotions deter me.

I appeal to all future voters who are willing to open their mind to move past what is happening. Whatever side of the political spectrum that you fall into, be it Democrat, Republican, or Independent, when it comes the time for voting, have your values, but never give way to extremism. When voting, find your mindset voting after objectively weighing out the pros and cons of the candidates. Look at each candidate, analyze their past, their level of telling more truth than lies, of respect for the office, for the law, for all the people, for the American experiment, values, how well they treat our allies, etc. If they have that one policy that you don't like—a policy which is more an opinion of yours but does not affect the nation harmfully at all—then you still should vote for them. Understand that there is more to the equation than just your vibes. It's about everybody.

Extremism is never the solution. Have your ideals but remember what the Greeks said: All things in moderation. When you do that, you make better choices in life. And even if the candidate you voted for lost, you still feel the comfort of knowing that you supported the right cause.

On YouTube, a commentator said it best:

'I believe voting for Kamala was the same thing as Passover. Those who voted for Kamala had the protection on their doors, and even if we had to endure grief and pain our endurance wasn't going to last long the way those who voted for the felon. It feels like a very parallel situation.'

Another person online echoed the same sentiments but left a chilling prophecy.

'I am a 77-year-old, white male, republican and veteran... voting for Kamala Harris was the easiest choice that I ever made. I don't want to hear your reasons for doing otherwise—if I easily overcame my racism and misogyny to vote for her, your excuses are lame, so shut up. I know what's going to happen. And stop saying the whole 'it would have been just as bad under Harris' crap. You know you're lying to yourself. You just say it because you are not brave enough to blame yourself and admit this is all your fault. Own what you have done, understand that we are going to be mad at you for a while, but then be patient with us, stand with us, and vote better, with us. Believe me, when Harris lost, and the Orange Turd won, it will lead to our country dying. Karma is going to hit us so fast.'

———

This next section of this Afterword will be concerning the trigger words that are used, even during presidential campaigns.

In presidential campaigns, there can be name-calling. The 2024 campaign was ugly, with the victor being the worst when it came to slander.

A part of his arsenal of using words incorrectly to hurl insults was to call his opponents fascists, communists, Marxists, and Socialists.

When it came to the first insult, it fell under the category of 'every accusation is a confession' concept. He acted like a fascist and ran his presidential campaign on fascism but called others that.

With the other words, we must go further back.

Communists and Marxists are words that are meant to scare Americans. It works, while many don't even know what those words mean.

Research them before you let politicians deceive you.

But it gets worse.

Some of those words are not negative things. In fact, they are positive aspects that work well, *with capitalism*, and were demonized so that people could keep their wealth and trick the poor into staying such.

Villainized by right-wing influencers and red politicians, for decades, Marxism and Socialism are there to help the poor, but many don't want you to know that.

Marxism is a political, economic, and social philosophy that analyzes class struggle and the role of economics in human history. It's not commonly used and is not harmful.

It's not an evil movement. It was there to get the common masses thinking of economic balance and imbalance.

But the main thing that I will focus on is socialism.

Socialism is often the right-wing go-to word to slander the left, or the centrists. They literally treat socialism as a demonic word to trick you into not looking closely at it.

To put it best, I will used the words of our 33rd USA president, Harry Truman. Truman was the President after Roosevelt, and here is what he said in Syracuse, New York:

> *'Socialism is a scare word they have hurled at every advance the people have made in the last 20 years.*
>
> *Socialism is what they called public power. Socialism is what they called social security. Socialism is what they called farm price supports. Socialism is what they called bank deposit insurance. Socialism is what they called the growth of free and independent*

labor organizations. Socialism is their name for almost anything that helps all the people.

When the Republican candidate inscribes the slogan "Down With Socialism" on the banner of his "great crusade," that is really not what he means at all.

What he really means is "Down with Progress— down with Franklin Roosevelt's New Deal," and "down with Harry Truman's fair Deal." That's all he means.

— President Truman, October 10, 1952

To help you more, in the USA 2025, we have all benefitted from a socialist program for decades: Social Security.

Americans, in my time, literally cannot survive without their social security. It was something created by democrats, for the people.

It was first founded by President Franklin D. Roosevelt, and his democratic colleagues in 1935.

After many attempts to block the legislation, the republicans eventually voted for it, it passed, and now we have social security. So, before you hear someone use the word 'socialism' in a derogatory way, research it, and you will find that it provides free programs to the needy.

And again, I reiterate, socialism can co-exist in a capitalistic environment perfectly. In fact, it works better in a capitalistic society, for many do need those programs.

People use fear to keep you from educating yourself. Always embrace learning more. President Kennedy said it best:

'The ignorance of one voter in a democracy impairs the security of all."

— President John Kennedy

————

The last section of this topic is a list of warning signs of how to detect a dictator, who is trying to rise and undermine your democracy and your republic.

Dictators and fascists often try to gain power through a particular method. It was well articulated by Joseph Goebbels, the propaganda minister for Adolf Hitler's Third Reich. Goebbels was a Nazi.

Successful at helping a man rise to power who would go on to commit the greatest atrocities in Germany's history, Goebbels laid out how you use propaganda to help a tyrant rise and deceive a nation:

1. 'If you tell a lie big enough, and keep repeating it, people will eventually come to believe it.'
2. Accuse the other side of that which you are guilty.
3. Propaganda works best when those who are being manipulated are confident that they are acting on their own free will.
4. It is vitally important for the state, to repress dissent, for the truth is the mortal enemy of the lie, and thus...the greatest enemy of the state.

Among that, Goebbels promoted the ideas of getting people to love you by appealing to their emotions. He advised to constantly repeat just a few ideas. Use stereotyped phrases. The next thing to do was to give only one side of the argument. If you give that one-sided belief, you can practically brainwash someone into not accepting another perspective.

The next step is to continuously criticize your opponents. If you do that, your supporters will think that their contempt is justified, that the opposing side are villains, and you are the victim. But in fact, it's quite the reverse.

Here comes to the last, but not the least: pick out one special "enemy" for special vilification.

Reader, I can tell you that this is what happened between January 6th, 2021, and still is occurring in January 2025. The president-felon, who now controls the government, used ALL of these tactics.

Another thing to consider is a list created by Lawrence Britt, a political scientist. It's a list about the chief characteristics of fascism, and what it entails. You can easily look it up. If you care for your nation, and your personal well-being, read it. I shall give you the first three aspects:

1. *Powerful and Continuing Nationalism* - Fascist regimes tend to make constant use of patriotic mottos, slogans, symbols, songs, and other paraphernalia. Flags are seen everywhere.

2. *Disdain for the Recognition of Human Rights* - Because of fear of enemies and the need for security, the people in fascist regimes are persuaded that human rights can be ignored in certain cases because of "need."

3. Identification of Enemies/Scapegoats as a Unifying Cause - The people are rallied into a unifying patriotic frenzy over the need to eliminate a perceived common threat or foe: racial, ethnic or religious minorities; liberals; communists; socialists, terrorists, etc.

> — Lawrence Britt, 2003, Free Inquiry
> Magazine

Here, in the winter of 2025, we are watching these characteristics unfolding and might potentially come to fruition. I know that, when looking back on our time, you will ask these two questions:

'How did you all let this happen?'

'Why didn't you stop it from happening?'

All that many of us can do is give you the best answers that we can. We cannot explain away the choices of the American people that wanted this.

Right now, amidst all this, I do not know what may happen. I hope for the best, and that our government will fight to not be overcome. But I also know that the worst might occur.

If we continue on the road that lays ahead of us, then the times will be dark. This era will be the United States of America painted in all its mistakes, and all its failures.

All that this work can show you is that there were many of us, a large number, that tried to stop it. On November 5th, 2024, 75 million Americans—among those were women, men, people of color, white people, democrats, republicans, and independents, in all fifty states, stood as fellow countryfolk and tried to prevent this, in solidarity. We lost to millions of others who voted in the opposite direction, or did not vote at all, not protecting us. But please, remember our fight. If our failure has repercussions that affect you, in the time period you are in, it is not what we wanted. From what I can tell you, at this time, it is that when you step into a voting booth, to cast your ballot... choose wisely. Do your research. Accept that no candidate is perfect, so choose the one that accepts their imperfection, but tries to be perfect. Choose the candidate who cannot control the press, who respects the laws, who does not have a criminal history, who cares for people, who has experience, and when they make a mistake, you have the right to protest them and list your grievances. Choose the candidate who is not above the law and can be held accountable. To quote a character from an iconic book, 'There will never be a society anything like perfect!'. It's the character Jessup, from the novel 'It Can't Happen Here', by Sinclair Lewis. If you ignore everything that I have said, read that book! All in the USA, from late teens to onward, should read that book.

And do not trust anyone who claims they will take you back to a golden era, where things were better.

This was put best by the tv show, <u>Doctor Who</u>. In the episode, 'Invasion of the Dinosaurs', the lead character was talking to a man, who had been sold a lie of better times gone by:

Mike Yates: We shall find ourselves in a golden Age.

The Doctor: There never was a golden age, Mike. It's all an illusion.

Historically speaking, there never really was a golden age. Anyone who tells you so, was selling you a dream—an illusion that was never real.

But to have a presidential candidate who knows their

common flaws, but has the confidence to strive to be better and care every day, who respects our constitution, has taken economy lessons, who has respect for their fellow citizens, loves their nation, comes to serve but not to dictate, believes in equality and our rights, and has much experience working in the government—that's the one you pick.

And vote—that is what I will leave you with. Always research, and vote, for your sake and for everyone else's.

And now, currently, I leave you, uncertain of where our future lies. For those in the future who will read this, please remember that we were here. We tried to prevent this. We tried to protect you. We tried. We are sorry that we failed.

In hopes of giving you a glimmer of hope, against the weight of giving you all the best advice that we can leave you with, I shall end with a quote from our 46th US president, Joseph Biden, in his farewell address to the People of the United States:

> 'And my eternal thanks to you, the American people. After fifty years of public service, I give you my word, I still believe in the idea for which this nation stands, a nation where the strengths of our institutions and the character of our people matter and must endure. Now it's your turn to stand guard. May you all be the keeper of the flame. May you keep the faith.
>
> I love America. You love it too.
> God bless you all.'
>
> — Joseph Biden, January 15th, 2025

Friends, I bid you a good day.

THANK YOU FOR READING

Did you enjoy this book?

We invite you to leave a review at your favorite book site, such as Goodreads, Amazon, Barnes & Noble, etc.

DID YOU KNOW THAT LEAVING A REVIEW...

- Helps other readers find books they may enjoy.
- Gives you a chance to let your voice be heard.
- Gives authors recognition for their hard work.
- Doesn't have to be long. A sentence or two about why you liked the book will do.

About the Author

B. J. Quander is an American History enthusiast, who has always been compelled to learn about the origins of the USA, as well as all the countries that created the nation, and the cultures who have inspired it.

B. J. also has a great respect for the US Constitution, the law, and it strictly being upheld, she comments on the current times that she has observed.